THE TOBACCO BARN

KYLE HINTON

www.kyle-hinton.com   @kylehinton

Hardback ISBN: 9798993418643 | Paperback ISBN: 9798993418681
Large Print ISBN: 9798993418612 | EBook ISBN: 9798993418605
Audiobook ISBN: 9798993418650

Printed in the United States of America.

the tobacco barn

For Momma

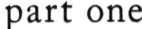

part one

chapter 1

For the longest time I'd thought the old man saying grace up on the wall in our dining room was a painting. A loaf of bread and cup of soup, the Bible and his spindly eyeglasses crisscrossed on top of it, all together placed at his end of the table, with his elbows on it—same as I always have, never told not to—and fists folded in prayer. His flannel jacket looked a lot like the one my granddad wore to supper despite visible soot around its cuffs and brushfire smell permanently stained into its pattern.

Too poor to own an original work of art, this I knew for sure, even before I realized it was a colorized photograph hanging there all that time, screen-printed onto thin paper like cardboard and textured with fingernailed swirls to give the appearance of brushstrokes. That somehow the picture was more special than it actually was I've since become well aware, and of my belief in its existence as anything but, whenever I find another one lying in a thrift shop with bits of the man's pensiveness peeled away and tagged for a couple bucks. This old man can been seen all around town, in the next one over, across state lines—going back decades he's been. And the Bible had actually been a dictionary and the whole lot staged in some photographer's studio, in Minnesota, where the town painted 'Home of the Picture "Grace"' in bold lettering on the side of their iron water tower.

The man as it turns out was poor too, a peddler, and someone they'd have called a drunkard in his day, like my dad—though *he* was not a man as beloved and mythological as the one depicted in the picture. Dad wasn't one to sit still long enough for a picture to be taken of him let alone a whole painting. Just another drunk is all he ever was. Stout and shiny, hair greased and neatly combed as always, as if it really mattered; he stinks even now, in every memory I have of him, smothered by the smell of his breath that breathed not only from within his mouth but seeped out from his sun-leathered skin. He wasn't at all special for it, either, not unlike everybody else's dad I knew growing up, but as far as one got from the dads I watched on TV. And more than just a sip here and there and from time to time, he'd less than owned up to, but never a day gone by without drinking, to excess, with as many blackouts as brownouts, whenever he'd come in half-on half-off, short-fused and upset about something. Scream-ing and carrying on so much until sometimes, most times, he got to where he couldn't see two feet in front of him, never mind tomorrow, stumbling and falling over himself and his words. Forgetful of how he got to where he was, not only in the moment of forgetfulness but all the years leading up to it, worsened his hot temper. Fed up and vengeful as ever and holding those around him into account, always and mercilessly. Standard Issue. Run-of-the-mill. Really the same ole make and model found inside every other broken home kit across America. Trademarked. The "If you don't shut it up already!" type who begins with a slap in the face and sober "I'm sorry, I'll never do it again . . ." and ends up leaving bruises or broken bones the next time.

And this isn't to say Mom didn't play her part—short of saying she flat out asked for it—willing and able as she ever was it seemed to me as a kid hearing her confess that this is what she'd signed up for, her hands always tied and yet at the same time still capable of doing something, anything about it but never would, having long since given the man, or any other man, a pass for all the terrible deeds he'd done and kept on doing. Maybe once or twice she even took some bit of responsibility, more a cross she could bear and let no one forget how heavy—another syndrome yet to be coined and before long given a proper name in their honor by those suffering without it. It wasn't her fault, though, but it was *his* dad, Landry Wains senior, Granddad, who'd made him the way that he was—and I guess it was his dad before him, and so on, or so someone else always spoke up to maintain the men in ways better than I could, explaining some kind of deal or another *he'd* made. Either that or it was the war's fault for making him some which way; blame always pointed in another direction. Without hindsight I didn't know the dimensions of truth in each of the lies I was made to believe growing up, a good man from a bad one, being told to love them as they were, and so I looked up to all of them to know how to be. If it wasn't for Mom and her constantly reiterating "Please, oh Lord, don't turn out like your daddy," contradicting herself the next time she was telling me "Do exactly as your daddy says or you-know-what's gonna happen," I might not've become the man I am today, who I'm still trying to figure out. Anyway: "He'll be home any minute now, you know, so you best shape up!"

As confusing as this picture I had already was, moreover whenever I thought my mind was made up, after a while it didn't carry the same authority, to do as I was told. Especially after that first year when Dad didn't come back home for Christmas, whichever time it was they'd nearly called it quits—not officially, not legally: "Not so fast, Lynn," he slyly spat off at the prospect of their divorce finalized on paper: "You ain't gettin rid of me that easy!" But Dad had already moved on and found himself a new job and what I presumed to be a new family to destroy several towns away from ours, near Fayetteville, a baby on the way with a woman who'd not yet known him long enough for history to repeat itself in bruises. And with it came all his talk of being reborn. A new man, changed, seen the light, living the life the good Lord intended, without a bad-mouthing woman dragging him down and his only son she refused to give his name but his same initials and then turned against him: his past life, he called us. Even so I knew our front door might fly off its hinges any day from the Wednesday before last when he'd gone out from it for good. And I suspected it must've been on Mom's mind every day leading up to it, too, his imminent departure and at the same time his ploy he'd no doubt made good on before any arrival ever came, keeping me behaving well after he'd left us there in that house by ourselves, forever fearful of his inevitable return for hurricane season. So in that way, consequentially he never really left.

By now we'd no longer gathered around that table for supper and so we definitely weren't saying grace. We'd had to have been out on the road late after stopping off at a drive-thru someplace in a town where nobody knew our name. Fishing through cold fries at the bottom of a cartooned box I'd find a bagged toy—Hamburglar driving a yellow convertible race car—to my cheap thrill. It would already be July, halfway through the year the heatwave took Mrs. Barnes, my elderly sixth-grade school teacher who also taught Sunday school and seemed to have just been reminding us to be sure and read lots of books over our summer break.

Sweat glued me to the front seat of our sky blue '67 Chevrolet Bel Air, more the color of an overcast sky by this time or the way I saw it, dull and dented, a family heirloom in Mom's eyes—"I took you home from the hospital in this car!"—parked and left without the engine running with the keys still in and the radio on but no A/C. Not all by myself, however, but with my best friend who lived across the street from me, Tommy Sellers, kicking the back of my seat and wolfing down the last bite of his cheeseburger. And not the first time we'd been told to wait out in the car, in whatever motel parking lot it was my mom and his dad prearranged to rendezvous, for them to finish up in whichever room they'd chosen this go-round: never the same number as the last, whether it be out of an abundance of caution or superstition who's to say.

"Whataya think they're doin in there, really?" Tommy asked, a grade under and a year and three months and three days younger than me so he had reason enough to ask the real questions.

"*You know,*" I answered back snidely, knowing he didn't though not without some idea as to what was going on but not really.

"Yeah, I guess so," Tommy said, sighing, picking at the piping around the car seat while pleading with the door he was making eyes at through the windshield to hurry up and open already. "But—"

"Here," I said to him, handing over the yellow race car, free from its plastic baggie, not entertaining enough for me to play with.

"*Really?*" Tommy asked. "You gonna let me have it?"

"Yeah, go on. Take it."

I was tuned out, tuned in to the radio playing "Roll With It" and a condom that looked more like a busted bubble gum bubble on the sidewalk's crumbling crack between the asphalt parking lot. Drips of brown water turned to mildew on the metal siding of the motel beneath a buzzing window unit and continued into a wet line on the sidewalk before evaporating around that same crumbled crack where a tin-roofed overhang stopped. A liquor bottle with sweat and a spit swallow left inside stayed wrapped in its silvery sun-bleached label that mirrored the low sun.

"When're we gonna go already?" he said, knowing exactly when.

This time hadn't yet been long enough a wait outside in the car for the sky to start turning; although the days, as long as they were then, it was still late enough to be considered "after dark," when by now, if both of us belonged to someone else's family, it might be bathtime or bedtime, time to be read a story and nod off safe and soundly to sleep. But instead I was itching with sweat and to go already, reading for the umpteenth time the side of Tommy's dad's truck parked beside us: *Sellers Fix-its* and a phone number to call stenciled in white letters on both its pea-green doors, along with Siler City, the town where we lived, painted by hand in cursive beneath it like a slogan I could repeat forever.

As the neighbor from across the street, Todd's fixing things around our house began logically and simply enough, when if ever something tore up, seeing as how no other man was around the house to help, *he* was. And Todd's pricing was fair and reasonable enough, so Mom made a point of reiterating to Dad when it came time to pay the man, bolstering the frequency of his visits to our house. Did a decent enough job too—not to mention Tommy's mom would give me haircuts for free out of Todd's conversion of their garage into *Pam's Beauty.*

"*Hey*—is that your momma?" I asked, causing Tommy to squirm and squiggle and stop steering Hamburglar over the door paneling.

"Oh yeah . . . What's *Momma* doin here?" he sighed, straining from the backseat to better look over the front, clearly unaware of how dire the situation.

"I dunno," I said, without saying I had my suspicions about why she was there, though with no clue how she found us.

Pam must've pulled her car into the motel parking lot without either of us noticing at first because just then she blurred right past in front of the Chevy, pounding the pavement in flip-flops and her balled fist against every motel room door she selected at random. And because she didn't wait for anybody to answer each time she did, when she finally chose the correct door numbered 14 and Todd answered it, other guests staying at the motel had begun to collect outside to watch what happened next, like a studio audience of excited next contestants on *The Price is Right.*

Todd stood stupid, naked in the opened doorway, cupping only a washcloth over himself, flushed red and sweaty in the face. Looking both ways for who could've knocked on the door he caught sight of Pam, and at the same time she stopped and saw him. His dumbfounded stance instantly swiveled as she came barreling into the room with both arms swinging, screaming and yelling at the top of her lungs.

Tommy reached forward and climbed up and over the wide front seat and landed himself there in the center next to me. With every-one out from their rooms watching on in amazement, awed and in a scramble to get a better look at what was going on, we had a front row seat to the action: his dad falling out onto the floor and losing hold of the washcloth and my mom sitting there unfazed on the edge of the bed with only a stripe of golden sun in the shape of the opened door covering her up.

Neither one of us knew what to say, but since Pam was doing all the talking, cussing and ranting and raving, and rightfully so, we didn't need to. Still I wanted to say something, instead of holding back the urge to shout out the window at her. And I figured his mom had to have known this was going on, so why act so surprised? All this time, how could she not? Whether warranted or for no good reason, a bit of theatrics was at play here for sure, acting like she meant it maybe more than she did because everyone was watching to see what she was going to do about it. Best I stay out of it, though, so I did.

"Get up," she shouted at Mom. "Whore!" She slung her arms at the walls and pushed Todd away after he'd gotten up.

Mom snatched the bedsheet off the mattress and wrapped herself in it before standing and then traipsing across the carpet that showed the passionate way the two of them had taken off their clothes, follow-ing the trail leading to the door. The cheap ply of the sheet allowed her nipples to fleck through it like stains, and for a sunburned man in a cowboy hat to whistle at her from the parking lot, another to again call her a whore.

"See there—trash! That's right. Get out, filthy whore!" Pam shouted.

"Look who's callin who what," Mom said to her, pointing a thumb at Todd, laughing.

"Lynn, don't you start up."

Mom kept her smirk and went on about her business.

"Pam, you too, now. Shut your trap already, willya!" Todd said, grabbing his pants and hold of her thick arms like it wasn't the first time, as though they'd been here before. "Come on and let her leave, now . . . Quit pitchin a fit! She's gettin herself together."

Seeing the state the two of them were caught in, the room's and their infliction onto it—beer cans collected on the table in a corner, a lamp shade off-kilter, pillows tossed, coverlet strewn aside—and finding my mom among the mess with Todd in this way, proof positive no less, and backed by strangers without a clue who these people were but not without some ideas, Pam became even more enraged. Before anybody was going anywhere the door slammed shut.

With Tommy there was no need to then try and speak to what was really going on, nor the shame that Mom brought onto me or for him of his mom and dad's onto him; we knew of each other's well enough. His was evidenced not just in moments such as this one playing out in front of us but also those unseen, physically, the past: a black eye he'd gotten or his brother's broken arm, both their blisters across the backs of their legs that scarred like the one on my knee. And it didn't seem to matter much, his dad's sleeping around: a man is a man. "They are what they are. Men. Who they've always been and will forever be," how both our moms looked at it, speaking of our dads. "You'll grow up to be one. Just you wait."

In the final minutes of muffled shouting going on inside the motel room, it'd seemed a good idea for Tommy to go on ahead and get back inside his dad's truck so that when the motel room door finally flung open his mom would have no more insults to add to her already injured self: her son she'd assume an accomplice and guilty by association, when seen through her raging lens, still out there sitting in "the whore's car."

"Ya better go on, now, Tommy, fore she blames you for it," I told him. "Get—"

And when the door did open first Mom appeared, bare feet tip-toeing on the sidewalk out front for everyone to gawk at as she strode to the car, her blue jean cut-offs half-buttoned up under his ribbed wife-beater slung over her mess of curls; nude-colored bra straps dangled out from her opened pocketbook with the ends of a neon elastic exercise band.

People were shouting at her by this point, taking Pam's side, including I guess it was the manager of the motel, out from a dingy office in her big zebra-printed T-shirt and all legs, like she showed up to work wearing what she'd slept in the night before. Mostly just shaking her head and scratching her saggy, sun-spotted arms at first, sucking a cigarette, but then she was dragging her flip-flops over the cement toward the room and started up, choking on it when she said: "Go on then, honey. You heard the lady. Get back in the trashcan you done came from."

Everybody burst out laughing and Mom shot them all a bird.

"*Momma* . . ." I yelled out through my downed window. "Come on already. Hurry up. Let's go!"

Onto the center of the front seat, over an impression of Tommy's butt not entirely gone from the depressed cushion, she slung her pocketbook.

"I'm sorry," she sighed, just as Pam came out from the room after her, Mom's shoes strung from her fists, determined through tears and sweat burning her eyes to catch up with our Chevy before it pulled away.

"Gimme a smoke outta there, willya?" she asked, erratically steering in reverse to avoid Pam's wrath.

"Bye . . ." Tommy yelled, one arm waving, his body hanging over the downed window of his dad's truck.

Pam hushed him, scolding: "Don't you dare say another word!" and at the same time she was slinging Mom's shoes through the air toward our Chevy, landing the heel of the left one on the windshield, glass cracking like lightning.

"Ah, shit," Mom said, swerving out of the parking lot, just as the right shoe dropped down on the trunk of the car with a *pock!* and the sound of thunder reverberating through its metal, before she was hitting the gas and sending one after the other off on to the glossy asphalt with a clink.

Pam stood scowling, bent out of shape in the empty parking space screaming at the sky; Todd shirtless behind her in the motel room's sunlit doorway, his unfurling denim waist and that paisley-tooled leather belt he beat Tommy with slung loose through its loops.

Feeling around inside her pocketbook for what seemed forever, under bra cups and between little glass bottles and blotted tissues and opened and shut makeup compacts and sticky applicators, I finally rattled her last cigarette out from her empty pack of Pall Malls. And with its filter stuck impatiently tapping up and down between her smudged lips, kept shut otherwise since she'd white-knuckled us out of the parking lot, I waited for the lighter in the dash to pop back out. Not only was the glove box open-and-shut with its busted lock and handle, and a window in the back didn't want to budge—now the windshield with a spiderweb of broken glass—but the red ring of the cigarette lighter that had always lit up well enough until now was deciding not to. No heat was felt in its metal rim after I pulled it out to feel for the burn.

"What? What is it?!" Mom cried.

And I tried pushing it back in again, hearing it click the way it would so I knew I hadn't done it wrong, and waiting for it to work, but still it didn't. The lighter, like everything else, was broken.

"Fuuuck!" she wailed, pounding the steering wheel with both hands. The cigarette left her lip hanging angry, landing unlit on the dirty carpet mat between her tan-lined toes, painted with a colored nail polish to match her fingers.

I don't remember if I read a single book that entire summer before the seventh grade. Or maybe I was never much of a reader anyway, not picking up where Judy Blume or Betsy Byars left off, my own adolescence more than enough to keep me occupied.

chapter 2

I was seventeen and halfway to Tennessee when they found me and brought me to Polk Youth Center back in Raleigh. Led down a long, narrow, bricked corridor, I'd been handcuffed at both my wrists and feet so that it was hard to balance my foreshortened steps, like a penguin's, patting against reflective floor tile checkered on and on for so far up ahead I'd swear I could see myself looking back on it now. When we finally reached an opening at its end my eyes were only just beginning to adjust to the bright lights overhead and coming back into focus after being blinded by all the flashing cameras staked outside the prison's main entrance—only in my head, of course, as no one cared who I was or where I'd come from, how I'd gotten here, much less what was going to happen to me next. Not only were there no photographers taking my picture for the papers, I wasn't asked by any reporters for comment or any part of my side of the story, unlike how I'd seen it play out on TV and I guess the way I imagined it would have for me up until to the moment when it was actually happening. Though inmates such at these arrive with grave offenses requiring expensive attorneys who refer to them as their clients and ask that they keep their mouths shut, out from the spotlight, and dress in these clothes they picked out for them to wear from JCPenney. Made-for-TV movies or the nightly news this was not; this was real life, at least once the bus had made it behind the front gate as high as the window downed next to me, where planted beneath it in manicured beds pretty colored flowers in full bloom reached for the sun.

Hot as hell inside and out. Any other day than this one, I thought. Couldn't it have been winter? When instead of being stuck sweating on a bus for a whole lot longer than the last hour since I began to wonder to myself if I was ever going to get off I'd at least be acclimated to the cold already. How much farther did I have to go? Not only now but later? One day to fourteen months—how long is *that*? More to the point, how long would this period of confinement last after I was no longer locked up? A lifetime? Which is how long?

Within this endless uncertainty, however, along the way toward Raleigh I'd recognized every town we were driving through, altering the passage of time into a standstill I was able to more consciously process. The map in my head eased any discomfort I might otherwise pile on from not knowing where I was going. It wasn't until I didn't recognize anything at all that I realized there was no going back to where I'd been and what I'd known or thought I knew, what I felt familiar with, the semblance of something akin to normal I'd been running away from for so long it actually felt good to sit and stare a little while. Though to be somewhat fair to myself and my memory, how it worked or wasn't or isn't any longer, every whistle stop in these parts looks like any other not big enough to name or map, let alone remember. Highways stretch wide for pull-overs and truck stops, litter to cumulate, and hitchers to have the right of way. It certainly wasn't room to grow. Most everything remains as it always was and forever will be—if it hadn't already been torn down or left standing only as a reminder. As many churches as there are gas stations. Vacant motels and barred pawn shops and pool halls. The one roller rink that by the looks of it is either thriving or struggling to make ends meet, or both, depending on the time of year. Putt-

Putt always open for business, even in the pouring down rain. Chain grocery stores, too many and way too big not to shut down the little guys so they did, each one selling more food than whole counties can even stomach. Kit homes and single-wides and double-wides and subdivisions few and far between but coming up quicker than most people said they would. So on and so forth. Like the Top 40 on the radio, on repeat.

Raleigh, on the other hand, is the notable exception. There's a mix of old and new, not so forward but not stuck behind either. And you feel it coming miles before you get there it's so big, when, before you know it, I-40 off-ramps you into the middle of it, what for me was my final destination, where alongside the prison eastbound and westbound lanes kept on going forever. There's no escaping the sound of it, the sight of freedom as it passes by on either side of you at all hours of the day, other people getting to where they're going while you're stuck in the middle. The whoosh of it took me back a step as I climbed down from the bus, how I wished I could've stayed in my seat and ridden it back, but truly there was no turning around.

First things first, they asked that I strip naked: "Everything off!"

This didn't come as big of a shock to me then as it could've, had it not been for the policeman who first arrested me before bringing me to this prison asking me to do the same thing in his. But it was much smaller, the town, and the jail he put me in, too, makeshift or out of an old movie, *Andy Griffith*. And not as thoroughly a search was performed after doing so as the one was here. There I didn't feel anywhere near the degree of confinement that I did now, standing here shivering even on what was perhaps the hottest day of the year, in a room reeking of sweat from the stripped inmates and uniformed officers alike, having not even yet reached my cell—not assigned to me for another week or longer. In that lazy jail cell there maybe wasn't even a window to see out of and if there was I didn't think to look for it. It was probably nerves keeping me seeing a way out somehow, my body's natural defense in anticipation for what was going to happen to it here that had expanded an inner world where I might could still see myself free from it, outside of myself, past the present predicament I was in and ahead into the future. I felt more vulnerable in the span of the first five minutes in Polk than I had ever before in my life, even when stood staring up at my dad, fearful for whatever wrath he was bringing, without control over any outcome and at the hands of a couple gluttons in uniform checking and double-checking over and under and in and out for drugs and weapons, any paraphernalia of a past life they'd been trained to find but rarely ever do.

"Ain't you *pretty* . . ." one said and I pretended I hadn't heard.

Moving along through what I'd not yet understood to be day one of the intake process, next a pile of neatly folded blues and whites slid across a metal table towards me: a cotton t-shirt and boxer shorts, a chambray button-down—all sized medium and anchored by a pair of faded blue jeans marked with a 29-inch waist to start me off in my own uniform; a pair of socks and grayed sneakers pulled from marked plastic bins handed to me completed it. Putting everything on it felt soft and worn against my skin, so much I knew it wasn't my own; of course these clothes wouldn't be brand new but were hand-me-downs from whoever it was my same size and fit that had them handed down to him with his sentence. Not long after a stent in the boiler room washing them I'd learn how to cut and sew these garments, too, though mostly mending.

"Come time, someone'll give you a jacket for the yard," said one of the officers. "Any other requests outside of that must go through whoever it is that's over you first before you get it."

"—If you get it," another officer, between his handlebar mustache, carried on, inking my fingertips in assembly-line fashion.

Down another long hallway I was on my way, accompanied up a short concrete staircase that had chipped off and exposed rusty rebar in places. The brick walls along this stretch had been painted sloppily over and over again a yellowish-brown, umber color, and the floors and fixtures were not as nicely maintained as those in the entry. My guess was they didn't need to be as much as we were beginning to pass through to where admissions—they called us inmates "admissions"—were housed in open dormitories non-segregated but monitored by security level: minimum, medium, close or maximum. Unseen and unheard no matter the threat, and what felt at times like being left to our own devices, it was truly about survival. Not at all unlike *Lord of the Flies,* irregardless of persistent rape and murder (disregards to Simon, and to Piggy). The tone set at this intersection was sinister to be sure, a line in the sand, more ominous than anything, if still life-threatening, like gazing toward the deep end of the pool. But only a glimpse it was, of the young men I'd in no time share such deteriorated accommodations—twice as many of us in total as there should have been and not supposed to be, triple-bunked in dorms, where we slept and shit and stood and sat collectively at the mercy of the men in charge, who more often than not were the oldest inmates, or correction officers culling favors. A pretty straightforward function was served for the rest of these detention interiors, cordoned halls, various levels of respected authority, add-ons to the earlier entrance and its landscaping done well enough for a postcard. By contrast, these rougher passages officers and staff referred to as "the old" versus "the new," a distinction that became clearer only after the whole complex eventually shut down, remained void of any reminders of nature, certainly nothing to promote anything that reached beyond its impenetrable walls. With no plans for capital improvement, even after negative press attention, its mission of instilling a hopeless sense of what would ultimately expand to a lifelong sentence of detention remained foremost, accomplished.

By the time I was brought here to serve my sentence there had been some measures in place to address matters of morale and wrongdoing, at least on paper. One such measure being psychologists, who, 'admissions' aside, seemed as though they were there to help incite change inside a system of certain inevitability. Whether hired as a front to deflect from the public sentiment of the prison's lacking in our general welfare and reform or in some combination with a spearheaded campaign toward a future funding operation for the new industrial prison complex underway was hard to know, having had no idea myself what was going on as it was happening. They did ask a lot of me is all I took, questions on top of questions.

On day one: Explain what it was like growing up, the situation between my mother and father, and what did I believe had led to their separation and did I take any responsibly for it on myself? And how had it been without him in my life versus with? To the next: Was I ever abused as a child? Describe the kind of upbringing my mother provided to me as a young boy. My father? And now? Had either of them ever broken the law? And any in particular that I could better recall and explain further? Did either of them ever do drugs, or drink alcohol in excess?

Did I?—come day four, picking up wherever it was we last left off—which led to more questions about me and less about my parents: What was *I* like as a young boy? What did *I* want to be when I grew up? Where did *I* believe I had gone wrong in my life? Explain my criminal history, whether charged and convicted or not, anything and everything that I could think of as deviant and immoral that might better their evaluation. Did I believe myself capable of change?

While regulated to what I can best describe as a purgatory prison throughout this judgment period, in addition to days of further and far-reaching psychological questioning, which didn't go on consecutively but intermittently and what made it seem prolonged more than I guess it ultimately became, I was also given a physical examination, aptitude and IQ tests. Whether the results were good or bad I remain in the dark about and maybe didn't matter. But by the end of these preceding evaluations and tests I'd taken and other's note-making, I was ingrained with the strictest rules and regulations I had ever come under by an officer and by unshackled supervision I was to abide at all times and determinative of my sentencing structure.

"You will serve your time under medium security"—was the result

I was being given by a staff member, speaking without looking at me but at a carbon copy on the desk in front of her—"which allows for certain privileges, like permission to work, longer allotment of hours spent in the yard, extended visitation time."

Another officer, who'd not spoken a word, startled me when asking in a voice that didn't match her face: "Do you understand everything that's been relayed to you?"

And unlike the other officer, barking at me, I'd come piercingly into her focused sightline when I answered back: "Yes, ma'am."

I turned eighteen the day before my assignment, making me question whether my age played some part in why I'd been waiting so long for the next morning to arrive, when I was finally taken into the dormitory with everybody else where I belonged.

It was quick and swift, cutting me loose like a wild animal into a pen. "This is you," the officer ahead of me said, stopping at the first open cell we encountered on the right.

Positioned inside were three empty bunk beds, each made precisely the same and surrounded by the smallest of breathing room equally as tidy and appointed, what for me immediately spoke to how the rules were absolutely meant to be followed and not the least bit half-assed. Bars painted creamy white divided these sleeping quarters from the ones adjacent to it, after another and another, a long repetition of gridded panes of steel and concrete that made privacy impossible. Though why it would be any different, why comforts of home should be made a priority here, I understood the reasoning for neither.

"You can take that one—the bottom bunk. They'll all be returning from the yard soon," the officer continued, pointing his finger at it after pulling his attention away from a scratched-off clipboard in his hand.

I froze, stood stoned just past the opened gate of the cell, smelling myself, my fear, sweat and a singe of Borax in my nose leftover from the clothes I'd just slid into.

"Alright, then," the officer said, leaving me this way.

I nodded back in some kind of mannerly way and then looked up and down at the other inmate's beds, resolved I was to picture the faces of the guys who slept in them before I was really faced with them, and I was telling myself their stories already, of how they landed themselves here. And what version of my own was I going to tell? Who was I now? Aside from the rules laid down by the staff, what were those unspoken and adhered to by inmates and how would I know what not to do, who not to be in here, in order that I might endure.

In this quiet moment, between before and after, freedom and captivity, still alone but for my swimming thoughts, no matter I was drowning in them, I saw myself as a part of the framework made up within this larger cage of concrete and steel that had divided me from the open passages of hallways leading me to it. Back to those tedious days I'd spent being asked who I was, out through the front entrance I escaped in my mind, wearing my same clothes I'd arrived in and that I'd worn for the past several days. Back on the bus, taking the interstate, through every town, every place I'd ever been and again making every decision I ever made, as though I might could choose differently. But of course I couldn't. Here I was, dressed like somebody else, everybody else. More than alone I was all of us put together, a larger body now, a whole, a constant, inescapable hum. It was the tapping against my car seat and the knock on the door, the slamming of a fist, a gunshot gone off, the beat of a heart. I could hear all of it, all at the same time, when at last the feeling overwhelmed me, and true confinement sank in.

chapter 3

The motel incident haunted me throughout the rest of the summer and well into the start of the next school year, when by October, more timely, on Halloween, our teacher sat at her desk grading quizzes, glancing up on occasion to check whether we were still reading silently at our desks. A tall and skinny, black witch's cap, the shiny plastic kind, stuck out from the top of her head. Two mummies slouched alongside the wall of windows lined with radiator coil overlooking the faculty parking lot. Another witch, good like Glenda, sat directly across from Ms. Roundtree quietly nodding her pointed head over our assigned pages. And near the middle were these two vampires, sat on either side of Lindy Graham dressed like a cheerleader, Tyler Green and myself, pretending to read and passing a note whenever the bad witch wasn't surveilling the classroom. Of course, Tyler, he'd come to school that morning already looking the part of a real vampire; for me, having had no costume to wear, I'd squirted ketchup on my chin at lunchtime, popped up my shirt collar, and wet back my hair in the boys' bathroom.

We were writing back and forth about what this high school party he'd heard that someone his older brother knew was having later that night might be like. Did he think somebody's parents were gonna be there? Or anyone else our age? Drinking? Smoking? Tyler's older brother had planned on driving and agreed to let us come along with him and some of his friends so long as Tyler didn't tell their dad and how I figured all along was why we must've been invited, not technically. For what other reason could there be to want us tagging along. But Tyler said to me it was cool, don't think too much, and that the worst that could happen is that we'd throw up. He wasn't as persuadable as his older brother, but I'm sure I circled yes, that yeah I wanted to go, if only to get away from home for the night. Although I'd circled yes so many times on so many notes passed around in class I may have actually circled no. It doesn't matter, though, I never made it to any party.

The classroom door swung open and every head lifted from the page.

"*Momma? . . .*" I spoke up under my breath.

Yeah, it *was* her, though she could've easily been a flesh-starved zombie, haggard to the point of appearing like an anomaly of human nature she was so skinny, wearing her coral-colored corduroys and white blouse slung low around the neck and clinging to her bones for dear life. She'd done her hair the same as she always did but her face was not as pretty as it usually was. And her eyes were bloodshot and circled red and blue, smudged and faded into the runny makeup around them and caved in as deeply as her sunken cheeks. She'd been crying and still was in between gulps of breath and sniffling coughs and the shakes, like something scary she put on to mark the calendar, except for she clearly wasn't in costume. And though she looked pretty bad, she didn't always look *this* bad.

"Excuse me, um, hello! *Ma'am*," Ms. Roundtree spoke up, scooting back her chair to stand.

"I'm taking my son home," Mom stopped her. "Travis, come on, hon."

Ms. Roundtree looked stunned like she'd taken one in the gut, and the classroom too, the air sucked from it, fell even more silent around her.

"Go on and get your stuff. We're goin," Mom went on without any explanation.

"*Mom . . .*" I tried, pretending to be as shocked as my classmates.

"Trav, get movin, now."

"Come on, stop—stop—please," I pleaded with her, standing from my desk and waving my arms to try to keep her from entering into the classroom any further than she already had, passing right by Ms. Roundtree like she wasn't there.

"*What are you doing here, Momma?*" I whispered.

"Here," she said, reaching around me, and instead of the stench of rot and gore trailing after her, a smack from her liquored breath plastered my own face with embarrassment, heated it up and made my eyes itch and cross.

"*Momma . . . Wait . . .*" I tried, but there was no use.

Up close I better understood just how bad her condition really was: her left cheek was swollen and not made-up to look bruised the way that it did, without any makeup at all; purple, smeary skin around the one eye socket was on purpose and not by her own hand; blotchy impressions were evidenced up and down both her arms like she'd been grabbed, more man-handled.

"Sweetie, come on, now, get up! Don't make me ask a third time. We're leavin," she shouted out over the gawking stares, commanding everyone's undivided attention, the kind of attention I never sought but rather avoided. She was not having it any other way.

I did as I was told, collected up whatever I had out on my desk with the other things I'd put away inside of it, and I began to move.

"Hurry up, already. Get everything. Don't leave nothin behind."

Hearing her say that I wondered if maybe I was never coming back and it only slowed me down and pissed her off.

Although she wasn't looking at anyone other than me, her anger directed nowhere else other than in my direction, her eyes were crossed and crooked, unfocused, even when she pointedly rushed through the rows of desks toward me, and so I was unsure of myself, where I stood.

"Are you mad at me?" I asked. "Why're you mad at *me*?"

Before Mom was even aware of herself and my questioning, the teacher spoke up again. "Ma'am, *ma'am*," more scolding in her tone, standing her ground this time when next she said, "Who do you think you are? You can't just—" but was quickly shut down by Mom's drunken slurs, her flailing, misdirected arm that tethered itself to mine, her then incessant snatching at what she could of my shirt and jacket slung over my elbow, managing only to retrieve my backpack at first.

The sound of those white heels she always dragged under her feet, clacking across the tile floors, cut straight through me as we moved out.

Not putting up any more of a struggle, we were then finally exiting the stunned classroom as quickly as she'd entered into it, only stopped by her foot catching on the leg of Priscilla Whitaker's desk, that and her swaying, stumbled attempts at walking faster. Everyone, even Ms. Roundtree, kept silent the whole time we did until when the door slammed shut behind us and the kids erupted with reaction: small-throated laughter mixed with groaning sighs and grumbles. I didn't need to ask, though I wondered what they were saying, but knew I'd find out for sure come Monday morning.

I continued after Mom down the emptied hallway. Mortified I was but thankful the bell had not yet rung; at least now not everyone in the entire school had witnessed "that seventh-grade-kid's momma," the one everyone who had would be talking about and without any need for stretching the truth.

She turned and wrapped both arms around me, tucked her hands into mine like she was cold or my date to the dance. Under the fluorescent overhead lights I could see in greater detail the bruising under her eye and how red her arms looked.

"What happened to you, Momma? What're you *doin* here?"

"That fuckin piece a shit . . ." was all she mumbled and then she walked with determination, steering us in the direction of the bathrooms: the girls' bathroom.

"Momma, no! Stop, stop! What're you doing? No! We're not goin in there . . ."

I tried my best to pull her away and keep us on a swift path toward the exit doors but she succeeded in dragging us into the bathroom instead. Luckily it was only the two of us inside, though every noise we made I knew announced itself into another kind of intercom system, our voices amplified by the floor-to-ceiling tile everywhere, me as her accomplice instead of hostage in a holdup.

She looked at herself in the mirror, panting, almost panicked it seemed by something, not to be confused with someone, because never did she show fear of another person, at least not in front of me. Even on his worst day Dad looked small in front of Mom, her defiance overpowering his.

"Oh my God. Would you look at this . . . He really did it to me this time, huh?" She closed her eyes and bore down onto a sink basin. I thought the fixture might just sever itself from the wall it clung to, having never struggled against an adult person's weight before.

"Who? Was it Daddy? Is he back?"

She wasn't giving me any answers.

"*Momma*, why are you here? What happened?"

"What, am I not allowed to just come and see you because I damn well won't to?"

"No, you can't. Come on, now. Not like this! Not with everybody else, in class, Momma. What is it? What happened? Tell me."

In the mirror I watched her like a rerun on TV.

"I wanted to see my child—my baby," she cried, sobbing, swiping at her face with toilet paper, tenderly pressing it into the skin under her eyes. As close as we were to each other now, I could smell her and only her: perfume mixed with sweat, dried beneath more sweat, burning with alcohol. She was beside herself, unable to stop her hands from shaking, and an induced hysteria illuminated behind her eyes.

"Where're you coming from? Who did this to you?"

"I'm sorry, sweetie. I am," she continued, turning herself away from the mirror's reflection and propping herself completely up onto the edge of the sink.

I imagined the entire bathroom caving in around us, starting with the sink mounted to the wall that my mom saw fit to fully sit onto like it was made for her. Although she probably weighed as little as the fattest girl in the seventh grade—who also shared my mom's endurance for being called names—I still watched for the bolts to loosen. I pictured pipes bursting and ceramic wall tiles flying off like shingles in a tornado, the toilet stall doors collapsing, *smash!* after *smash!* around us.

Her face was blotchy, and sticky, strands of sweaty hair dried stuck. And her arms shown more clearly the grips of hands much larger than my own. Dad's hands were three towns away on a job, incapable, I was sure, and so it had to have been Tommy's dad who'd done this to her. I took a deep breath and braced myself.

"So, Tommy's dad, then? Was it Todd? Did *he* do this, Momma?"

"Yes," she sobbed. "Son of a bitch. I guess it ain't that hard to tell? Right? Tells me he's gonna stay with that sow of his."

"You mean Pam?" I asked, because it could have been any number of women she was referring to. Todd was as much a whore as the woman sitting next to me—Todd's branding, not mine, and Dad's too, and by everyone who didn't know her; she'd probably been called a whore even when she was still a virgin.

"Sweetie, I'm sorry. Do you forgive me? I'm so, so sorry," she said, starting to cry again, slumped over like a sad sack. "I messed up. I'm shit. I'm sorry I came here to your school. You hate me."

I ignored her bellyaching and nodded along, felt of her arms, twisted the loose, hanging skin to better inspect the pattern of bruises. "Momma, these . . . these are not light hits. You've really got some sore spots on you."

"Todd, he's, well . . . you know. And you know, little ole me . . . here I am. But hell, I hit him back. I sure did and real hard!"

The muscles on her arms felt soft and spongy, and I could feel down through it to the bone, cold and solid and unbreakable, like how the sweating copper pipe connecting to the condenser out behind our house did, wrapped in soggy insulation foam, that Dad needed Todd to repair that one time, back when they were still together, Mom and Dad. And I remembered how I watched him, much younger then, unaware of any double-dealing that may have already been happening. How could I've possibly known, though? Still, I blamed myself for not seeing it coming, he and Mom, Pam and Mom always at odds, me and Tommy in the middle of it, all of it.

Snot hung on to her upper lip. I tore off a length of toilet paper and handed it to her, put my hand on her shoulder, kissed her swollen cheek, still thinking about how the bell might ring any second.

"Come on, Momma, let's move on now, get you outta here and into the car. You know we're in the girls' bathroom, right? So please. Can we? Please . . . Can we just go? We have to leave before somebody comes in here. You got everything? Get your pocketbook."

"So what if I was hitting him first. He just shoved me off, and I kept on going. Buddy I gave it to him good. Best I could. I just couldn't stop. Kept on hittin the bastard. He wadn't happy about that . . . No, no, no," she said, laughing through a throaty cough, tears slick and shining up her puffy under-eyes so much she looked like she'd been in the ring. "The man thinks he can just, what? Push me aside like that. Like I'm trash. Dirt up under his feet. You know something, he done told me things . . . shared stuff with me he hadn't told nobody. Yeah, so . . . But I dunno, I—" She began to trail off, lose herself and tear up again, though something trained her eyes almost instantly and she stopped it, focused for a moment on whatever it was in front of her that I couldn't see. Maybe it was a reenactment of some story Todd had told her—made up to tell her, how I saw it. Dad was always telling her stories, too, like a future she could depend on.

Either that or disciplinary action had been taken against her and she wasn't allowed to break. Don't say a word. Put up or shut up. Scolded how a teacher who hated children did, or a dad like mine who wished he'd never become one: "One of my greatest regrets is havin had you. Second only to your momma and her makin sure it happened."

Mom laughed it off and reached for her pocketbook, nearly knocking it off the edge of the sink plundering through it.

"Momma, you ready? Come on, wouldya stop already, please." I took her pocketbook away and tried pulling her together, giving her more toilet paper and hugs. "Let's go home now," I sighed. "Can we do that? Please, can we, Momma? . . ."

She exhaled long and cool and pressed her hair back, stilted up on her heels and checked her appearance in the mirror one last time.

"Alright," I said.

"Now he wants to go back to that—"

"—Momma. Let's go. Is that it? You got everything?"

The two of us walked out, finally, with me talking her down, continuing to speak to her in a consoling tone of voice. "Let's get you home, Momma. Get you cleaned up."

We made it to the edge of the front steps of the school when the bell rang. She continued to lean on me, the right side of her body folded over my shoulder like a prize-winning stuffed animal I'd won at the County Fair. I hated the County Fair.

I found our car in the parking lot. She slumped over in the front seat when I let go of her, blocking the door from shutting when I tried.

"*Momma* . . . Mom!"

I came around to my side of the car and got in and slammed both doors shut, sealing us off completely.

"So?" I asked her.

"*So?* So what?"

"And then what happened?"

"Whataya mean? Here I am."

"I know that, Momma. But what'd you come and get me for?"

"Well, Trav, I just took off, come straight here. I wanted to get you. Take you outta there. Take you home. With me. I needed you."

I couldn't blame her for it, her showing up the way that she had. It was my own damned fault, for being as agreeable as I was with everything she'd said, like nodding my head with a frown, answering her, "Yeah, Momma, it's awful. I hate it. That they're making me go. Anyplace else. I can't wait to get outta there," when she asked: "Don't you hate school, Trav?" I didn't hate school and I couldn't wait to go every day. Now, I didn't love school, either, and was actually beginning to feel the way she thought I did about it, but anyplace else other than home was fine by me.

I sat back in my seat and looked out at the woods waving in the field next to the school parking lot, a smattering of deep red and orange only just beginning to show. In a month they'd look dead and gone, skeletons, their bones picked clean.

"Let's go home, Momma," I said, catching my breath.

She cranked the Chevy and gassed it sideways out of the parking lot, stalling behind lines of school buses before going around and then idling us between groups of costumed students ready to cram into them, some who could very well be my own classmates, snickering and walking alongside our car windows as we rode past. We weren't nearly far enough away from everyone, onlookers and storytellers, from Monday morning. I'll bet they must recognize her, I thought, and me with her.

I slid down and kept my head lowered, ashamed though determined still, feeling through her pocketbook. I couldn't find what she needed, what she didn't need to ask for.

"Want me to run in somewhere? Grab you some smokes?"

chapter 4

I don't remember falling asleep but I dreamed I was walking through Granddad's house. I'd found my way in the dark through the long, piecemeal hallway reconstructed around me like a puzzle, or more a maze, changed so much over time that it was somehow all the different versions of it with every add-on and remodel ever constructed and now finally made-over into one singular vision of theirs combined— with my own. Rooms were where they would've been: he and Grandma's, his alone in the way I was seeing it, feeling like she'd died and gone without a trace; Mom's old room that they never changed since she left home at sixteen; Aunt Sharleen's used for storage; and the blue-tiled bathroom with its clawfoot tub ringed in iron scum. These led to what was this even more vague image in my mind, of what I remember as the informal living room where company sat and talked and the kitchen and dining room connected to altogether span the back of the house.

At the hall's end, a picture hung on the wall that I can't place, and a door to the right was left open into the living room even though I was always told to keep it shut so the air wouldn't let out or come in. Seeing the opened doorway and recognizing it for what it was I walked through it as an adult and no longer a child. The arrangement of furniture inside appeared the same as how I'd seen it last: my grandparents' chairs, arranged around the wooden TV, with their upholstered backs facing toward me immediately upon entering the room. But before seeing these chairs I'd looked left and up the carpeted staircase to see a large floor-to-ceiling painting of angels, the one that leaned against the landing wall.

I could feel heat warming up against my face, hear crackling pops and sizzles from what in my subconscious must have been the source, and I saw how the living room was dimmer than usual with the TV set cut off. The room turned gray and spotlit with an amber glow against the ceiling of one corner. Turning my view toward the chairs, circling around to face them, as if I was going to walk right over to Grandma's, have a seat on its arm—as I always did—I instead looked to his. The brown chair was ablaze, engulfed entirely in flames. The room around it was so dim and turned darker still, oddly unharmed by the fire that raged. I felt myself entirely alone in the house, oddly unafraid of the sight of my granddad's chair on fire, staring at its emptiness for another moment, smoke billowing around its sides from underneath the seat, mushrooming up onto the ceiling. Taught springs were exposed through the charred fabric and bits of its cushioning smoldered away.

Then I felt my face illuminate, my eyes burn like I'd been standing there too close for too long without doing anything, staring directly into the fire. And I touched my skin and sniffed the air in the room but smelled nothing burning, nor did my fingertips feel anything, when I knew none of it was actually happening. I squinted with the realization, that I'd only fallen asleep, that my granddad was not dead yet, although he would be soon. I took a step back and shook the feeling of the fire and instead detected myself, sweating in bed, my surroundings: the bunk, the solid wall beside it, this place, Polk, the window.

Wide-eyed and quick to acclimate, I wrestled myself up from the bed and looked out at a cloudless, deep blue sky. Lights overhead were

still switched on in the dormitory, glaringly bright and recasting the
glass window into a mirror that I wanted to better see myself in, for
assurances that I wasn't still dreaming. Like a sudden thunderstorm,
the mattress over my head started to rumble and the strips of sprung-
out metal holding it and what was actually the person creating the
disturbance in place above me rattled.

"*Hello*," I heard him say to me—no one else around for him to say
it to—with no emotion, and I quickly turned over in a swath of sweat
to place him. "Yeah, *you*. Wakey, wakey."

"*Hi* . . ." I spoke up, having to say something, and cowering when
I did, dazed I'd not discovered him lying there sooner, as in the
moment I awoke to find *I* was still here.

"Sorry about that. Didn't mean to scare you. If I did. You don't
scare easily, do ya?"

"No . . . I don't," I said, stiffening up, straightening my back to
become even an inch taller. I wasn't ready to face him just yet, or
better yet, to look my reality in the face. I felt the wall I was up
against, fortunate to have its safety stacked beside me and to have
been assigned that first cell and not one dead-centered without any
kind of protection. I folded inward, waited to be put out of it. Flick-
ering there like a fire under him I waited until he slung his torso over
the edge of the mattress with his head upside-down to look straight
at me.

"Good. Cause otherwise you're in the wrong place, my compadre."

His dirty blond hair hung stringy and sheened oily under the light.
And his breath, speaking very breathy to me, I guess because of the
heaped position he was in over the bed mashed his diaphragm—and
also turned his face red to purple to blue and popped out veins too—
was stagnant and sour. Maybe he'd not said a word in some time, or
he'd said so much he'd dried his mouth out.

He and I simply coexisted for another moment, breathed the same
air, and it got me wondering how he knew that I awakened below
him and why he had not gotten me up when he first came back from

the yard. Aren't inmates supposed to assess fresh meat and figure out how best to devour it? He must've felt me moving around in bed. But was I? When I was walking around between the rooms in Grand-dad's house? My impression of sweat in the bed evidenced otherwise. Could he hear me?

"You were out like a light. But don't worry, you didn't miss nothin. Yer up just in time for dinner. And if you don't eat *you don't eat*."

No sooner than he said this, a loud buzzing siren echoed through-out the dormitory and he was hopping down from his bunk.

"You gotta stand," he said, motioning me, so I did too. "Just follow my lead, alright."

I nodded and glanced over at the other bunk, wondering where the other guy was.

"And don't go worryin about him. The quiet type. Maybe a mute. I dunno. But keeps to himself and that's good for me *and* you. Out of trouble. Though, maybe those are the ones you really oughta worry about, huh? No—I'm kiddin, kiddin . . . Or maybe it's more the one tellin you not to worry." He grinned. "In all seriousness, basically do whatever they tell ya to do, the officers, within reason, and every-thing'll run smooth."

Just as he said this two sets of officers entered through opened doors at both ends of the silenced dormitory, shortly followed by another officer, unaccompanied but holding a stick out in one hand and whacking it in the palm of the other. This began the nightly routine of showing anyone else straggling to keep up in his vicinity where they needed to be, put in their place into the larger group of us that moved out single-filed, as another officer was counting and checking each and every inmate off on a clipboard.

"Alright! You know the drill," an officer said over our heads.

None of the bars were closed, even still, everything wide open, and in an orderly herd everyone did as they were told.

As he'd instructed, I followed the movements of the bunkmate up above me—now in front of me—walking a straight line, with his arms taught and flat-handed, almost marching, briskly, militarily. Trained or not, I thought, he might next belt out in sync with his footsteps: "Left. Left. Left—Right—Left!" I didn't dare mimic him, not this early on, his marching to the beat of his own drum, literally. There was humor in it, though, some glimmer of joy to be had out of watching his level of seriousness and ecstatic adherence to every rule. Projecting confidence or playing the part or not, it was sometimes hard to keep up with, for me to know if he was really that serious or only doing it for a smile. Even the slightest amount of humor seemed at odds with the situation at hand, and any detection of it in mine or anyone else's behavior because of it I feared certain repercussions. I carried on as if this was the introduction to part one of his unpublished guidebook: *How to Succeed in Prison Without Really Trying*.

We stepped forward into another hallway that merged with other inmates in line, collectively passing alongside more emptied dormitories with opened cells showing the same kind of stock-stillness as a classroom during The Pledge of Allegiance or the minutes after a steam whistle. Only then did I understand just how many of us there actually was. Out in the open this way, during these orchestrated walks to meals, arranged around stringent scheduling and shifting officers and their wielding power, new admissions stood out the most, and I felt it; eyes were on me then, in those early days, sizing me up and down.

"Don't look at anyone for *too* long," my bunkmate said ahead of me.

When we sat down with our trays the first thing I asked was his name.

"Jacob," he said. He set his fork down to reach politely across the table and shake my hand, the one I wiped off on my knee before reciprocating, firmly like it really meant something. And he eyed me straight and narrow, too. "I'd say it was nice to meet you but under the circumstances I guess it don't make a whole helluva lot a sense to."

"Any other kinda way than this, I suppose you're right," I said.

I'm not sure what sort of odds I had stacked against his likelihood, but with Jacob I did get the feeling that somehow I had gotten lucky. It was during that first meal, watching him speak to me, in his quiet, careful choosing of words, that somehow eased my anxiety, I knew something had to be off. I didn't want to think negatively of him, to worsen things, as bad as they already were, the circumstance I was in—we both were—I just couldn't understand how someone could remain as honest and sincere as this guy was towards me, having been surrounded by the chaotic day-to-day life that essentially turned men back into the animals we'd been brought up to grow out of, and being made to feel like one, like it was the only way to live.

"And what should I call you?" he asked me, chewing and smacking.

"Travis."

"So, then, Travis, what brings you here?" His mouth was a big grin full of bright green peas that looked like a boy half his age would show his momma to make her proud, his daddy mad.

I shifted in my seat and looked around at all the other tables first before answering him, more whispering the one word: "Murder."

He swallowed the peas and stared straight through me, stupefied.

Even whispering I'd said the word less matter-of-factly and more as if to let him know that I was going to tell you, but it might not be the answer you would expect from me, and so don't expect you can take advantage of me if that was your expectation.

"Oh, well then how the hell'd you get assigned *here*?" he said, wide-eyed, snapping out of it. "You won't be for long if that's the case. Not in here." And he took his eyes away, spooned at his plate like it didn't mean anything what I'd said.

I wasn't sure how to answer that, if it was a question he was asking me or one he was trying to work out on his own.

"Does anybody else know—besides the pigs that put you here? Did you tell any of em in here, I mean?" he asked.

"No. Just you."

"Good. That'd shorten your time even more. String beans get snapped. And how old are you?"

"I turned eighteen the day before yesterday."

"Well then we should throw you a birthday party or somethin. Maybe drink some beer? Go down to the creek. Invite some girls." He grinned and held his stare at me, with a subtle pause, making sure I understood that he was only just pretending and wasn't going to make that happen. "Naw, but, for what it's worth, ain't much I know: *Happy Birthday?*"

I laughed. "Thanks. Not a very happy one I don't guess but it's reason enough to think on, another year." Maybe then I'd stepped my foot in it, instead of overlooking the obvious, making light of the troubles I made for myself. He wasn't saying another word. "And you? How old are you?"

"Nineteen, closer to twenty. And you know somethin, most of em in here ain't much older, give or take somewhere around there. Not too many as young as you—some, but still, not older by much," he explained. "I know of some though, maybe twenty-one, -two—the elderly in here they're called. Yer young and seem even younger," he said, drawing his face into a frown. "I guess that could also mean you've got many years to look forward to."

I shrugged and tried not to show any more emotion, to be as optimistic as he was trying to make me.

"But not for you to worry, not in here you won't. Most put in yer position'll serve their time elsewhere, after moving on to another prison. Out-of-state maybe. A kicked can. I don't know. I mean, obviously you ain't gettin out any time soon," he said, picking at a roll on the corner of his dinner tray. "They'll have you outta here and on to another one before long," he continued. "Guys come and they go. A lot of em come right back."

"What I said—that's not why I'm in here. I—I said that—I don't know. I thought I would come off differently I guess."

"Oh. Alright, then. I figured. That makes more sense. Yer story wadn't making any. So what *did* ya do?"

"Well, I took all the cash out of the register where I was workin at—had been a good while, too. Them folks didn't deserve all that, neither. But yeah, went off with it, whatever else I could take . . . Gone for a little while, on a bit of a spree I guess you'd call it. Had got in a bit of hot water before, but things had cooled off . . . Still, I just couldn't keep on doin it, you know. I had to get the hell outta that place—fore I got stuck there forever."

"Ah, yep. 10-4 to that! And ain't nothin wrong with a spree. Done been on one a couple times myself. See, now that's better. That checks out. You know, you shouldn't tell a story like that. Lets a man make up his own ending to it. Unless you *are*, making it up . . . If you are then you should keep tellin it. Makes a lot more sense. That's what you say if anybody asks. Can't nobody make you prove you stole something in here. Ain't no place to hide nothing."

"No, yeah, you're right." I took a long sip and swallowed tightly. "And what about you? What'd you do?"

"Well, I stole my daddy's car," he said with a "shit-happens" shrug and smile. "Simple as that. Don't get much easier to make sense outta what I done to deserve my time."

"And how long you got left? How long you been in already?"

"Well, I guess it's not *that* simple. You see, it ain't the first time I took it but my daddy only reported it this one time—I caught him on a bad day, and for the last time—and so I got a year on account of me only being eighteen when it happened, but not a first-time offender so I didn't get as little as I mighta could had I been. I done some time before, something much smaller, pettier. Then after that I broke bad, got caught with drugs, which is why I stole the car in the first place go figure. So now it's been . . . goin in-and-out for about two years almost, and then some more left to go ahead of me. Don't get me wrong, though. After I turn twenty-one next year I intend to keep myself outta here for good. And you gotta do good to be good. At least better, right?"

"Yeah, no, you're right. And same goes for me, once I get out . . ."

He snickered at my wishful thinking, like it was something he'd heard not only himself proclaim before but everyone else in here for the first time.

"But is it hard to do that?" I continued. "Being good—in here, I mean."

I was thinking that maybe I had figured him out then, the secret to staying sane, safe, surviving the way that he had, and with what looked like, if not his head held high, his chin up. Was this warm-hearted act of kindness simply that: an act? I can understand the will and motivation to remain optimistic for one's future, combined with a record shining as spotlessly clean as possible to achieve it sooner than later even more so.

"How do you mean?" he asked, looking at me now through hair in his eyes. "I don't follow."

"Well, I guess I imagined you—well not *you*, not exactly, but whoever it was you were going to be, my cellmate—would be someone, I dunno, sorta different. Honest to God, I think that's what scared me the most about coming here."

"Different, how do you mean?"

"Angrier, aggressive, and violent, especially towards me. At least to me you don't seem to have an angry bone in your body. And nobody else around here has bothered me yet. Not even come up to me. Aren't they supposed to?"

Jacob laughed out loud at this and finished the last bite of his dinner roll before saying, "Man, you got me all wrong. They call me crazy in here! Crazy-ass Jay . . . First time I was in I came in swinging at everyone, everything, and since I'm back in it, yeah, they know their place. Counselors or whatever, even they labeled me insane. Nobody messes with me, and since you are with me, they ain't messing with you neither. You see?"

I hadn't seen it, not until he spelled it out for me, and I paused to take everything into account, our every moment together leading up to this one. It was more an ease that Jacob navigated himself with and less his jolly clownish behavior, his air of confidence—or was he a confidence man? How only the two of us were sitting at a table set for six, surrounded by mostly tables at capacity or over, not one of them brave enough to burst this unspoken bubble around us, suddenly it clicked.

"Crazy Jay . . ."

"Yeah, but maybe don't call me that. To tell you the truth I don't like it all that much. Really I'm not who they say I am. All my life I've been called all sorts of things. And you seem like somebody who wouldn't so—"

"Jacob it is, then."

I faced Jacob, Mr. Happy-go-lucky, cheerful with a spoonful of mashed potatoes in his mitt, and I understood him; we had an understanding. And maybe I was both the most unfortunate and luckiest man alive. A man because I was now eighteen, and because I was considered one among the many stuck here in this place, seen as capable of things only men could understand and grapple with, an image contrary to the version outside, where I was no one. In here, however, I was someone not to be messed with, even if only by association. On the flip side of the coin I called tails that I'd been handed, this guy might just soon kill me in my sleep.

"Don't worry about it, yer safe in here," he reassured me. "And you can call me Jay if you won't to. Just Jay. Only my ma ever called me Jacob."

I nodded and kept my head down, conversation to a minimum until dinnertime was done, when in whatever recreation time remained in the day, dinner tables transformed into card tables and guys on full stomachs flexed their strength for other inmates, what I guessed were further means of marking territory, seeing as how we weren't allowed to piss on table legs.

I wasn't up for any card games and didn't have much muscle to flex. I just wanted to return to my bunk, even though I didn't have to, not so soon, but I didn't want to be anywhere alone. And what a pussy I would've looked like to the other inmates, I worried, had I just gone and closed myself off in the cell on my first night. Sticking close to Jacob was the only plan I'd devised so far, and the circus around us was a spectator sport he savored, along with his last sips of milk or tea or water he was nursing.

Before long, guys went from poker-playing to arm-wrestling, to exchanging stories about girlfriends they missed at home, some their wives, another his five-year-old son. And whenever commiserating over how badly they'd missed sex it was as if they had never had it before, but clearly they had. Urges didn't go away just because they were locked up and were satisfied no matter the cost. The cost of doing business, they called it, which, in order not to pay the price, cost you.

"You gotta give em something right upfront," Jay said. "Either commissary money or a black eye. A broken jaw is better but more consequential in the long run. Initiate yourself before they initiate you."

I tried to play it cool, "Yeah, yeah, definitely. I understand," but inside I was terrified. Might I maybe had; money I did not. Nor could I see myself capable of walking up to any of these guys and hitting them at face value. Stick to the plan, I reminded myself, standing up from the table after Jay did, walking like his shadow back to our bunks.

By then it was almost lights out, "a time when you least expect it, always, no matter how long you've been here," Jay told me. In suspense I propped up my head as best I could with the curdled pillow I'd been given and waited for it to happen, but eventually became convinced it never would. I tried wandering off, rechanneling my thoughts away from their anxious tendencies toward stupid things, like how the layers of foam separating my spine from creaky metal springs underneath looked like two flat rubbery pancakes and gave no relief. Above me I could see Jacob's squeezed out between the slats, and I wondered if in the morning we both would have red patterned impressions made across our backs. How this passed as a mattress, I don't know. And with it a thin, itchy sheet and woolen blanket moths wouldn't even give a chance, a proper bed fit to sleep in?

Onto my side I curled and turned to face the wall, and I tried making out old scribbles and markings left behind in the painted brick. At first nothing made any sense, not legible enough to read in all the dingy cream-colored chicken scratch. Even had it been, I don't think it could have been interesting enough to take my mind off tomorrow. Then, in a heavier hand, inscribed deep down to a past paint color, a whole paragraph of scrawl could be read, line for line, and it was getting interesting, until the rest of the story disappeared behind the side of my bunk. Pulling back the covers and the edge of mattress I continued to read another sentence or maybe it was poetry, until I was reading something even better: the title of an actual book. It was probably one of Jacob's, taken out of the library against the rules, forgotten about and fallen between the wall and my mattress or purposefully hidden there. Maybe it could've even belonged to someone before him, or another me, who had occupied this very bed.

I held of it firmly in my hand right as the room cut to black with a loud pop of the breaker, echoing as quickly as I could hear it—"Lights out!"

I wasn't tired at all and continued looking through the dark at minor details reenvisioning before my eyes: the metal framework of the bunks finding light from lampposts outside the wide windows, indentions in the sheeny brick. I could have very well slept as much as I'd needed before dinnertime, wide awake but still dreaming it felt, now more worried than I was then, about everything I knew.

I peeled open the now unreadable book to a page bookmarked with a paperclip, half uncurled. I spun it around and watched tiny fragments of light chase up and down its sides. Some things could go hidden in here after all. Carefully I wedged the book behind the mattress in the spot where I'd found it, wondering where I could next hide the paperclip, but along the wall, in an unmarked plot of brick-work near my head, I first scratched in my initials 'TLW' and the year ''93' underneath. Its tip seemed sharpened because of it, a long buried tool that had since been forgotten about, destined to be found. Who had it belonged to? Had they left it there knowing someday someone like me, perhaps like them, would need it? I pressed the bent point to my fingertip, instantly drawing a droplet of blood, and with it came the unfamiliar sense of accomplishment, sparked by such a discovery I'd made inside this strange and I'll admit scary new place. It spoke to me like the first word of some hidden language I was only beginning to learn, an understanding among those of us who've experienced it firsthand and need to know, how I was going to have to live from then on in order that I might survive.

chapter 5

With the exception of *Pam's Beauty*, the Sellers's house across the street was a mirror image of our own: homely, single-story, hip roof, combination horizontal-vertical lap siding, big picture window, built brand-new twenty years prior. Ours, however, had not retained a kind of vibrancy pictured in the same catalog it was likely purchased from, not in the way theirs had. Its shutters looked to be just painted even years after they had been and when you might soon suspect to see signs of needing a fresh coat but not yet. The windowpanes never showed cracked or broken, always reflecting a kept-up yard, too, where, because Tommy had a little brother, Brian, there seemed to be some kind of bright spot out there on the front lawn or side strip of clean-cut grass. Up and down the driveway, stretched long enough for two parked cars, Tommy had first learned how to ride his bike before taking it out into the street. Inside the house, however, I knew spelled another story, as far from home for the two of them as mine had been for me.

When Mom and I got home from school, Tommy and Brian had pushed the curtains back from the window in their front room and shoved up beside each other to watch us park and get out of our car. Todd's green truck was parked in their driveway and I tried distracting myself from it, Mom too. She'd cooled off some from the drive but couldn't stop herself from stewing in it a little longer after we got out, idling her own engine and glaring across the rain-spat asphalt at the truck and then, catching sight of the boys glaring out the window back at us—at her—she was revving up again, shouting out loud: "Fuck you. And fuck you too!"

"Momma . . . What're you doing? Stop! Don't . . ."

"No, no, I'm not shutting up! Fuck your daddy! He's a piece of shit," she yelled at the house, flailing her arms again like she had in the classroom, still slurring.

"Leave it alone," I said to her. "Just come on inside and talk about it some more, Momma."

"Come out! Todd! Get your sorry ass out here!"

"Wouldya just—"

"No! He's not sittin this one out. No way, no how. Bring yourself outside, Todd Sellers!"

"Stop," I tried again, seeing as how another scene was being made, and as warranted as it was, one I'd wished I were strong enough to make myself, I didn't want to be making one. Not us, not like this, not now. "Yer only gonna make it worse, Momma. Just come and get in the house. We can settle down and watch somethin on TV. Come on . . ."

But it was too late to compromise, as Todd had emerged, beelining from their opened front door she'd been shouting at to standing stiff at the end of the property line with a sharp glare at Mom.

"Lynn, what in the hell do you think yer doing?" he spoke under his breath. "You *don't* wanna do this, you hear me? Don't try me, woman."

"*So what?* You come straight home afterwards to be there for em? Is that what's goin on? She done put a guilt trip on ya? That's not what you told me you was gonna do, Todd. *You know.*"

"Hey!"

"Hey what?"

He was seething red in the face, more than Mom was, even more so than he had been in the motel room, but trying to keep it together as best he could I guessed, for the sake of his family maybe, I didn't know what it mattered. He looked back at his house like he had some ability to hide what was happening. Tommy and Brian snatched the curtains shut.

"I'm not doin this with you no more, Lynn. I done told you that."

"Hah," Mom laughed, and she circled our car, dropped her purse and then skipped across our driveway toward him. "*Did you*, now?"

"Momma, come on, now. Stop! Don't go over there. Get back. Come on."

Todd walled himself right up in front of her, stopped her dead in her tracks, put his foot down. "Don't."

"What? . . . You gonna hit me again? Does that make you feel good? Feel like a man? Huh? Is that right?" She kept her volume turned up, echoing between our facing houses, off the side of theirs and onto ours, back and forth until she was screaming over herself: "No . . . I know what makes you feel good . . ." And she rubbed her hand up against the crotch of her cords. "Pathetic."

"You're only embarrassing yourself, now, Lynn," Todd spoke over her.

And then Mom pointed at Pam, who'd come to the open doorway to watch but with nothing to say about it. "It damn sure ain't that lard-ass you keep locked up in there. Yeah you! What're you staring at, bitch?"

Pam didn't talk back but continued her stoic stance from inside the house like she knew it wouldn't be only words that came next out of Todd, that her best bet was to keep her mouth shut and stay out of it, at least for the moment, when the two of them were hung out to dry the way that they were.

Near the storm drain where grass edged and browned into the road Mom seemed to have forgotten all of a sudden what she was gunning for, like she was waiting for the rise out of him that wasn't coming.

"That's right. Keep your fuckin mouth shut," Todd shouted at Mom. "Don't you say another word to her. Just turn around. Walk your little ass back across that road, now, Lynn. Go on."

Mom didn't like to be told what to do, especially not when she was drinking, and she laid into him, slapped and pounded his chest the same way Pam had done at the motel but more violently, directed, purposeful. Mom was more feisty, scrappy, all arms and legs swinging around, belligerent, too, but Todd simply rose above, towered her, took her hits in stride, no differently than he had before. He could have just as easily ended her right then and there but he didn't; instead he smiled.

Tommy and Brian now stood staring out the doorway behind their mom. I didn't know what else to do but stare back. It felt like we were on opposite sides, entrenched while at the same time exchanging intel across enemy lines through only the coded expressions we managed to form in our faces.

Mom was not letting up and Todd had had enough and so finally backhanded her. She'd been stumbling around, trying to find her footing all the while shouting and swinging at him, and with that blow to her left jaw, she found herself immediately dropping to the grass, unable to keep balanced.

"Hey! What are—" I yelled, and I came around the side of our car, rushing toward him and feeling my insides churn, as though I might develop the strength to do something about it.

"Your momma's trash, son. She needed it. Just look at her take it . . ."

My focus reduced to a viewfinder's where projected inside was a slide showing nothing but Todd and my mom. A rage resolved.

"Don't you talk to him," Mom said, getting up onto her hands. "Don't you fuckin speak to my son. Not ever!"

Around his feet she was slowly rising to her knees—faced with his—and she started hitting on him again, as best she could. He shoved her off with his foot with little effort, like he'd maybe given up on her and an idea of her doing him any real harm, as though it wasn't a fair fight after all.

"Just stay the fuck away, you hear me," Todd said, walking back to the door and grasping Pam by her arms to turn her around inside the house. Tommy and Brian made way for them to enter before the door slammed shut, severing our line of communication.

"He can't just do that to you, Momma . . . Not anymore," I said, reaching down and hoisting her back up onto her feet. I could feel she was tired of fighting but still had some left in her. "Listen, willya? Don't do anything. Just stay right here."

I ran back to our car and swung open my door and fiddled with the broken closer of the glove box, again and again, until it finally sprang open. Mom had kept a pistol inside, fearful she was on late-night drives home from work and wherever else she was going at night. It was still in there, the outline of it shown soft beneath a wrapped cotton rag I was told never to look under, concealing the rigid cold of burnished metal. I snatched the rag off and quickly gripped the gun in my hand. Only in dreams had bullets been fired from it, and still, even then the touch of it was unfamiliar to me, not real. But this was really it. There wasn't any bit of shaking or trembling in my wrist either. No sweat in my palm. Laser-focused and determined to do what I had to do was all I felt, seeing this as something playing out in reality as it had in my dreams.

Todd answered the door immediately after I banged on it.

"What do—" he said, shortened by the sight of the gun in my hand aimed at his chest. I knew his stance, his height, what best position for the barrel to be pointed in for only needing to fire a single shot to drop him dead.

"Listen, now. You can't talk to my momma like that. You can't keep on hittin her neither."

I didn't recognize the sound of my voice, if the words had come out right, but I knew he heard me because he started slowly stepping backward. I walked in toward him, trying my hardest not to let the tingling sensation coursing through my arms spread any further.

He hadn't spoken a word so I continued to talk. "Not anymore you're not. And them too, you can't hit any of em." I was eyeing past Todd's shoulder Tommy and Brian, standing up from the couch in the living room. Then I was seeing bags of Halloween candy split open and scattered out across the coffee table next to half-filled bowls of it for giving away that evening. Fun-sized 3 Musketeers bars and tiny boxes of Nerds and every color Tootsie Pop.

"Stop," I heard Mom shout outside. "Don't! Travis, no!"

"No, Momma. Look at what he's done to you. Look at her," I screamed.

"And so what're you gonna do about it, kid? You gonna shoot me now?"

"Maybe," I said. "Maybe I will. You can't just keep on doin this. And gettin away with it . . ."

For reassurances, in hindsight totally unnecessary, I looked over toward Tommy and Brian again, now directly to the left of me and Todd's right, requiring more of my face to turn away to do so, when in a blink of my eye, Todd knocked the gun from my hand and shoved me into the wall, indenting it with the shape of my body.

"There you go, that's right, you dumb son-of-a-bitch," he said.

And he punched me in the stomach and slammed my face with his elbow, slumping me over like a rag doll. Down onto the cold linoleum entry I collapsed, against the weight of a bag of play sand burst through my stomach and chest. I thought I might suffocate on breathing too much air too fast. My face felt numb and not like my own, like a mask.

Mom screamed and jumped on top of Todd, with Pam slapping her and then clawing at her face, the three of them each against the other.

"Look whatcha brought into this house," Pam was yelling at Todd, then stopping, herself out of breath.

Todd slung Mom off and into the same wall I had my back against, when I felt the rumble of it go through my spine. He kept her down by punching her square in the face. And she seemed out of it but pressed her hand under her smeary nose and at the same time consoled me by wrapping her bony arm around my side.

"You think this is some motel," Pam kept going, "with a revolving door where you can do whatever the hell you wanna? No! You don't bring your trash into our home!"

"Ain't just me that's done it, but yer own damn doin too, you know. I wouldn't a had to go out lookin for it elsewhere if what I needed was at home."

"Oh, fuck you," Pam sighed. "Not like I ever got what I wanted and you see I stayed put, doncha? You good for nothing piece a shit!"

Todd slapped her across the face and shoved her up against the wall. "Shut it, wouldya already?" She looked down with his backhand already red across her cheek, shifting aside in submission. "And she's right, too, you know. You *are* a lousy lay." He laughed at his own insult, shook his head in dismay and reached around her body like she was still in the way of the open front door. "Always have been. I'm done. With all of it."

Todd was more than fed up, slick with sweat and stink, clinching his fist tightly as he walked through us, finding and then fumbling his keys in his other swollen hand. That's when a loud shot went off and my ears started ringing with it all at the same time. I felt the sound as a forced pitch penetrate my eye sockets and knock me back, even though I knew I wasn't hit. And I saw it was Todd, dropping his keys and twisting back around, half-stepped over the threshold like an actor in a Western.

Then it was Tommy, standing there as gray as the sky outside, stunned by what he'd just done, his own capability, as young as he was and having never even been in a fight before, breathing so heavy I thought he might pass out. Adrenaline had him shaking, like he'd just swung the first punch, which I guess he had, with the gun held tight by his little fingers laced together.

"Fuck . . ." Todd garbled out, beastly and frothing. And he fingered his right side where his shirt showed red and black with soot, stunned at the color of his fingertip, though hardly impaired by the bullet Tommy had put there. "So *yer* gonna shoot me now, then? You little shit, come here!" Something super-human he was, Todd, when he lunged at Tommy.

"Todd, just, wait, now—Don't!" Pam hollered for him to stop, but there was no need, as another bullet shot out and stopped him cold, straight into the chest: to the heart I thought he took it.

Tommy fired the gun again, out through the open doorway towards the sky. Then again and again—the smell of smoke so strong now and stagnant—one through the thigh and into the side of his dad's face before it tore out into the wall with shredded skin and blood spatter.

This finally dropped Todd to his knees. He keeled over next to me on the floor, instantly quiet, motionless, his long gaze strained onto the ceiling or what I imagined must have been his whole life up until that moment. He was holding himself together, though, somehow, his arms folded to his chest, maybe groaning, maybe silent, I couldn't tell, for my ears were covered but my eyes were open the whole time. Even when Pam let out a scream it was inaudible after so many gunshots gone off, and seeing her face lit with terror, I wondered if she could even hear her own self as I watched her hands coming up over her mouth in slow motion.

Sirens already whined in the distance. And neighbors. Gossip.

"*Tommy?*" Pam whimpered when she eventually could, after working up the strength to get up, red sprayed across half her shirt, not only visibly shaken but seemingly scared of her own son. And when he didn't respond she crept over and carefully freed the gun from his frozen hands, settling it down onto the coffee table after clearing off the spilled candy.

Blood had begun to spread out from underneath Todd's body, flowing like a water hose left on in the yard, over the linoleum around us. Glossy by the light of the opened door, it pooled at the edge of the beige carpet in their living room, soaking in, where, because Tommy's mom always told us to take our shoes off whenever we came inside to play, had kept spotless and clean until now.

chapter 6

Columns of slanted white sun beamed down in a haze the morning of Jay's release from Polk. "Just in time for Thanksgiving," he'd exhaled excitedly after first getting word of his earlier than expected release, on account of what, exactly, was as good a guess of mine as much as his own.

"Oh yeah, right . . . Thanksgiving. That's some kind of way to look at it," I'd said to him in turn, really reaching, not for any real happiness or excitement because there wasn't any of that, no matter how deep I dug, or at least shallow enough to fake even a fraction of the thrill heard in his voice telling me the news; but no, still it wasn't there. "Yeah, well, congrats." I knew he knew I didn't mean it. He couldn't very well apologize for his release, nor did I think he should; I wouldn't have.

"Welp . . . Just a couple more weeks left, I guess. Why it takes em that long, hell if I know," he said as if speaking his thoughts aloud.

The two of us had always steadied ourselves in the same spot up against a wall outside, and it was no different now, watching like any other day a heated basketball game turn violent. Fallen leaves whirled around and gathered at our ankles, crunched under my feet thrashing through them in frustration when he'd gone back inside after telling me. And how was it that I could possibly be mad? Selfish is what it was, my acting out this way, or not showing it but rather what was my misplaced aggression, so a certain woman with a skirt suit and desk to sit behind and me in front of would have me believe. Too, that the degree up on the wall was more proof she knew what she was talking about when she said I needed to try harder to identify this side of myself. I should've been glad for the guy, and I was, sure, but I was not happy about it either. Up until this news it'd seemed our paths would run parallel a while longer before they'd eventually crossed and gone off in their separate directions, whenever I was meant to leave Polk before he did and never come back. But no, this was not meant to be. At least I had a couple weeks notice.

It took another day or two but I did finally say it. "I'm happy for you. No lie."

"I know you are, just not right now you're not," he replied with a smug, toothy stare. "It'll all work out the way it's supposed to."

Waking up every day at five-thirty meant more time for us to say our goodbyes this morning, against a clock that would most likely run out for him sometime after noon, and for me to better prepare myself for it—least that's what I should've done. It's in this last hour before breakfast the dormitory remained mostly calm and quiet, light beams turned to dark shadows barred across the cold concrete floors, against an air of something swept more clean and crisp over everything now, after so many months spent suffocating through heatwaves and dry spells, brought by the change of season, the first of many I'd not yet come to realize.

Jacob had already put the final touches on his perfectly made-up bed and was collecting a small pile of things, mostly creased letters he'd received, some he'd written and never sent, and a couple of photographs, leaving behind only scotch tape residue along the walls around his bed for the next inmate to peal off.

Over breakfast, trying to make up for the support and encourage- ment I'd lacked in the days leading up to this one, I asked him with a look on my face like I really cared to know the answer: "What will you do, then? First thing, I mean?"

"Well, first . . . first I'm gonna take a shit—alone, all by myself!"

We laughed, so loudly we took on looks.

While Jay kept a smile on his face I silenced any outward appearances of excitement because I felt I had to. Everybody in here had heard the news of his release by now, short of turning twenty-one and a lot less time than he'd thought he'd have left to spend in here. Not just since he told me he was leaving early but every day since I got here, leading up to today, I'd been wondering about what it was going be like to not have him around, no longer sleeping above me, eating across from me, listening to me talk—talking to myself mostly, and yet I swear he always heard me somehow, let me know he did. But more to my point I worried how I was going to keep myself protected without him around. Whether he knew it was coming or not, he never spoke to this fact, only about how odd it was going to be for the both of us to go back to doing all of these things alone, and worse, eventually, for me, with a new inmate after him.

Then he had to go and say it, without coming right out and saying it at first: "Just hope he's not some pussy. Woo boy, you'll really be in bad shape then."

Of course, before I lost the chance to move up in the world, I'd ask an officer to let me switch places with Jay, to bunk above his replacement—authority given to those who'd earned it seemed a fitting motto one of the officers might appreciate enough to grant my request. And I wasn't really going to take Jay's place, at least no more than his sense of superiority I hoped I'd also earned in my short time here. No way was I going to fill the void of his absence in the ways I'd already brought to mind, most especially the one I dared not dwell on too deeply, the elephant in the room: me sitting in this same seat at this same table alone, as soon as tonight, without so much as one other guy to talk to, never mind the one who'd practically been my bodyguard.

"No, but for real," he said, "yeah, *that*, for sure—a big shit—but I'm gonna eat something. Really eat something. But even only some halfway decent meal'll be a whole lot better than the ones they've been feeding us in here." He flopped his spoon up and down in a blob of brownish slop. "No, you know what, why not go all the way. Red Lobster, yeah. I'm gonna go to the Red Lobster."

The nervous anticipation I had for his final date of release was like candy for the crowd of other inmates that sat around us during meals. Throughout this last day of his, I caught them making eyes at me if ever I looked away from Jay and his excitement, sending me threats through gestures with their hands, swiping them across their throats.

"Really I just wanna see my momma, and hopefully my girl, if she's still around, if her momma'll let me. Doubt it though."

"You never know. Maybe she'll be out there when you leave. Like you never left. I know she hasn't come since your birthday, but—"

"No, that I know for sure. Not a chance. There's been no more letters, nothing! I think she's moved on. I can't say I blame her."

I didn't know what to say to him. I couldn't say I blamed her either.

"Whatever man," he said, switching gears. "I'll be a free man—through and through."

I'd lost my appetite and so I picked at my tray of food with its pattern of vegetables, brownish-orange piece of something like meat, plastic cup of nothing left to drink, divided out and so repetitive by then that I could play a game of memory with the different types of beans and potatoes we ate, and on which days of the week they were served to us.

"What about you?" he asked.

"What do you mean?"

"What's the first thing you're gonna do when you get out?—Cause you will, and it won't be long now, I imagine. What about *your* girl? You think she'll come around, eventually, maybe?"

I laughed nervously, having not thought much about what I was going to say to her in all honesty, though not admittedly, not owning up to my selfishness for being here in the first place, with only me, myself, and I taking over most of my day-to-day thoughts. For some time now it had been this way. "I dunno what I'm gonna do next," I told him, like it was the first time. "Never come back here, that's for damn sure."

"Well, that right there's the only thing that'll keep you going man. Keep you from coming back. You gotta remember that, how, once you're out, and before you got in here, the way it feels to be on the other side. The air . . . it's different, you know. It doesn't get any better than when it's your own, when you got nobody tellin you when you can and can't breathe. Nothing like the air out there in the yard. It's not the same. Smoke is all it is out there, blown out of the ass of this prison. I'm talkin about the real deal. The taste of freedom."

"Yeah, yeah . . ."

"No, really. It sounds silly to ya now, I know. What, you think I don't wanna mess up all these fuckers in here. All this time dealing with all this. Idiots, dudes who want a death sentence, they can have at it. I mean, you learn real quick. I definitely did. But then, you see it's the only thing keepin you from your future, yourself. Thinking about tomorrow. Don't fuck it up."

"You're lucky that you can say that, *it is* tomorrow," I said, smiling.

"True. But, you've got, what is it you got left in here, another year—two at the most . . . or I guess the most is still a lot," he said, half laughing. "But let's say a year. One year. And it could be worse. You coulda gotten life—for what you did but didn't do. Don't forget that. If you had never stepped foot in here before today and killed tomorrow, you'd be stuck forever. No way out. Coming in here at seventeen the way you did, turned eighteen not but a few months ago, you know, you could be outta here early like me."

"More like when I'm twenty . . ."

"Hey, well, you know, you gotta start somewhere. Just don't worry about anybody else. Focus on yourself. Forget about what these guys are doin. They come and go too. The worst of em prolly gettin transferred out and over, even another state depending. Just don't get your-self on the same trajectory. You already dodged one bullet."

The prospect of having a new cellmate was overwhelming enough. And now, thinking about a new prison, a "real" prison, with "real" inmates, my scope narrowed in on itself. If I *was* to ever be trans-ferred there I imagined it would be for a lifetime and for offenses a lot worse than the ones committed in here: double murder, triple murder, serial killers.

"Good behavior can only get me so far," I said softly.

"Look where it got me."

"Yeah, maybe so," I said, doubtful I'd make it long enough.

"Listen, break the circle. You're just holding the spot for some dude who's gonna steal a lady's pocketbook a few months from now. He'll come in, same age as you, and be let out, and he'll probably hold a gun to the head of the next unlucky person he takes from and'll end up right back in here."

"Do *you* think if there's a next time, *you'll* be come back here?"

He gave me a look of dismay, as if I hadn't built up any faith in him and his release. "Only if it's as a reincarnated fly on the wall. But that sounds like the worst possible way to come back. No. I'm done with this place. I can't be a part of the system no longer. I just can't."

I could see his own anxieties for his freedom and the potential for coming back, and so often they do. Come tomorrow his world outside would be much larger than the one he'd lived in for the past several years. He was just as nervous about entering into that world as I was about him leaving this one. But I wanted him to be a citizen of another world.

"Stay free," I said, encouragingly.

"Yeah, thanks, man," he said, tearing up. "I just don't know how it all happened. What I did to get here—not really, but *really*, you know? Why? And how can I not be here again. I can't. It's like I don't know how else to live or something."

"Come on, it hasn't been that long. You've got time. You'll be fine."

"Only when you've been in here do you see how out there clock hands spin so much faster, man. It's not easy to keep up. It's hard, you know. We can only hear about all the stuff going on, or catch it on TV sometimes if we're lucky. But mostly we're just left to imagine all these things happening out there, to a place that we're not a part of," he said, finishing the last bites of food on his tray. "The world keeps on spinning, as it should. With or without us it does. And you know what else, in here it's like we're not a part of it or something. Like they don't want us to be. Like we're stranded on some kinda deserted island, but there's no sand or sun, no clear waters to swim in, to escape to. The sun goes on shinning there. Storms, they come and they go. How bad things are, but at the same time with how good it would be to not be stuck in here, if given a chance to at least try, it'd be nice. Nice dream. Good and bad. In here we've only got the bad, though, always to fight against, it seems, ourselves and other inmates, so it's easy not to expect the good. But when you get out there, let me tell ya, it's so hard to have both, to try and figure out which is which. There's a lot of good going on, but there's still so much bad too. I don't know what I'm saying, I just wanna experience that good, man. Am I making any sense?" he finished, laughing.

"Oh yeah, definitely. I get it."

"Yeah? You ain't just shitting me?"

"No, no. I'm not. And you're gonna be alright out there. But really, my small world in here, it's about to get smaller— *Crazy Jay*," I answered, laughing to cover how I really felt. "I'm gonna miss you."

"No you won't. You'll be fine. Just keep to yourself, let em know you don't mess around with any of that shit. Keep your eye on the finish line, and when you do get out, we have to meet up."

"Will I recognize you?"

"I hope you don't," he said, standing up from the table.

"I hope I don't either," I said, and I picked up my tray and followed after him.

The next day came the sound of clanging metal, dangling in rhythm against a waistband and squeaky, patent leather shoes, making its way through the empty dormitory. Jacob turned to me and smiled wide, raising his eyebrows as if to say, I guess this is it.

Two officers walked toward us, then one tapped on the bars with his baton. Like he even needed to wake up him up on the morning his release, having heard the sound of it coming for weeks, Jacob was already standing at attention.

"Welp. Don't be a stranger," he said with a smile. "And I'd send books but I know you won't read em. If they'd even give em to you."

"Until next time," I joked.

"Yeah, *right*." He laughed and, bending down beside the bed to grab his things, whispered at me, "But I did leave you somethin to hold on to, til yer outta here, too." He then straightened up and followed the accompanying officers.

I sat on my mattress and wondered what and leaned forward to hold sight of him walking away. "Alright. Good luck out there," I shouted.

He sent back a thumbs-up over his shoulder and continued onward, his silhouette eventually turning into a keyhole in the distance, walking through the sunned hallway until he reached its end and disappeared.

After that, the afternoon spent without Jacob was a break from the routine I'd adhered to throughout the last four-some-odd months, one that began with me waking up to realize I was still here. Everyday, without fail, even going back as far as summer, my second morning here, I needed the daily reminder. By then Jacob would've been up already, before everyone, having already had his way with the toilet, and he'd be quietly making up his bunk. Then I'd leave to take my turn on the toilet, or try to, leaving him alone to pencil down any thoughts he was still having from the day before—he was always thinking, scheming—that he'd sometimes share with me whenever I returned.

Home was mostly on his mind, how he was longing to return to it, how he might get there, if he ever would when the days seemed so long that they might never begin again tomorrow, and how it might be for him once he ultimately made it there, because he believed he truly would. I'd maybe share with him some of what I had either dreamed about or dreamed for my life outside Polk—on a good day, whenever there was a dream for him to try and interpret for me or when I was feeling hopeful about tomorrow.

We'd have finished squaring away our cell just in time to stand for showers, and breakfast that followed soon after: oatmeal, eggs, toast, sausage links, coffee or orange juice, and an orange. I ate eggs and toast everyday, and I grabbed an orange to take with me in my jacket pocket for a snack during breaks at the cut and sew, where Jacob and I had both worked, but mostly we talked when we weren't supposed to, while we mended shirts and jeans, laundered them, sunup to sundown if ever we could.

Not here in Polk but in the newer, bigger prison, I heard how companies contracted the inmates to manufacture their clothing, in addition to the uniforms they wore when they did, and for peanuts, for big profits, enough to get the occasional commissary visit—if you saved up. I wondered if I'd ever worn clothes made by a convict before I came there, if I'd been wearing some part of another uniform I was wearing then, a long time ago.

The work wasn't all bad and it made the days go by faster. I don't remember ever watching the clock, something a nine-to-fiver would envy, I'm sure. But I was in detention, so time wasn't real, and I had nowhere to go after five o'clock, and well, maybe they did, and maybe they had more than five o'clock to look forward to. Or maybe not. Maybe they were just like me. I got along pretty well with the others I worked with and I saw that I could actually do something like this for real if I ever had the chance. I'd find myself work at a factory once I got out, that's what I was telling myself, if in the future people were still wearing clothes like these. I'd already imagined the ways I could streamline my floor, making for a more productive and profitable garment production. Maybe I could run an even bigger team, manage, get along, kill time, until the time came.

Some days, if I started early enough in the morning, I didn't have to continue working for much longer after lunchtime, only another hour or two, and then afternoons would be spent freely. Still, I alternated this freedom to wander around between time out in the yard and meeting with a guidance counselor. And, while I wasn't required to, I even took some of the high school-level classes offered here, an alternative version of the real thing. Whatever kept me sane, separated from the majority of the others, was where I found myself. While most sat around and watched TV, stationed to whatever channel it was that always stayed under the control and watchful eye of one inmate, others were always up to no good.

For this reason the opened dormitory was a place I avoided. Time spent in the office or classroom, out in the yard, with Jacob, these were safe zones. Even on the hottest of days it was better spent outside than inside the dormitory, where it smelled like a locker room and felt twenty degrees hotter. With the coldest days ahead I thought it would be no different, even without Jacob.

The basket of oranges was empty this morning and so I had to go without a snack during my break at work. And when my shift was over I walked alone by the rec room and saw reruns of *MASH* were playing on repeat with no one watching. Between my granddad's house and Dad's, I'd seen every episode before ever coming to Polk, so passing by I recognized Corporal Klinger on the TV screen, afraid he was going catch the mumps, saying, "If you get em as a kid, you don't get em as an adult. But if you get em as an adult, you don't get kids!"

I continued down the hallway, replaying the next scene in my head as I made my way outside, when the door to the yard slammed shut behind me. Immediately I felt my face get punched, twice, from both sides, and my leg kicked from behind, knocking me down to the ground. I covered my face so that I couldn't quite make out who was doing what—the two, maybe three of them—kicking me in the ribs, punching me in the back, stomping on my feet. I curled my body into it, wrapped my arms tight over my head.

"Look at ya, now. Yeah, that's right. Not so tough, huh," one of them said, as another spat on me and nudged at me with his shoe, trying to get a rise out of me. "Get up!" he yelled, kicking me harder.

I wasn't going to take it lying down so I raised up and faced them, bloody lip and nose and all. There were two of them, another watching and laughing, still as involved as the ones throwing the kicks and punches. Blood was spilling in a stream down my forehead, stopped thick in my brow, and I knew a cracked rib when I felt one. I gave them as menacing a glare as I could muster, saying nothing. I didn't feel the pain as much as I did a burning rage inside numbing it.

"What are you gonna do about it?" one asked, laughing, leaning over me. "Ya gonna kill me now?"

Another one chimed in. "That's what you're in for, right? Murder."

"Where's your boyfriend?" the other one asked, and he kicked me in the side. I could feel a sharp pain branch off around to my chest, my heart. The tightened stitch when I breathed worsened.

An officer ran up and separated them from me, and broke up the circle of onlookers. They made eyes at me as they were taken into the dormitory, for what I assumed would be a light tap on the wrist. These were the same guys from dinner the night before, gesturing what I had coming to me, warning me of this very moment. And it wasn't only then, but ever since I'd come in here they'd had it out for me. It didn't make it any better that Jacob had beaten one of them up a long time ago and without him they'd needed to make some kind of example out of me for the other inmates, proving themselves again. I'd watched as new inmates after me were softened and then hardened, broken before being put back together. This was how it must have happened. How it was going to be.

I wiped the blood from my face and cleaned my hands off in the grass. Inmates who'd watched either laughed along with those standing next to them with more authority or turned away seemingly unfazed—and maybe they were, as if this rough-up was assurance of their own disconnection from reality and that they must continue to keep appearances, be the constant bystander until the day arrived when they could become a real person again. I stood, continuing my glare at them across the yard, and with my fists clinched I slammed them back against the rough brick wall, over and over, until my hands were dirty with blood again.

My face was throbbing that night after I kept myself quiet. And my entire backside was bitingly sore, even against the good-for-nothing mattress, the worn-out pillow a cotton ball for all the blood. Turned onto my side for relief, the side without the footprints, I adjusted my weight as best I could to relieve those places that felt like they'd been tenderized: torn shoulders and tingling spine; ribs that stung like stitches. Lifted up from the added discomfort of those metal bands holding me still, I looked at the underside of the bed sprung above me, empty, having no give in it, the same feeling sinking in slowly now. No puffs of foam pushed through its frame as it did whenever Jay was up there. My hands still trembled with rage from the reality of my afternoon, and with the emptiness of my surroundings, I couldn't keep my mind focused on anything else long enough to begin again my first day of freedom, so I imagined his, and I was happy for him. I wondered what he was doing right that second and if he'd thought about me at all, how I was managing. Had it been me, had we traded places and I was the one on the outside, I wouldn't be wondering about me. I hoped, for his sake, he'd forgotten about me already.

I didn't think I'd ever see Jay again, that his promise he'd made with himself was one he'd keep for good. He never did send anything—if he'd even been allowed to—and I never got word of how he was doing. Though I missed our talks at night, whether they be serious or only to lighten the mood, and always with his certain way of understanding, I was still listening to them and holding on to the them as truth. The fact that I could trust someone, especially in here, a compadre, was something to reflect fondly on. And I believed in him just as much when he said he wasn't coming back. Hopefully he'd no reason to be consumed with thoughts of remembering this place, his longing to stay out, that it just came naturally enough on its own. Hopefully he found himself changed, enough to realize that where he'd been, who he'd been, and the people he'd spoken to, were no good. Nonetheless, during those first several months in Polk, he taught me that sometimes in order to be yourself, you had to do wrong by it.

Then, I thought long and hard about what I'd say to myself as I was now, no longer in that place. The day would come, no matter how hard it was to see, I might've tried to convince myself. Nevertheless, it wouldn't be enough. No explanation could talk me out of it, pleading with myself to sleep that night, to picture a better tomorrow, to today. And in time, I instead turned back toward the events that had led me there, wishing once more that I could prepare myself for what was to come, because I couldn't take it back. But even if I could I didn't want to. I wouldn't change a thing.

After a while the dormitory began to get very quiet and the lights flickered off. With the summer well behind me now and the days getting shorter, the sky outside wasn't blue but black. I took hold of my breathing, tried to be still and steady my pulse, and focused my eyes through the dark on anything that might have been left behind. I felt along the side of my bunk where the book had been and discovered nothing wedged between it and the unflinching wall. But when I relaxed my right hand and smoothed my shaky fingers over the rounded side of the mattress, I felt a thick lump, raised and shorter than the length of a ruler, inches from a clean slit cut into its seam that I could poke my finger through. Hidden between the spongy, mealy chunks of foam I found it, gripped something long and rigid, like plastic, maybe even tape-wrapped. It was a handle, and melded into it were several thick sewing needles, razor-edged, that he must've collected from our mending job.

chapter 7

Sometime in the month after Tommy shot his dad, a carpet man's truck pulled into their driveway. I saw wide rolls of new beige-colored carpeting going in and the old coming out, the last being the blood-stained portions from the living room. With time the blood had turned from cherry red into a rusty, almost brown color, and it looked like his entire body had bled out there was so much, a lot more than I'd remembered.

Since no criminal charges had been brought against him, an eleven-year-old considered too young to be a "juvenile" and defending himself and also his mother, except for her forbidding him from seeing me again, Tommy continued the sixth grade that fall like nothing happened. And that really didn't stop us from seeing each other, not really; being out after dark every night wasn't against the rules and so we'd meet up on our bikes at the end of the block where his mom couldn't see us together, ride around until midnight sometimes. So between the two of us picking up our bikes where we'd left them, and his dad arriving home from the hospital not long after the carpet truck, the way I saw it, nothing *had* really changed. For Tommy, however, it seemed there might've been some kind of aftereffect, like maybe he was still shell-shocked, and whether it was words with me, I didn't know, but there were some things left unsaid, or maybe he just didn't want to talk about it.

"Did you feel anything, you know, when you shot him?" I asked.

"How do you mean?" he said through heavy breathing, and he was whipping his bike around like he was competing or only showing off all the same. Thanksgiving break had started and it felt like no time had passed, so letting off steam was probably all it really was. But finding extremes in every act as a kid I guess is how I confused his, seemingly angry and aggressive, taking it out on the bike instead of me or his mom, his dad, I couldn't tell.

"Come on, Tommy. You know you can tell me. Talk to me."

"I don't know what yer talkin about."

"Like . . . I don't know. You know, like, inside of you . . . Come on, you know what I mean. What'd it feel like?"

"I dunno," he sighed. Then he turned in the gravel and booked it, skid out onto the road, way up ahead of me.

"Wait! What're you doin? Stop, stop. Slow down willya . . ."

"You gotta keep up!" he shouted back.

I raced forward, out of breath when I reached him. "Tommy."

"*What?* What!"

"I'm not the one after you or nothin."

"Okay, okay . . ." he said, winded but still pedaling, though not as fast. "Well, you know what happened. You were there."

"Yeah . . ."

"I dunno, it just happened so fast. I don't really remember."

"What're you talkin about? You remember. It *just* happened. Don't give me that."

"No, I do, I just mean . . . I dunno," he said, circling me. "I don't know how it—the gun—it just . . . shot off so quick. Like maybe it wadn't me who pulled the trigger, or I dunno what."

"So you mean . . . you didn't mean to do it?"

"No, no, that's not true. I did. I wanted to shoot the fucker."

"But you didn't shoot to kill him—or almost kill him? Did ya wanna actually kill him, Tommy?"

"I don't know. Maybe I did. Maybe I didn't know if it was gonna kill him or what. It just happened. You were there. You saw it all, too."

"Well, yeah. Duh. I know *that*, but I also know that if you shoot somebody chances are they might die from it. What'd you think was gonna happen?"

"I know, I know . . . It's just, I just wanted him to stop doin what he was doin. All of it. I just wanted to make it stop. You know?"

"Well you got what you wanted. At least for the time being you did."

"I didn't know that's what was gonna happen is what I'm trying to say. Honest. I didn't wanna *not* have a daddy. I didn't want *my* daddy. Still don't. And I can't say this to nobody, but I'm glad I did it, though. I shot him. I did that. And he'd of messed me up pretty good for it otherwise, had I missed. But he didn't die. I still think he's gonna come after me one of these days. Once he's up to it."

We'd been riding out in the open until light from Mr. Hickson's opened garage fanned across Tommy's face, sweaty even in the chill of the nighttime air, and the reflectors on the frames of our bikes lit up and gave us away. And so we rounded a corner and circled back to a stop, decided to keep on going through the side of the woods, up a hill that overlooked our street, where houses had stopped being built, careful not to get turned over by a beer can or bottle in the dirt.

"You know what, I actually thought he might be different," Tommy continued telling me, nearly out of breath but not so much that he couldn't laugh about it now. "Maybe someday, I dunno."

"I don't know about that," I said, trying to keep up again.

"Now I'll never know if I could've just left things alone. Maybe I'd get another daddy. Maybe not a better one but at least not one like him, I mean—somehow different."

"You mean if your parents split?"

"No, well, I dunno. Just, maybe he'd've changed on his own."

"I wouldn't hold him to it. Even after you shot him."

"Well not *now*, no way he's gonna change. That's what I mean. He just might kill us all." He laughed after saying this so I knew he was kidding, but not entirely. "It's one big mess."

"You know none of it was your fault, doncha?"

"What difference does that make whose fault it was? Even if it was, it don't matter. Not now. I did what I did. I almost got him, too. It woulda been so much better off for everybody had he died. *We'd* be better off. My little brother, he'd have had to suffer through it without him but it's ten-times worse with him still in the picture. That's my fault. And I wonder what it's gonna be like with him, still, having a daddy versus not having one, I don't know . . . Which is worse? I guess I'll never know."

"Without mine around, it's no different, though. Not really. Momma ain't the same, but I don't know if *I* am or not. But I do think it's better. He's like yours, he can come back as soon as he wants to. So I guess it's no different. But it'll be better for you, Tommy. One day. You'll see. You won't be ridin that bike forever. Stuck on this street. In that house."

We'd reached the highest point, which was probably only a mole-hill in retrospect. And now that both of us had tired out we slung our bikes down, sat in the grass until we weren't seeing two sets of stars. Tommy was huffing so heavily, more so than he ever had before during these routine night-rides.

"Are you alright?"

"Yeah," he sighed, looking off. "It's not too hot. Not too cold."

As we got to talking, I saw him in a new light. Not just because of what he'd done but because he'd been trying to make sense of it. Maybe I hadn't realized then, but here was this kid, processing as best he could, alone, what had happened. And not only what had just happened, his almost killing his own dad, but all of it: Todd, the man who'd made him do it by beating him and his mom and little brother. The weight of the whole world was on his shoulders. The silence between Tommy's words felt like a void he couldn't fill.

Finally he spoke up. "Momma's not talkin, neither. Just stays in her room all the time. I fixed breakfast for us every morning this week. And who knows who's gonna do what or what's gonna happen when we start back at school next week. I don't even *wanna* know."

"So nothing but peanut butter and jelly, then? For a week . . . And what're you gonna do on Thanksgiving? I'd tell you to come over to my house but it prolly won't be any better. But you can if you want. Ah, but you can't can you?"

Tommy laughed. "Screw that. I don't care what my momma says no more. And I bet you, give it another month, she'll be done with the whole thing. Fake grounding me. How does she even know? She can't tell. Doesn't care. And what about you, what'd your mom say to you? When you got back from the police station? She do anything about it?"

"No, just that she wadn't gonna be there holding my hand the next time. And if my daddy found out he'd go psycho. You could've been held liable for what you did, she told me, for my part, bringing the gun to you."

"But it wadn't *your* gun . . . You didn't do nothin."

"Tell *her* that. I think she thinks she shoulda been the one to take care of it. She did say that I was to keep my ass away from you and your fucked-up family."

Both of us laughed.

"Naw, but she didn't really mean that. Doubt she remembers she did."

"They asked me about all the bruises," Tommy mumbled. "And more about him, Daddy. What he was like. What happened that was so bad I wanted to up and shoot him. I don't even know why they did. Like they even listen to me when I tell em. They know him good and well, what he did. You know. All those times."

I looked through his stunned expression, to all the times I could recall the need for a warrant being out on both our dads but never were. "Shit. Pretty crazy, Tommy. You shot a man!"

"I know. It's weird. I don't know how I'm supposed to feel about it, neither. How come I feel normal about it, like how, I dunno, I guess how I think people that kill people do, I guess. Like a soldier does. Maybe I don't know what's what. I think you're maybe supposed to feel powerful. Maybe I do. I stopped him, and even though I wanted him to become like someone else, I don't think it coulda happened any other way. So it's over. I mean it's not. Not yet. Not really. It coulda been. One more shot and he'd be a dead man right now instead of sitting in his chair in the living room drinkin beer and cussing. Honest, that's what I can't stop thinking about. I coulda taken his life *and* his chair."

"You still can," I said to him, seriously and not for any other reason than it was the first thing that popped into my head.

"No, too late now," he said, like he'd thought of that already.

We sat there, our backs curled against the dark night, in silence for another minute, allowing each other to process everything. Our breath was coming out from our mouths like smoke did from the barrel of the gun after. How the smell of it had too, the gunpowder stink, hung over the scene for as long as we kept our mouths shut.

Out of nowhere, with no pressure from me for him to, he spoke up. "So are you scared of me now?" And he was laughing, I guess to make it less a serious question, but I knew he was dead serious.

I laughed too and looked over at him, his face haloed by his panting. Of course I wasn't scared of Tommy but I did feel this certain special power he'd described. It's not something you're able to acknowledge in someone without knowing how they were before they gained it. And, too, when it's not as easily recognizable in yourself you can see it more clearly in others. He'd done something that I'd been incapable of. It was my shot to take, and instead, he took it.

"Naw. Get over yourself. Yer still small."

"Not *that* small. And maybe you've stopped growing. I'll catch up—no I'll pass you."

"Fat chance."

When we rode back down on our bikes, Tommy hopped off and walked his through the rest of the way toward his yard and slung it down along the edge of the dim house. I watched him crawl into his bedroom window, the same way he'd come out that night, before waving his skinny arm at me and then quietly pulling it down shut.

Parked in our driveway was a car I didn't recognize. It hadn't been there when I left the house, and lights were still on, showing the kitchen and living room through the front window. Laughter and voices sounded from inside when I reached the front door.

There was no sneaking past my mom, and whoever this guy was she'd let in, talking in a deep tone of voice, slurring, really, who I must have met before but couldn't remember who. Together in the kitchen they slouched, like they'd been that way for a while. Mom, in her blissfully drunk state—whenever drunk and in the company of strange men—got up from the chair when she saw me and started banging things around, searching for something to cook with.

"Where ya been?" she asked. I didn't answer.

The guy at our dinette table watched the way her body moved around the counters, how she bent herself over more than she'd needed in order to open cabinet doors, using her butt to slam drawers shut, every few seconds peeking over her shoulder to sure up his still sitting there, watching.

"*Momma*—it's late."

"Your momma says she's gonna fix us up something."

I sat down across from him.

"With Tommy? Amirite?" Mom asked, not answering me either. "I thought I told you—"

"Come on, leave the kid alone," the guy said.

"Hey, now . . . We were getting on just fine," Mom snapped back, slamming a pan down on the stove. "Don't talk unless you know what yer talking about, dipshit. Not another word. Ya don't even know."

"Don't know what?"

"That *Tommy* shot his daddy. Not me. And how it was his momma first, who told us that we can't hang out anymore."

"Oh . . . Wait, wait, wait . . . That's *you?* With them folks from across the street, that's—"

Mom cracked eggs into a bowl and slung it aside, turned around quickly. "You see there. Now what'd I just say? But least you see what I gotta deal with. I can't leave him be, not for one second. Before he's off doin what's he's not supposed to," she said. "You wanna nother beer? Something harder?"

"Beer's fine. Wow. That's tough kid," he said.

"Hey, don't go feeling sorry for him. It coulda been him. Imagine the man getting shot by my own kid, the fuck. Deserved it. And with his daddy's gun no less. Now, the other boy, he got it passed off to him, basically is what happened. But this one here—*my* boy—you're sitting across from the real perpetrator. Or almost."

"So you didn't do *anything?*" he asked me. "What, you scared to pull the trigger or somethin? Is that what happened?"

"Hey! What'd I say?" Mom shouted.

"What, Lynn?"

She carried plates of food from the counter and set them around the center of the table. "Don't go mistaking him for a pussy. You hear me . . . He'll take this knife," she said, lifting the one she was using to halve toast, "stab your ass right in the chest."

The guy raised his eyes and reached for a piece of toast and Mom slapped his hand.

"He goes first. Get you somethin, honey," she said, nodding at me as she emptied a pan of eggs out over several plates and set too many forks and knives, spoons for no reason, on the table between us. I took what was mine, added to it a couple triangles of buttered toast, and kept quiet.

"Thank you, ma'am," the guy said with a smile.

"I got some taters comin up next. And you know what else, he'd only hurt somebody if he really had to," Mom carried on, sloppily spilling out hash brown patties from a box in the freezer. "We take care of each other, don't we, sweetie? Besides, they'd have hauled my boy away were it him who shot the son-of-a-bitch. Who'd be here then, when he was gone?"

The guy stood from the table and slouched up behind her and grinned, scrambled eggs in his teeth.

"Stop! You know it sure as hell ain't gonna be you," Mom said, giggling, swatting at his reaching hand. "No man—never—not one of em never ever could replace my boy."

The guy, though sleazy, seemed nice enough. Not memorable, but not such a bad thing considering. He acted and looked to be on the younger side for Mom, no more than ten or twelve years older than I was at the time, and I remember wondering if he'd graduated from high school. I wanted to ask him what it was like, what I could expect, because even though it wasn't for another couple years I was looking forward to it so much, to getting a car and graduating and turning eighteen and getting the hell out of there, but never did.

chapter 8

Cuts and bruises on my face had barely begun to heal when Dwayne arrived at Polk, admitted into our dormitory the day after Thanksgiving. He took the bunk below me after I'd been given the go-ahead to take over Jay's, dragging his feet and then slumping down without a word, though brought with the odor of food grease, a smell I'd once distinctly possessed myself working in the kitchen at the restaurant; but where exactly he'd gotten it from I couldn't figure. Maybe it was just him, the way he didn't properly look after himself, his hair being *that* dirty, his face scratchy with scruff and pale. How he hadn't bathed throughout all those days of intake I wanted to ask but would never. I didn't want him to know I'd even acknowledged his presence, by sight or smell or otherwise. Nor did I speak, thinking how it was going to be the same treatment for him as I'd received: not being spoken to, not at first. Either that or I was just embarrassed by my own appearances and lack of taking care of myself, at how colorful my face looked and if he might have suspicions of his own about me. If *I* could, than I knew, like a cut-down tree, he could count the rings of purple fading to black under my eyes, greenish yellow smudges over my cheeks, with the assumption I was incapable of defending myself. Most of the swelling had gone down, though, but a needlepoint of blood-crusted slits where knuckles had broken the skin was more evidence to confirm his hunch. Truth be told, in my own defense, I didn't put up much of a fight. Had I, I might not've lived to tell him all about it.

"I see they musta got ya pretty bad . . . " he sighed, finally, after what seemed an eternity of silence, standing out from underneath to say this before saying hello.

"Yep," I said, no longer playing dead. "But you should see *them*."

"Oh, so it was two of em, then?"

"Three."

"Six fists and six feet . . . Shit. Ain't much you can do about that. Well, I guess my next question is who should I be lookin out for?"

"Oh, no one, naw," I mumbled, sitting up, knowing what payback would come both ways if I pointed him in their direction. I could just as soon tell him everybody in here was against him but why make matters worse. Maybe he already knew that. "No, it's no one person—or three people—worth your time. Not really. I mean, I haven't even been in here for all that long is all. Give it time, though. Haven't had enough of it to leave my mark yet. You live and you learn, right."

"Well, sure. How long *has* it been?" he asked.

"Four months."

"Ah, yeah. And how much longer have you got?"

"I guess about a year, give or take. The guy whose place you took, though, he got out early. It can happen. With my luck, though . . . who's to say."

"Yep. Go figure."

"At any rate, what about you? How long?"

"Ten months or ten years from now. Who the hell knows? But no, ten months. You know how it goes—or, I guess you don't do ya . . ."

"So this isn't your first time, then?"

"No, it is. Jim, my older brother, he's down in Brown Creek. He started here, though . . . And so it goes."

"Oh."

"Yep."

So then I didn't need to give him the same crash course on the prison that had been given to me. Reliving every moment of my experience up to now didn't seem necessary either, nor was it cathartic for me to tell it to myself. Even just thinking about it makes me feel the same way I did then, like some things that happen to a person should remain frozen when and where they took place, especially during this particular time period, having had no control of it and always up against it, what would probably be better left unsaid forever.

"I'm guessing then you didn't have nobody tell *you* how things was gonna be, huh?" he asked, now searching in my face for some kind of reason as to why it was so badly beaten.

I traced a fingertip over the tender spots and dried my eyes in a staring contest with the wall.

"Don't sweat it," he said.

"You think one thing," I started to say, "that you're all set, but you never really know when somebody's gonna be waitin for ya."

"That's precisely when they are, bud. That's why you gotta prepare yourself for whatever comes your way. Never get caught with your pants down."

No matter the hurt it took to do so, I smiled. So did he.

"What's your name?" he asked. "Or what I should call you."

"Travis."

"Dwayne."

Dwayne was nineteen and said he'd been involved in a bank robbery gone bad. His older brother, not the one already locked up, had used a loaded gun in the robbery and when caught up in the moment shot a teller in the shoulder and a woman in line accidentally in the knee before fleeing on foot, leaving his little brother, Dwayne, waiting in the getaway car for the police to apprehend instead.

As a baby, in Wichita, his mother passed he and his two brothers around a lot, before they moved to North Carolina when he was five, having since lived all over the state. Dwayne was smarter, street-smarter I should say, and much rougher around the edges than anyone I'd ever met before. Still green, though, and maybe not wet but damp enough behind the ears to be nervous about something. A recovering speech impediment, perhaps, detected now and again in certain words or turns of phrase. Or maybe he was a recovering addict or still addicted, in how he was carrying himself, more crawling, with eyes never aimed at one thing at a time for too long. I couldn't tell which, only that whenever we got to talking about something long enough, whatever it was seemed to bother him. I figured this was why it had taken him so long to begin with; he didn't want to be found out. I doubt my busted face that I lied about had made him feel any less at ease, however, and I thought, after his series of lie-detecting questions put at me, he'd know I didn't want to be found out either, that I hadn't put up any real fight against those responsible for my face being the way that it was.

"So, these guys, they got it out for you or somethin?"

"Pretty much, I guess. They didn't like me from the minute I stepped foot in here."

"Yeah, but you say you got em good? Did you really, though? Or like you said, before they got to you."

"It's not always that easy. You have to find a balance in here, man. I actually wanna try not to stay here forever, you know. Not any longer than I have to. I've tried to keep to myself."

"So what happened to them, did they get moved or anything?"

"Well, no. Because I never said anything."

"So they just beat the shit out of you—and . . . that's it?"

"Pretty much. That's how it works," I answered, again feeling as if I was speaking in circles and losing his vote of confidence.

"Damn . . ." he sighed. "That's some real messed up shit."

"Yeah, you see. Didn't your brother ever get into it in here?"

"Well yeah, but—" And he stopped himself from saying anything else, looked at the ceiling and the cement floor, out the window.

"What? Tell me."

"No, no. It's just, well, he's a lot bigger than you."

"I'm not that much smaller than *you*," I blurted out, as if I'd been thinking it the whole time, unconsciously, since I sized myself up against him.

"So," he said, "I'm not the one with his fist in your mouth neither."

He'd taken offense, clearly. "I didn't mean nothin by it."

"You shouldn't sell yourself short. There's more than one way to skin a cat. My brother taught me that."

"Yeah, you're right."

"Besides all this, you ever get beat so bad you wanted to do something about it but ya couldn't?"

"Yeah."

"And what'd you do about it? You had to do somethin. Even doin nothin is doin somethin."

"No, I know what yer sayin. What I did was I waited til I could."

He looked at me with a pleased smile. "There you go."

Dwayne's line of questioning aroused in me my own suspicions about why I hadn't tried to fight back, or at least make some meager attempt at retaliation if only to secure my standing in Polk, or more to establish one, to rewrite the script. And it went deeper than that, too, back to when I was a kid, unable to do anything about it. It wasn't that I didn't understand how it was necessary to do something, to not stand idly and watch as bad things happened, I just didn't know what, exactly. Not only had I witnessed the outcome of violence firsthand and what scars it left me but also to someone else, to Tommy and *his* brother, Dwayne and his, and Mom. Going on in the household outside of this one here but all the same, by other inmates inside.

I think this place only intensified the feeling, projected the memories back at us, confronted us daily. Having had a cellmate who'd already presented himself as a psychopath to the other inmates in turn made me seem guilty by association and so that I didn't think I had to prove myself. I guess I hadn't realized that the other inmates knew all along who I really was, less like his shadow and more the defenseless lightweight when it came to defending myself. If they only knew. If only I did.

At first it might not have seemed Dwayne and I shared all that much in common, but we did come from a similar background, knew exactly who each other's dad was without having to meet him. This alone made it easy to connect, to level with one another, and I sensed right away that he felt he could trust me. Not to necessarily take care of him, of course not, as evidenced by the bruises, but that I was someone he could talk to, and that I heard him. Even so, I didn't know who to trust, and I had no reason to share any more than I did. Once I told him what I was in for I knew any doubts he had, if he had any, about his safety sleeping beneath me disappeared, though I had every intention of making him feel the opposite, in case he had plans of his own he wasn't telling me.

At dinner that night, the guys who had beaten me up were sitting a few tables away from where Dwayne and I were, having already watched us walk in, smiling. I tried not to make any sudden eye contact with them, to ignore theirs, and so I began eating in silence. Dwayne didn't know me well enough to tell something was off, but I couldn't hide my eyes any longer and Dwayne turned around to see what I was looking at. He met with them squarely in the face, unflinchingly, and while they didn't immediately say anything, I knew they would sooner than later.

"Is that them," he said.

"Yeah, that's the ones."

He took a bite from his plate before turning around for another look, and when he faced back forward I could see zero intimidation or fear behind his eyes. It seemed more like we were in school again and they were only bullies that needed to be dealt with.

"Wonder what they're in for," he said.

"I dunno."

"They stick together like that? All three—four?"

"Yeah."

I must have been six inches shorter than the guys were and half their weight, when wet and hung to dry, and Wayne wasn't much heavier. Stretched up and down his right forearm he showed me a tattoo of thorns, "a piece of Christ's crown," he'd said, a present from his older brother in prison who had another piece of it on his left arm. And on the back of his hand Dwayne had a blob of scar tissue shaped like a scull.

He took another, bigger bite of his food, swallowed without chewing. His eyes zeroed in on their table.

"Fuck em," I said to him. "Don't give em any satisfaction."

"Naw, yeah. It's hard to take how they can just get away with it is all, you know?"

"And so it goes . . ." I said, looking at them without blinking, how Jay did, how Wayne was now, watching on as one of them stood up from the table, angrily and shaking his head.

"He's coming over," Dwayne said, strengthening his arms, all of himself really, into something like a stone statue. His sleeves were up, and so was his head, in anticipation.

I felt a pit deep in my stomach start to burn, my face tingle, my arms quiver from my shoulders down to the tips of my fingers. I settled my fork to the side of my tray and tried relaxing.

"How's your face, faggot?" the inmate said, in his thirties by the way he looked but probably barely old enough to drink, a teenager by the way he carried himself.

Dwayne's fist tensed up and I looked at him as if to say don't.

"And who do we have here? Your new boyfriend? He looks *real* sweet. Tell me he's sweeter than this pudding," he said, now stepping up to our table, looking down at Dwayne and at the same time dipping his finger into my dulled brown desert cup. "Think maybe it's about time we have another go in the yard . . . And you and I can get to know each other. Whataya say? Show your boyfriend what it's all about?"

Dwayne picked up his fork and glared outward.

"Or maybe we oughta just go right here," he said, slamming his fist on the table.

"Inmate!" an officer yelled out from across the room.

"Relax, I'm going," he said, laughing. "See ya later," he said over his shoulder as he walked away.

Dwayne sat in silence, had stopped eating his food, and I thought he was about to explode. I was so focused on him that I'd not realized my own guts were boiling over at this point. I'd waited long enough to do something and now seemed as good a time as any.

I slid back in my chair and waited a second to stand, to catch my breath, up with my heart.

"What're you doin?" Dwayne said.

Gnawing at my fists could go on forever, and they would bleed every single time. I looked at Dwayne, shifting my focus, my stance, my entire being it felt like, to becoming someone else, who I had to be. I'd not been left alone to fend for myself, though, for the waistband in my jeans was an easy place to hide it, kept within reach, where with only a couple stitches one could easily conceal something small enough. In an unseen second, I'd be able to slip the shank out and put it into my front pocket if I needed to, and I did. Dwayne's mouth slowly dropped at the sight of the sharp tip in my hand, along with it the red in my eyes that he didn't think I was capable of seeing.

I walked around the table and it wasn't only Dwayne who was watching, turning around to see what I would do, but everyone else, drawing a quiet room all of a sudden.

The guy who'd punched me first, nearly knocked me out cold, had already sat back down and was laughing, looking up at me. "Oh, look. Now you're mad? Oh, you gonna do something, now, little bitch?"

"*How's my face?* . . . How's my face," I said, standing over him, and screaming, "I'll tell you how my face is!"

"Inmate!" the officer yelled. "Sit yourself back down!"

The guy dropped his fork and flattened his hands on the table.

"What the fuck? Who you talkin to?"

He was about to stand just as I pulled the shank out from my pocket, gripping its handle as hard as I could, hoping it would hold together well enough whenever I slammed it down into his hand. And I must have done it again and again, continuously, over and over, for as long as I could, because when an officer finally pulled me off, screaming and cussing, I could see his right hand looked like battered, bloody meat, a butcher's, with deep holes and mangled bits of flesh down to the bone. Broken-off needles still stuck in to the torn skin of his useless hand, held to his chest with him screaming and crying out in pain, while another guard restrained me, pulled me away in the opposite direction to stop me from going after him and anyone else sat or standing around the table.

And my own hand was covered in blood—his but also mine—cut in several places and no longer under my control; it felt possessed; I did. Dwayne stayed put in his chair, stunned as the guards threw me onto the floor, restrained me and then pulled me back up for my walk to isolation, where I was going to have to sit and stand and sleep and shit while I thought about what I'd done, for however long it took me to come down.

chapter 9

Dad had driven up from Fayetteville that Christmas, only after he'd caught wind of what had happened on Halloween, or so I assumed was the reason why he rode all that way. I'd not heard Mom say a word over the few phone calls between the two of them, nor did I slip up if he and I ever talked—for no more than a minute whenever we did, those times I answered the phone or when Mom handed it off to me to listen to him: "You ain't given your momma a harder time than she does herself, now are ya?" "No, sir." And too, by now I'd assumed he was oblivious to all of it, not just the shooting but what had been going on long before then, throughout that summer and into the fall, another something we just weren't going to ever talk about, like it never happened. But in the way Siler City works its magic, it wasn't two seconds of him riding through town before somebody tooted their horn at him and stopped and fed him earfuls of intel, these enemies of ours who'd always been vouching or praying for him—the ones on *his* side he'd rattled off from a short list for Mom in another shouting match like they'd owed him one—enough that he took to drinking about it before he ever walked in the front door.

"Whose car is that?" I asked Mom, seeing this Dodge something or other parked in our driveway.

"Whataya mean?"

"*Look.*"

She lit a cigarette and came over and looked out the window in the front room, stood right next to me so I knew I wasn't seeing things.

"See. And there ain't nobody sittin in it."

"Huh."

She cracked open the front door and waited a second before stepping out onto our small porch, more a slab of mossy cement, with no shoes on and wrapped herself up tightly in a coat she liked to wear every year around this time but was too thin to keep her skinny self warm.

"*Momma*, get back in," I whispered.

She turned back at me with a funny face and then tip-toed a ways away from the open door to get a closer look at the Dodge, how ugly its shape was, the color dirt. And she started shivering, so bad I thought she would get herself stuck out there that way, unable to move another inch, or worse, fall out on the cement, one or the other. I'd seen her get to shaking before and end up sick the next day, for days. I'd also watched an eighth-grader at school shake so bad I couldn't unsee it, the first month back when leaves were still on the trees and him sweating bullets so he wasn't shivering because it was cold. His blue eyes went back, went white, and his face, too, popular with the girls before it happened, the last time we'd ever see him again, all stretched out and stiff on the waxed floor between the lockers, stricken by it. But before I felt any panic set in over whether it was her time to freeze up and fall, she quickly bolted back toward the house like she'd seen a ghost, her shoulders curled over, looking both ways into the night to sure up that she really hadn't before coming on inside.

"You see anybody?"

"Nope. Not a soul, you're right. Just sittin there. Empty. I don't see nobody, Trav," she said into a short breath, still trembling, standing in the dim doorway.

"I told you."

"Well, whoever the hell it is, the son-of-a-bitch's blocking me in," she said, stepping back and reaching inside for her cigarette still burning in the ashtray set on an end table beside the couch. She took a long drag from it like she was making up for all the ones she'd missed in only seconds without it and flopped down onto the couch like she was brain-tired.

Then, just as I was about to slam the door shut, in walked my dad. "*Dad?*"

Mom blew smoke and got up from the couch. "*Landry?* What're you doin here? Whose damned car is that?"

"I come all the way from Lumberton and this is the welcome I get?" Dad said, and he leaned into Mom with a side-hug and big wet kiss on the side of her face. "Figures. I done heard all about it two doors down. From across the street. Down the road. Back at TJ's, too, fore I could even take my foot off the brake."

"*Lumberton?*" she sighed, clawing the kiss off her cheek. "I thought you said you was staying in Fayetteville."

"Well back and forth, yeah, Lynn, but closer to Lumberton. It ain't no Unsolved Mystery or nothin, come on, now."

"And that car?" Mom asked, rolling her eyes and walking off.

"It's a Dodge, Momma," I said, like I knew more about it than she did just because I knew its make.

Dad raised his eyes, wrinkled his sloppy mouth and licked his lips in a way that I knew what was coming out next. "Trav, won't you fix your daddy a drink? Your momma too. I'm sure she wants one—another one, I guess I oughta say, by the smell of it," he scoffed, and pointed for me to shut the front door already.

"No, no, his momma don't want no drink. Not with his daddy." She sat down on the chair I'd not pushed back under the eating table from when we ate supper and sucked on her cigarette. "And Don's still fixin em up for ya down at TJ's, so come on, then, why're you here? You damn sure didn't drive all that way—from *Lumberton*—to come have a drink with *me*."

"Don't sell yourself short," he said, smiling, gazing around the living room like he might find something new to look at that wasn't there the last time; and there was nothing to see, except for maybe the TV, what I'd thought had been left on layaway for good up until only a week ago, for six long months, before Mom finally went and picked it up. *A Stranger In The House* on USA was screaming mid-stream and Dad yelled for me to turn it down. "Whatcha got it on, boy? God almighty . . ."

I dialed it down and left them going back and forth about it and whatever was next on his agenda. In the kitchen I fixed him a drink—hers too, knowing good and well I'd be asked to no sooner than I set his down on the table between them. Dad wasn't staying awhile, anyway, or hadn't intended to, sitting down on the couch without first taking his jacket off at the door, nor his dirty boots, and smelling like he'd already smoked his last cigarette whenever it was he'd actually pulled up in the driveway, before he already had to get going, before ever making himself known.

"So Lynn, tell me something, wouldya? Help me set this thing straight," I heard him say, like it was the beginning of something he'd rehearsed in his head.

"What's that, Landry? . . ." Mom said, walking back towards him.

"What's this talk I'm being told about you and that pencil dick over there? You got it for him that good that ya can't go outside your bounds a little further—just a *teeensy* bit?" And he put up his thumb and index finger to illustrate his point of just how little. "Like at least, I dunno, outside a mile radius of married men to roll around with? Ya figure that's too much?"

I settled down their chattering cups and myself on the floor next to the TV turned low.

"In front of the boys, no less," Dad kept on, and he laughed to himself. "The whole world and God. Where's your dignity?" He was slurring, leaning forward and taking a sip of his drink. And Mom was laughing, masking another emotion, surely—both of them were—and she reached for and took a swallow of hers, eyed me with a big gulp.

I didn't tell him nothing, I eyed her back, angrily like she could even think I ever would. I didn't want the man to show up here the way that he had—no kind of way, really, like a magic trick on us is what this was, hearing him repeat how Mom, his sometimes-wife, sometimes-mother to his kid, was moving on in spite of him and his having done so a long time ago. How was his new family? I'd have asked him were it me, to change the subject. But I couldn't very well speak for Mom, nor could I tell her how her appearance alone was saying a lot more than I ever could, or for that matter the neighbors—the square-shaped Peters next door and probably Miss Wendy with the wigs next door to them: the usual suspects—and a lot louder, too, when one look at her was all it took to confirm: "Your momma's a waste, son."

He read how wrecked her future was reflected back in her eyes, crystal balls lit up by the abusive affair with Todd and his subsequently being shot by his son with her gun—"the one I done gave you, Lynn!"—with no words needed. Even her usual thinness had lost weight, mostly in the face and what retention had remained in her arms, left gangling now; her skin sickly, the complexion of cereal milk. And it wasn't just the way she looked, but it was more her behavior's erratic response to what had happened, living in a state of existing only part time and made worse by her at-home remedy of even more daily drinking, pill-popping, but to no real success. Reality had sunk in is all, that's what it was, in the sockets of her eyes, behind the thickness of her skull, that her world was not as disguised as well as it usually was or how she believed it to be. No it was for real, and it showed.

"Look at ya," Dad sneered, shaking his head. "You're somethin."

"You didn't mind it fore you went and moved on to yer greener pastures you call em."

"Don't you go gettin on that, now. You definitely don't wanna talk about what you don't know."

"But *you* can?"

Dad set his drink down loudly, with such force I thought the glass was going to shatter. Then it was him leaning back and rolling up his sleeves before spitting out every detail of what had happened the day Tommy shot his dad as it had been relayed to him, in addition to those forgotten days leading up to the incident at the motel and those following it.

"Yeah, you see, I can. Cause I *do* know, dummy."

Not only did he know this much but he went through even more, all of it, a play-by-play he was getting from Billy Wexler down the street, how it was his ex wife's fault, her sleeping with Todd behind *his* wife Pam's back—and he laughed while saying this, a "you're pathetic" laugh—how their altercations out in the front yard, not for the first time, had gotten everybody talking. And the motel parking lot scene she'd made but also several more. In the grocery store when nobody was around and it was just her, outbursts. Outside TJ's, her smoking, and talking too much, random encounters with strange men "that red-headed S.O.B." Gill Erickson recounted for him like she was some kind of dirty movie star.

"You been all over the map, darlin. What'd you think I whatn't gonna find out?"

I heard things I'd never heard before and probably wasn't supposed to hear. Dad wasn't as secretive as Mom, at least when it came to telling the truth about her, whether it was a lie or not. And maybe I was too little to know any different anyway, had I known what was real.

"That's not all. I'm not done," Dad spat off.

Again, at TJ's, where anybody who's a nobody has a stool with their name on it, this one guy, some dipshit Dad knew little of but well enough after they got to drinking, he told such stories that Dad would think enough about to recall for Mom now. And he was taking

the side of this do-nothing, his opinion as his own, which said something else.

"He had a lot to say," Dad sighed. "Seen some stuff to back up
every word of it, too."

Like how Mom was apparently doing drugs—more than the ones
he'd known about, even given her once or twice before, to shut her
up—hard stuff, that he'd been there whenever she was snorting it or
smoking it right out in the open and buying some from this guy and
some more from that one.

"Spending my own damned hard-earned money on this shit. With
the checks *I* sent you—for *him*," Dad would clarify, pointing his ciga-
rette-holding fingers at me like I was the reason for anything. "No,
you done took it too far this time, Lynn. It ain't cute no more."

It was no surprise Mom wasn't herself, or more who she'd worked
hard to present herself as, but I'd known nothing of this arrangement.
I was under the impression that even financially we'd been left to fend
for ourselves. Either way, it didn't matter much. It couldn't have been
a lot, my dad was always a very cheap man, even when he didn't
necessarily need to be. And his jobs were always odd, and suspicious
in the way money magically appeared—again, my dad the magician.
These days he'd mostly been into cars, clunkers and lemons, tore-up
trash he could fix for next to nothing, always at the repo auctions,
flipping through Auto Traders, and connecting with contacts he'd
put out feelers for, on anything he could buy and sell.

"Hey Trav, listen here . . . Yer . . . What are you now—"

"Thirteen."

"Old enough, then," Dad said, biting on his cigarette. "Here." He
tossed me his keys from his jacket pocket. "Go on and pull that one
back and around and park the Chevy in its place up close behind it.
Do a switcheroo for me, wouldya . . ."

"What?" Mom said, finally speaking up for something, if not
herself.

"The Dodge," he said. "You were right about that one, son. It's you and your momma's now."

"The hell it is," she said.

"The one who's paid for the car you been going around town in, doin whatever the hell you wanna call it, oughta have a say as to who's drivin it, now, doncha think? That seem fair to ya? Since you and me ain't nothin no more I'm takin what's mine. That car's worth more without your driving it."

Holding the keys in my hand, warm and smelling cold, the ring of metal, I gripped it harder. It wasn't only the key to the Dodge but it must've been a half dozen other car keys with it, which was which I couldn't tell. Of all the cars, why ours, why take the Chevy, I thought but wouldn't dare ask him. Why did you have to take our car? Mom loved that car. I loved that car.

"Here, boy. Gimme those," Dad said, and he took back the keys.

My hand held the impression of them, their toothmarks still white in my palm. Of course I wasn't going to go out and crank the Dodge he'd driven up in, nor did he expect me to. He was only using me as an exhibit, for show, but he had meant what he'd said. Come hell or high water he was taking the car. Not only that, he was taking me with him.

"Yes, ma'am. You bet your butt I am! The boy needs his father."

"No hell yer not," Mom said, and she grabbed at the keys in his hand but was shoved aside and pushed back onto the couch.

I think he thought that this was his way of showing that he cared, about me, about his family's well-being, but he cared only for himself.

"Trav, I'm taken you to Lumberton. You wanna come and live with your daddy? Meet your baby sister?"

I didn't say a word. I only looked at him, glared, through tears I couldn't show. I just sat down beside Mom, waited and watched to see what was going to happen next.

"That's fine, too. But yer going."

"But why?" I spoke up, following after him.

"You ain't gonna be somebody your momma made alone. Not if I can help it. No siree . . ."

"Whataya mean, Daddy?"

"Ask your momma, Trav. She knows what's what."

She was barely speaking straight by now, if at all, and between the moment Dad walked back into the house through the front door and when it slammed shut as he and I were leaving the next morning, Mom was either stumbling over herself and her words or so high that her eyes rolled back into her head and saw nothing of it. She might as well have covered her ears.

"*Momma?*" I asked her, only to get a waving and then reaching hand in return, for something to hold on to. And it wasn't me but her empty glass.

Even without his being here and watching months of this gradual progression of abuse or any sort of context for it, for Dad, I'm sure she presented herself as a woman teetering on the edge of total collapse, a version of Lynn much further gone than the one he'd last seen in the spring. Then, he'd come into town only for the purpose of rekindling a flame he'd had while he and Mom were still together, perhaps more a fling or even his mission to Mars, his visit to another world. He was trying to find something with the woman that was impossible for him to see, so Mom told me. But, as she later explained, he'd been unsuccessful in his attempts at keeping that fire going as well.

Miss Lells, "the other woman," was a teacher at my school, and someone who had shown real potential for a fresh start. "No denying that," Dad had said, spitting out the window rolled down. "Anyone that pretty. That young." And she *was* pretty, and she *was* young, the youngest teacher I'd ever had. "Skin smooth and tanned like a brand new fancy car seat," how Dad described it, an image I couldn't get out of my head, even still.

Fortunately for her, unfortunately for my dad, the Miss Lells he'd known had since become Mrs. Gilbert, a married woman. Still she was petite and blond and young enough to think about her any other kind of way than as a mother. But she was now, and this had made her breasts that much bigger and worked like charms on men like my dad who were easy to please, men like her husband, Mr. Gilbert, a man Dad had never met before but knew just by looking at him that he was dumb as dirt and didn't deserve her. Fortunately for me, back when she was with my dad, she'd only just started at the school, teaching first-graders, and so I'd narrowly missed being one of her students.

He walked outside and got in and cranked up the Dodge, quickly reversed it into the grass. Then he steered the Chevy back and out into the road, left the door open, not saying anything, instead focused on getting the Dodge pulled back up and parked where the Chevy had been.

Mom was on her feet again and at the front door seething mad.

"Here, you're tall enough to see over the wheel," he said to me, tossing the keys to the Chevy my way. "So then you can pull it up for me. Can't ya? I've gotta deal with your momma. Put it in park right up close behind this one and give me back the keys so she can't try nothin."

I didn't answer him, only lowered my head after looking at Mom and walked towards the Chevy.

"Get back in the house," he yelled at her. "Fix yourself another drink. I know you want to."

I came around and sat down in the driver's seat and slammed the door shut. And I took a minute and thought of what might happen if I just drove off right then, right there, no looking back, if they'd even bother trying to find me. Or would I maybe lose myself along the way to nowhere? Because I couldn't think of a place I could go, nor did I have a dream of one to lead me toward. Even though I'd no say in the matter—literally, not saying anything—I knew it surely wasn't Lumberton, a place I'd never been so never would I ever dream of calling home. I really didn't want to go, and I couldn't bring myself to move another muscle, let alone crank up the engine and move the car.

I slumped in the seat, turned and gazed out the window at the house across the street, to see if Tommy was having an okay Christmas Eve. I wondered when, if he ever looked back on his own memory of this day, would his version of it look anything like mine? Or would it reflect back more fondly for him versus years past, with his dad still not fully himself and therefore better because of what had happened.

Through a split in their pulled curtains I could see the TV screen light up the walls, jolting against the steady flash of multi-colored Christmas lights, no different than the night before or since three weeks earlier when the spruce as tall as his dad went up. Did Tommy and Brian have presents from their parents underneath it to open in the morning? Or did Brian still believe in Santa Claus and Tommy needed to keep pretending?

Somewhere kids were sleeping with remote-controlled cars to wake up to, dreaming of speeding them up and down the driveway. WWE wrestlers and the ring for them to wrestle in. All four Ninja Turtles *and* Splinter. Their doorbell rang non-stop tonight with guests stopping by to wish them a Merry Christmas, and even more had written the words in greeting cards since Thanksgiving, giving the mailman a shoulder cramp.

Looking back up at our house I could see Mom and Dad inside, the front room orange like it was on fire, their arguing on mute, with the radio playing over the final seconds before I made the decision to do as my dad had told me. No multi-colored lights flashed. No tree stood up in the corner. There certainly weren't any presents to exchange in the morning. Even if there had been, I imagined Mom had forgotten all about them.

In years past I think they must have somehow made up for the miracle of Christmas, because they'd fought regardless, but we'd be opening presents under the tree in the morning. And Mom would've actually spent time decorating it, we both would, together. I remember the last one, with its spiny top that swept the ceiling when we stood it up in its place it was so tall, much taller than Dad. It bent and scratched against the popcorn ceiling, and so there'd been no space

to crown the angel I'd made in the fourth grade. I'd constructed her
hair from glued-on silver-spray-painted macaroni noodles. A crunch-
ing sound she made whenever being mounted up onto the tree came
from dried corn husks I'd taped together for her robe. She was pretty,
and sparkled next to the strung lights, but her face had a funny way
about it, those plastic googly eyes I'd given her, too big for the Blow
Pop head and crossed from how I glued them onto it. Off-kilter, so
much so that Dad saw that it was only fitting to give her a name
that matched, calling her retarded. "The retard angel, made by the
retard," he said. And this set Mom off: "You're the fucking retard,"
she snapped back. She took a swing to the jaw for that one too, though
not as hard as the one she took this Christmas.

Of course I didn't know then that it was the last Christmas we'd
spend living together as a family—however way that was, it was ours,
the only way I knew. Though we'd not looked much like a family for
most of my memory, even when seen from the perspective of somebody else, looking in on us from the outside, or down on us, perched
atop the Christmas tree, there was no hiding it. Bad things lived
here. Happiness did not. But I think it may have been without Dad,
happy, and I wished it had been his last Christmas, only Mom and
me after that, because at least new memories stood some chance of
being different, even better, if he'd just stayed put, found a bar to go
to in wherever town he'd been sent for whatever job he was on at the
time. Then, she and I could've been rocking around the Christmas
tree that night without him.

After I parked the Chevy I walked back inside the house to them
having at it worse than I'd ever remembered. She was cussing and
ranting on about the Chevy, and me giving him the keys to it only
made it worse. Again, I had no say in the matter. Then, Dad was
handing her the keys to the Dodge with a smug grin, when she lost
it. She threw them back at him and landed them like a foul in his
stomach. It seemed to have knocked the wind out of him, enough that
for his turn, he backhanded her so hard she fell out on the kitchen

floor. And he kept on yelling until his voice was hoarse. How horrible a job she'd done raising me on her own, and had he known it was as bad as it was here in Siler City, how it had been ever since he left, thinking all that time she'd been doing for me what he couldn't, he'd have never left me here.

I remember seeing the cigarette she was smoking fly through the air from her lips when he hit her and land on the carpet in the dining room, more like a nook right outside the kitchen, nothing formal. Had it not been for me seeing her get slapped right then, had I rushed off to my room instead of watching the cigarette burn with the stinking smell of singed carpet fibers, our house might not have still been standing come Christmas morning. Mom was stone cold and Dad wasn't paying any attention from above her, staggering some, with one boot on either side of her head and arched over her like she was something he'd chased after or frightened to death.

With a crisis averted, and without the two of them even knowing it had been, the argument over me and her poor excuse for not being a mother to me ensued. By now I was tired of hearing it, tired in general, and I picked the cigarette up from the carpet sneakily so I wouldn't attract any more attention. But as I crept onward toward my room, the bickering interrupted with Mom coming after me, then ahead of me, slamming herself into her room. Dad gave a look and threw his hands up, got a beer out of the refrigerator and sat down with it on the couch.

"I didn't mean for any of this to happen, when I took the gun out of the car, pointed it at Tommy's dad. I only have myself to blame. Blame me. Don't blame her. It wadn't Momma's fault."

I'd already said it to myself just like this a million times in practice, like I said it to Dad, as a last ditched effort to change his mind about taking me down to Lumberton. I didn't understand his real reasoning in wanting to take me, but that he seemed to hate Mom that much that it was what would hurt her the most. Had that been it? I'd only grow up to hate you one day, I'd wanted to say to him, though I didn't have to, I didn't think. And if I had any say, he would hate me more than he hated her, if he hadn't already. Who's to say? Just the word, *hate*, it felt a lot more heavy as a kid, the weight of it enough to squash out all other words in the English language, like there was no taking it back. Would it be enough, to say it, to tell him to his face just how much I did? Really it was truly only as strong as my little fist was against a man like my dad. And I'd seen how strong he was.

He took a deep breath and patted the cushion beside him for me to come and sit, so I did.

"See, now, my question is why weren't *you* the one who shot the son-of-a-bitch? You didn't protect your momma. Some kinda sissy, I guess. I didn't teach you that. You had your chance."

He took a big swig from his can and slammed it down onto the table.

"No, sir, I was there. Not you. I defended her. Me. It was me who was holding the gun at first—*your* gun." And I could see the anger in his face rise and red, smell the sweat bead in his hair. I changed my tune. "So you see, Daddy, it wadn't just me, you were there too. Right there with me. Just like you taught me. I coulda had him, too. Just, don't take it out on her. Momma didn't do nothin."

"That's my point I'm making, Trav. Now get me another beer and then you need to go on and get in your room."

After the combative night between Mom and Dad seemed mended and gone to bed, I was up the next morning as early as I should've been as a boy on Christmas morning, only to find myself gazing down, sleepy-eyed, at my hands kept to myself. Made small again, no longer the man of the house, but under his thumb, I was doing as I was told. "Stop scratching at the rubber!" he'd shouted. Picking at the Chevy's paneling kept me calm, my sights off the road ahead, frosted fields and steam rising in pockets of overgrowth, from a thaw under the clear sun after the hard freeze overnight. The past didn't look any less bleak, and so I tried to listen to the radio but he'd turned it to a station that was playing songs I'd never heard before.

Anyway, I'd exerted all of my energy in holding back my desire to insert my opinion into their spat over what to do with me the night before, so I could barely keep my eyes open on the road this morning. Much as it was for Mom before we got into the car and drove away. More than hungover, unable to get out of bed or say goodbye or put in any last fighting words to try and keep him from taking me. Whether she'd remember it or not I'd said to her, whispered when he wasn't near us, that I wanted more than anything to stay with her and that living with him would turn me into him. I was afraid. This hurt her feelings more, the thought that though she'd see me again, she might never see *me* again.

"I'll figure something out, Momma," I told her, wiping the tears from her face. "Some kinda way to escape."

part two

chapter 10

"Your granddaddy died," Mom said, not in the kind of sober way most would expect these heavy words to be spoken but rather matter-of-factly. "People die, that's what they do," she'd once explained death to me. So then I was reminded again, now, when it came time to see if she really meant what she'd said, hoping Granddad's death—her own father dying—wasn't as simply put as that. But it seemed to be. And at the same time somehow a sort of a revelation it was, that I could understand she must already be grappling with, and in turn, in telling me, it was possible she felt some burden would be lifted from her and passed on to me. At least in some small measure, that could have been her reasoning, if there'd been any, however much a soul weighs, if enough to feel heavy. Knowing he was going to die, that that's what people did, not necessarily today or tomorrow, never mind yesterday, I knew the day would come; she had prepared me for it. However, I didn't expect I'd hear it in here, in Polk.

"He did?" I asked, in the way she might, like it was gossip I was responding to, somebody else's granddad who'd died.

It was the first time she'd come to see me since I was put there, just before Thanksgiving, before solitary. And it was towards the end of her visitation, almost time's up, when she said: "Listen here, Trav.

I've gotta tell you something." Only then did I realize that *this* was what she'd had hidden behind her eyes for almost the entire time she was sitting there, saying not what it was she wanted to, thinking about it, though, but not enough to actually say the words out loud. I could tell from the moment she sat down that something was there, another way about her. She never started off anything she ever said with telling me that she's got to tell me something, no matter how bad it was. So I knew it was really something. But still, she was never good at hiding what she was thinking well enough, not from me. It wasn't just her response to seeing me this way in Polk I was seeing, no, nothing shocked her, not really. I imagine she could've pictured me in some kind of uniform, even hoped I might be by then. Maybe not the denim one I wore but anything other than plain clothes that might set me apart, or I guess more aside, though not so soon, so young. A cap and gown had never crossed her mind, I'm sure of it, but I think she'd have liked it if I'd returned home from the battlefield as someone to brag about, without a scratch on me, with a metal, to prove something. What, I can't say for sure, maybe something to myself, because she knew I needed to believe in me more than she already did.

"Sounds like he woke up like it was any other day—the morning before last—made it into the kitchen, and then gone. Right there. Left your grandmomma behind. She's the one who called me. Not your Aunt Stace. Nope. Well hell, I don't guess she'd be the one noway. I didn't even think to ask if your grandmomma'd called her to tell her. I guess I should."

Mom felt further from me than she ever had before, not only by the distance between us, but somehow through time, like enough of it had passed to make us estranged. Maybe that made it easier to digest the words coming out of her mouth, too, the two of us sitting across from each other and limited to ten more minutes at the most. Both my arms and legs were kept to myself, not cuffed but underneath the metal tabletop as I was told, so even our body language was unable to speak. We only held glances at that point, after we hugged and sat. And I could tell, listening to her and her listening for my response to the news, that she wanted more from me as much as I did from her. But we were stuck.

"I guess I'm gonna miss the funeral."

"Yep," she nodded, putting her hand on mine. "I'm sure he'll understand, Trav."

"He doesn't care," I said. "Right. Not anymore."

Mom put on a smile for my sentiment, nodded her head again. "If you're thinkin your granddaddy's the one gonna come and tell you how it is don't be."

I told her about the dream I'd had my first night here and listened to her interpretation of it. Something to do with my own death, maybe hers, I don't remember which, I just know it was her belief that I'd dreamed up the fire, the feeling that Grandma had died when she really hadn't, not as prophesy but as a way to remind myself of my family and where I'd come from—the good side, or at least better than his, how she'd always described hers.

"He never liked your daddy and it made things rough between us for a while. But we got to say our peace. So there's that. But no use in dwelling on those days. That's all over now." She shifted in her seat and locked eyes with mine. "So go on, then. Tell me more. Sorry I didn't come sooner. You know I didn't even know til I guess it was two weeks you was in here that you was. I mean, you up and leavin the way you did, how was I gonna know? And so what about the boys they got stayin with you? The one up over you while you was sleeping? He ain't botherin you is he?"

"No, no. Jay. Yeah, he's not like that. He's been nothing but nice. I think had I been bunked with somebody else, things woulda been a whole hell of a lot worse in here these past few months. That's for sure."

"Well that's good to hear. And you're eating? Bathing—"

"Momma. I can look after myself just fine. Even in here."

"You ain't gotta tell me twice. Bout four months it's been since your birthday—hell, six or seven done gone by without me seein or hearin from ya til today. I will say, you did go and get yourself caught without me. Who was lookin after you then? I coulda given you some money, Trav. I'm still holding the last one down, believe it or not."

"I can believe it."

She fumbled through her pocketbook for a pack of cigarettes and stuck one in her lips and lit it. "Can ya now? How so? Go on, tell me. Or are you just shittin me?"

"No. Just by lookin at you, Momma. You're still skinny as a rake but your color. Your voice, it's different."

She smirked, pleased with herself or not believing me.

"I'm tellin the truth."

"Alright. Well, you just need to watch yourself. Watch where you walk in there. You know your Aunt Sharleen, she did some time. Was a long time ago, and I know a women's prison ain't nothin to compare to no man's—"

"It's not *real* prison, Momma. I mean, I don't think it is."

"Well, still, same rules apply. Most of em in there with ya are headed straight for it anyhow. Learnin how to live in it is what they're doin to em. But not to you, though, Trav. Don't you for a second go thinkin you're meant for it. That that's all there is for you. You're eighteen. You have your whole life ahead of you. And it coulda been worse, you know. Least they didn't go and—least they got you for somethin petty is all I'll say about it."

"Yeah. Don't—"

"Don't you neither. Keep your mouth shut. Head down. Look ahead, Trav. Be planning for your future. I don't ever wanna have to come here and see you this way again. Not anywhere else. You hear me? I want you right where I can see you, the way I always have." She bit down on her cigarette and reached out and touched me.

"Yeah, I do. I hear ya."

"For something so stupid. Musta not been more than a hundred dollars, huh? Two at the most. None of it was enough, though. But I guess it didn't matter. You knew that already, before you took it."

"I guess so. It was more than that. I got by alright.

"For what? Another month, maybe?"

"Cause somebody ratted me out. That's what I think."

"Was it Tommy?"

"*Tommy?* No! Why do ya say that? Tommy'd never do that."

"I dunno. I haven't seen him is all. So—"

"You haven't?"

"No. Have you?"

"Well no, course not. Not in here, Momma."

"I don't know, Trav. Hell, maybe he come in here to visit same way I did. You ain't gotta bite my head off."

"I know, I'm sorry. He hasn't been. But before, yeah, sure I did. Ever since, no. You really hadn't seen him?"

"Not once."

I thought maybe she'd have seen him coming or going from his house in all the time that had passed between now and the last night I'd seen him, which had been a while even since the time before that, since—

"You keep your mouth shut, you hear me?" Mom said.

An officer was stepping up to us, a shadow cast over the tabletop, with doubt, Mom's, and my own. Her eyes darted at him and stuck there.

"She just sat down," I said with a tone I shouldn't have taken.

"No I hadn't neither," Mom intervened, standing and brushing up beside the offensive officer to soften him, cool him off before it was my turn to be guided by his determined walk, when after she and I said our goodbyes the memory of her would reconfigure itself before getting back inside my head.

And I held hold of it, six weeks afterward and a month to the day in solitary, even though I'd wished to rid her of my life entirely; she was all I had by then, this impression she'd left me with to remember her by, telling me to remember myself. Now, stuck between two places at once, I was seeing her sitting there in the flesh across from the table, in a room without one, with little to no light to make out if I actually was or not and only enough air to breathe that I might soon suffocate if I became conscious of just how little I was breathing, if I panicked, believing I no longer could.

"*Momma?*" I heard myself whisper. It was like every boy who'd ever been brought to this hole was speaking through me.

It was cold and I was shivering but that didn't stop me from feeling the body heat of another person, maybe people, who could say what was real? Around this time, after about thirty days in solitary, your mind begins to play tricks on you. I only know this because I'm no longer in there and can see my way out of it. Not everybody does, though. The ground starts to move under your feet, like you're walking on water, or sometimes through quicksand they're so tired. If you allow yourself to you'll cave in.

"Whataya want, Trav?" she said back at me. "There ain't nothin I can do for ya. Not now. Look what you done got yourself into. Knowing damned well you shoulda been keepin yer nose clean."

"It's not all my fault, Momma. You know that," I spoke out.

And suddenly it was everything I ever wanted to say to her, just between me, myself, and I. Every word I never said. Her voice echoed against the walls like it was stuck inside a telephone, inside my head, and couldn't get out, couldn't speak up enough to be heard.

I wanted to say something so badly when I saw her last, sitting at the table, her hair bleached and brushed and pinned aside, make-up on the same way as she always did if ever we'd get to go to Kmart or the movies. And I could smell her, how she did when she had a date with a man or a bottle, either way, special or not, something she was looking forward to.

"Here, dab a bit of this on your neck," she whispered, turning up the bottle of my dad's cologne on her finger, shaking it, then smearing the way he smelled on me. "The girls'll go crazy for ya."

And it was the first day of school, a chance to start all over again. "But don't tell him, you hear me?"

"I won't," I whispered.

I didn't tell her then that I'd already started thinking of how I was never going to come back home and that my mind was mostly made up about it. It may well be the last time I'd see her, I thought. Maybe this was why the memory was so strong and one that I reached for through the darkness of my days in solitary. For so long it had been Mom and I, but no more. Never would I escape if I didn't let go.

I felt myself more upset at the thought of this than by the news she'd brought me. Granddad's dying, though it was what people did, eventually in life, in actuality I figured it must be true, too, that it was written in the stars that something would need to die between she and I in order that we might go on living our lives. Of course this is more in hindsight, thoughts like these I'm having, but even still, then, under the tabletop, my hand was twisting the leg of my pants so tightly I thought my fingers might burst and so I knew I was feeling some kind of way.

And then, alone again, only weeks had passed in here and already I'd forgotten everything that happened to me throughout those first days, even some of the ones leading up to it, all those thoughts I was having, these memories of mine I was recalling. By this point there was no time or space to speak of and that ground I once stood on, as shaky as it seemed, was gone. Along with the walls, a window to see my way out of and the door to open, all of it a blur in my eyes no longer focused. My body was tired, broke-down and empty. And it seemed like there was nothing that I could do to make it any better, to make things right. Nothing was going to pick me up: food, water, words, my imagination, much less a thought of a better time.

Days had begun bleeding into one other and I was talking aloud to see if I could hear myself, if I could understand what I was saying. I didn't know what time it was, and I forgot what the weather felt like when I was in the yard last, what it looked like from inside the dormitory. I couldn't even think of how much better the bed out there felt versus the one in here. If out there it had been hot or cold when I last slept there I had no recollection. Was the purpose of this time spent separated from everyone also meant to isolate me from myself? Without much to look forward to, with my memories changing from color to black-and-white to static, I could think of no other time when the present was all there was to think about.

A lone oak leaf, or maybe it was paint peeling, fell from the ceiling and it changed from green to yellow to red, landing on my chest. A thousand more fell after it, surrounding me with scratchy dry parchment, like Granddad's rolling papers. All at the same time they crumbled to dust and dirt and snow was falling. A squall it was, blurring the horizon line in my mind, far enough away from here for me to contemplate its force to be reckoned with, slowly but surely making its way over the hills. Even such a diversion like this, a glimmer of the world spinning outside these four walls, it does nothing to keep a man from his obsession with what's going on inside. How I pictured it, an old house of rooms, each one with every wrong I ever did and kept inside. Lock and key. Hallways connect them like timelines and reflect locked doors that repeat again and again and keep going until it's its very own consciousness, one beyond my own, anyone's. Beyond simply keeping me deprived and desperate, quiet—how I had to be but haven't always been—with my mouth shut.

Lying frozen stiff on the floor in the center of the place I'd been forgotten, I outstretched my arms and legs and began flapping, as if I was making a snow angel in the concrete. I was shivering, my teeth chattering, with only a holey blanket and a furnace that didn't make it this far, or so they'd told me. Take it or leave it. With or without it I was on my own.

chapter 11

When we arrived in Lumberton everything was closed. And not just because it was Christmas day but also Sunday.

"Yep. Always on a Sunday, course, but on Mondays too. Some of em even wait til Wednesday to open up. Some never do. Like they never was. Ain't much, I know. But what'd you expect?"

Something more, I thought.

Dad thumbed from his stubbled chin dip spit strung to the amber bottleneck poking up between his thighs. "It ain't like Siler City got much more than what they got goin on here, anyhow, Trav," he said, in defense of the place he couldn't for a second admit was not worth the gas it took to get to.

"I didn't say nothin," I said to him.

"And ya ain't got to neither."

But, if I had added my two cents, it would've been that Siler City's got living in its limits only a fraction of the people Lumberton has, and less buildings, a lot less. Half as many streets criss-cross through it, and red lights, maybe two, three at the most, keep you from going over the slower speed limit and past it before it's gone. Stop-and-go pretty much summed it up—not just his driving but how the conversation carried on between us in Dad's last half-mile of touring me through to see the rest: not much more. And maybe it *had* only been because it was Christmas that it looked as empty as it did then. Right? I sure hoped so. Hardly another car on the road. Not another soul.

Fayetteville, now, where we'd gone through miles earlier, would've had *something* to look forward to—no Raleigh, no, not even close, but more to discover—enough to stop and stay awhile. Why not live here? I thought when we'd made it that far. Was it out of his range? Work or self-worth or otherwise? Even moving on, judging where he'd ended up living, in a two-story strip of apartments that seemed to suddenly arrive out of nowhere, I still wasn't at all sure I knew the reason.

"Home sweet home," Dad grumbled, putting the Chevy in park.

Home was situated right next to the highway, closer to the gas station lit up across from it than any other houses, a neighbor to call, or even a park to kill time in. Nonetheless it was something to look at. Already I saw myself staring out the front window in his apartment at the pumps, folks pulling in and filling up, getting to wherever it was they were going. Wishing I was one of them.

His front door was one among a half-dozen or so others, not unlike any one of the motels it brought to mind but clearly with no road sign nor a parking lot with riffraff the way I was used to seeing them.

"You get everything?" he asked me, keying open the door. "Make sure you ain't done left it in the car—whatever it is yer gonna want."

"Yep. Yessir."

He looked over at me like I was a kid who'd never belonged to him, whose possessions he'd not recognize regardless if I'd actually been here toting them around with me. I'd honestly had no time to think about where I was going let alone what I'd need once I got there.

"The door sticks," he sighed as I was coming in after he did. "Just give it—Kick it." I tried to. "Kick it, willya, Trav. Come on now, dammit."

"Sorry . . ."

"Don't say yer sorry. Ain't nothin to be sorry for. Just get on in."

"I'm in. I'm in."

He seemed upset, and he always did, but more than usual. Ticked-off at not just me, and frustrated and fidgety. Focused someplace over his shoulder instead of on what was in front of him. On the lam is what he looked like. A man who'd robbed a bank or just got done doing something he shouldn't have been. Hiding something or from it.

The apartment was always left without the heat on so the bill wouldn't run up too high, and so our breath was showing, his even more with cigarette smoke.

"Back yonder's another room," he pointed. "I suspect you might could call it a bedroom. Ain't got no window, though, but hell, it's a place to sleep—But shit, no bed, not yet. We'll run up the road and get one for ya."

Not only that, there was no food in the fridge. And not that I was expecting anything, but nothing new for me to play with. I needed an even more overactive imagination to make that happen for sure, because I couldn't even picture Dad at a store picking out something for me like maybe a bike to ride, a ball to toss around, or far more dreamy a Nintendo system—and another game to go along with the one it came with. I imagine in his mind this trip down to Lumberton, to live with him, his saving me from Mom and who he thought she was turning me into, was my Christmas present that year.

Further in we went, setting things down on a beat-up couch, and the floor because there wasn't anywhere else to sit, I wasn't surprised by his lack in taking care of himself, having not provided more for me. Everything looked about how I'd expected. Only, after so much time, it still seemed as if he'd only just moved in or was getting ready to move out. Beyond spare in the way it was furnished and with its walls still blank of any pictures or posters or even a calender to keep track of where he was and where he was going. Some boxes stacked against a wall, though, so I thought maybe it was just that most of his things had not yet been put away and if there was a proper place to put them he'd not yet figured it out.

"Ain't a whole lot, I know," he sighed, fingering out a cigarette from a pack stuffed in his shirt pocket. "And it looks just like it does. I've only moved in here not too long ago. It's just a helluva lot cheaper out here so I did what I had to do. For you and your momma."

"What're *you* doin for *Momma*?" I shot off.

Without a second to think about it, he popped me in the lip with half his fist. I felt it sting like a bee, split against my sharp and crooked lower teeth. Blood felt cold on my lip as it swole, and smeared my chin when I wiped it off, along with any look he told me I had on my face.

"I gotta pee," I told him, and I did, after the ride, after holding it. But more than that I needed to get out from under him, after being so close to one another. The reality was that I wasn't going to be able to.

"Trav," he sighed. "Come on, now."

"I'm just peeing, Dad," I echoed.

In the bathroom mirror, hazy from his handprint smudges and spotted with sink spit, I checked to make sure I was okay. *Do as you're told*, I told myself. *Speak only when spoken to. And don't ever talk back.*

"Are you hungry? I can fix you somethin," he shouted. "Come on back and sit down. Yer fryin my nerves with all yer movin around."

When I came out I said nothing, already going against the words I'd reminded myself in the mirror to not forget. But I did sit down, on the couch. Across from it was a rinky-dink TV set on top of a Jim Beam box markered: Important. *How* important? I thought. More important than me? Than us?

"Where were you living before here?" I asked him, genuinely. "Was it ever actually in *Lumberton* Lumberton? I mean, it's been a year almost, hadn't it?"

"Oh—well," he paused, and I thought I already knew the answer based on his expression breaking apart. "You know, yer momma musta done told ya bout it, I reckon. Stayin with this woman I was with. Yep. And so, well—didn't work out, so there it is. She had other plans. Ideas of her own, which whatn't mine."

I didn't question him and he went back to playing house in the kitchen, cracking eggs into a hot pan on the stove. I'd better get a stomach for it, I thought.

Then maybe it was the sum of it all suddenly sinking in, and I couldn't stop myself from taking a bucket to my thoughts so I wouldn't sink too. "So what about school? What am I gonna do when it starts back up? Where am I gonna go? Did you tell my new teacher I was coming?"

He slung the pan from his hand and spit back at me: "Boy! Questions are like—hell, I dunno what. Just . . . Listen here. Listen to me, wouldya? Wouldya just . . . Find you somethin on TV and stay put. Keep quiet. My head hurts. You oughta know enough about a hangover livin with ya momma to know what's what with yer daddy's, now, Trav. Let me do this. This one blasted thing for ya. Wouldya? Can I do that? Can I, now?"

"Yessir," I sighed. "Sorry."

"Don't say yer damned sorry, boy."

I looked away from him, into the TV, the black screen. I still hadn't turned it on, unable to focus my attention away from the new place I found myself in. Which he was right about: it wasn't much, a lot smaller than spacious, and not even close to a place called home. Nor was the man I was to be sharing it with making it any more so. Looking back it was the sort of place I'd guessed a man like him, someone without a family, a woman telling him not to, would pick to live in. And if he was on a kind of mission to impress this thirteen-year-old, he wasn't. That's not to say it took much, but more than this, definitely. I knew then he'd no intention of taking me back with him when he drove up to Siler City, that I was wagered or won or even somehow pawned off, having had no other way to judge the condition the place was in. I doubted anyone with enough sense or another dollar to spend on something elsewhere would choose to live here. Dad wasn't some genius but he wasn't stupid neither. And he wasn't poor—wasn't rich but not so much without that he had no other choices. He got by was how he put it.

"Glad yer here, son," Dad said, with scrambled eggs and a couple sausage links on a plate he set beside me on the couch cushion. And he finally sat down on the other end of it, eating from his own.

It was nice of him to say, whether I needed to hear it. But still I wasn't confident that my coming here had been the result of persuasion on his part, that maybe I'd actually been only a last minute afterthought, along for the ride, collateral maybe.

I picked up the plate, turned the TV on and let whatever it was play into commercials, the two of us eating in silence, before I tried talking to him again.

"So you're gonna sell Momma's car for real? I'm not asking you cause I wanna bother you, Daddy. Just curious is all. You don't have to. You already got a car." And he gave me that look. "I'm just sayin."

He stewed in it for a few seconds, lit himself a cigarette.

I didn't push, and although I did want to know, I didn't want him to know that I did. How were things going to be from then on is what I should have asked. There was never the question of how we got here.

He blew smoke long and slow, deliberately, knowingly. When he did this it made whatever he was going to say seem more serious, thoughtful, like me and Mom needed to listen up. It was no different now, just the two of us, though I didn't have her to cut through the bullshit.

"That car out there yer momma was drivin done been through hell. What's gonna happen is it's gonna be fixed up—for cheap, mind you—and then sold to one of the guys I got in my pocket. If not then the highest bidder."

"She loves that car, Daddy."

"It don't show it. Don't tell me it does. When you love something you take care of it. Let it be a lesson to you, Trav. And if she don't keep that roof I bought for us to live under—for the both of you to keep on at it—she's gonna lose it too. It's all under your daddy's name. There's another one: never let a woman have anything that don't belong to her in her name. She can write her name anywhere else she wants to, so long as it ain't on nothin she don't own out right. That car. That house. Me. Hell, you, even you, Trav. Yer momma don't own you. You're almost a man. And in my absence you were, you hear me."

"Yessir."

"Now, go on and finish yer breakfast. I gotta hit the road."

"*What?* What do you mean? We just got here. Yer takin me with you, right? *Daddy* . . ."

"No. I'm not takin you with me. I got work I gotta do. What'd I just get through tellin you? I got things I gotta take care of."

"Come on, can I come?"

"No. I done said it once—twice—don't make me say it again."

Then he was off. Just like that. And I was left alone. I was old enough to be, sure, but it wasn't any other day, it was Christmas. Not only that, I was in a strange place, where I knew no one. Where Tommy wasn't across the street whenever Mom left me alone. Where the familiarness of it felt safe—most especially whenever Dad had gone. There was *that*, I thought. I didn't have him to worry about anymore.

Because there was an earache of quiet to it, a stillness that tickled me on the inside, I turned the volume up real loud on the TV, so I could hear it in every room of the apartment I inspected and not the sound of my own blood pumping. I was looking for evidence, anything to tell me different, some proof of who this person was without us. Really it seemed like someone had died here, suddenly, been out jogging and run over by a car, a hit-and-run, and the contents of his place had been kept the way they were, untouched, ever since. Dad wasn't a runner. He was a marathon drinker, though. And by that evening I figured he wasn't doing work but was out tying one on—another one, and another.

It was nearing dark by five and so when I next pulled back the curtains in the front room—clearly bought and hung by that woman who'd had ideas—I saw the highway outside alive again with a steady *whoosh!* And myself, too, I could see standing there reflected back at me in the window with the TV left on looking out at the gas station across the road. Rowdy with dented pickups idled at both pumps and cars parked every which way, I listened to the rise and fall of their engines, doors slamming shut, car radios playing. A man with a grisly beard hung out from his downed window shouted at a woman walking up to meet another woman waiting for her. Her ankle boot propped against the station's cinder block wall painted in racing stripes the colors of Florida. I couldn't make out what he was saying but understanding her reaction I could imagine.

A pad of dust looked like lint along the window I was glued to. Seeing it, I sneezed, and then again. It had settled on top of most everything around here. Made sense. I traced it clean with my fingers and brushed them off on my knees. The woman who'd last thought to before me must've parted ways with him a lot longer than only last week. Not that it was her job to clean up after him, just evidenced by the effort of hanging a curtain, I was reminded how Dad felt it was. I never saw him so much as lift a finger around our house and so what made his own any different.

When I looked back up and out the window, I saw one of the women now standing at the edge of the highway, suddenly cross-ing it, skipping across the center line toward the apartments. Her ankle boots sounded out, almost glowed in the dark by the dim light trembling under metal awnings crinkled over every door including our own. And she was heading straight for it. I ducked down so she couldn't see me, or at least I thought she couldn't.

"I can see you!" she shouted between the sound of her knuckles against the door.

I stayed put, didn't make a peep, crouched with my back curled against the wall below the window.

"Landry! Lan*nn*dry*yy* . . . I know you're in there. Open up! Come on, now. I can see yer TV on, ya fuck. Come on and open this damned door. You owe me thirty—no forty—forty fuckin dollars you owe me. It ain't like I'm workin for free, ya know."

I covered my mouth with both my cold hands and squinted my eyes shut, waited awhile in hopes she wouldn't know it was me. And after the sound of her seemed to have finally gone away I raised up.

"Hey! Gotcha!" I heard her start up again, this time banging her fist on the window pane, the butt of her cigarette lighter against it sharp and sudden and sent down my spine. I thought she'd shatter the glass if I ducked back down now, seeing her see me, standing right there in my face. "*Yer* not Landry. Who're you?"

"Travis," I said from the other side of the glass.

"*Travis?*"

"*His son*," I answered, like she oughta know.

"Oh. Well, still. Yer daddy, he owes me. Least let me in, wontcha?"

She walked off quick and I didn't need to lean forward to watch or wonder where she was going because I heard her back at the door. Knowing I couldn't hide, that she knew I was in here, not *of* me, clearly, but clearly that she did my dad, I opened the door for her.

"Thanks, kid. It's colder than a witch's tit out here," she said, rushing in and shutting the door behind her. She shook her coat off like it was a burden from her shoulders. "But whew, ain't much better in here, is it? Whatcha got the damned heat cut off for?"

"I dunno," I mumbled, watching her move the way that she did, antsy or itching to leave already, coming in like she lived here. She smelled like the cold stuck to her, and cigarettes, hairspray, too. Whiskey was on her breath or maybe it was only the chewing gum she was smacking, even whenever she spoke. But she wasn't all together, not on her feet the way she might be if she'd not been drinking. Or maybe it was just her: "Gloria, but my real name's Gail," she'd tell me.

"Cause yer little I can tell it to you. Gail's not sexy. But you wouldn't know anything about all that."

I stretched my back to make myself stand taller and didn't say anything to her about it, only listened as she rattled off a story for me about how she'd met my dad not long after he'd moved down here—from Raleigh.

I shook my head and smirked.

"Oh, no? He didn't come from Raleigh," she asked.

"Nope. He and my momma, they didn't really divorce yet neither I don't think. He has a baby, too, you know, with some other woman," I told her. "Did he tell you that?"

"This is why I don't make it personal. Or I try not to. Yer daddy, though, he tended to steer it in a way I wadn't always willing to anyhow. Which is why I just want my money so I can go. But I see you prolly didn't even know yer daddy was doin what he done."

"What? What'd he do? Tell me."

"Oh, no. Nothin I can think of that might make him any worse than any of em are—just that he's a john is all I mean to say. No more. I'd never change a boy's impression of his paw."

And then I thought she'd maybe confused my dad with another man. *"John?"* I said. *"Landry's* my daddy's name. Turner Landry Wains. But—well, you knew that," I sighed, hearing her shout out for him mere minutes ago outside. I didn't know what a john was then and she didn't have to explain it to me.

"So, you see. I just need to take what's mine and be on my way— fore he comes home."

She plopped down on the couch where I'd been sitting, glared crookedly at the bright TV screen. She didn't look much older than the girl on the Coke commercial. Even as cold as it was she wore a skirt, but her pantyhose were not torn like they were on women in the movies who did what she did. And her makeup wasn't done up the way theirs had been. Her hair was like Mom's, even though she couldn't have been old enough to drink.

"How old are you?"

"Yer momma musta didn't tell you it ain't polite to ask a lady that?

Old enough, though. And *how old are you?*"

"Fifteen," I lied, though only by about a year and half. And she smirked like she knew the truth but didn't question it. "For how long have you been lookin for him?" I asked. "I mean, how long's it been since he's owed you the money you say he owes you?"

"Well, I—"

"I mean, is he gone all day like this most days?"

"Most Sundays, yeah, sure. He said he works nights a lot, and days . . . I guess a lot. I dunno. I don't hardly see him parked out front. Unless he wants me to is when I come over. But on Christmas day I thought sure I might catch him here."

I'd forgotten all about it being Christmas. And I'd not noticed how the front room she said she wasn't leaving from had turned dark as night, lit only by the TV still on that I myself had stayed put in front of, pretending like I cared about whatever commercial it was playing when my real interest was stuck on her.

"How long *are* you gonna stay? Really," I asked.

"However long it takes for your daddy to come home. I ain't got nowhere else to be. Why, do you?"

"No. Just wondering. What if he never comes back?"

"Oh, he will. One way or another, he's hittin that bed—or I guess it could be somebody else's, now that you mention it."

"Whataya mean?"

"Nothing."

I stood up from the couch and looked out the window. A car came by and not another one right after it, not for a minute, maybe longer. I felt myself sway a bit, my head heavy.

"If yer tired, by all means . . . Don't let me keep you," she sighed.

"I'm not tired. I'm not a little kid. I don't even have a bedtime."

"Oh, well, there you go, then." And she shuffled in her pocketbook before lighting her a cigarette, with her head held back to blow the smoke from it at the ceiling instead of me, like it might bother me.

"I don't care about that. My daddy and my momma smoke, so—"

"Whataya want one? You *are* fifteen."

"Yeah. I do," I told her, though I really didn't. I'd only ever smoked one of my mom's cigarettes, never my dad's and never a Kool like hers.

I sat down and she pushed the pack next to me with her lighter centered on top, turned her gaze away so as not to make a show of it as I tried doing the same. As foreign as it seemed then to smoke, even to hold a cigarette between my fingers, it should've come as natural as cussing did in my family.

"Thanks," I said, after I lit and sucked on the filter and blew out, without so much as a rasp in my throat. This made her smile.

We faced the TV screen, smoking in silence. I wanted to enjoy it but all I could think about was how Dad would kill me if he came in—kill her, too. The both of us were as good as dead if he'd walked in that door right then. But he didn't.

Gail stayed and chatted with me for a good while, chain-smoking and biting at her nails, going on about nothing in particular, until I really was tired, from the long day I'd had, from waiting forever for something to happen. Even if it seemed nothing had, it did. I think I'd fallen in love with Gail, or Gloria, whoever it was she wanted me to believe she was. I'm sure it was her I dreamed about that night. And when I woke up the next morning, it was some other woman in Dad's bed beside him. No sign of my Gail, or his Gloria.

The next day, and into night, it was the same thing. And the night after that. Dad would roll out of bed, up and leave me sometime mid-morning, sometimes sooner, only a couple hours of seeing him after not seeing him at all the day and night before. Either all alone or, if he was feeling sorry for leaving me, with a five-dollar bill to go buy myself something to eat at the gas station, I stayed in the apartment like he told me to. It took him until the next year to get me a mattress to sleep on, and actually was only a few weeks from the time I watched the ball drop on TV, but 1989, still.

The merry-go-round of women didn't stop, the apartment being more the whorehouse Mom had described. I didn't care so much about that, though, nor did I see them the same way. The months wouldn't have passed by the way they had were it not for Beth, a waitress in town, or maybe Jill, a thirty-something just passing through, who ended up staying a week after I met her the next morning after Dad took off. Then there was Misty, a beauty school beauty, Dad coined her, from whatever town was the next one over in no need of naming. Misty got along well enough until she didn't, leaving when snow was on the ground. Mary Beth, another waitress, Beth's replacement, she left with a black eye and a bag of Dad's clothes—his "good shirts," he called them—and if he ever saw her again . . . Kelly, assistant manager at the Piggly Wiggly over in Laurinburg, a woman he'd been seeing now and again but hadn't since the spring. And there were definitely more, only these were the ones whose names I knew and who took interest in me, even drove me places on occasion. Or the morning after another one of Dad's benders, if they stopped themselves from taking off too quick, to stay and chat awhile longer with me, like Gail did, back again that summer or nearing close to it. She and I sat out front on plastic lawn chairs that just showed up the same way she did, smoking cigarettes, watching the highway alive and well.

"This'll prolly be my last time," she said, and she had before, many times. "But really. This is it. I'm gonna be moving north."

"Where?"

"Don't know yet. Just that I am. Wherever's not here's where."

"Take me with you."

She laughed out loud, hacked out her cigarette smoke.

"I wadn't being funny. I mean it. For real."

"Even if I did, there's breakin the law and there's *breakin the law*."

"What's stopping you?"

"*Me?* Well, what's stopping *you?* You can leave anytime you want. I'm sure yer momma'd be happy as a clam to have you back. Where she can see you. Know yer all right. And you are, ain't you? All right."

"When do you leave?" I asked, ignoring her question.

"I dunno yet. Soon though. I won't be comin back here to this place. That I know for sure. So—"

"Before you go, can you do something for me? If you won't take me with you will you take me to the bus station?"

"So what, you can take it God only knows where? And with what money? You ain't got any do ya?"

"Yeah, I mean, I dunno."

"He really don't give ya nothin does he? If yer gonna do it, well, you best take it while he's got it. It comes and it goes. Fore he's out the window with it."

"Where *does* my daddy get his money from? What does he do? He said he was gonna sell my momma's Chevy but he never did."

"Well . . . I can't say for sure but he spends it so he makes it. Sellin cars, sure he does that. And other things, too . . . He's not set up in an office everyday, yer daddy, you know that. He puts in the miles, that's for damn sure. Probably done seen every county in North Carolina."

The truth was I *had* saved up *some* cash, taking a loose dollar bill here and there whenever he'd left his pocket change laying around. Although I wasn't so sure it was enough to get me anywhere but here. It was a start at least. And not some bright idea but dulled down some ever since day one when I'd started thinking of the day I'd leave.

"Go on inside. Let's see what we can find," she said, standing, scraping out her cigarette on the sidewalk. "You already checked the box of rubbers in his drawer?"

"*What?* No . . ." I answered, following after her, beating me to it, already in there looking.

"Shit," she sighed. "Ain't nothin but a buck left in it. Ah hell, but listen, when yer good and ready, next time he's sleepin, get that billfold of his and take off with whatever's in it. Take what he's got— what's yours. He won't know the difference. Trust me. Won't know what hit him. They never do."

"You won't tell him, willya?"

"What? That yer takin from him, *hell* no."

"No, that I'm gonna leave."

"Oh. Course not. Cause you ain't tellin him how *I* am. Or that it's *me*"—pointing at her chest—"who's helpin"—and to mine—"*you*. It's our secret. Ya hear me?"

I nodded and then watched her go through the rest of my dad's drawers. The bed was a mess beside her, where they'd slept the night before, where his impression remained in the pillow, his smell, too, hers. The room was a picture of the two of them together, and I felt myself jealous of him.

The next weekend I tip-toed into his bedroom early in the morning when it was still black out. His pants were wrestled off onto the carpet and in the back pocket his billfold was fat. And it wasn't all cash, but business cards, notes on napkins torn and tucked inside it. There was also a bent and folded picture of me and Mom, and him, the three of us. I must've been five or six at the time, grinning—all of us were. We looked like strangers now, a family that might be in the dictionary under the definition for it. I stopped myself from thinking too long on it and quietly folded it back, rubbing by fingertip over his initials branded into its soft, worn leather. To go with what I'd taken and my decision, Gail ended up giving me a ten-dollar bill and a ride to the bus station in town.

I told myself then it was going to be the last time I ever saw or heard from my dad, there in that bare apartment, passed out on his bed, good as dead, as alone as he came, having been out so late the night before that I knew he'd not be up to read my note about me leaving until I'd already made it to the last bus stop. I don't even remember what it was that he said to me before then, or if he said anything to me at all the day before, but I'll always remember him telling me: "You ain't nothin but a bad hangover that won't go away from a good time me and yer momma had a long, long time ago."

chapter 12

Time spent in solitary wasn't all that different from the time I spent in that apartment. A stranger I'd been in Lumberton, not just to my dad but to myself, and again when I first arrived in Polk—or how best I could make sense out of what had really been periods of great tribulation. It took finally making it to the other side before I was able to look back this way and see myself for who I really was.

Those outsiders, too, going their own way and not by accident into my life at thirteen, and eighteen, it was my understanding how they were no longer strangers. And even though I'd lived with Dad, without Mom, knew at least in part some things about him that I hadn't before, he still was. It was almost as if whatever impression I had of him only muddled more after those months spent getting to know myself, getting to know him through the women he'd wrangled into his orbit. Just as I had, for them, I think they must've thought they knew themselves enough to know a man like my dad. Though not enough to know to stay away from him. How they could be what he wanted them to be or possibly change him, like my mom believed herself capable once upon a time, this must be what held them in place. Maybe he just liked the attention they gave him. But it wasn't enough for him. They weren't enough. Not for me, either, keeping me company whenever *I* was alone, to myself, kept there the same way I was and then again while in Polk. Who's to say that maybe my dad wasn't in some kind of exile of his own making.

Even before Polk, already I'd become another person, and once there, and in solitary, I was changing into someone else entirely. Someone I no longer recognized. I took it hard on myself. Harder with every day that passed. Remembered more than I wanted. My mind wasn't through playing tricks on me neither. I'd seen ghosts Mom had told me not to believe in, walking circles in the hole. Back from the dead. Risen while I slept, there to wake me in the mornings and then keep me up late most nights. The lights were out but I could still see everything.

A cold hard reality had settled in. Colder than that apartment. Colder than the front seat of the Chevy driving down to Lumberton. His shoulder, all those times he had nothing to say to me except bad things, mean things. Sometimes unspoken with a fist. Back of the hand. Busted lip. I felt it in my stomach, the blow, the wind knocked out of me.

I was freezing before I knew what hit me next. So then it must be Christmas, I thought—somewhere, because it wasn't happening in here. No joy. And then it was New Year's in another timezone—hell, a whole other dimension. Nothing new. It must have been February, when again I could see myself no longer alone, slouched up sideways next to what appeared to be the decomposing body of a man my same height. In no time like the present, after a bout of heavy snow, there he was emerging from it, whiteout or my own blackout or even my memory's mistake in thinking I could hold on to something long enough for it to be there.

"Hello? Somebody! Get me out of here . . ."

Curled up under the filthy toilet bowl he stunk to the heavens. Each of his limbs nearer to the bone as they folded into the other, with muscled arms clinched tightly around only cartilage and tendon left for knees, bare knuckles to booted feet. And his sheen of hair, in strands that could have been spider webs so much time had passed, sparkled under the bright overhead light that suddenly flickered on. In the blink of an eye all that was left then were bloody boot prints planted along the floor beside my cot and growing up from those seeds I'd sewn for harvest, before I was convinced I would wither away without ever getting the chance see it for myself. I was under an avalanche, caved in, left numb, through until March, and it started to melt, my mind.

In April it rained so hard the concrete floors felt wet all the time and the walls swole up with it, reeked like a bog I was fixed in feet-first, unable to move an inch. Food didn't stick to me and so I'd gotten as skinny as the bars I stood and slept and squatted behind. They watched me, too. All of me. Every move I made. Made threats. Made me do it. Made me. In the space between my arms and legs daffodils began to bloom, around my head and neck. Patches of grass sprung up and rested my body in peace and filled the cell with the sweet sick smell of it freshly cut in the Sellers's lawn across the street. And it was tulips coming up from my granddad's grave I never got to go see. All around me they grew, so many I couldn't help but crush them whenever I felt like getting up on my feet again. I had no way of knowing if they were really there, of course not, if springtime had come. So I imagined it. I must have. All of it.

From inside looking out, as every hour of it came and went, each season gone to the next, I wasn't sure which one or for how long or even how old I was. Had I even aged? Did it really matter anymore? Birthdays. Holidays. Days. Weeks. Months. Years it could have been and I'd have known no difference. Maybe I'd never leave, I thought. Maybe I never left. To be sure would have required of me an under-standing of time far greater than my pined-up calendar spelling it out. Maybe, just maybe, I thought, it was myself I was seeing in my cell, the man with blood up to his neck, a face I could no longer recognize.

When it was summer I knew the day I'd turn nineteen hadn't come yet. I squinted and raised a hand over my eyes, blocking them from the blinding hot sun that beat down on me. I was trying to see the future. I didn't know for sure what day it was, how much longer I had, only how it could have only been sometime during my sixth or seventh month in there and so more still. The floors were hot and the air was heavy, my skin soft and not scaly like it was in the drier months prior. I didn't remember back to then, not with any sense other than how one wasn't like the other: before and after. It was time for a haircut but I could not for the life of me recognize when it had grown so long. And if I couldn't recognize the dead things growing how could I my own self, turning another year older?

But I did, when the heat became so unbearable there was talk of letting me out—or even letting me out for a little while, to come back, like a house cat or maybe a dog behind a chain-link fence. Heat this bad only happened when I came along. Mom had told me how she'd have soon sweat me out than give birth it was so hot the day I was born. Without any proof, other than my mop of hair dripping wet against my face and neck, I imagined myself now nineteen years old. That wasn't so hard, I thought. So then could I make myself believe I was any age, anyone? Maybe I'd been here before, made myself believe less time had passed and in actuality it had been twice as long and I was twenty. Twenty-one? How old *am* I? If a man has to ask himself, has he not lived longer than the one who forgets to?

It wasn't so much a case of how my birthday came and went without incident; it wouldn't have been possible any other way, really, not in Polk. There was never going to be a big stink. No party or cake. No lit candles blown out or wishes made that I couldn't tell anyone what so they'd magically come true. And even had I not been in solitary, being able to tell someone, Dwayne I guess would have been my only ear, he'd have said Happy Birthday, maybe, and only if I told him it was. The long and the short of it: the day I turned nineteen. All of these things I already knew, on the day, the day before it happened, the day after it had come and gone. So sure I was, it would feel like I remembered them happening before they ever had. But how much different would it have been out there than in here, on the outside, had I not been locked up?

A fly landed on my cheek and I swatted it away. Was it brought with the smell of August? I thought. Decay, blood and guts, the gore? And it wasn't just the one fly but a swarm of flies in the hole with me. The buzzing became as deafening as the silence in my ears without them there, when I had nothing to think about but what I had done. It pained me to hear myself think, so then I listened for the beach, summer's end, and felt the hollowed seashell sharp against my temple, the sound of it closing in tightly around me. Echoes inside unable to escape but that when I stopped listening, for a second I was exploring: the Outer Banks: ocean spray in my sunburned face and wide mouth, salt mixed with spit and sweat, and a gull calling out from the clouds. But again arose the smell of something far stronger.

A smell, as they say, can be an easy trigger for recollection, sometimes great enough to unlock a memory capable of bringing you right back to a place in time and to remembering even more: minor details that collect and enlarge into something so specific it begins with a moment of silence and slowly amplifies, becomes louder and louder, so loud it can't be ignored. Brought by the touch and feel of something that maybe didn't seem as memorable until the moment you begin to experience it again, with everything all at once colliding with the other as it quickly rushes through a narrow passage in the brain before making its way to what feels like the eyes in a matter of milliseconds. And just like that, there it is and there you are. And here I am, brought right back to where I started and when I could taste it as strongly as I could smell it. It remains everywhere, all over me, no matter how hard I tried to shut my eyes to the sight of it then, to make it go away. Make it stop. I'm reminded of it, and I was then, of why I was there, how I made it here today, by the pungent smell of another man's insides. The downright mess it made. All the blood. His body beaten and stabbed to a pulp. It still hangs heavy, here and there, in the floor drains outside the hole, leveling the blood out into the hallway so that we could all see it, smell its thick, ironed stench permeating the air, so that I can still taste it when I breathe. Was it that someone let him in, into the hole beside mine? To let him out? Was it my turn?

Not only was the blood there, a puddle in Polk, but it was across the street at Tommy's house, his dad nearly bleeding out on the carpet again: a lake of blood. I saw myself in its reflection, heard Pam's voice shrill, screaming at him. Mom was seeing stars the same way I was. Gun smoke laid still over it like a white sheet over a dead man.

It was more real then than it had ever been since being put in solitary confinement—than any other reenactment of mine in all the years since it actually happened. And what if it had *not* happened? Or what if it had happened not how I remembered and everything I was seeing, had seen, was my own imagining? An illusion? The carpet had been ripped out and replaced after all. I needed to keep seeing things play again and again this way to know for sure. And if ever I wasn't able to, I felt an intense deprivation. Especially now, when I was alone and without proof. I could have been anybody if it weren't for the reels replaying for me against the cement walls of that hole I felt too weak to climb out of. In need of more than my own hands, I realized. That I was going to have to dig even deeper to find my way. The sensation of being touched by another person, knowing good and well enough that I was truly alone in this place I'd locked myself into, that would have helped. I never needed my mom more than I did then. It was only her face I could see, stunned, not looking at me, when all was said and done. And the smell still lingered, like the hollowed brain contains in it the very rot of a best laid plan gone horribly wrong.

These thoughts sounding out like unseen animals in the woods at night are what kept me awake. Though alone, through the stillness of my exerting all efforts to get out of it, from making no sudden movements to call any unwanted attention to myself, it was easy to mistake what each noise was and where exactly it was coming from for another. More than that, who had done what to who? And was it even worth a man's time trying to work out a reason why? Or where? The here and now, or going backward, how it is we find ourselves in such a place to wonder who we really are, what's it all for? Not only are the sounds of Polk called to mind, the what ifs, but the way it felt to wonder what was going to happen next. A constant vibration in my ear, the thumping, the heart of the matter. It did me no good to dwell in the past, I supposed. But easier said than done.

When I thought I'd run my course, had nothing left to live on, I could see myself alive inside solitary. I'd stayed up so late and for so long, sweat every last drop of it I had in me it was so hot, that my head felt disconnected from my neck. Up above the hole I looked down on me. I must've been a kid again, wearing the clothes I'd one day grow into and then out of. Blue jeans dirtied with red handprints skid up and down the thighs. Laced up boots too big showing prints leading the way out. The floor was sinking and I was too, up to my waist in blood or the bathwater I'd thought to drown myself in at that motel off I-40 I holed up in for days like some kind of fugitive junkie. Sirens sounded. Lights chased over the walls. The boy found in a manhunt.

Tommy's whisper brought me up from it, the muck, and my head down to my shoulders, out of the clouds. I wasn't sitting on the bed with no give in it where I'd laid my worries to rest but the raggedy cot I'd just sweat every ounce of myself out onto, breathing heavy in some kind of faraway state.

"I wished I'd killed him."

He must've been eleven, almost twelve again and sat across from me, staring out between blood spatter over his face that began to form a smile as soon as I recognized it. The whites of his eyes, glints of crooked teeth under his turned up lip, they stole what little sight was left inside this place, shined like a flashlight over every last detail before it was gone. But one thing I knew would never go away was the body. Bones and all it turned to stone, stardust that blew away in a sudden gust of wind. The chill woke me up in a cold sweat, up against someone's hollering: "Wains! On your feet. It's time to go."

chapter 13

"Wake up, hey! Kid . . ."

Frustration in the man's voice, and his poking at me, too, pulled me out from the tunnel I was slumped deep inside.

"*What?*" I asked, shaken and startled so much I'd forgotten where I was when my eyes adjusted to the wide window beside me with a view of a parking lot and highway intersection. Mid-morning sun was hot in my face and a bus seat hard against my back. I looked out and stupidly asked the driver where we were.

"You gotta get off. I can't let ya keep on at it," he said, motioning with his hands for me to move. "I had seen ya back here hunkered down the way ya was before but now you gotta buy yourself a ticket if ya wanna keep on thataway."

I straighted up and stopped slouching, stood from the seat.

"Where's my bag? I sighed. "I had a bag with me!"

"You put it in the seat next to ya?" the bus driver asked.

"Yeah."

"Well then it's gone."

"*Gone?*"

"Fraid so. And you gotta go. Unless you got any money. You can get a ticket in there," he said, pointing at a convenient store with bars over its windows and signs for cigarettes and beer.

"Wait. What happened to Raleigh? I thought this bus was going to Raleigh . . ."

"It was. It did. Done came and went, kid."

An elderly woman was yelling for the driver, knocking the steps leading onto the bus with the rubber tip of her cane.

"Hold yer horses, ma'am, I'm comin . . ." the driver said to her, then to me again, "And yer goin. Come on."

I got out from between the empty seats, still only halfway remembering ever sitting down. I looked back and then in each seat we passed for any sign of my bag. A change of clothes and a Walkman Dad never touched was all I'd packed—and two or three tapes I'd never listened to—but still, it was enough to wonder about. The bag alone was my backpack I took to school. It felt like a piece of me was gone without it. How could I have been so stupid? I swore I'd never fall asleep on a Greyhound bus again, that I'd take in every mile regardless of the unmoving scenery.

The driver waited until I was out of the way to help the old woman onto his bus. But as I was walking off it he stopped me. "Hey, kid—"

"Yeah?"

"Ain't you got a momma? Somebody you can call?"

Funny, I thought, his not asking if I had a daddy I could call. He must've known, sensed in me something he had in himself.

"Yeah. I do."

He fished in his pockets and handed me what must've been the change from buying a fresh pack of cigarettes he tore open, standing and staring as he packed it against his scrawny wrist.

"Thank you, sir."

"You get on, then, to wherever yer goin. You ain't supposed to be here," he said, parting his dry, chapped lips for the filter to tuck into.

"Hey, can I have one of those?" I asked him.

He chuckled, the unlit cigarette bobbling. "How *old*'re ya?"

"Old enough," I answered.

He turned the pack up and slid one out and delivered it to me, lit it before lighting his own.

"Thank you," I said, in a tone as deep as I could muster.

"So, then, where're you off to? Where're tryin to get to? Was it Raleigh or was it somewhere else?"

"Hm. I thought maybe it was but I guess it wadn't meant to be."

He raised his bushy eyebrows like it was gospel I was speaking.

I shrugged my short-sleeved shoulders, smirked and blew smoke.

"You some kinda highwayman?" he said with a gruff giggle.

"Naw, too young to be doin all that, mister."

The old woman inside the bus was barking at him again and so he turned away real quick and went on up the steps to tend to her without saying another word to me.

I finished the cigarette slowly, watching for several minutes as a half-dozen or so passengers loaded up onto the bus, until it pulled off. Roads opened up in its absence and I took in a long hard look at the kind of town I was now stuck in. Unrecognizable, though that didn't matter much, as another stop in another state and these very coordinates would look a lot alike. However, "First in Flight" on the plates of every car or truck that passed by, parked in the lot around me, spelled out which. And it being flat I supposed we'd not gone far enough west to notice otherwise.

A hole in the wall next to the convenient store was bustling with folks eating breakfast. In tight blue jeans a waitress set a plate of hash browns, bacon and eggs over easy, and a cup of grits down on a table pushed up next to the window, so it was like she was putting it right in front of me. I could taste it, feel my stomach growling just looking at it. And as I watched her step away she smiled at me, before she was on to the next table, asking what they were having.

I was starving, long rid of last night's slice of pizza leftover in the box from the night before. Days with Dad began with breakfast more often than not, oddly, considering every other meal was forgotten about or became an afterthought when someone else brought up how he should feed me something. This morning had been unlike any other morning, though, and I was feeling it.

On the T-shirt another waitress wore I noticed printed underneath the restaurant's logo and name was the town's: Sanford, NC. So there, here I was, in Sanford, the first stop on the southbound bus out of Raleigh, maybe halfway to home—my old home, not the new one I'd hoped to make in Raleigh. And, really, what was I thinking? Did I actually believe I was going to make it on my own?

I remembered how if ever I threatened to run away from home, which I often did, my mom would remind me of the first time I'd said that I was going to, when she'd asked who it was I'd talked to and been convinced that I could, the kid I knew who'd actually, successfully, succeeded in running away from home and lived to tell me about it.

"Not anyone you know. . ." I gave her with attitude. I must've been eight, nine maybe.

"Of course I wouldn't know them—no one does. Nobody runs away from home and lives to tell about it after, Trav," she'd said. "Whoever the boy was in whatever movie you saw and figured you was gonna be just like him—runnin from home and finding yourself a new one—that one, yeah. Do ya know what happened to that boy?"

"Yeah. He's happier now."

"Well, he is because he's an actor playin some poor boy's sob story and gettin paid to run away from home. But no, the real boy, I'm talkin about any one of em done got took, like down in Florida, he's dead. *That's* what he is."

"Nuh-uh."

"Uh-huh, yes he is, too. That's why nobody hears from little boys that run away from home. Not ever again. They either got snatched, shot dead, got hooked on drugs or died . . . People are out to get em. They are. Everywhere, all over. It don't got a happy ending. Is that what you want? Leave me without. You wantin me to try and survive somethin like that? Cause *you* sure as hell ain't. These old, dirty men out there lookin for you. They are, Trav. Ain't nothin but bad for a boy like you out there on yer own. You must want both of us dead."

I shook my head no, told her that I didn't.

"I don't write the rules. And children, they don't come up with things on their own neither. They gotta come from somewhere," she said. "Like the movies. Something ya seen on TV."

She was right about that.

A bench stuck out between the restaurant and convenience store, next to a payphone with a waterlogged phone book dangling from underneath it. Taking hold of the phone book I was reminded of the fatness I'd felt of my dad's billfold, how worn and wrinkled it had been, and the way it'd shaped in time to his backside pocket. Metal panels on both sides of the payphone were marked up and down with crude doodles and cuss words, stickers and scratches. Cigarette butts and chewing gum wads and the wrappers they came in mashed into the grooves running along its edges. I kicked an old rusty oil can out of the way and took the phone off the hook, realizing I'd no choice but to call Mom at this point, tell her where I was and that I needed her to come pick me up.

I waited and watched until I knew nobody was looking before I slipped in a quarter. The phone felt warm in my hand, sun beaming down over the town like we were ants under a magnifying glass, and the receiver, even more so, burning a circle in my ear. I dialed our number and waited for Mom to pick up, but the call didn't go through. So I tried redialing the number, slowly this time and as accurately as I could, knowing I knew it by heart, blaming the frustrating heat if I'd forgotten.

"I'm sorry, your call could not be completed as dialed. Please try your call again," I heard a second time. With that I slammed the phone up onto the hook and plopped myself down onto the bench.

What if my mom had finally moved on, without me, I thought. The minute she realized she'd no longer need to try to take care of me she was out of there. The day after Christmas was too soon to know for sure, but for as long as I'd been gone since then, why not? Dad didn't have a phone hooked up and so it'd been more than a month since I heard from her. Then it was on the payphone at the gas station across from the apartment—her calling me, at a time she told me she would—and so there was no way of knowing if she'd cut out or simply lapsed on the bill. And I'm sure that's what happened, had our service disconnected just like the one time we'd come home without a dial tone. It took a week before it was back in business.

Ways I might could stay here, in this town, began swirling through my head. How I might start over and become someone else here seemed a good enough idea to keep on thinking about it. And maybe I wasn't old enough, but still I could get a job, possibly working at this place. Busy enough it was to not be thought about for more than another second, my age and where I'd come from, how it came to be that I'd gotten here. Easy money. How hard could it be? And if taking orders was too much to start out with then I could be a busboy. Save up my wages for a car I could drive as far as I wanted when the time came. I was a student at the high school, surely, they'd assume and not question, as convincing as I was a smoker, even more a kid in a school. Who got C's and B's and tried out for the football team? I just needed to try. Apply myself. Show up. Do the job. The tables I'd end up picking up after, dishes I'd clean, and looking under my shoes at the floors I was sweeping, suddenly I was holding a broom in my hand and smoking a cigarette on the walk to take the trash out at the end of the night. But how would *I* eat? With all the money I was making going to a room I'd have to rent. I couldn't sleep on the sidewalk and plate scraps could only get me so far. I might find that I needed to pull tips from that jar by the checkout register, to seeing how easily I could get myself to go as far as pulling more: directly from the cash drawer. But it would be an angry scene of waitresses catching on to me quickly, even eventually leading to them calling the cops on me. American dream my ass.

I tried the phone again: "Please try your call again."

I thought I could call Gail to come and pick me up. Surely she had a phone but I didn't know her number . . . So . . . Maybe then I'd walk, I reckoned. Arrive sometime after breakfast tomorrow. Not actually considering long enough the idea of walking the forty miles and the many hours it might take me to get there, I got back up on my feet and began to, northeast, towards Raleigh.

Driving me to the bus station in Lumberton, Gail had to have known I was lying about getting a ticket straight home, just like she knew I wasn't fifteen. Like how all these folks probably suspected I was some kind of lie out here, squirreled up next to a payphone. Other than getting out of that apartment I'm not sure what she suspected I was actually up to, what plot she ultimately knew she'd be a co-conspirator in. Well nothing so far as to call her that, not that she knew of, sure as she was I wasn't going to blow up a building or rob a bank. But I could tell she knew something was up because of the way she talked to me in our short drive, like her way of persuading me to think for myself without any kind of negotiation.

"You know something? Ain't nobody I know got a perfect family," she told me. "And if you ever met anybody that tried tellin you different, don't believe em. They're a damn lie. I took off not much older than you, maybe halfway through high school—*if* I made it *that* far. My daddy's a son-of-bitch. And after Momma died, I just couldn't anymore. Left my sister too. That's what kills me. Alone with him. She didn't see it, though, him, how it is. Not the way he really was."

"Whataya mean? Why'd she stay?"

"Cause she wanted to, I dunno. Said she did. She whatn't old enough noway. But you are. Smart too. You got sense enough to know when yer not supposed to touch yer hand to something you ain't supposed to. It took me a couple times but I caught on. She never did. Or maybe she whatn't gettin it like I did."

"You're smart. And you ain't much older than me. So—"

"Right, right . . . Anyhow, I suppose I got about ten years on ya. It ain't always about how long you been alive, but how much you got left to live, how bad you wanna, you know? Take it from me, that's how it always is. How it's gonna be. You probably blame yourself and you shouldn't. Thinkin it's you who's gonna change him, asking yourself is yer daddy gonna be less the bastard that he is if you can help it. Or your momma . . . Can I make *her* stop? Not just the harm against you but herself, too."

"I don't know but I sure didn't have a clue about all of the stuff he told me. I can't understand, why my daddy, though. I always thought she was tougher, I guess. That she couldn't have nobody pull nothin over on her. But—"

"Hey, you wouldn't be here if she hadn't met your daddy," she said with a smile. "And, I get you. Adults can't always make sense of things the way kids do. I dunno, I—"

"It ain't always black and white is what yer tryin to say."

"See, *yer* tellin *me*. What'm I gonna say to you that ya don't know already?"

"Okay, well, why're you with my dad?"

"Shit . . . You got me there. Mistakes, I got some, more than a couple. I dunno. I'm young. Stupid," she said, laughing to cover the pink filling in her cheeks. "I—"

"He's not good. He's a bad, bad man. I'm telling you."

"Who are you tellin? Yeah, your daddy's a piece of shit and all, but from what I've heard—you and your daddy—sounds like your momma ain't much better."

"Well, she was younger than you when she had me, so at least you haven't repeated some of hers."

"Hah! Don't fret over that either. Everyone wonders if they were at some point or another. Whether our parents' or one of our own, though it's always neither. Trust me," she said. Her eyes were beginning to glaze, fixated less on the road in front of us and more on a road she couldn't see. And as she continued to speak, the sound of her voice gained an even greater warmth, maybe tar in her lungs and last night's whisky left coated in her throat, consoling, lived-in, and not just for me but for herself.

I looked away from her and leaned my head against the window and watched the highway start to build up around us, out of nowhere and back to the middle of it.

"Here you are—and here I am. But not for long. Take care of yourself, Travis. Yer one of the good ones, you know that . . ."

It seemed like she'd precluded this plan I had to escape from my dad to go back to my mom. What was I going to do? I couldn't go back now.

A half hour into my walk, more just to see what might happen, I decided to stop walking to Raleigh, turn around and walk the rest of the way home—no matter how long it took. And I must have outlasted the heat but twenty minutes or no more than two miles past the last landmark in town, a dilapidated barn, the last of whatever stood on the lot that now housed a cluttered mess of mobile homes planted in the red dirt and worn-down grass.

It started to rain, then pour, but I kept on walking, in my sopping wet clothes. My shoes squished with it and I barely saw a way down 421, let alone myself, a homeless teenager who only wanted to get to a home that I didn't know would be there for me even if I made it. Where was she? Was she with some man? I wondered, moving across a railway overpass, stopping halfway to peer over the edge at empty train tracks running both ways underneath. Then the rain just stopped. And the highway was widening ahead with the sky opening up above it, like the Emerald City was near.

When I made it back to the convenient store I went inside with my pocket of change. Passing racks full of food I salivated seeing a honey bun and had to buy it.

"Phone's given you trouble?" the cashier asked. "I saw you out there. It's tore up sometimes. Most of the time. Numbers stickin. Keep on tryin, though. Long as you got the number right it'll call it."

I thanked the man and went back outside to sit on the bench to eat my lunch in peace, sure I wasn't going to get a hold of Mom. But after I unpeeled my fingers from the honey bun wrapper, felt it sick in my empty stomach, I thought why not? When I knew the cashier wasn't looking, I scratched my initials 'TLW' and ''*89*' into the metal before I put in the same quarter I'd been using and dialed home— each number so deliberate and hard that my fingernails showed how much I meant it. This time it was ringing, more than once, and then Mom answered.

"Stay put. I'm coming to get you," she told me after hardly any explanation at all, before hanging up.

Gail was wrong about my mom. And so was I. She *did* care. I was relieved, hearing her voice, her worry, hanging up the phone with proof that she was nothing like my dad. Although I didn't know what to expect when she eventually arrived, I knew that she would. Whether I'd recognize her or not didn't matter, she'd recognize me and in my voice who I needed her to be: the mom who once lost me at the lake in Siler City, when I was little but big enough to remember. Like how the water looked brown and thick and so I didn't want to get in it. The smell of barbecues going up in smoke all around, with some benches filled up for a birthday party and the sound of other kids playing. And then my mom when she finally caught sight of me after what must've been only a half hour. She ran full steam towards me, grabbed a hold of my shoulders and started shaking my little body to the point that I thought I'd done something wrong. She said to me then, stressing that I never forget it: "If you're ever lost, no matter what, I will always find you." I know now that she was shaking me so hard because she knew *she'd* done something wrong, and she wanted to remember how I felt in her arms after she'd found me.

chapter 14

Jacob Porter had a friend waiting for him in Raleigh when he got out of Polk, a guy called Miller—a last name stuck as his first ever since fifth grade PE. He drove a dark purple '77 Pontiac Trans Am—*not* a Firebird—and before he was taking Jay anywhere, they were heading straight for the family restaurant outside Raleigh somebody had told Miller served up the best damned fried chicken in the state: "Whoever it was wadn't lying to him, neither. Case yer hungry when it comes time for you to taste yer own first bite of freedom. And trust me, yer gonna be." The sky's the limit after that, when the two of them were riding high the rest of the way back to Hoke County where they'd both grown up: "Been friends ever since we was babies." Raeford, fifty miles or so south of Siler City and bigger, getting bigger by the day with a bunch of new business coming in, was home and seemed someplace smart to start over again. Jay'd find himself work at any one of the mills, and Miller, already in line at a factory, said either one of them he'd have his pick. Easy money. A wife who wasn't so easy. Raise some kids instead of more hell. And if it wasn't the best life, it was good enough at least. Easy living.

Growing up in trailers side-by-side up on blocks, going nowhere between the tall pines and wide open lake, not but ten minutes from the surnamed streets of Raeford, meant they'd always been getting into something, usually no good. Until Jay's stent in Polk never did a day in their lives pass by without one seeing the other, even if it was only to cuss and spit out the cranked-open windows, practicing being grownups. And so more than a homecoming it was a return to life as he knew it, the only way to live it, perhaps why it soon led him inevitably back to his old ways.

A get-together for Jay put on by Miller and some of the guys was planned the next night after he got out. Though it was an alright time, with a rowdy crowd they'd all got to drinking too much, music turned up too loud, and too many girls for their own good so there came a lot of showing off, whenever things got out of hand. Pistol shots into the black night and donuts in the gravel, the smoky stink both brought, someone screaming at somebody, always, came with more attention they didn't need. Eventually the cops showed up, but fortunately for Jay, underneath their starchy uniforms these guys were cool enough to stay for a cigarette and swig of something, welcome him home, making nothing more of the call they'd received other than to ask that the party end there. They overlooked the disorderly conduct, any underage drinking and pot-smoking going on, and whatever else was happening with those in attendance who they themselves had gone to middle school and half of high school with. Anything else they saw and it was "nothing to see here," stealing away their time with party favors in exchange for whoever it was in charge's obedience to shut it down as soon as they were gone. By then it was nobody's charge to lead, but Jay didn't want to go back to where he'd just come from, so he whistled and waved his arms, told everybody to get on to wherever it was they were going, that they couldn't stay here. It didn't end there, out by the lake, under the stars and between their breath showing in the biting cold, but only relocated to one of the two bars still open at that hour and where this guy knew that one who didn't care which of them was coming or going.

Between rusty games of shooting pool and darts stuck into the wall instead of the cork, Jay met a girl, Ruth Ann, a senior in high school he ended up talking to until time was up. They left together, in Miller's Trans Am, making out in the backseat with the radio dialed low against the slow sunrise that spread toward them like fire across the glassy lake. They agreed not to leave it there, to meet up again that next night, and they did, then again, and again . . .

"Long story short," Jay said, "I got the girl pregnant."

"Oh—" I told him, short with whatever words were right to say to him, instead of the wrong I could see coming. This was days after I'd gotten out of the hole when I wasn't expecting to find him back in Polk. He'd expected to see me, though, and was just as surprised when he hadn't.

"I thought sure you was gonna be sittin right here when they let me loose back inside this corner of hell."

I was adjusting to not being alone every minute of the day—to days, really, and hours and weeks and months—even to the light beaming in through the wide windows that still stung my eyes. But, I guessed, seeing him didn't need much getting used to; he was just there when I'd last been out with everybody else. It was like we'd picked up right where we'd left off.

"How long *has* it been," I'd asked him, "since you got put back in?"

"I was out there, what? I guess it was three months—almost four since they let me go early—not even . . . So middle of March, maybe. Hell, I don't even keep track anymore. What use is a calendar now?"

"Shit . . . I don't know," I'd said to him, sighing in sympathy, though I knew I'd be getting out soon and that *I* was never coming back. "Well—"

"Ain't got nobody to blame but myself this time," he'd said, reading my mind, what I'd never actually say to him. "I mean, at first, when I got locked up in here, I used to think it was cause there were things that happened to me, you know—but like they do to everyone, really, to you too . . . So that's no excuse. But I didn't have to go and let it make me into somebody else, somebody I ain't supposed to be. That's the thing, see. I know I'm not this guy sittin here in front of you. I know better. What I done—it's real strange, like I ain't makin no sense, I know. And you know what I'm talkin bout, but with you, with your momma, you didn't let that life change you. Or did you? Maybe you don't know yet. Not through and through noway, that I'd be able to tell if it was. And me, I think it was losing mine the way I did, havin a daddy not worth shit—seems we all do, though, now duddn't it? I mean, when I stole the son-of-bitch's car I had fun doin it. I did. And robbed that place . . . For who knows what? It whadn't just the money? To feel the fun of it? Wadn't fun though, Trav. Sometimes these things just happen, someone'll say. Even sometimes like they was supposed to happen. I don't believe none of that though."

"Maybe you couldn't have done what you did, sure, instead made different choices, but you don't think you were meant to be locked up in here, do you? Not for the way you were raised."

"No, naw. Well—now, I'm not so sure. But I don't even care to wager with myself no more. Not over what kinda man I coulda been. What's the point? I see no future for me now noway. Nothing more true to say than that. How could it not be?"

There really was no hope for him. I didn't see any, not then. He was not getting out of prison, not any time soon, not if the laws weren't rewritten. It seemed our paths had crossed once more only to grow the divide between right and wrong, increase the pain brought on by our predicament in judging between them. Neither of us would have what they called "the good life," or much of one at all, most especially Jay.

Ever since he returned home he'd been having a tough time finding work after all, and then, with Ruth Ann, a baby on the way, he became desperate to leave the trailer he grew up in and shared with his dad. His real mom died when he was fifteen but still haunted the place, so he told me. More his dad, though, who'd remarried. Jay's mom, or her spirit, rather, didn't agree with his choices, Jay's dad kept on telling him. He'd wake him up every night or keep him awake for days without sleeping, blaming Jay for everything. He took some of the blame, as the hellion he'd admit he was, but said it was more the meth's doing. Still, his dad accused him of muddying things up for he and his new wife, Jay's little half-sister that looked nothing like him or his dad. It didn't help matters that his dad still held a grudge against him over his car being taken so many times and without his consent: "You can't just take another man's property—especially not his car—regardless of kin," Jay owned up to, "even if the worthless hulk only took me two miles over the South Carolina line before it tore up on me."

Jay leaned back and stretched his arms around himself and held tightly. "The only way I'm getting outta here now is in a body bag, my friend. I gave em what they want is what I did. My daddy, too. To keep me in here: mission accomplished. Even when yer out there, shit's rigged. Trust me. I know. Just because you can walk the streets like everybody else don't mean the chains are off."

"It wouldn't be that way if you, I dunno, got a good lawyer."

"For what? I did what I did. No need for false hope, not anymore."

I didn't know what to say to that.

"Look at me . . . Who knows where I even stand at this point. And if it's freedom that's coming for you, and not the rest of your life spent in here with me, it'll be there. You're already where yer gonna be."

"I just wish there was something more that I could do."

"Do better. Or, you know what, who fuckin cares?"

"You *are* still alive, so . . . And you're gonna be a daddy!"

"Who? *Me?* Oh, am I? I couldn't tell. This hell we're living in, case you hadn't seen the fires burning everywhere. Look around you . . ."

I gazed at the faces of men sat around us, saw Dwayne alone at a table, looking up at me from his tray as my eyes passed his, wide-eyed for a second with an ease of fearfulness and gratitude for what I'd done. The guy I'd attacked was nowhere to be found and I couldn't even picture what his hand might look like now, if he still had one.

"That kid's never gonna know me. I didn't do it just for me. It was all for my kid I prolly ain't never gonna meet. You ever had somebody besides you who you was lookin out for? A girl?—Wait, what am I sayin—yeah, you know exactly what I'm talkin about . . . With what's her name?—"

"Tiffany."

"Right. Tiffany. Listen to me now when I say this: Whatever you do, don't get her pregnant."

I smiled. "I doubt I'll ever see her again anyway."

"Don't be so sure. And oh, *hey*," he whispered, "*just in case . . .*" He reached his arm underneath the table and looked down for me to do the same. In his hand was a little shank made from a toothbrush. "I got my own and so this one here's for you. I know they're going to be all over you, non-stop. It ain't like the one when you first come in."

"That's what got me spending all that time alone."

"No, that fucker's hand you tenderized is what did that, Trav. And I thought you said it wadn't bad in there noway."

"I didn't say it was good, neither. I gotta be better, be more careful."

"Naw, I get it. You made it out though. And you will again."

"Yeah, well, once was enough. I don't know how I did it, honest. Maybe it ain't the same for everybody, but for me, it was like torture. Time drawn out so much I couldn't think, and still it was nothing but these never-ending thoughts of mine. And seeing things, too. Stuff I saw and don't wanna see again. Didn't want to to begin with. Yer hungry, starving, then less hungry, even less, until you don't even wanna eat anymore."

"Damn. Yeah, I don't think it's like that for everybody."

"What I did, it came back to haunt me."

"Well, sometimes it goes down like that. I think that maybe it depends on what you did." He looked at me like he knew more than I was telling. "But I believe you. I can tell you this, I know now that I'm not going to make this stay any worse on me than it already has been, but I ain't layin down dead neither."

"How much worse can it get?"

"Hah, I wonder the same thing. Once I leave here, though, I think a lot more. Now you see what was in it for me?" he asked. "Why it wadn't just another stupid mistake I made."

"Yeah. I get it, I do."

We sat silent for a minute, and I tried to hide the feeling of pity I had for him. He'd hate anything like that. I just continued to sit and listen to him spill.

"I had a choice," he mumbled. "I've yet to meet the man I coulda been, who woulda had it any other way than I had. But I did what I did. I'd probably fuck up again, over and over again, if I got the chance to.

"And you know something, Miller, he's comin from the same place as me, the both of us was, but now, he was doin alright for hisself, had saved up enough to move into a house he rented right off Main Street in a wrecker's backyard. And that's when he invited me to come and stay with him a while, when I was broke as hell, to try my hand there. Course I agreed, not thinkin anything of it, though. Miller, now, see, he didn't come right out and say strings was attached, but he'd definitely been hatching a plan and needed his trusty accomplice. And *I* needed more money. That was it. That's what I was trying for, really. Honest. An honest living. A baby ain't gonna be cheap, I knew that much was true.

"Now I was makin *something*—next to nothin is what it was— workin every odd job I got. Few and far between. That wadn't gonna float. And I coulda been makin more if I'd done like everybody else was, these guys workin up at the Pizza Corner. Even the delivery boy was in on it. Pizza wadn't what it was all about, that's for damned sure. Makin some real money, I coulda done well, as well as Miller'd been doin. Cashier my ass. That's what he was up to. But I didn't. I didn't wanna do none of it no more. The bad stuff, you know."

At fifty past eight, on the Thursday they'd planned to do it, Jay walked into Pizza Corner in his cobalt ski-mask he'd not worn since he was a kid and Miller's Members Only jacket the same color as his Trans Am. Like clockwork, between eight forty-five and eight-fifty, the manager came in to collect the cash tills before closing time at nine, every time carrying along with him those zippered bags from Pizza Corner's two other locations in Fayetteville he'd already gotten. "In the back's the safe—where he's gonna put em—every time he does, and in the same spot. That's where yer gonna come in."

"When I went inside, Miller was sweatin bullets and makin eyes at me. I guess cause there was customers in there, even when it was near nine and they's supposed to be gone. Still, 'Get on the fuckin ground!' I shouted. And they all did. Dropped like flies around me. And Miller, he was grinning, slumped down behind the counter, just like we'd planned, after pretending he was scared of the man in the mask, with a gun—yeah, he gave me that too. But he was kinda givin himself away whenever he'd keep on lookin at things in the front of the place, watchin the door I guess, for the manager to come through, cause he hadn't come yet like he was supposed to. And I was supposed to just take off with the bags—all three of em—when the man got there. Whatever else was in the safe, too.

"It felt weird to hold Miller at gunpoint—all of them folks in there, like the family on all fours by the windows—when it wadn't supposed to be anybody else in there. 'Open the register!' I shouted at the other guy workin there. Tremblin, too. Close to wettin his pants it seemed like. Miller, he seemed surprised how convincing I was. How good a job. But I didn't know it, cause I was shakin too. Adrenaline takin over. It definitely wadn't his first rodeo, though, his first time seeing a gun pointed at him."

I shook my head hearing the details of the story Jay was telling, knowing already it hadn't ended well for him. Though he'd played his part, I wondered if it had been at all hard to do what he'd done. He was describing it so casually to me now that I couldn't help but think if maybe it was easy? Because he'd done it before? Would I, too, pick right back up where I left off? No, I was telling myself silently, assuredly, zoning out as Jay continued telling me what happened next.

"Right as I was telling the guy—a teenager prolly—to hurry up,

'Move faster! Faster! Empty it. Do it,' with Miller's eyes egging me on to yell at him, the manager walked in and I had to keep it up, the act, shouting at him to get himself back here, too, pretending I was mad. Maybe I wasn't by then, because it was very real for everyone else who wadn't in on it. And the manager, he was quiet, patient with me, did what I said, but only up until a point. When it was time for him to come back and empty out the safe, plans changed.

"'Fill this bag up, mister! With all the cash you got in there,' I shouted, tossing at the man what was actually Miller's backpack from high school, and I was sticking the gun in his side. Only for effect with the bullets taken out—or so I'd been told. When I got what I came for I was supposed to jump back over the counter with it in the backpack and Miller was gonna stay afterward. That way neither one of us would be found out. He told me he was gonna park the Trans Am out behind the place, where there'd been an easy grab and go out the back door. That musta been mistake number one, assuming he had and that there'd be one. I was so caught up with the role I'd been told I'd get enough money to play, so much I wouldn't have to worry about baby food til the baby was ten, that I didn't see what was actually playing out around me.

"'Get it all,' Miller'd said to me before, when we was planning the whole thing—when *he* was. Now he was quiet as a mouse, and ghost-white, while the manager looked like he was seething, red in the neck from what musta been coursing through him, what he was gonna do. And I coulda seen it had I not been so damned blind. 'Empty all that into this bag, here,' I told the manager, 'with the rest of it!'

"He opened the safe and reached in for a bag of money, put it into the backpack, before he done reached back in again and brought out his own gun. My gut turned seeing it, too, buddy. He shot it at me but missed, instead hitting one of the windows, shattering it. Everybody's screaming. Running out like it's an earthquake or somethin. I'm losin it, not knowing what to do, when, stupidly, I fired back, fraid I was gonna get shot myself. I caught the man in what I thought at the time was his shoulder. Then Miller's shouting at me, and I'm shouting at him, seeing blood when I shouldn't a been. The manager fired off again, aimless that time, his arm like a spaghetti noodle, though he got Miller, who was runnin off with the bag out through the front. It musta been his plan all along, I thought then, leave with the money and me stuck there, here the way I am. Only, Miller'd not planned on him being on foot and gettin only as far away as the next intersection. Been hit in just the right spot, they said. The manager, too. Both of em dead. Both of em my fault."

"Wow. Jay—I'm sorry, man."

"Wadn't nobody but me to refute it. And honest, I didn't try to. Just gave in. But yeah, I got plenty of time to think about it now. And nothing personal, but I was holding onto hope I'd never have to see your ass again," he said with a snicker, turning the grim storytelling into something lighthearted, like he might start to cry if he didn't.

We weren't sharing a bunk anymore, nor did we work together, and so I'd heard segments of his story again and again. Even still I'd not heard the whole thing, and I never did. Thinking back, again to when he first saw me after I was out of the hole, sitting there stunned and sighing in disbelief, he looked at his own hands like they'd never come clean, and he said: "Who woulda thought? Amiright? Was you thinkin it? I sure wadn't. Though, whenever I got back in here, I thought sure I was gonna see you. But instead of thinking about myself, you done had me wondering where the hell *you* are, like maybe they done cut you loose early too. I had something nice to dream about in those days. Even if they weren't mine to dream, it was nice while it lasted."

I nodded my head and half-smiled, hid my eyes from his. It seemed odd to thank him for it, though maybe, I thought, those nights I was unable to sleep it had been because Jay was doing all the dreaming for me and at least there was that. It was nice to know I wasn't all alone.

"You wanna know what I dreamed about?" he asked.

"Don't tell me," I told him. "It might not come true."

chapter 15

When we returned home, the house was no different than how I'd left it, even though it did seem somehow changed. It had to be me, I thought, the way *I* was, seeing it again: myself bigger, it smaller. And once inside it was how I felt out of place, unsure of whether I should sit or stand, acting like a stranger who'd stopped by only for a visit or maybe to try and sell the Encyclopedia Britannica. Even the smell, what I hadn't smelled before, I asked myself if it had always smelled this way. So had *I*, then? And what'd I smell like now? Dad's musty apartment? But then I opened the refrigerator and saw it stocked up with all my favorite foods, and Mom was telling me not to fill up too much, that she was fixing my favorite for dinner that night. During our drive back to Siler City from the gas station in Sanford, she'd made no mention of these efforts of hers, to I guess make me feel more welcomed, at home, where I belonged. At least a heads up or what would've seemed her way of telling rather than showing, had it not been for my absence, didn't happen. Nor were there any other claims to her own betterment, like announcing to me and the world that she herself had changed. Both came as a surprise to me. For my part, there was little to no expectation as to whether or not she'd be driving drunk or high whenever she'd pull up—if she would—and if so if she'd be alone when she did or with some strange man riding shotgun. And would it even be the same house that we'd arrive home to? I wondered. But no, I got in, up front, right next to her, and I hardly recognized this side of her: the good mom who'd nearly erased herself entirely from my memory and who I was not expecting I'd ever meet again.

Almost immediately, maybe because it had been so much time that had passed since I last saw her, it was clear something had changed. It was hard to put my finger on it at first, but I knew it wasn't just the absence of our time spent together. It was something else entirely, more her than me. I could see clarity in her eyes, the whites of them whiter than a sheet of notebook paper. And her skin wasn't tired and depressed but vibrant, even behind the suntan. When she looked at me, her gaze no longer disconnected from mine, and it searched me, as if she was seeing me as her son for the first time. Sitting down beside me was the type of mother I'd envisioned in paperbacks and saw on TV, no longer some kind of vision or actress playing the part but live and in the flesh.

Cigarette smoke drifted in and out of the car from her arm hung over the downed window, and with warm highway air I inhaled it with a smile. "Thank you, Momma," I mumbled to her, looking out at the sunny side of the road.

"Course, Trav. Anything for my baby. I'm just so glad you called me," she said, in a voice that sounded clearer, without any doubt that she meant it.

I hadn't seen all of her then, slouched in the seat, smoking, smiling. It wasn't until we'd made it home and she was getting out of the car, walking me to the front door, that I really saw her. Maybe on the straight and narrow she was, still smiling, and so sure of her steps. Had she put on weight? I wondered, though I'd dare not ask, knowing for sure she must've so why pretend I wasn't? It looked good on her, too, only ten pounds at the most, maybe halfway to getting back up to where it probably needed to be. And in the way she moved I could see something living in her, move through her body, beginning with the sunspots on her cheeks and then to the corners of her mouth, molding itself into a gentle calm, an ease like peace, her spirit.

And maybe I *was* taller, or she'd shrunk, seeing as how we fit together differently now, hugging once inside the house, with her head and neck cupped into my shoulder, like how it did with Dad's in the good ole days. Even so: "Wrong pieces of a puzzle that somehow got stuck together," she'd described the two of them. And similarly, how Dad saw it: "Can't fix something broke that whadn't never put together in the first place."

Now it felt final, my coming home, away from the other side. There didn't seem to be any going back to the way things were. And over dinner, Mom was sipping from a tall glass of what looked like liquor but was actually sweet tea. (It didn't smell like anything when I sniffed it, when she walked into the kitchen to get dessert.)

"I hadn't had a real drink since you left," she said, lighting her cigarette. She leaned back in the chair, not prideful as much as she was pleased with herself, for her achievement, and she watched for my response. It couldn't possibly be true was what I was thinking, but I didn't let on to it. Again, seeing her appearance and hearing words I'd never heard her speak before, somehow conjured up in me was this belief that it could have been. More than could've it had to be. I couldn't live any other way. Anywhere else but here.

"I started going to these meetings," she said excitedly, "and I got to talkin to these people, strangers—that's what maybe made it easy. I listened to their stories, and they did mine. So it was something, I dunno. I realize that I done made a lot of mistakes, Trav, too many to count. But in order to rectify, I got to, make em count."

I got out of my chair and put my arm around her neck, squeezed her tightly. I felt her tears warm against my skin, and heard her heart in her chest, and then her cough, laughing at our sentiment, her being sober for the first time in she didn't know when.

"When you was a baby, even then . . . I mean, not a lot, but some, enough. Yer daddy, he had me hating myself. It didn't take much, though. I might notta made it this far had it not been for you, Trav. And when you was gone, I couldn't see the point, carrying on like I was. I had to do something. They call that 'rock bottom.' That's what. And I told em I done been six feet under before, the walking dead."

I sat back down across from her at the table, thinking back to the year before, to Halloween, how she looked then in comparison to the way she did now, and I smirked.

"What're you smiling about?" she asked, flicking ash off the tip of her cigarette onto her barely touched dinner plate. She smiled too, like maybe she knew what, if not explicitly which time it was that I was recalling—with so many it could've been—one of them had me reeling.

"Nothin," I said. "It's just, I'm happy . . . I dunno . . . cause yer happy. I can tell, Momma. This time's gonna be different."

"It is. It's gonna be. I promise."

I outstretched my arm, slid my hand over the table toward hers. Our fingertips touched, what had always been sort of our thing.

"Your birthday's comin up. Be thinkin bout whatcha want, alright?"

I nodded and pulled back from the table, took our plates into the kitchen.

"Well aren't you a good boy."

I ran the faucet and started to suds up a sponge, when I heard a knock at the door. I felt my heart sink into my stomach. Had it been Dad, I worried, already after me, right on my heels the whole time I'd thought I was getting away clean. I knew I'd have to take his belt for what I took from his billfold—worse if he drove here drunk. A car ride, or even a long walk, "idle hours" Dad called them, any length of time spent thinking too much about something, always seemed to make a not so good situation turn bad with him. Catch him in the moment and he might soon change his mind, but wait a minute, a second too long, and God only knows what way he'd go.

"It's Tommy," Mom said, opening the door wider so I could see.

"Trav! That really you?" he yelled into the house excitedly.

I stepped back from the sink and turned to face him. "Yep. Who else was I gonna be?"

"Somebody else is what," he said, running at me.

I looked at Mom, unsure if it was okay that he was in here.

"We done patched things up," she said, raising her eyebrows. "Pam's alright." And she shut the door. "—I guess."

Tommy swung his arm like he was going to put his fist into my stomach, stopping short to instead pat me. He was inching taller, in only the six or seven months since I thought he might've stopped growing altogether.

"Yer bigger," I said to him.

"You didn't grow any," he said.

"Yes I did."

"Yeah, he sure did," Mom said. "In more ways than one. Say, why don't you boys go out, bike around a bit? I'm gonna clean up some."

We ran out into the yard where late July was keeping it hot as hell. I missed the fireworks that popped off every year up and down our street. Embers of backyard bonfires making the air fill with fear of somebody's house burning down, like how the Littles's did when I was nine. Though it was Mr. Little who started it, to get back at his wife, still I was reminded of it and prayed ours never would. Hot dogs and hamburgers burning on the grill had gone away, too, or maybe it wasn't the weekend yet.

"How'd you know I was here?" I asked Tommy.

"Cause you was gettin out the car, dummy, going on inside."

"You watch Momma's house like that? Even since I was gone?"

"Every day. I just knew you was gonna come back. You had to."

"Why do ya say that?"

"Cause you never said goodbye to me."

"Ah, you're right. I'm sorry, Tommy."

"Ain't nothing to be sorry for."

I found my bike tossed up against the side of the house, fortunately with both its tires still tough enough to ride on. We figure-eighted, or what we called "infinity-ed," round and round in the street between our houses, over and over until we got dizzy.

"When'd my momma and yers make up? Did they, *really?*"

"Yeah. Your momma used to cry—right after yer daddy come and got you—every time we seen her she was. Gettin in and out of the car. Smoking on the porch. Sometimes just walking round the yard. Sobbing. And my momma finally couldn't stand seeing it no more, feeling sorry for her, talking about how men'd made em the way they'd been. At each other's throats. And my daddy, he went to work in West Virginia, said he'd be gone for he didn't know *how* long. Been there for a while. After that, Momma said it was gonna stop, *your* momma's crying all the time. She knew why she was, being a momma herself, and so she went over to your house one day and was there til dark."

"*Really?* You're makin stuff up."

"Yeah, no. It's true. I ain't lyin."

"I wanted to walk over and see you sooner, but I didn't know. It seemed like a bad idea, I dunno. Man, and here I thought—"

"I know, I know," he said, huffing and puffing, pedaling hard up a hill.

"I hadn't ridden since the last time you and me did," I told him, keeping up the best I could.

"What'd you do then, where you was at when you was gone?"

"Nothing. That's what I did. I started smoking, though."

"Nuh uh."

"Yuh huh."

"Why'd you go and do that?"

"Everybody does, Tommy. Women do."

"So what, yer a man now?"

"Basically. I'll be fourteen in twelve days."

He slowed his pedaling, eased himself back closer to me. "You ain't a man but you do look different."

I laughed, and I didn't want to give him the satisfaction of knowing it, but so did he. His expression was turned sideways, maybe the heat's doing or perhaps a culprit I couldn't accuse so easily just by looking at him, which was Tommy, but not *Tommy*. He seemed to be in the shadow of the kid I knew before I left. It might take time, I reckoned, before I'd see him in the same light.

"Maybe you did get taller?" he asked himself aloud. "Somethin, I dunno what."

"I mean, it's only been—"

"Seven months," he shot back. "It's been seven months since you took off." Saying it, he sounded more angry than tired.

"Well, now, I didn't exactly *take off*."

"Whataya call it then? Didn't tell *nobody* before you left."

"I know, I'm sorry. I apologized already. My dad, you know how it is. Well, he and . . . I don't even wanna get started on that. I've tried to put that out of my mind. I keep thinking he's gonna pull up any minute. But honest, it happened so quick. Overnight—no planning at all—I'm sittin next to him on my way down to Lumberton, against my will."

"So then he kidnapped you? Is that it?" he said gruffly.

"Well, I don't know if somebody's daddy can kidnap them, but maybe? I didn't wanna go. I told him that."

"So why'd he take you, then? They get into a fight or somethin?"

"Yeah, something like that," I answered vaguely. And because he'd asked, I thought of how people say the word 'fight' like it was only words exchanged, not blows, not an actual fight, though Tommy knew better than that. When my mom and dad fought, they really went at it. If only they'd ever raised their voices, my dad's hand like he wanted to use it he was so mad but never actually did. Squabbles over minor disagreements like doing the dishes or taking the trash out, him working too much and coming home late, which would mean she'd actually wanted him to be there: Why wasn't he spending quality family time with us? And could he take me to soccer practice the next time? "Nearly burned the house down," I added for Tommy, for color.

"Oh, shit. That bad?"

"Is that bad?" I said, laughing. "What about you? What happened on Christmas morning? You get everything you wanted?"

He chuckled. "Went to my grandma's house."

Tommy cranked his sneakered feet, blew past me and I struggled behind him. For several more stretches of street he bound forward, just as soon as I could catch up with him.

"Are you mad at me?" I hollered.

"What?" he asked, his head back and mouth wide.

"You heard me . . . Slow down!"

He pulled back. "I don't know," he said, breathing heavy. "Maybe I was. I'm not anymore, though. I wasn't gonna talk to you when—if you ever came back."

"I did, you see."

"For good?"

"Yeah, I hope so."

He half-smiled, still short with me, not his usual, brotherly self.

"My momma seems better than when I left, too," I told him.

"You think so?"

"Yeah. Don't you?"

"I guess. She's been nice lately, yeah."

"What about yours? What's it been like with your dad being gone?"

"What do you think? Basically I took over for him. Lookin after Brian. She has me doin everything. It's a lot. Specially with school out. Still, I'm glad he's not around. But oh well. Who gives . . ."

His bruises had fully healed, those welts I'd seen, all faded now along the backs of both his legs. But those were superficial, I thought. The real wounds, gashes from the incident, it would take longer than a few months for what really hurt him to go away, for him to dig any deeper to actually grapple with what had happened—if they'd ever heal. That's how Tommy had changed, I was now realizing. Though he'd not grown much taller since he and I'd last stood on the same pavement together, he had this tough guy attitude about him that wasn't an act.

"You know, you don't have to be like that, not with me. There's gonna be plenty of that come fall when you start the seventh grade."

"Like what? What're your talking about?"

"I dunno, Tommy, maybe I'm seeing things."

"I think maybe you are. Whatever."

"And I might be joining you."

"Whataya mean?"

"The seventh grade."

"Yer going in to the eighth grade, aren't ya?"

"I dunno now. It's so messed up! I didn't really go to school in Lumberton."

"*What?* . . ."

"Yep. I missed something like half a year of school, so I don't know what's gonna happen. If I'm gonna be held back or not."

"So you mean yer gonna have to start all over again?"

"That or try and see if I can make it up somehow. I don't know how, though. Summer school's started already, Momma said. She didn't know til I told her on the ride back."

"Well if you do, maybe we'll get to be in the same class! I can't believe we're gonna be in the same grade."

"I mean, I *hope* we're not."

"Yer right, for yer sake I hope yer not. They'd sure come up with something for ya if you did . . . Hoo boy!"

I tried not to think about it as we kept on biking, making our way up the next to the last hill we'd always used to climb. It was so hot I was slippery in my shorts and T-shirt. Sweat dripped from the tip of my nose onto my knees and wet the back of my neck, my messy, uncut hair. I felt my face heating up, too, even though it was getting late, after dinnertime and when we'd usually be inside. When we made it to the top, I could see the last clouds stretched east like taffy in the sky above our street.

"We should be gettin back," I told Tommy. "Do you wanna come over for dinner? I'm sure my momma won't care."

"I don't know. I ate already."

"Alright, then."

"I mean I can eat again," he sighed.

We both smiled and launched down the hill, when it seemed something had shifted back into place between us. The feeling of having a true friend I could rely on returned, the old Tommy, the old me. Even as we slung our bikes down in the grass and walked toward my front door, it was like only a day had gone by since we'd last done the same thing. Or maybe it was more what somebody might've called déjà vu.

"Hey, Trav . . ."

"Yeah?"

I turned back to see him stopped cold in his tracks, glaring ahead at me. His eyes were held onto something, like an idea, or something as simple as a thought. And with an intensity I'd recognized in him once before, he said, "You know, if I was you, I'd've used the gun on *your* daddy instead of mine. Maybe it's not too late, neither. Or then, I guess you would be *me*, and you'd've done it already and I wouldn't've had to do it for you."

Even had he waited for my response, I wouldn't have known what to say to something like that. Stark against the dim grass the shape of him skinnied down as he picked up and kept on ahead, when instead, I responded the way he did, without another word.

When we came into the house, I waited a moment, looked out the opened front door at our driveway with that ugly Dodge parked in it. The popping sounds from our long drive under the sun had stopped and I hoped I too would be able to settle down, remain parked here on this same street. Everything seemed just the same as it had been before, how it might always be, should I ever leave and come back again. Like the Sellers's house, still standing, unchanged. Accept now, when I looked in through the picture window, I saw nothing: no life. The Christmas tree had been taken down, of course, along with the colored lights. The world spun. Seasons changed. This great big sycamore tree, towering over the edge of the street between our houses, it was fully alive again. For the first time ever, I'd not been here when it woke up, to see it come back to life and turn green. I'd missed its scraggly blooms that hung down like "grapes with the grapes missing," how Tommy and I'd described them. But I was just in time, before long, to see the tree send out its "golden nuggets." Then, the two of us would start swinging our sticks at its low-slung branches in hopes of knocking enough of them down so we could both live like the kings we were, that is if we'd not outgrown them.

Come fall, I'd wondered, what *were* the kids at school going to say about me starting seventh grade over again? What would they call me? I reckoned something like Dad would coin if he only knew: "repeat seventh-grader retard, you know, the one with that broke-down drunk, zombie-lookin momma." That's what I'd be, who I'd forever be known as, that boy who failed seventh grade because he got kidnapped. At least I'd have a story to tell.

It's been my experience, whenever somebody calls somebody else a retard, it's only because that person throwing it out there, seeing if it sticks as an insult or not, is themself bothered with his own lack of smarts, no matter that of the person they're intending to make fun of's. Like my dad, using it so loosely the way that he did when I was growing up. Now maybe he thought it would make me smarter, or maybe he thought I'd already outsmarted him, even as a boy. If kids in school were going to call me retarded, I told myself it would only be because *they* were the dumb ones, not to let it bother me. I wasn't who my dad would have me believe, and so why give somebody my same age the same satisfaction.

"Don't listen to a word yer daddy says," Mom told me, and I listened. "He's full of shit—shit for brains."

Knowing this, even at thirteen—soon to be fourteen—versed in the insights my mom gave me like it was truth—the word had no effect on me, not anymore. Nor was she a drunk, not anymore.

"Sober as a judge," she said. "Sworn off all them pills, too—and anything that's gonna make me any other way than your momma."

I turned fourteen in August and started September as a seventh-grader, again. But not long after speaking to the school counselor, then the principal, a man Mom knew already from way back when, I was taking some tests and reading required reading and being asked if I was ready to go, that he'd go on ahead and admit me into the eighth grade if I was.

"You bet I am!" I shouted, kicking my feet across the carpet, unable to sit still in the principal's office.

In the car, Mom told me that she and the principle had come to some kind of an agreement, how that Saturday night he'd be picking her up at the house and I was to stay the night over at Tommy's house.

"And the next weekend, too," she said, smacking chewing gum. "Just ask his momma if it's alright. It will be. And don't you *dare* tell her what I told you. You was smart enough to skip half a whole damned school year is what happened. My boy's a genius."

But really, more than some kind of genius, I reckoned, I was just one lucky kid. And I was beside myself, so happy I could cry. Not only was I getting taken out of the seventh grade and being put in the eighth where I belonged, but *this* was where I belonged, right here in Siler City, with Mom: my home. Furthermore, Tommy and I had the next two weekends to stay up late, to talk about it, everything.

It wasn't all about me, though. Maybe that was why I'd not gotten the attention I'd expected I would those first couple months back to school, only hearing once or twice about how stupid I was for having to repeat a grade—never given any official new name to call me by. I'd actually heard more about Tommy, how in elementary school he'd gone psycho and tried to kill his whole family and nearly did kill his dad, and didn't I know the kid? Didn't I live on the same street as him? Now that he'd started middle school—news to some of the eighth-graders—he was that boy who got himself arrested on drugs and thrown in jail for a whole week—or was it a month? And didn't he try and kill *himself* too? What was he *really* like?

More than what actually happened, the stories toughened him up. And he *had* grown taller, I noticed, seeing him in this new light, when by the time school started he looked skinnier, somehow also hardened, too, like he'd been troubled and sent away someplace far away that maybe even I'd not known about, with most of the blond faded from his messy hair and his skin not suntanned but pale from not enough time spent playing outdoors. He wasn't saying a whole lot, adding to this overall effect of his being the outcast family killer, apprehended. While both of us were outcasts, it was for different reasons, making it seem like we were different people versus the boys seen in school, even when he and I were back to normal on our street and the marks we shared showed as one and the same—same as they always had.

"They say you tried killing yourself?" I said with a smile, not trying to be serious in my line of questioning, though I knew it was serious. I knew something like that did happen to people, but I was sure it hadn't been given another thought for Tommy.

"They say all kinds a things, Trav."

"Did you make up stuff? When you was tellin em the story about what happened? With your dad?"

"No. I didn't even tell nobody, neither. Not really. I mean, I did, when I had to. The police. Even then it whatn't every detail. Like when they asked me where I got it, I never told them it was your gun—or yer daddy's. The one I'd used to do it with."

I shrugged it off, looked past it.

"I dunno," he sighed, looking at the ceiling. "I hate the seventh grade. I hate that they took you out and put you in the eighth."

Based on what I'd heard about Tommy now, I imagined him as boastful in his telling, making a show of himself in the new school cafeteria versus how he actually was after Halloween happened. I hadn't known then as much as I did now, like how he just as well might've made up parts of the story, describing his dad's brains splattered out on the carpet and the cherry red blood spilled out everywhere like an R-rated movie, whenever I was out of school down in Lumberton, "unable to be reached for comment," as someone trying to get their facts straight might report. But nobody asked me.

Since I'd been gone, and ever since summer ended, speculation grew rampant and more stories were told to support the ones that had already been: Mrs. Everrett's missing cat that Tommy had found and skinned, strung up in the trees behind Margaret Carraway's house by his shoelaces; Brian, his little brother, pissing and shitting himself during a long weekend trapped inside of a closet Tommy had locked him into, nearly starved to death when they finally let him out; Tommy was a devil-worshiper—his whole family had been—and that's why he did what he did. None of it was true, of course, or so I continued to believe. So convinced by their own stories they were telling each other that I found them convincing myself, though I knew the truth. It was only an act that Tommy was putting on, his way of coping with the bullying that started happening, like snatching the laces out from his sneaker in the hallway for everyone to gawk at, meant more as a message to leave him be but instead fanned the flames.

A year had passed since the incident, and on Halloween we didn't talk about it. We didn't dress up or go door-to-door trick-or-treating. I wondered what might happen when the stories were no longer anything worth telling, or listening to, reduced to useless memories of his own recalling, about who he used to be, or who kids in school thought he was. And which was it?

"You ever think about that?"

"Do *I*?" he asked, like maybe he'd not been listening to me talk.

"Yeah *you* . . ."

"Well, yeah, sure I do. First thing I'm gonna do is get the hell outta here. Soon as I can drive . . ."

"The world better watch out."

"That's right," he said, "I want things to be different, you know. I don't want the same ole thing no more. When I'm old, things can't be like they are now. They can't be."

"They won't. It'll be different. You'll see," I said to him, as if I could see the future any better than he could. But in some respect I could. I knew, even at fourteen, that nothing lasts forever.

Tommy smirked and then looked back up into the night, shined his flashlight into the black sky as if to search for a future through it. I realize that it was out there, that somewhere it'd already happened. And while I didn't have any reassurances that he wasn't going to be who he was that day, I knew he wasn't who people said he was. That he'd not tried to hurt himself, nor would he ever anybody else. Maybe I knew him better than he knew himself. He was still my friend Tommy, the one who wanted to bury our fallen toy soldiers in the dirt after they'd lost the battle.

chapter 16

Christmas came early in '94. Ten days early. After one more night spent wondering when, if ever, I would be let out of Polk, I was. The next morning I got on a van heading toward wherever it was going, downtown Raleigh, I guessed, where I'd have to make my mind up about which way *I* was going. It wasn't Siler City, I knew that much. And I had some ideas, some clues as to my own whereabouts, my past catching up with me, so to speak.

"Sanford, please," I told a little man inside the ticket booth. He wore a big sweater over his uniform, a cap and gloves. The glass between us was so fogged with his breath it covered up the rest of him.

"*What's that?*" he asked me. "Yer gonna have ta speak up, boy."

Had he sensed my second-guessing? I could still change my mind. It wasn't too late. I could tell him anyplace I wanted. Anywhere in the world—at least the first leg of a long journey to get me there. Though I'd been afforded nothing further, still, North Carolina seemed bigger than it had ever before.

"Sanford!—sir," I shouted. "One ticket."

"Well, now, I know that much, don't I. Who else ya got standing next to you? Here," he said. "And you better get if you wanna catch that one. Otherwise—"

"Yes, sir," I cut him off, seeing his finger pointed at a bus being boarded behind me, without wasting another breath. "Thank you."

The Greyhound looked old inside but kept clean, was sparsely filled with only a half-dozen or so passengers. Even with the last trip it'd taken and its engines vibrating underfoot it was as cold inside as it was out. I took a seat near the back, where diesel fumes drowned out any lingering smells, and curled up next to the window, as icy as it was to the touch. Although Highway 1 wasn't Highway 421, looking out, I wasn't going to miss a thing.

Standing inside Polk, nearing my exit, I'd expected snow to be on the ground, for travel to be iffy. This wasn't the case. The bus driver was no nonsense, too, on schedule and, I could tell by looking at him, always on the road. "Good morning, folks," he grumbled to middling response. The bus jarred forward and knocked my stiff shoulders back against the soft seat.

"You want some?" an older lady asked excitedly, tilting a torn-open pack of crackers at me across the empty aisle between us.

"No, thank you, ma'am," I answered with a smile. I did want some but I didn't want to open the door for conversation.

"Yer about my grandson's age," she said matter-of-factly. "I don't know about you but I sure need somethin in my stomach or else I'm gonna be sick, you know. You sure you don't won't some?"

She was younger than my grandma, or how I remembered her. This woman's hands weren't as defined, shaky, nor did she cough when she spoke, not once. "No, ma'am." I smiled again and nodded. "That's alright."

The van that brought me here was toasty. Almost too hot. Heat burned as it rushed out from vents like a blow-dryer, so close to my legs that I remembered how I'd forgotten what it felt like to be so warm, to be sitting in front of a fire but actually on the road with air-conditioning that did what it was supposed to do. The van's driver had said nothing the whole way, keeping the radio on to do all the talking. An airplane had crashed overnight in the woods not but ten miles from where we were driving. Fifteen of its twenty passengers had died tragically. I thought only of the five survivors, wondering if they were awake yet or in comas, if they'd known how they'd survived a plane crash and felt the impact of such a thing: a miracle. As the reporter gave further details, I could see in the rearview mirror how the driver was hearing it, blowing air through his cheeks, shifting his gaze out the windshield, like it was tough, like maybe he wanted to say something to me about it, share in it. Sleet and fog were to blame.

"Last night's American Eagle crash was the forth plane incident to cause causalities in the US in the last six months," the radio went on to say. "On October 31, another American Eagle commuter plane went down while waiting to land at O'Hare, killing all sixty-eight on board. Thirty-seven of the fifty-seven passengers aboard USAir Flight 1016 were killed in a crash outside Charlotte-Douglas International Airport in North Carolina back in July—two months before another USAir Flight's crash in September, which resulted in the deaths of all 132 of its passengers."

I shivered, slumped down in my bus seat, still thinking of the news I'd heard on the radio. With it, and the old woman sitting diagonally across the aisle, no longer eating her crackers but closing her eyes slowly and blissfully like maybe she'd soon fall asleep and never wake up again, I thought some more about my own grandma, how she'd once told me, when I was little, that it would all be over soon.

"What will?"

"All of it. Everything, hon. Every last bit of it. It's almost time. You'll see. Fires are gonna scorch the earth clean. Creeks and lakes and rivers, even oceans, they're all gonna dry up. Dry as a bone. And vegetables aren't gonna wanna grow no more cause of it neither. Won't be nothing left for nobody—not me and you, though." She pinched my arm with a toothy grin when she said that.

Stretched out over her waist I looked up at her, her fuzzy chin, her eyes glassy in the way they glued to the TV screen she was watching whenever she'd talked over it to me—always she did. *Donahue* and then *Sally.*

"Planes . . ." she sighed, "they'll start fallin right outta the sky. The highest thing we got to heaven, and the first that'll go. To show us, you see. You just wait, hon. Watch em fall."

"You ever been on a plane before, Grandma?"

"Course I ain't been on no plane. Where'm I gonna go to?"

"I dunno."

"What, you wanna get on a plane? Is that what you want?"

"I'm not scared."

"Course you ain't. Where're you gonna go? Where's that airplane takin you to?"

I thought of all the places it could take me, destinations I'd only seen advertised as prizes on TV, on *The Price Is Right.* They didn't seem real, so far away from where I was, seeming impossible to get to. Airplanes didn't seem real. Only when they fell did they, proof that just another person had invented them and made a mistake. I thought if I never went anywhere else, the world outside of this one would stay as it was forever, like a fantasy, keep on going however I imagined it, better not worse. Never would I know just how real it actually was.

"We're not birds, Trav," Grandma stressed, coughing into her fist. "We ain't supposed to fly."

Out the wide window I watched Wednesday morning traffic crowd the highway alongside the bus. A sheen of dew glittered under the sun, and the horizon looked hazy, steam rising up from scraggly ditches and open lots of yellowed grass where I'd seen a stray dog the last time I paid attention.

Further along the hour or so route southwest, out from under Raleigh's stretching belt of civilization, the highway eventually gets surrounded on both sides by pine trees, for miles. Never-ending it seems. Nothing to see here, not even a little town or sign to point at, something to remind you that you were here. And I had been before, I remembered, though seeing it now for the first time, I got why it was that I'd fallen asleep.

The exit ramp into Sanford came on suddenly, my heavy thoughts having carried me most of the way. A truck stop was a wall of Fords and ugly bricks, a crowded restaurant I could smell when we rode past. Buildings were industrial, long and low, rigid metal, until it was empty parking lots across from little houses like the ones on my street, only dotted between gas stations and churches, mechanic shops and frozen-over red clay rubble, where I guessed the town was either expanded or had stopped, given up. I didn't recognize any of it. Whether this was the road I'd walked on, believing it to be in the direction of my future, I couldn't say. But then the bus turned and suddenly I knew exactly where I was.

"Alright, *Sanford*," the bus driver piped up, easing onto the brakes.

He pulled into the parking lot of the same convenient store, busier today, right across from the restaurant beside it.

The old lady was digging through her pocketbook when I stood from my seat, and she stopped to say, "Merry Christmas, darlin."

"Merry Christmas, ma'am."

And she went back to it, feeling with her whole hand like at the bottom of a popcorn bucket, and mumbled, "Now, if I can just see what I'm doin."

I kept on past her, my legs half-asleep, and I hobbled down the short stairs out the bus. I stood and stared off for as far as I could see, both ways. In front of the restaurant sat the bench, next to the payphone. I set my ruffled sack of hardly enough to get by with, not enough to remember what, onto the bench and picked up the phone. Muscle memory perhaps, my fingers dialed the first four digits of my home phone number, without thinking. Again, I told myself, it's not too late. Go on and call her.

I hung up the receiver and bit my lip, dug deep into my pants pocket for the scrap of paper I'd kept hidden ever since I'd scribbled on one side of it:

harnett county

- off hway 421 somewhere

before crossing cape fear river — gone too far

And on the other side, between torn edges and rough folds was a list of names:

Mallory
Dunlap
Hill
~~Clap~~ Clapp
Tillett
White

There'd been more names, I was sure. But I'd accidentally got it wet, lost a few from the bottom of the scrap. The ink bled, too, and where the paper pulp got torn away I could make out a J and an O, easily Jones, I figured.

Luckily that phone book, along with everything else, had remained as it was, how I'd hoped it would be, and I opened it like I knew what I was doing, so as not to be suspected of doing anything.

Mallory was somebody's last name and I started with it, fishing for a quarter in my other pocket, flipping through the white pages of the phone book only to find there was not one but three Mallorys in it. And what if none of them were the right one—what if the right one wasn't even listed in the phone book? Hell, what if none of them were? What if they were in a phone book but just not this one?

I slammed the book shut in frustration, sat down next to my sack. I could hear the breakfast being served inside the restaurant behind me, feel heat radiating off the foggy windows.

Call your momma, boy, I heard somebody say to me. Not really, but it sounded real. I looked over at the payphone, thought again about the only number I knew by heart. There, on the metal part that stuck out on the side, I saw where I'd scratched my initials 'TLW' and ''89,' dirtied over a bit and burnished but legible, proof that I'd been here before. I could give it up and get a job in this restaurant, I thought, same I had before. But I was older now, of age as they say. Legal. I could buy my own damned cigarettes.

I unfolded the piece of paper and found a Dunlap in the phone book, only one, so I called it.

"We're sorry, you're call cannot be completed as dialed."

Alright. That wasn't so hard. Next: Hill. Too many to count. For the same reason it made no sense to look up Jones. There was no Clap or Clapp, but I did see one Tillett. Okay, now there's a phone number I could try. And it rang, the phone was actually ringing . . . And kept on ringing.

"Hello?"

"Hello?" I asked back stupidly. "Hi, yes, hello. Is this Tillett—the Tilletts?"

"Uh, yessir, yes it is."

"The Tilletts who live somewhere off 421—in Harnett County?"

"Um, welp, that depends on who I'm talkin to, don't it?"

"Oh, I'm sorry. I didn't mean—"

"Didn't mean what? Who is this? Ronnie? Ronnie, is that you?"

"No, ma'am, my name's Travis. I'm not . . . from here, I'm—"

"Well then why're you callin me for?"

"I'm trying to find—"

"Listen, my husband, he's got his brother livin out that way but no, you're callin somebody in Sanford, honey. Another Tillett."

I know I sounded deflated, realizing the list was likely of no use, but I wasn't expecting she'd hear it in my voice, respond to it.

"Wait now," she said. "I guess you must be callin for work or somethin. The farm. Is that right?"

"Yeah, yeah that's right, ma'am."

"Well then here, lemme give you the right number to call. I know they've been tryin to get somebody over there. Stead of takin in strays, I told em. Stop lookin for it and just let it be. Good things'll come, right?"

"That's right, ma'am."

"Here—you got a pencil?"

"Um, yes, ma'am," I said, though I did not. I did however have a piece of glass on the ground I could use to scratch with as she read the phone number, digit-by-digit aloud to me.

"There. You got it?"

"Yes, yes I got it," I told her.

"You take care, now. Alright?"

"Yes, ma'am. I will. And thank you."

I hung up the receiver, listened to my quarter, went into my pocket for another to dial the number she'd given me. It rang too, and after two times, I heard a click before a long silence.

"Hello?" I said.

"Uh, scuse me. Sorry bout that. *Who's* this?"

"Oh, hello, sir. Yes, my name is Travis. I was calling to talk about your farm."

"Yes. What about our farm?"

"Um—well, I'm coming through, from—I'm on Highway 421."

"Are you lookin for a place to stay? Work?"

"Oh, um, yeah, well—"

"Now listen, I have to tell you, we ain't one of them big-business, oil-run machine, bank-bought types. Done been hit hard last five-ten years, and so we ain't what we used to be, but listen, we got chickens, a few goats left, and a cow that's good for nothing these days but she sure'll bat her pretty little lashes atcha. Either way, even if you ain't spent no time on a farm, boarding don't require work. Long as you got *something* to give, that'll work just fine. Least til you get on yer feet."

I didn't tell him this but I'd named chickens before, neighbors next door to my grandma and granddad. Breaking and chopping their necks the way they did, passing them off to a woman slumped over a stump with blood up to her boobs, I could never. A girl my age plucked every feather. Grandma fried their skins, made me shell peas and at least try to peel potatoes, as bad as I was, at least at first. I was good at *that*.

"I'm a fast learner," I said with a sigh. And the man continued to ramble on, in a voice that sounded raspy or under the weather, telling me all about the farm in a broken, roundabout way, muttering details that pertained to what seemed like every job that he'd ever hired somebody for, even those that had long since gone away, like twining and drying tobacco leaves. I broke in, "Well, but maybe I could—"

"Em hm, I hear ya," he said, like a long-delayed response to what I'd said. Maybe the connection was bad, that it actually was delayed, every word I said. "Well, listen—Say, what day of the week is it?"

"It's Wednesday," I told him.

"Alright," he said, like he was thinking about it, not anything I had said in particular but what day it was. He then began to speak in what I guessed were thoughts he was having with himself or maybe it might be words with somebody else, in the room beside him.

"Sir?" I mumbled. "Sir? . . ."

"So when're you wantin to? Today? Tonight, or . . ."

"Hm, well," I said, not sure what to say, how to carry on any kind of conversation with him. "I think if maybe I could see where yer at, I'd get a better idea of—"

"Where'd you say you was from?"

"I'm from—I'm actually calling from Sanford. I just got off a Greyhound bus and—"

"Em hm. Ah, yeah, I hear ya. Well golly, I don't know what to tell ya, who told you to call, but yer a ways away from Lillington, where we are—" Then I heard the voice of a woman break in over his in the background.

"Yessir, no, yeah, I understand—"

"No, no, now—I'm not sayin you can't come out this way, just—if you can't get yourself here yer gonna have to get somebody to I guess. And if you can't then *somebody's* gotta come pick you up then, if yer ever gonna make it out here. I've got my hands full right now, but—" And he broke away again, to listen to the other voice.

"I wouldn't expect you—" I began to say.

"How bout I get my nephew to? My brother's boy, yeah. He's got him a taxi cab business over there in Sanford. Doin alright I hear. Picks up some colorful characters."

"You don't have to do all that, sir, really."

"It's not a whole lot, son. It's just a ride. Ain't but a dollar's worth a gasoline noway. Some supper for him oughta do it—naw, I guess it ain't time for that but Mae's got *somethin* on the stove—yep, she's nodding her head, or are ya shaking it? Anyhow, yer choice. But someone like him'll take you for five dollars otherwise, I suspect."

I didn't have but five dollars on me and I didn't want to tell him, so I told him okay.

"That settles it then. Now listen, I don't know how long he'll be. And I'm not gonna lie and say he's the sharpest tool in the shed, but he'll get ya where yer going in one piece."

"What's his name?"

"What's that?"

"His name? Your nephew I should be expecting?"

"Oh, Ronnie. Yep, he'll be there."

chapter 17

A glass of wine. That's all it took, what started it up again. If it had been anything else before it then I surely didn't know what. Had I missed it, not thinking I needed to bother looking? There must've been something I hadn't put together. Big bottles under the bed, slid carefully toward the middle of the mattress so my edging foot or reaching hand wouldn't sound the clinks. Tiny bottles in the top drawer, stashed underneath panties and bras, so as to go undiscovered without being in the trash I took out every other night. I should have smelled something, not just on her breath but when I got switched to dish-washing duty sometime after Thanksgiving. That was probably when the whole mess got cleared away, while I was toweling dry our mismatched plates and chipped bowls, shinning the glasses that up until then had only had milk or tea or tap poured into them. When I think about it I guess lugging and then stuffing the noisy bags into the bin was akin to Santa Claus and the chimney, so practice or pretend or make-believe all the same, and in secret, too, as I put away dishes neatly—neater than she ever had—into the kitchen cabinets, once or twice with even a smile on my face.

"Just something to sip on," Mom said. "To celebrate. Can you give me that? *One* glass, Trav."

The silent treatment never worked on my mom but I didn't know what to say. So easy it was for her to make her mind up about something that I knew she had, that she was going to have a drink tonight regardless of how hard I pled for her not to. And her mind had been made easier to make up because she'd already started drinking again.

"Fine. You don't care then? Neither do I," she said.

"Do you have a preference, ma'am?"

"Like what?"

The waiter pointed at a list on the menu, two columns.

"Oh, red or white?" Mom said, unsure of herself. "White, then."

I'd never seen her drink a glass of wine in my life. And why now? To celebrate what, exactly? Christmas? We never celebrated anything, at least not like this, not formally, and never at a restaurant. Only once, and recently so it seemed this was going to become a regular thing, about a month and a half ago after she got home from work Mom said, "I'm gonna take us out for a chicken dinner," with big news on a Friday night, "to celebrate." The new job she'd gotten, a promotion, it wasn't so new anymore, and so what? In the time since she'd started, had it made her feel fancy enough for a glass of wine or something? I wondered.

It was coming up on a year since last Christmas, since she'd last impaired herself with anything (to my knowledge) and hopeful I'd been that this version of her would outlast the one before it, into the new year and beyond, forever, if it existed. And I'd not let go of the image of her Tommy had described to me when I came back from Lumberton, of her being so sad, like I'd died, seeing her cry non-stop without me there. Christmas morning this year was supposed to be different than how it was then with me on the road and left alone in Dad's apartment; Mom bruised and hungover in bed and finally waking up without me long after I'd left. I guess because I believed her when she said she'd been sober ever since then that I felt sorry for her and was determined to make it up to her this year, because she'd done her best to make it up to *me*. More than anything, I didn't want to see her cry. It shouldn't have taken a Christmas miracle for her to be sober.

Since school had started, she'd gone up two dress sizes—"I'm gettin fat, Trav."—and looked better than I'd ever remembered. She complained about her closet, though, still filled mostly with clothes that weren't her right size: "juniors sizes they're so small." Her pants wouldn't fit her, and her shirts clung to her. When she'd dusted off her jackets and skirts, though, they revealed a time in her life that I'd not been a part of, when she was a secretary, "doing the books," she'd said. These clothes fit her perfectly, like she was another person then, and again today. She pulled out as many as she had, her "fat clothes," but there'd been too few to get by on, she'd said, and we needed to go shopping. She put it all on plastic, not because she wanted to, she told me, because she had to. Outside the fitting rooms, in a big three-piece mirror, she poked at her stomach and sides, pinched her skin and slapped her butt. To me she was beautiful, looked the way I imagined she should, normal, like a mom. But for her, she was every bad thing in the book. Kids at school called each other things she called herself, things I'd never imagined adults were capable of holding on to and repeating. She bullied herself is what she did. For months, always comparing herself to how she used to look, wanting no part of what she looked like now, sober and off the pills or whatever else, it should've been taken as another clue.

After that night, after the glass of what to me looked like sparkly piss was set down in front of her and she lifted it to taste, the less shit she gave about drinking again, and the more she receded into her old self. One glass was then a bottle before long, usually two. A beer became a six-pack and then ten, and a tallboy in the morning on the way to work. Liquor bottles were out in the open again, without hiding it, her drinking. No shame. It was quicker for her to get back to where she'd been than who she became that year, the mother who answered the phone and picked me up and stocked the refrigerator, helped me with my homework and listened to me when I told her what had happened at school, because she'd asked me to tell her.

When next I saw the bag of her fat clothes stuffed in the trash can outside, at least I knew what to expect. I'd not been well-enough acquainted with the woman who'd worn them, discarded, and ill-fitting in more ways than one. At least it meant there'd no longer be eggshells to tiptoe around or sly attempts at conversation surrounding her "recovery" that more often than not had become heated and uncomfortable or dead silent. Awkward was never our thing. It was one way or the other. Her way or the highway. She'd ditched talking with the other drunks, hearing sob stories that couldn't hold a flame to her own, she'd told me. Things I didn't even know about. And she was right, I hadn't a clue all the things she never told me. I was no genius and I damned sure wasn't some kind of mind reader.

In some ways a drunk is easier to manage, less of an ordeal than dealing with somebody sober who doesn't want to be, pretending to be when they weren't, no surprises there. Anyway, the guessing game had gotten old, too. Mom made me feel like a parent taking care of their child, like a grown up when I wasn't, when I shouldn't have been wanting to be one already. This was not something I knew that I needed to learn at the time, but looking back I definitely did, seeing as how my eye was on the door before long, before I was even old enough to drive. And whether she was drinking or not wasn't the real mystery worth solving, I reckoned, but the reasons why, this plagued me as a child, still it does. Then it was mostly myself I blamed. Maybe Dad, maybe not, not when it was just the two of us without him in that house, once he'd made it clear he wasn't coming back, when I didn't see how he could possibly drive her to drink like she said he did—and me, too: "Just cause yer a boy don't mean you ain't gonna be a man one day—just like yer daddy. You and yer shit, Trav, yer drivin me up the wall. Drivin me to drink from this bottle, boy." She could hardly see well enough to know who she was talking to so I didn't listen. Dad would say the same thing about her, about me.

Putting Mom's puzzle pieces back inside the box and up on the shelf, looking up to the sky like Grandma told me to, my hands together and talking to it, at someone else outside this world, "the spirit in the sky," as the song goes, was more mysterious than all of it. I couldn't help but wonder, was God mad at me, looking down on me and laughing even, seeing this little boy looking up at him and asking him, *What did I do wrong? What had I done to deserve a daddy like mine?* . . . Who beat on me, told me I was stupid and reminded me whenever he wanted to remember how much it hurt me, to tell me that I wasn't his son but that my momma was a whore and so I could've been anybody's bastard—a son of a bitch, and I most definitely was not *his*. Or a mom that didn't love me enough to leave a man like that, to stop drinking long enough to see life any other way than this, another way, to let me be enough for once, to take some of the fault, maybe make the world that felt so heavy up on my shoulders just a little bit lighter. I was only a kid. Even had she told me it wasn't my fault, in those days, I wouldn't have believed her. Everything was *not* going to be okay. It too shall *not* pass, whatever it was. Everybody around me seemed to only be pretending it would in order to wake up in the morning, like she did. How Dad lived his life away from ours, a double life, just like Mom. Maybe, I thought, maybe that was how she was able to keep going, by making herself believe whatever it was she was telling herself. Truth was, what I really needed, more than anything, was the truth. No more lies to cover more lies. It wasn't coming out of her, I knew that much was true.

I couldn't have known it at the time that nothing in the world could take away what had happened to her, the damage that had been done to her not only by my Dad but men just like him, before him, and after. What it did to a man, she'd tell me, how it made them feel strong to hurt a woman, make them weak and powerless, like she couldn't possibly live without him, needing him to take care of her. This wasn't the sort of position I pictured my mother in for all those years leading up until when I realized how hard a hold men had on her. Not only my dad but Tommy's, Todd, and men whose names I never knew but knew well their place in her life, what void they were filling at the time. No, it was going to take something supernatural to heal my mother, just like Grandma'd told me: "Our family's got a curse on it. Only the good Lord above's got the strength to cure what's been done to it. Not just to me but your mother. And to you, too," she said, tears in her eyes. "But really Trav, honest to God, I've lived enough years to know, we ain't no different than nobody else."

Repentance would come years later, in stages. First it was Mom and I sitting across from each other once a month at Polk, surrounded by strangers, both of us guarded from the "man's world" she was at least only halfway still living in. Almost staged by then, like the two of us were sat there under hot lights for a reunion on TV, a talk show in the way we'd been separated by so much time, everything that had happened and what we kept unspoken.

"I'm so sorry," she said, her voice quivering, beginning to cry.

It was several visits after that first time she'd come to Polk with news of her sobriety and Granddad's death, when she began saying her sorrys, that I'd heard it so much it meant less and less. She apologized almost every visit since, for everything she ever did, even the things she couldn't remember doing.

"It's okay, Momma," I reassured her, as I tried to do every time, shaking my head and looking squarely at her. "You did what you did and it's done. Nobody's perfect."

"No, no, Trav, yer Grandma, she died on Tuesday."

I didn't believe her. She was pulling for more sympathy than I'd already given, I thought. "Yer lyin," I said. "Momma, don't, don't . . ." But I could see in her eyes that she wasn't, and that she was okay with it, that she'd made peace with Grandma.

Maybe it was our surroundings that allowed it to just exist, her death, how it had come and gone already and with nothing I could do to stop it now, but for Mom and I to share in it. It wasn't the same as when she told me Granddad had died. I didn't even bring him up. How close apart they'd died never crossed my mind, and in some strange way it seemed one had enabled the other, to be less resistant to it. Which way, from whom, I didn't know. In the moment I just slumped in the chair and cried. I knew I couldn't for long, with our time ending, time to go back, time to show my face. I had to go back to being somebody else. So did she. Every time she had.

"I'm sorry, Momma," I garbled out.

"Me too, sweetie," she said.

I watched her take another sip from the first glass of white wine. Each swallow took away from her, gutted her, set every piece of her she had left out on display across the fancy cloth between us like it were an undertaker's tray table. I was watching her die. Already it seemed her eyes had glazed over, and when number two came, they were seeing past me, to the next one. Her objective had not been to celebrate her promotion after all, but rather to obliterate her conscience, that little voice inside telling her that she didn't deserve it, not just the job but all of it, everything that she was, and she was worthless, not enough for anyone and in need of more even when she was enough without any of it: the drinking, Dad, whatever else she'd been telling herself.

When the check came her face was flushed with sentiment. She looked no different than when I'd last seen her drunk, only then she was never much of a wine drinker, and the skin, once stretched thin across her cheekbones and now soft and gorged, I'd never seen so red. I took some cash from her pocketbook to pay the check, and inside I saw several emptied mini-bar bottles, one unopened. I glared across the able at her with such disdain. Hatred seeped out from every piece of my body and into hers, over there slumped in the chair, like a scene from a movie I knew well enough by heart. Our plates were picked at, nearly every bit of it eaten, only scattered chicken bones left gray and gooey. She ashed her cigarette off over the mess. Smoke threaded her freshly-painted fingers and I smelt her without having so much as a whiff.

I made her let me drive us home, and I listened to her tell the truth for once, about what had really happened at work. Her own skills and powerful plea, and nothing else—though the sixty-seven-year-old married toad of a boss differed in his opinion of Mom's qualifications—is what got her the promotion. It would be a one-time thing, a retirement gift, he'd said. He'd already groped and felt and slapped and fondled every bit of her on the outside so what difference did her insides make at this point, how he'd framed it. What was left of her?

"That depended, I said to him, how deep did he wanna go? Did he want my brains, my heart, hell did he want my soul too while he was at it? *That* wasn't for sale. Nor was any of it. I'd had it, Trav."

She beat her fist against the door panel. Lit a new cigarette off the last one she'd smoked to the filter.

"I'm sorry, Momma," I said, listening to her go into more detail about all the times she was made to do whatever he wanted— "whatever any of em wanted."

"I didn't know . . . I had no idea," I said, not knowing what else to say to any of it.

"Like the son-of-a-bitch at your school."

"What? *Who?* What're you talking about, Momma?"

"Come on, Trav. You know that. Your principal. I mean, he was different though. He's not 'the principal.' I knew him since I was yer age. And we'd gone on a couple dates before."

I started to cry, quiet and with my face frozen, my body paralyzed. As she kept telling me what happened at work, how she'd gone in to see him four more times since he'd asked, since she'd told him no, it was now with this new promotion versus her termination he was dangling in front of her. I felt so sad, sad for Mom, for myself, for all of us.

"Momma, don't tell me any more. Stop, stop, stop!"

She looked over at me, saw I was crying and so she started to.

"You need to hear it. It's the truth. This is real life, sweetie. I'm sorry. I'm sorry I'm such a lousy piece a shit. A momma that won't give it up, baby. I'm sorry. But listen, I just want ya to hear me, I ain't told nobody none of this. How the man drops a hotel key in front of me on my desk. Tells me: if I'm a no show than there's no reason to show up tomorrow. What am I gonna do? It was either do the job or you don't have a job.

"So I snatch the curtains shut, make him keep the lights cut off. Mouth shut, too—no kissing. Hell if I don't wanna hear the man say another word to me. No talking, neither. It was before he showed up that I was downing two of those mini-bar bottles of vodka—just like that!" Black tears ran her cheeks, telling me all this. "And next thing I'm slipping two more into my pocketbook on the way out, once it was over with. Ain't stopped ever since."

Right before she'd come home that night, to celebrate, she'd been fired for her "erratic behavior at the office, and an unsatisfactory job performance" in the position she'd only just been promoted to, one I still wanted to believe she'd gotten from the power that came with her winning the mother of the year award for 1989.

chapter 18

It was after lunchtime when Ronnie showed up. I'd never ridden in a taxi cab before, nor had I recalled seeing one, not in person or not like the ones on TV. His wasn't yellow and it wasn't checkered. It had writing along one of its dented and beige-colored sides, though, something to the effect of Such and Such Cab Co. and a telephone number to call. It screeched to a halt like it wasn't sure if it was me. Then a window rolled down.

"Are you the kid I'm supposed to be takin out to Uncle Joe's?"

"*Lillington.*"

"Yep, that's right. Hop in," he sighed.

I got into the back, like I was a real paying customer.

"You ain't gotta sit back there if you don't won't to," he told me.

"I don't mind," I said, and I did mind, sitting up front that is. I could smell the front seat from the back, a collection of trash littering the floorboard: Pepsi cans and candy wrappers, drive-thru bags filled with more trash, crushed cups and emptied ice baggies, old and faded newspapers that he must've kept up there since before the last time I was around here. The heat turned up only made it worse. "I'm alright sittin back here," I assured him.

I hadn't even checked a map in the gas station to see how far I was going. Wasn't even a thought until I got into Ronnie's car, figuring up how long I'd have to hold my breath.

"Won't take us more than about half an hour noway," he said. "Still, twenty-somethin miles out there. Woulda been a pretty good fare had it not been my uncle calling me to come and get ya. And I have to say, though, I'm thinkin it might be a first too. Ain't nobody ever told me to pick em up to go out yonder before."

"I'm grateful for the lift, really. Thank you."

"Don't thank me. Uncle Joe's the one with a ticker made of gold."

"Yep, seems like it," I said.

"Where're you comin from anyway? Yer at the Greyhound stop or comin outta Jimmy's restaurant—one or the other—whatn't the gas station cause you ain't got no car." He laughed and then sipped from a big crinkled straw stuck into an even bigger cup before mashing it back into the center console.

I didn't want to tell him where, not specifically. Even if I didn't say Polk Youth Correctional, Raleigh alone might raise an eyebrow. He was waiting for something, though. "I come from all over," I told him. "From just about every county—lived in three, or four I guess."

"So what, yer just passin through then?"

"Yeah. Maybe. Maybe not. I don't know yet."

"Tell the old timer what he wants to hear. But don't tell him where yer from. Everywhere ain't somewhere you wanna be from, kid. I'm sure I can place where, too, but I'm not somebody who's gonna judge nobody. He tell you I was dumb as dirt?"

"*What?* No."

"He's a good man. Fearin kind, you know. Cover up your ink if you got any. It ain't new to me. Boys like you come through, faces like they from some kinda milk carton or phone comp-ny pole."

"Sir, I'm nineteen years old, and I ain't no missing child."

"But yer lost, all the same. I may *be* dumb, sure, but sure as hell if I can't see who somebody is. Not everybody's got a talent for it, neither. I do. Maybe's cause I drive em all over—all sorts of types."

"Maybe so," I mumbled, unsure of myself in the back of the man's car, not just where I was sitting but where I stood once we got to where we were going. Surely he wasn't going to tell his uncle whatever it was he was getting at. "I'm with you, there. Most don't know *who* the hell they're talking to. Just talkin. To hear themselves talk is all."

"Now watch that, too, yer swearin. Even the small stuff, Uncle Joe sweats it all. Hell most especially."

I shut my eyes, as a clue he could take, to stop carrying on the way that he was, but it didn't do any good. Besides, if it wasn't him it was the radio.

"You hear bout that plane crash round Raleigh?" he asked.

"Yep, sure did."

"Just awful. People up there minding their business and don't even know what's what—and boom. Least *all* of em didn't get took."

"Yep," I gave him. "A silver lining."

"Them clouds musta been mighty dark for em not to see two feet in front of em. With all them gears and gadgets they got. Some are talkin like it was no accident."

I turned my face to the window, away from reflecting back at him in his rearview like I was listening to him talking. I should be paying more attention anyway, I thought. The route, or as I was remembering it, how I'd tried calculating it, was the same drive time and nearly identical distance the other way, toward Siler City. Lots of towns came up on the map along Highway 421, and it went all the way to Wilmington this way, to the beach if you wanted. We'd never have made it that far, not even by a long shot.

I looked forward. "Is . . . Cape Fear River coming up?"

"Oh—whataya know bout *Cape Fear River?*" he asked, half-excited, half-suspicious. "You musta seen that movie, huh? The new one not the old one—I know you ain't seen one as old as me. But it come out a couple years back, got De Niro in it, fore it was on the TV this summer, I think is when it was. Whatn't all that bad. Me, I like what they call classics. Just like this car."

"I haven't seen either one," I told him, trying not to recall where I was when it came out, either on TV or at the movies.

"Just as well. But naw, the river's *way* over yonder." He pointed to his left, tapped the window with his fat knuckle. "And I mean, the bridge, yeah it's comin up, but that's not for a good ways, til you done left from Lillington—which we ain't goin to noway. Uncle Joe and Aunt Mae's farm ain't in town or on the highway but a piece back in there some before you get to it. Yeah, boy, they in the boonies. Ain't but a couple more of em around, neither. Ain't much else."

We'd been on the road for maybe ten-fifteen minutes, and because nothing ever changed, not unless it had been a whole lifetime that'd passed, especially not out here, I thought I would begin spotting markers in my memory of the joyride. The skies opened up in places, stretches that went on for more than a mile, without pines to murky the waters I was wading into. Too, because it was probably as cold then, if not colder than it was now, colors looked similar, gray and brown, leaves already about where they were this time of year. And a stink hung over the highway, unlike the one whirling around the front seat but familiar. A paper mill must be close by, that or the river he said was far wasn't far enough not to smell of stagnant swamp water alongside it, like death.

After ten more minutes we turned off the main highway, passed a hand-painted sign selling cow hay, then a rusted metal one for a church up ahead. Then came the church, though it looked unfit to worship in, like it hadn't sounded of a sermon since the 70s. Not just the church but some of the houses, too, both the old ones and newer, caved and covered up by kudzu, either poorly built or built to last forever but couldn't take it anymore. And farms, a silo and different outbuildings, they popped up like relics, better times, worse now. One old barn after the next, I saw, plain as day, out in the open and more than I could count on one hand. But the only thing making one stand out more than the next was a particular way it had been sided, crooked clapboard in an up-and-down direction or what seemed without any, another half-fallen off but still careful in its construction. And black-colored, and brown, rust-colored red, blood red. Each one we passed felt heavy in my stomach, to my core, but I didn't let on to it.

"Yep, hit hard," he sighed, seeing something in my face, I guessed. "I mean, most of it, all round here, been like that since, well, far as I can tell since they been put up to begin with. Like a person, dying since the day they was born." He squinted at me in the rearview mirror. "You ain't gettin sick or nothin are ya? We're almost there."

I know, I wanted to tell him, but of course I couldn't. And even if I thought we were, it was hard to know for sure. Dirt roads went every which way. Roads with no names. Burn piles in yards I'd swear I'd never seen before. And a gas station that looked brand new, about a half-mile from the one nailed up shut with moldy plywood. Signs for this and that, deer coolers and legion suppers and auctioneers coming to town with livestock and ag equipment, private property and no trespassing, leading me off in every other direction but the right one.

After taking a left on one of the roads and then another right, Ronnie slowed down, turned the radio low. I could see he knew exactly what he was doing, that he maybe knew this dirt like the back of his hand.

"You seen a big ole house? Somewhere near here . . ." I asked him. "With one of them smaller, stubby lookin barns."

"A tobacco barn, you mean?" he sighed. "Course. You been dead or just asleep back there or what?"

A steely, tattered mailbox jutted out on the right side of the road, silver spray-painted and written in white was: Whites. Stuck in my head I thought it was something to do with the klan, skinheads, not surprised to find something like that, but then a quarter-mile from it there was another: Hill. *Names*, stupid, I told myself. I took out the scrap of paper from my pocket and read the list of last names again, looking out the window for another one, but I didn't see one, not until Ronnie was stopping, turning beside a black plastic mailbox with stickered-on numbers and the name: Tillett.

The gravel drive was overgrown along both sides with browned weeds, and I could see a small pond ahead, on the left, in the distance a roof outlined through a gray haze. Trees grew huge, grass overgrown.

"There they are," he said to me, sounding more like himself.

An old man got up from his chair pulled close to the end on the wide front porch, walked down a short stack of steps toward the car. The house built up around him stood two stories, plus a basement or maybe a cellar with a hatch door nearly rotted off so it was hard to get to, like the one in *The Wizard of Oz* that Dorothy got locked out of. The house itself was in disrepair, too, with peeling and chipped-off paint—spots with no paint left but brown, wet-looking wood—and the windows, big and tall, waved the reflection of the sky across them as we pulled closer and parked.

Two dogs rushed up to Ronnie's door, before I opened mine and they came running around to greet me.

"They won't bite. Don't worry bout em," an old woman hollered out from a porch swing. A blanket wrapped around her and I could tell she was a larger woman underneath, how maybe it was a comforter from a bed as big as my mom's.

Ronnie got out from the car and yelled up, "Aunt Mae, what're you doin out? Yer gonna freeze to death."

"Oh hush. I only come out when I heard the gravel pickin up."

"She's tellin the truth," the old man said, eyeing me while at the same time shaking his nephew's hand. "You done a good thing, Ronnie. I sure ppreciate cha. Now maybe sooner, but beggars can't be choosers. And anyway, yer aunt's done finished up if you wanna go on in the house and fix you a plate."

"I would but I ate already. Besides I gotta get on back. Got somebody else waitin on me. Two more after em."

"Oh, well. Guess you done got too big fer yer britches, hadn't ya?"

"Bye-bye, now, Uncle Joe," Ronnie said, tipping his head and smiling at the old man's pat on the back before quickly running up the porch steps to kiss his aunt goodbye on the cheek.

"Boy, you take people round in that thang?" Mr. Joe asked, looking at the car as Ronnie ran down and got back in, glaring through the front window mostly, at what I'd turned away from.

"I know, I know," Ronnie said, slamming his door shut after him. "I got that and ten more things I gotta get done."

"Make it a priority, wouldya?" Mr Joe said.

"See to yer comp-ny, Uncle Joe," Ronnie said, backing up and steering himself straight, having never turned the engine off.

"Where are my manners," Mr. Joe said, stepping toward me, extending his hand. "What was yer name again, son?"

"Travis," I told him.

"Joseph Tillett, and that there's ma wife, Mae," he said, pointing.

"Ya'll come on up so I ain't gotta come down, woncha?" she said with a hand held out.

"Nice to meet you, sir, and thank you for getting me here. Awfly kind to go and do something for somebody you don't know like that."

"Well, works that way sometimes, don't it. And thank my nephew. What'd I tell ya?"

"Still in one piece," I said, smiling, watching the rear end of Ronnie's car disappear in the gravel dust.

"You can see—though it ain't much to look at this time a year— got a lot of land needs tending to out here. Over yonder we have our coop, what's left of it," he said, getting right to it. He wore belted blue jeans too baggy for his bony legs, his hair kept, a blondish gray color. His face was chiseled and clean-shaven, a long, large nose, cheeks creased with deep wrinkles. And his arms were bony, too, bare even in the cold, the loose skin hanging from his elbows as he pointed out across the yard to a dirty little pump house he said needed fixing.

"Yeah, they lay alright, when they wanna," he said, watching me walk back to the chickens, more to see how I looked on a farm, I guess is what he was eyeing. "But you ain't about all that, are ya?"

"Well, now, I didn't say *that*. I had some chickens on my family's farm, so that shouldn't be a big deal."

"Now, where was it you said you was from again?" he asked, walking us up the front porch steps.

"Oh, I didn't, sir." I wanted to use his memory as an opportunity to backtrack in some places, ending any further questions regarding where I came from. Folks from around here are pretty territorial and can go on and on about tiny towns only they know about, counties and their registers, creeks named after them and streams they were knee-deep in when they were little, mile markers dented with rocks they themselves had thrown at them. Most highways looked like they did anywhere else, but not here. "Like I told you on the phone, sir, Sanford—a Greyound dropped me off. But I spent most of my life in Chatham County."

"Well, that's alright. Ain't a lot of life under your belt noway. You look like yer—"

"Hungry," Ms. Mae broke in. "Come on . . . Let the boy be, Joseph. What he's got is time. Lots of it. Don't cha, darlin. More than we got left, Lord willin," she giggled, wallowing out from the porch swing.

She kept the comforter on, gripped it in her fat fists like she was afraid it would fall and she'd freeze. Something was childlike about her, even as old as she was. Smile lines lifted and pressed in around the corners of her thin pink lips, and her blue eyes widened with excitement under thick glasses that appeared discolored or tinged for the sunlight.

Mr. Joe stood like he wasn't sure what to do with me. He didn't wear glasses, but seeing him now this close-up, his pupils were blurry, fixed in a position of a solar eclipse just when the sun begins to hide itself behind the moon, with a blue hue spread across it. I'm sure he was as stubborn as my granddad had been, needing glasses for half his life and never so much as tried on a pair.

"Well, invite the boy in for some lunch, Joe," Ms. Mae said from the other side of their bent-up screened door, slamming it shut in a hurry like it was protecting her from the cold.

"You heard her," Mr. Joe said, urging me on. "If yer not thinkin you're gonna stay then least stay for some cookin. How bout it?"

"Actually, if it's not puttin you folks out," I answered.

"Course it ain't," Ms. Mae shouted.

"Oh, OK. Well, great, then yes, thank you, sir."

He and I followed after her, into an open hall where a dark wood table sat covered in mail and a vase of dead flowers off-centered and long dried up of any water. Maybe they were never alive, I wondered. The lights were dimmed down and shadows carved the walls. It smelt chemically, maybe like carpet cleaner, and something cooking, more a mix of burnt biscuits and Mop & Glo the further into the house we went. A room opened up to the left and looked like a place people would sit and drink coffee or tea, more formal, more fancy the way the furniture had been arranged, but was half-filled with boxes now, clothes strewn over the arm of a couch and more stuff in a chair, not so much you couldn't tell what was underneath all of it, but enough for me to notice it being out of place in a room this nice. After we passed a tiny bathroom in the hall, under the big wraparound stairwell that had pictures lining its walls, I stopped waiting for that déjà vu feeling and just took it all in like it was for sure the first time. A light was on and the tile sparkled, along with the toilet. If the carpets were covered in crumbs and dander, it was because more time was spent cleaning the bathroom—and the kitchen, I could see, once we got there: not a pan out of place, or a dish that didn't already get put away properly, tile floors reflecting the ceilings.

"Have a seat wherever you won't," Ms. Mae said as we came together. It was just big enough for the three of us, maybe one more, around a table off to the side. "Had I had more time, I'd of set us up in the dining room."

"We ain't been in there since—well," Mr. Joe said. "It's been a long time, I'll say that."

"This is fine, just perfect," I said to them. "And the food, wow."

"It's like this every night," Mr. Joe chimed in. "Don't go thinkin yer somebody special," he continued, laughing.

"It's really not," Ms. Mae said. "Like I said. I'd a made us a real pie had I known ahead of time we was havin comp-ny. I ain't even gonna bring out what I got kept in the freezer. Shame on me for it."

I fixed a plate and sat down with them. "Are y'all not eating?"

"Nosir, naw. Go on ahead. We done ate ours already."

"Oh? Well, you don't have to watch me, then," I said, feeling guilty, feeling odd and not so much out of place as right at home. It suddenly hit me how I was sitting here in their kitchen, perfect strangers, enjoying their hospitality, perhaps taking advantage of it. But I didn't stop eating.

"When's the last time you ate like this, honey," Ms. Mae asked, slicing a biscuit in half, spreading jelly over it and pursing her lips as she ate it, keeping any crumbs from falling.

"I'd have to say . . . Well . . . I don't even remember," I told her, thinking of any occasion with a sit-down dinner like this one, the smell of steaming bowls filled with greens from the yard I imagined, butter beans, biscuits that I'd never admit looked better than my grandma's, meat and potatoes. "Maybe I never have."

Ms. Mae sighed. "Yer tellin a lie. Not even on Thanksgiving? What about Christmas? Your grandma musta fixed up somethin on Christmas?"

"My grandma died, ma'am, and well, yeah she did, before she went. So yer right. It was just for the two of us, though, whenever we ate her cooking. It whatn't like we all got together or nothin. I ain't got real big family."

"Oh, bless yer heart. I'm sorry to hear that, bout yer grandma," she said, her hand to her chest. "It's just Joe and myself, too, so . . . Oh here, let me get ya'll some more tea. And bless the food, willya, Joe."

He bowed his head and said a little prayer over the table, the two of us sitting there. Ms. Mae stopped herself from pouring for it, and I closed my eyes, hearing the old man's breath catch in his throat, and deeper in his chest, his soul.

During dessert, the store-bought apple pie that did end up being pulled out from the freezer, along with a cup of coffee, Ms. Mae seemed so happy to have him. Even just looking at me, sitting there at her table, like she'd wished I could eat her food forever. Had she been this happy even when I wasn't there, I wondered, when it was just the two of them? It must have been three o'clock, three-thirty at the latest, and I could feel my time ticking away.

"Hun, it's Wednesday, like I was tellin ya," Mr. Joe said.

Ms. Mae's absent face shifted, like she'd found herself with no clothes on, needing to get up and get dressed, ready to go.

"Lord, we've gotta get over to the church tonight," she said, creaking in the chair. Most of her was hanging off both sides of the seat, her legs wide, warmed in cotton pants that weren't her pajamas but something very close, as comfortable to move around in. And when she stood, her stomach sagged in her sweater, a pot of flowers embroidered over the front of it. "We got bible study on Wednesdays."

"I mean, now, I don't know what yer plannin on doin," Mr. Joe said. "I—"

"He's got a night to sleep on it, Joe, now. Least let him have that, fore he decides if he's stayin or goin. Try it before you buy it. Room's right up the stairs, honey. Two of em, too. Won't you have a look and see which one you won't."

"Or maybe he don't won't none of em, Mae," Mr. Joe said with irritation, a pause, cutting his eyes at her. "I'm sure this young man's gotta get on to where he's going. If it ain't gonna be here, I'm sure you'd like to know where, son. I ain't gonna pressure you, now, but yeah, we got some place we gotta be fore long—"

"Yer tellin *me* not ta pressure him, Joe . . ."

"Well, it's just, being round this ole bag-a-bones, I don't know."

Ms. Mae scooted her chair under the table and shot him a look.

"Yer a youngin. So, sure I could use a hand. And yep, we do got two beds ain't nobody slept in—not in a while. Clean. Dusty, maybe. Least the night. We can talk about how much."

"The church I saw comin in?" I said, instead of getting into any specifics about my stay, what might actually amount to outstaying my welcome, I worried. Still I was focused on the plate of food and how I got here in the first place. "It ain't up and running for people comin in and out of it . . ."

"Oh, naw," Ms. Mae said with a chuckle. "That church been a pile of wood and nails long fore you was born. We go into town."

"To Lillington?"

"Yep," Mr. Joe nodded, "that's right."

"Won't you come with us?" Ms. Mae said, with Mr. Joe looking even more stern and steely, like he himself was unsure of any decision other than having me sit down at the table with them.

"No, I don't know about that," I said, and I laughed. "I'm actually very full. I think I might even be sleepy or somethin."

"Yer right. You oughta be. Been on a bus and in Robbie's wrecked out model, I think I'd a done passed out if I was you," Ms. Mae said.

"And really, you've been so nice," I said, sure as I was that I'd never experienced hospitality so good, in a home I'd never stepped foot inside before. Although the land was familiar, it stretched well out from under this roof, and I might soon be on my way at finding where it was, more to the point, where I'd been.

"Well, I'll tell you what. Take yourself a nap, and when we get back from church, I'll fix us something, and then, if you wanna go, I know a cab comp-ny to call to come get ya," Ms. Mae said with a wink.

"You drive a bargain, ma'am," I said to her.

"See there, son, we've been on this farm for almost fifty years and you can tell who's really been runnin it this whole time, huh?" Mr. Joe said, laughing, sipping from a glass of tea rattling in his hand.

"Really, it ain't more than it is," Ms. Mae said.

"Well, thank you—both of you. That'd sure be a burden off me. Can I at least help with the dishes?"

"Well, there you go," Mr. Joe said.

"No you can't. I'll take care of that," Ms. Mae said.

"He won't?" Mr. Joe questioned.

"Yer just gonna be here when we get back and so we'll see about something then. Finish your pie. Have another piece if you wanna."

"Thank you ma'am."

She walked out of the kitchen, the soles of her bare feet black with dust and dirt, when Mr. Joe settled his glass down on the table in front of me, his pruney fingers wrapped around it. He only gave me an eye, like he had it on me, and not another word.

"Thank you, sir," I told him.

I didn't know how I'd been so lucky, to have a night away, a hot meal and bed to sleep in. Even if only halfway to where I was going, it was somewhere, a place to start. The sugar in the pie or caffeine in the coffee, one or the other I don't know, made me feel wide awake when the screened-door slammed shut after them. Or maybe it was that I was given a chance to redeem myself, to not prove myself wrong, or these kind people. If not, to search for it, for at least as long as it took them to get to their bible study and back.

chapter 19

Even though Mom and I never went to the fancy restaurant in town again, I did end up going back, that following spring, just after school let out. It was summer break and I had to get out of the house, away from her, her drinking. I lied and said I was fifteen so I could get a job washing dishes. Only a couple months away from the truth, it was time worth lying for, enough that I could get a head start on saving up to get away for good. I guess in that way, how I looked at it, working there wasn't a job so much as my ticket out. I thought that if I could wash and towel off a million of those plates, shine up each and every fork and spoon and knife, then I'd have enough money to cover my own way before long. I was going to find an apartment by myself and maybe finish high school or maybe not. Why'd I need to bother, I wondered, when I could keep working at the restaurant and eventually find work somewhere else, begin my life sooner than later. Wishful thinking it was. In hindsight, what else could it have been?

She hardly even noticed I was gone, and even without putting her first anymore I couldn't ignore how far gone she'd gotten. Maybe it was my fault, the divide and how much it grew between us, because I didn't want to see it for what it was and so I did nothing to stop it. I couldn't blame myself, nor would I allow it. Besides, Tommy never stopped looking, spying out their big picture window across the street, telling me all about what he'd seen throughout the rest of the summer. He tallied the cars and trucks seen pulling in and out of our driveway while I was at work most nights.

"Makes and models of every kind and color," he said. "And all different sorts gettin out and goin inside the house. Walkin her from the door, and later walkin her back to it."

"Well, least they have manners," I said, trying to make light of it.

At least when I got home and she wasn't there, I had him as a witness to account for her whereabouts, should the police ever get involved. That's where it seemed she might soon end up, the morgue, in jail, who's to say. And there was even the idea I'd started to carry around with me, trying it on so that maybe I guess it wouldn't come as a shock if and when it ultimately would be real, because I just knew how possible it could be, that she might soon disappear completely from my life. Most of all, whenever she was arriving home three days after I'd seen her last, I wondered if it was the last time. But it lessened, the weight of something like that, the feeling that there was anything I could do about it, to stop it, until I didn't even ask where she'd been and cared less and less about where she was going and more where I was headed. In the whole month of August, we maybe spoke two words to one another.

"There was this short, funny-lookin man once. Golly, you shoulda seen him. Most of em are taller, though. And then one looked like a Mexican, dressed in a fancy suit. And then this one man, he looked older than yer daddy was last time I saw him. She didn't seem to mind. None of it mattered. If they was ugly, had a limp, or a big fat stomach hung over his belt buckle, sharp and real clean-cut or downright filthy, don't seem to bother her either way."

"Are there any you seen more than once? Like the same one again and again, car or truck . . . Anybody I should be on the lookout for?"

"Oh, I don't know about that. I don't keep a video tape of em, Trav. But this one time, she fell out of the car, right on her ass, plopped onto the driveway. She was just a laughin, too. Like that time she wiped out on the front porch steps with a cigarette in her lips, slipping sideways like she lost count of em or somethin." And he got to laughing about it. "I'm sorry . . . I ain't makin fun of her."

"No, it's funny. It is. I mean it ain't when you really think about it. She was doing well for a while, you know. But shit happens, I guess, right? I mean, I decided there ain't nothin I can do about it. Not no more. It's best I stay out of it. What else?"

"You want me to keep an eye out for somebody in particular? I will if you won't me to."

"No, Tommy. I didn't mean nothing more. Come on . . . Besides, it really don't matter. I ain't gonna be around much longer noways."

His smile shifted to worry. "Whataya mean?"

"Well, way I figure it, once I save up enough, I'm outta here."

"*What?* So that's it, then! I mean, you ain't even old enough to drive. Just old enough to work. What're you even talkin about?"

"I will be. I already know how to, you know that."

"What about me? What am I gonna do? I can go with you, right?"

"I mean, you've got yer brother? School you probly oughta finish. Least somebody's got to."

"So what, you were just gonna take off? *Sayonara, suckers . . .*"

"No, Tommy. That's not it. Don't be like that. I just can't take it no more."

He looked at me cold, let what I was saying sink in a second.

Because of Mom's fall off the wagon, Tommy and I'd hung out more regularly, mostly during the day when I could. Even as we'd grown apart in grades, me going into high school, him stuck a year behind me, he was feeling more like a brother I never had. And I needed that, sure, maybe I did, but still, I didn't want him to come with me, not then, and of course I wasn't going to tell him that. Somehow I got in my head that even the good things were somehow going to turn bad. It was only more time before he and I would change, too. And maybe I would never be somebody if I always had this reminder of who I'd been, where I'd come from. Selfish, I know, even cold-hearted, but it was true. Sometimes I couldn't help but wonder if it had only been in each of our own miseries that we kept up the camaraderie. A horrible thought it was, one I kept telling myself wasn't true, up until I found myself asking the question of if he and I'd not lived across the street anymore, would we even make time to see each other?

"Sure, course you can come, Tommy," I told him. "Who else?"

After Labor Day, I answered my own question, when I'd started the ninth grade and left that fancy restaurant I'd been working at because they wouldn't work me in anymore. Maybe I wasn't good enough for it, I questioned, knowing I'd not been too good to do dishes. I needed more time, more money, more to do, and so I decided if they weren't going to put me in a position where I could make more, I'd find a place that would. I was fifteen years old and could count and didn't have a record or any tattoos and so I was hired on the spot at a busy seafood restaurant on the opposite side of town. Nothing fancy about it, I was familiar with the place, used to go there sometimes when I was little, when Dad came home and took us there if he was making up for something he'd done. And instead of working with people who felt like strangers even after all summer spent on the same clock, I was with folks I'd gone to school with, who I'd seen working at the same grocery store or gas station before they'd started here.

Only a month into it, just when I was getting the hang of things, swapping my sore feet between standing behind the register and over the fryers, someone I'd never met before came through the doors, someone who'd prove my escape plan faulty from the start.

Her name was Tiffany Rose, a sophomore at Northwood High School in Pittsboro. She came in with only a little bit of waitressing experience but right away looked as seasoned as some of the women who'd been working there ever since the place had first opened up seven years ago. She seemed more like a senior, and it made me feel more like the freshman I was, even less at first, like I couldn't handle even having a look at her, at how beautiful she was. It was possible, I thought, she may just be the prettiest girl I'd ever laid eyes on.

She'd finished her first shift before we finally shook hands, with my palm keeping soft and silky for hours afterward. From her pocketbook she'd taken out a bottle of spray and another squeeze tube of lotion. Something buttery and sweet it smelled like, and never before had I, nor had my grip glistened under the lights the way that it did. Next she took out a pack of cigarettes, leaned against the brick outside, and slipped one into her mouth.

"You need a light?" I asked, quickly following after her with a pack of my own.

"I got one," she said gently, smirking when it lit.

"Why'd you come all the way over here to work?" I asked her.

"Why? You don't want me here?" she said, smiling.

"No, I don't mean it like that, I—"

"I know, I know. I mean, well, twenty minutes ain't a whole lot, and Pittsboro done worn out its welcome on me. And really, Siler City, well, little more here than over there's bout all the difference I can tell. Still ain't enough."

"Yer right about that."

"Well whataya do on a Friday night?"

"Now, I guess it's the same thing as you: serving seafood platters and daily specials."

She smiled and blew smoke. "How long you been workin here?"

"Not long. Bout a month. I was washing dishes all summer at this other place before, though."

"And you like it here?"

"So far, sure. I don't hate it. I mean, it gets me out of the house."

"I'm talkin bout Siler City, yer home. I guess somewhere else then, is where you'd rather be, too, huh?"

"Oh, well, yep, right again," I slowly exhaled smoke and broke any silence, asking, "What grade are you?"

"The tenth, but I don't know for how much longer."

We had a lot in common, I could tell already, but I didn't point out the obvious. It wasn't remarkable, our facts, more common as they were among most people, the more you'd ask—if somebody just would. She'd grown up on a dirt road, though, in a house that wasn't a place I'd want to live, or how she'd described it, under his thumb.

"Times ain't what they used to be, my daddy likes to tell me. How gas was twenty-five cents a gallon when I was born, and men ain't walked on the moon since. Stopped lookin for anywhere outside this world gone to hell," she said. "Why bother, he tells me. Can't put it back in its box, once you done started burning women and children alive with napalm."

"Wow," I said with a long sigh.

"And he ain't even fought in Vietnam. Sure likes to talk like he did . . . You know they shot folks down in the streets and students protesting it on their college campus—peacefully too. And still."

"So he's some kinda hippie type?"

"God no. Or . . . I don't know. I ain't never met nobody like that. He *is* against the government, though. Whatever that counts towards. He's all I've ever known. And Pittsboro. My momma died when she was havin me, so . . ."

"Sorry," I told her.

"Ain't nothin to be sorry for. I don't remember her. I ain't even got no pictures to look at, neither. Daddy's description of her's all I got to look at. She had to've been blond like me. Daddy has dark hair, much darker than mine. Unless it'd turned by the time she had me. He told me once how she was starting to get grays already, that she was about as old as he was—and Daddy's fifty-somethin now, maybe almost sixty, so, yeah."

I thought of how much younger my mom was, how I'd never seen a gray hair on her head, couldn't imagine one growing.

"And her nose," she said, "I got her nose without a doubt." She squeezed her nostrils between her fingers. "I wish I hadn't, though."

I wanted to ask why? It was perfect. Freckles browned across it, then scattered over both her cheeks like stardust before they were gone. Her hair *was* blond but dirty, less young and innocent looking. The way she held herself, her cigarette, I knew, even at only a year older than I was, she'd lived a little bit more than most had at that age.

"Naw. But more than all that I wonder if we walk the same—talk, too. If somebody'd be able to tell I was her daughter or not. Daddy don't go into it much, so I can't but wonder. You know when you see kids and their parents, how they move alike. Stupid, I know it is, even wonderin bout it, whether I would see me in her. And what if I turned out lookin more like my daddy and he just won't tell me that."

"I know what you mean," I said, smiling. "I don't know which one of mine I look like."

"Least you got em—both of em. I mean, sounds like you do, right?"

"Oh yeah, I do, sorta. Sometimes I think it'd been easier had I not."

"I got a stepmom, not legal or nothing, since I was ten. But she don't count. She ain't nobody's momma—I mean she is, I have a sister, half-sister—she shouldn't be is what I mean. God, I can't stand the woman. Always on my case bout something or other."

"So Siler City, then," I said, "as far as you could get."

"Well, yeah, but reason I'm here's cause this guy's got it out for me or somethin, I don't know what. I thought going over to Tennessee mighta made him go away for good, since I got family over there, but I knew just as soon as I got over there, my aunt was gonna call my daddy and it'd all be over with. And then this guy . . . real piece a work—he's a *man* is what he is, not some guy, almost old enough to be *somebody's* daddy—ain't mine, though, regardless of whatever he got stuck in his head. I guess for some reason he thought ordering a bite to eat and tippin me for servin it to him was worth somethin more. I had to fight my way outta that one. Got this to prove it," she told me, lifting the tail of shirt to show me a scrape over her hip that had bruised.

"Oh—"

"*Shit.* There's Daddy," she said, stomping out her cigarette, slinging her pocketbook over her shoulder.

"Drive's damn sure too long, Tiff," he said, spitting brown out the downed window of his raggedy pickup truck. "Yer gonna have ta pick you a spot that ain't got me out here on the road so late for so long."

I pressed my foot up against the brick, watched her shoot him a look and pop the lid on a styrofoam container of seafood in her arm, on top of another one filled-up just as much underneath it.

"I can make up for it, though, can't I?" she said.

"Hello, sir," I said to the man, with a wave that felt silly.

"Marla's done made supper," he yelled, "so don't be thinkin it's some shrimp's gonna count against the mileage yer puttin on my odometer, dear—no matter how many you got in there. Smells good, though."

"Daddy, that's Travis," Tiffany said, after he'd not acknowledged my hello.

"*Son*," he grumbled, tipping his hat. "And *who're* you?"

"Daddy, he works at the restaurant with me. Come on, now."

I stepped away from the wall, closer toward his truck, thinking I was going to hear more from him. He looked as old as I pictured him, but grimier, like maybe he did hard labor, or hard time Tiffany hadn't told me about. It was too dark to tell what all he had tattooed on his arm hanging out the truck but it was a lot. Beer stunk on his breath, along with dip in his fat lip.

"Welp, Penny's at home hollerin for ya—Penny's her baby sister," he said to me. "She ain't gonna go to bed til she knows she ain't dead. Watchin too much TV . . . I told you."

He pulled the truck straight, reversed it and got ready to take off.

Tiffany cranked her window down quickly and called out, "When're you workin again?"

"Tomorrow night," I yelled.

"Me too," she said.

"No hell you ain't," I could her dad grumbling inside the truck as he drove out of the parking lot.

Tiffany leaned out the window, turned back and faced toward me, smirking with her finger up to her head in the shape of a pistol and pulled her thumb for a trigger before waving goodbye to me with the same hand. I watched with baited breath, holding on to something, I don't know what, as the pickup got smaller and smaller going down the highway, before it was gone.

chapter 20

Out of the blue Tommy visited me when I was just about through with my time in Polk. Any distance there'd been between us seemed to have doubled since we'd last talked to each other back before I left home. He was almost unrecognizable to me now, having not seen or heard from him in so long, and under such duress. Though I guess, if asked, he could've said the same thing about me, that he didn't know who I was anymore, that it was my fault. But I wasn't the one on the outside, with a telephone line hooked up and hung onto the kitchen wall that I could pick up anytime I wanted. I didn't have a car I could drive. He also had a life that he could keep on living, though, and I was glad he had been. Neither one of us were at fault, really, not in the least bit for somebody else's mistakes. Still, knowing him, I figured I'd have seen him sooner, heard his voice, surely. But I couldn't blame him.

"I asked Momma bout you last time she was here," I said to him. "The first time she was, too, and the time after that, and—"

"I know, I know. I shoulda tried comin to see ya, but you ain't no better at tryin. Even before you was put in here, Trav. Months'd gone by and not a word from you. Nothing. Nada."

"Well, now," I said, sitting up and looking side to side, behind him and around the open room. "I don't think you need me to tell you why. Do I? You know damn well."

"I mean, I do. I get it, trust me," he said, and he lifted the short sleeve of his T-shirt. There was a mark on his upper right arm, now faded and soft, discolored. Scar tissue is what it was, I recognized, like wax the color of his skin had melted and since dried up.

"*Tommy* . . ." I whispered, and my eyes widened at the sight of the crater-shaped spot, before he quickly brushed his sleeve back down over it.

"Let me tell you somethin," he sighed, "the way you just took off like that. Made me think I done something. Something to deserve it. I sure as hell ain't did nothin wrong. If being a friend is—"

"No, you're right, Tommy. I know. I was wrong. I'm sorry. Really, I am. Honest to God, with the way things went, I didn't know what else to do *but* run. I mean, you know . . . Or do you? I half don't remember myself."

"What do *you* think?" he asked, crossing his arms, tightening them.

"*I'm sorry*," I told him quietly. "For all of it, everything."

"Alright, alright. And speakin of your momma, she looks good, I have to tell ya."

"When'd you see her? She told me she hadn't seen you. Not once."

"She ain't. Don't mean I ain't seen her, though. She's been workin behind the counter at that tire place. You know I don't live with my momma no more."

"I didn't. How would I?"

"Well, yeah. There's that." He looked off, past me, like he'd seen a ghost. "It has been a while, hadn't it? You really did it. Just up and left. I'm not surprised you did, just *when* you did, *how* you did it—"

"I'm *sorrrry*," I sighed. "If it makes you feel any better, I got put in here for it—been here ever since. Doin my time."

"So what, yer some kind of a bank robber now?" he said, smiling.

"I didn't rob no bank, Tommy. I'm out of here soon, too. Least I think I am. I've been trying my best not to mess things up, you know."

"That's good. I'm glad to hear yer making amends with yourself, with them other guys they got locked up in there with you."

I just gave him a look like he didn't have a clue. Who I was, who we were. He didn't, truly, but he didn't deserve any of it, what I could say to make him sorry, what I could use to make him feel bad for me.

"Aren't you gonna ask me about somebody?" he asked.

"*Somebody* . . ."

"Come on, now," he said, lifting his hands, huffing and puffing.

"I ain't got a lot of time, Tommy. Won't you say what you—"

"Tiffany, Trav. Yeah, she's doin alright. I'll tell her you asked next time I see her."

"*How is she?* Really."

"I mean, I *guess* she's alright. She's still at the restaurant."

"Yeah. I messed that up pretty bad, didn't I."

"I don't know anymore."

"What about you? You got a girl?"

"No—I did—but not anymore. I've been sorta all over the place. Made sense not to keep going, you know."

"Yeah?"

"Well yeah. I'm sorta stuck, Trav. Just as much as you are."

"Well, I really am. I ain't got no place to go."

"Where'm I gonna go?"

"What about school?"

"What about it? You mean how'd it go? I'd answer ya if I knew. I didn't finish. Got close, though."

I felt guilty, and the feeling made me go quiet. Both of us were. Only then, seeing him familiar, recognizing where we'd last been and where we ended up, it seemed brave of him to come here. I'm not sure I would've had it been the other way around.

A guy sitting at a table next to ours began to fidget so loudly in his chair that Tommy and I both looked, watched him drag himself up on the tabletop in front of him. His uniform bunched around his arms flailing out, as he started to wail. And he shouted: "What?! No! No, no, no . . ."

"I know, honey. I'm sorry. I'm so sorry," a woman sitting across from him was repeating.

"Don't tell me that!" he yelled back, becoming irate and angry.

Then a guard approached, hovered the wall behind us.

Tommy was visibly nervous in his chair, watching, afraid to, but captivated. He curled his back and tried bracing himself to our table.

"Yer tellin me she's dead? She dead, Momma?" he hollered.

They both began to sob, and then the guy stood and kicked the chair and dropped his head. The guard stepped in and restrained him.

I watched as his mom pulled tissues out from her pocketbook, still sitting, watching her son kick and scream. Another guard left his stance to join the first one, to hold the guy and walk him away.

"*Hey*," Tommy whispered, eyeing the guards as they were exiting.

"What?"

"I think I mighta found it?"

"Found what?"

"You know, *the spot.*"

"*Shhh* . . . Tommy . . . What're you—"

"Here—" He was leaning back in the chair, reaching into his pocket for something, right as the second guard who'd left to help the first walked past us.

"*Stop, stop, stop,*" I mouthed, and when it seemed no eyes were on us, with his hand out from his pocket, I said, "You shouldn't've done that. I mean, you—"

"Hey, hey, now. *Hey.* Just listen to me, then," he said, lowering my temper, his voice. "*You gotta pencil?*"

"*On me?* No, stupid. I can't bring nothin in here with me, neither. Specially not no damned pencil."

"But ya got one of em in there?"

"*Yeah*," I said, looking around the room. "I mean, sure I do. Why?"

"Write this down, soon as you get back. Hear me?"

"You ain't sayin nothin, Tommy. What am I listening to?"

"I ain't said it yet, now, come on. Listen to me."

I leaned closer toward him, not so much that it looked like we might pass anything, if anyone was watching us.

"I done gone back and forth. Retraced them roads. Ridden both sides of the highway. Noon and night. And I swear to you, I ain't seen nothin. But I think I got close. I mean, maybe, maybe not. I ain't been on foot, though, and I ain't gonna be," he said, patting his arm. "But you, ain't nobody seen you before. Won't see you comin, neither."

"Tommy, no . . . No, no—"

"Just listen to me, Trav. You wanna start over? Here's how yer gonna do it. How the hell else are you gonna come up with that kinda money? You know I'm right."

I felt my heart in my throat, blood in my veins, out of breath. I must've turned red in the face, too, guilty, or still a suspect.

"I can't, Tommy. I can't even hear none of this," I told him, covering my ears, my face, hoping I wasn't acting out enough to be taken away like the guy next to me had been. Maybe I needed to be, to stop this plot from happening.

"Yes you can and you will. Listen to me," he said, pulling me out of it. "Once yer outta here, do this one thing, and sky's the limit."

Hearing him say this, same as how Jay had described his first day out, I thought of how sure he'd been that he wasn't ever coming back, when it was simply keeping himself away from himself he couldn't do.

"I'm not comin back here, Tommy. And they wouldn't bring me here noway. It'd be worse. I know it. You don't know what's it's like."

"Just cause I'm out there don't mean I ain't someway stuck in there with you. This is the both of us."

I sat up straight in the chair, took a deep breath and faced him, myself, and my future. Without even being let out yet I understood how easy it was for Jay to get himself brought right back to where he'd been, and how hard it was going to be for me. What was I going to do?

"Alright," Tommy said. "Now, Harnett County ain't so big it can't be found. And I know for sure it's off Highway 421 somewhere cause that's the one we was ridin on. And listen, there's a bridge I rode over, and I for damned sure know we ain't done all that then," he said, popping the table with his palm, before holding back his excitement. "*Cape Fear River*," he whispered. "Gone too far if yer crossing it."

I took another breath, didn't say a word to him then, only listened, or tried to, when next he said he'd had a whole list of names written down that he'd brought for me in his pocket, names he'd seen on mailboxes that he wondered about, whether they were ones worth looking into. The roads were not at all how he'd remembered them, though, and old barns were about a dime a dozen.

"Mallory, I remember, cause it's a girl's name. And Dunlap, cause it made me think of them fancy cigarettes when I saw a beat-up mailbox after with Hill written on to it. And Clap, like yer hands but with two P's. Jones, maybe. There's somebody named Jones everywhere, though, and that house I saw ain't looked nothin like the one we seen."

And he'd been right about that. A month later, my first night out, while Mr. Joe and Ms. Mae had their Wednesday bible study to go to, I walked up and down the road a ways, and I saw the mailbox for the Jones's, their house: small, ranch-style, and similar to the house he and I'd lived in, but it was without neighbors, and their front yard didn't have cut grass and kept flowerbeds, but a rusty tractor part that looked like it had been sitting there longer than the house.

I took from my pocket the scrap of paper I'd written on in a hurry, as soon as I'd gotten back after Tommy and my time was up. Now I didn't need to be sure what I'd remembered to be Jones, even half-gone from the list, or any of the others around it I'd explored and determined were not the right place.

"X marks the spot," Tommy'd said to me, "somewhere."

It was finally spring, only just beginning to green, months from that cold night, and still, I had my doubts about where I was, if I was in the right place or not. But it felt right, like maybe I was close. This was not the house, that I knew the day I arrived, nonetheless I'd stayed there, with the Tilletts, earning my keep ever since.

I turned off the main road and walked up the long driveway, back to the house. Through the woods that met the mailbox and blocked out most everything else, I could barely see the road behind me. And up ahead, leaves now hid any clue that a house was even standing there, only an impression of dulled white against a bright blue sky. The pond had thawed, with the occasional duck swooping in to float in it and flounder around in the mud. Sun had warmed the air up just enough, and there, up on the porch, Ms. Mae swung half-asleep in her swing, catching the breeze with her bare, chubby toes. The wood ceiling was struggling with how heavy she was, I could hear, creaking and twisting each time she swayed. It's a wonder the metal hooks holding the swing up hadn't given yet, the poor old woman.

"Hey, honey," she sighed, stretching a leg at me as I passed.

Mr. Joe might sometimes affectionately refer to her as "Big Mae," a nickname given to her whenever they'd had a granddaughter who their only daughter had named Maebelle—sometime in the 60s or 70s it must've been. The nickname had stuck, even long after "Little Mae" died, along with their daughter and son-in-law, in a car accident. "In a way it sorta memorializes her, you know," Mr. Joe'd told me. "We lost our family that afternoon on the interstate, any future fer it. Sure did."

I'd been shown the other bedroom upstairs, across the hall from where I was, still made-up for Little Mae, for the times she'd come and stayed with them at their house. It was all pink and frills, dolls rowed along the turned-down bedspread and piled in a chair under the window, all of it left exactly like it was the last time she'd been in there. The only thing that had touched it was dust.

This longing in them was there that first day we met, and I saw it, Ms. Mae's eyes locked on me at the kitchen table while I ate lunch, the same gaze she gave me now as I approached the front porch steps this morning, wishful as ever, that I'd perhaps never leave. Mr. Joe didn't seem put out by me, nor was he suspicious or acting strange with me around, more surprised is all, that I'd been so free with my time, "as young as I was," he'd said. "Ain't you got better things to do?"

And I surprised myself by how long I'd been there. One more night turned into a week turned into a month. It wasn't given a lot of thought, just seemed to happen naturally, a routine of waking up for breakfast and then helping Mr. Joe around a house that was way too big for just the two of them. Not only for two old timers, but it was especially true for Ms. Mae, her often needing help getting from room to room, and with lunch when it came time. I was there to help however I could. I fixed things that were broken and if I couldn't, whenever Ms. Mae went into town, I'd go along with her to get what I needed so that I could. I scraped and patched up and painted the siding, put up a fence for the chickens, after Mr. Joe thought since I was there we could get a few more. The plan was to expand in the summer, depending on what spring brought, and how long I saw myself there. "We sure can't do none of it without *you*," he said. "And why would we won't to. Two mouths to feed don't warrant all that. As it is, I can hardly keep up with what we got going."

Supper each night was the same as it ever was, no different than the first, only it *was* to me, as unaccustomed as I'd been to sitting down at the table by the clock. I minded my manners, did as I was told, like they were my own elders, hearing every story they could think to tell me, each one like they'd never told it to anyone before. And I listened to them like it was the best I'd ever heard, which wasn't hard to do; together, the Tilletts had lived so much, had more to tell than I knew I ever would. Even if I could live my life ten times over, it wouldn't compare. And even if I did I could never tell it half as good as they did their own.

chapter 21

It wasn't until a couple months later, maybe longer, that I tried making a move on Tiffany. I was already awkward around her, and I knew she could tell I liked her, but I knew she was waiting on me, maybe to make my mind up about whether I was going to do something about it. I didn't know if she liked me or not, though, and I wondered if I even stood a chance. And she wasn't going to wait forever, I thought, not a girl like her. I guess it was because she'd gotten hit on enough by guys that I thought I wouldn't be just like the rest of them. First I was going to be her friend.

Even though she had her driver's license she wasn't allowed to drive. She'd stretch her shift to be dropped off earlier, sometimes picked up later, so that we'd have extra time to hang out, take walks with no destination in mind, or maybe grab a bite to eat after work. It was innocent enough, indulging in this grand escape we'd longed for, where we could go anywhere we wanted. It was in this I felt us becoming more than just friends, more like Bonnie and Clyde. Even though we never ventured more than a half-hour's distance in either direction away from the restaurant, in our dreams there seemed endless possibilities awaiting us, should one day we decide to keep going, see how far we could get.

Looking back on it now, and seeing it then, as a teenager and through somebody else's eyes, Siler City really is a sad little town. Tired in the way an old dog keeps on going in spite of itself, how it used to be. Setbacks and all, it continued on, remained at ease, stuck in time. Business wasn't booming so much as it had gone off a long time ago. Even so, much like any town its same size, everything anybody needed was here. What else was there? And folks here had lives they were living, regardless of where they lived, just like me, like Tiffany, those we worked with and went to school with, holding out hope for it to one day be better than it was the day before. That feeling lives in everyone, I would think, even in the biggest cities.

All this talk about getting as far from this place as we could was how it started, her moving to a place neither of us had ever dreamed possible to reach, all the way to Alaska; and my hope to one day at least see another state, before deciding which one I was going to live in forever. But knowing it was unlikely, let alone impracticable, she reckoned, settling down someplace along the Pacific, maybe, might be far enough for her. I didn't think my plan was impossible, and soon she was discussing it more and more like it was her own plan, then it was ours.

It was November, cold out, and I gave her my jacket while she waited for her dad to pick her up after work one night. And it just sort of happened, right after I made sure the jacket sleeves weren't bunched but falling over her shoulders and was good for something, when I stopped myself from pulling away. She locked eyes with mine and didn't turn but stayed with me, as I leaned my face toward hers and kissed her lips. I guess because we'd started out friends, and a bit of time without knowing what we were had gone by before we kissed, laughing about it felt right at the time, and so I did. It was nerves, probably, and she did too. But then she quickly grabbed my face and pulled it back at her for another kiss, longer this time.

We held back, knowing it could go nowhere else, not tonight, not when her dad was due to show any minute. He'd warmed up to me only about two degrees and, from what I'd heard from Tiffany, there was no way he'd approve. She'd dated boys in the past, she'd said, briefly and not seriously, but more for fun, something to do, and it had always been in secret. Not even girls she was friends with at school knew about the boys she'd been with. "They'd be dead otherwise," she'd said. "Daddy says no man'll ever be good enough for me, so it damned sure ain't gonna be some boy."

Of all the boys she knew, she said she'd not met one who was like me, and that it was a compliment. "None of em talk the way you talk. About more than what's right in front of em, you know."

"Same for you, Tiff," I told her. "Different don't describe you, how you make me feel. Who cares how old I am—"

"I ain't any older, not really. I'm sixteen, you gonna like me when I'm sixty?" she said, laughing.

How easy it was to imagine. As simple a thought as that one, and an answer I could give her: "Duh. It's all I see."

She smiled. "All you see is me as an old lady?"

"No, you know what I mean."

"I'm not sure I do. Tell it to me," she sighed.

"Well, let's see. You got twenty-seven freckles on yer face—I counted—and they range from specs so tiny you can hardly see em, like robin's egg speckles, to some the size of a tick."

"Ew, *what?* I ain't got no ticks on my face."

"I know, I know. I can't think of another way to describe—that one, that one right there."

"Alright, then. What else?"

"You ain't afraid of the dark. And yer favorite color's changed twice since I've known you. Yellow, like sunflower—"

"Well, now, it was more a daisy—"

"OK, a daisy. Then, to purple, like the real faded—"

"Lavender. It's called lavender. The color I was gonna paint my room. But Penny didn't won't purple walls," she said, like she was frustrated all over again. "I tell you I almost smothered her to death?

When I was eleven. She was just a baby, though, and it was only ever a thought in my head—nothing more, promise. I cried about it, even thinking about doing it. But still, I did. I thought about doin it."

Penny was not her "real" sister. And Marla, Penny's mother, was only ten years older than Tiffany, so, how she put it, "old enough to be my other sister. It just ain't right." How she saw it, she was still only her real mother's daughter, and forever she would be, even if she never really was. Marla was not someone she would ever see in any other way than as the skank that took her daddy away from her, along with what little memory of her mom was left.

"You're lucky you still have a momma," she said, and not just saying it but reminding me again. Even knowing my mom's backstory, at least my telling of it, she seemed hellbent on changing my opinion of her, that or having me see past it to her own imaginary version she'd had of her own mother.

"*Whose* momma? *My* momma? Where is she? I ain't seeing one."

She laughed, before looking serious. "No, but listen, she wasn't always this way. And she can change. Be a real momma to you one day. You know that. And you know what she looks like."

"Yep, I do. Every which way. Sometimes I wish I didn't."

"Don't say that."

"It's true. Just cause she's somebody's momma don't make her pretty to look at."

Mom had actually met Tiffany and loved her, told me she was the real deal, that I'd be stupid not to marry her one day. She could tell, she said, just by looking at her. And Tiffany understood Mom in a way that I never could. Mom would be buzzed, sometimes picking me up at the restaurant, and she and Tiffany would sit in the car and talk, Mom slurring (the very first time they met) to my embarrassment, but Tiffany didn't care. She showed Mom the kindness and dignity that she said she deserved, the opposite of how she'd been treated—not to excuse any of how she'd treated me or anybody else, she was quick to point out—because treating her any other way was not only wrong but it was downright lazy, expected of everybody. Life wasn't like that. Things were never black and white.

"You'd miss her if she were gone. Trust me. If you'd never had her in the first place, too. I know you would. I miss my momma so much and I never met the woman."

"I know you hadn't, Tiff," I said.

"Funny, someone told me how when a daughter loses their momma in childbirth, as a woman, all grown up, she'll bear all those children that her momma never could. The ones stolen from her, they said to me. Like they'll become mine."

"Strange . . . That don't sound right."

"Yeah, it is, I know, but it's a nice idea anyway. I think it must be something someone planted into little girls' heads so they won't be discouraged from having children of their own. I was scared for a long time. Thought I was gonna die too if I ever did."

I looked at her and didn't say anything. I didn't have to ask if she wanted to be a mother, it was clear in the way she talked about herself, her future, how she saw a life outside this one. It wasn't going to be without the bond she felt she'd never had, I knew for certain.

"I'm sorry," she said, taking my hand.

"For what?"

"For everything bad that's ever happened to you," she said. "Go on and show me, then. Where's it at?"

"What do you mean?"

"Where you feel it the most. Where does it hurt? Show me."

I had no place to point to, where pain could be felt, because I wasn't in any. I touched my lower lip and she kissed it.

"Where'd you come from?" I asked her.

"Outer space," she said, holding back laugher. "They sent me to take over your planet."

After that, we still didn't go much farther than the restaurant parking lot, no more than a mile around it. And those times when we'd both be working she'd give me a note to make up for all the hours spent apart, between our last time together: a torn-out sheet of notebook paper folded into itself twenty times and wrapped in the stem of something cut from the yard. She'd hand it to me at the start of her shift, often when I'd already started mine and so I had to wait to take it apart. It was like a ritual, an exercise in perseverance like I was the karate kid. I'd take it from her and hold on to it under the pad I scribbled orders into, with eager anticipation, smell of it when I turned away from a table.

I never wrote her any notes back but she never minded. It was enough to know that I'd read what she'd written, she told me. Once, she'd been in a hurry, and *Hey* was all there was to read after I opened it, penciled in the center with all the creases patterned across the blank paper. Even that meant something to me. It helped that with it came a smile and a little wave from her when I turned around to look for her, to find her standing in a corner, watching me open it.

In school, I thought of her all throughout the day. Couples in the hall would pass by me and I'd imagine they were us. Even alone, without her, I'd walk the halls with confidence, pretending that Tiffany was right there beside me, passing notes to me in class, meeting me for lunch in the cafeteria. And just because I didn't write anything down for her to read, I'd think of things to say to her for the next time I saw her, to show that I was always talking to her, if only in my head. I was in my own little world most of freshman year, feeling myself changed by having a girlfriend to think about rather than what was happening at home. When people passed by me, I wondered, did they know someone was there even if they couldn't see her? And could they see me, beside her, at her school?

As young and stupid as we were, I was still able to identify what this was between us. With only my own parents to compare it to I knew that it wasn't something Mom had ever felt for my dad, what Tiffany had for me. And there was no doubt in my mind about whether Dad ever felt for another woman the way I did toward Tiffany. If this was what they'd experienced together, I couldn't for a second see how they could possibly manage life without the other, let go of it so easily as they had. When I tried telling myself the opposite, that it was me who got in the way of whatever it was they'd had—still, knowing it couldn't compare to Tiffany and I—making myself believe that this would've been some means to justify their split, their becoming different people from the ones they started out as, it cast doubt over everything. There was no way she and I were ever going to end up that way, I constantly reassured myself. Still, I couldn't help but read into us, the way we were, and wonder about our future, whether anything could be done now, ahead of time, to prevent something from happening that might have been destined already.

Mom was one thing, an example of how far someone could fall. Tiffany had never met my dad, nor would she, not if I could help it. Her own father was as bad an example enough, though if she didn't know how bad he could get, as bad as mine was, did it somehow prevent her from the truth.

I told her everything. About how stupid Dad had told me I was, made me out to be and believed I'd been, and that I was almost held back a grade to confirm it, how it had worked out, though, and how it was Mom, how she'd worked it out, and too, what she'd done to get hired and fired before she got the job she hated working at now. I described Lumberton, the women my dad had been with and who I met and talked to, what they'd told me and the things I'd seen there, and what the road between the two places felt like to me then. When she met Tommy I told her about Todd, Todd and my Mom, about Pam and how she and Mom had made up, like some kind of miracle performed. Everything I could think to tell her, I did. And I gave her a ring, something cheap I found at the jewelry store, where a teacher I had years ago stood smiling, recognizing me behind the glass counter when I walked in with money in my pocket. She helped me pick something out, to symbolize what it was I was giving Tiffany, a promise—however much of it I could afford to give her. It wasn't much, but enough to make her cry and then kiss me all over, to repeat what we'd already done together in the woods a few weeks back but that now felt different afterwards. With it, I told her, I would never lie to her, never hurt her feelings. I would treat her kind. And never would she feel the way I knew my dad had my mom.

"I love you Tiffany Rose."

"I love you too, Travis Wains."

chapter 22

Early Sunday morning I awoke to pots and pans, dishes clanging in the kitchen downstairs. It was so hot I just about had to peel myself from the sweaty sheet, with no A/C, not even a fan spinning above the bed. Heat's good for the body, according to Ms. Mae, keeps the blood moving in the right way. I don't know how she could be so cold natured, as insulated as she was, but I'd endured, nevertheless, throughout my first summer on the Tilletts's farm. It wasn't over yet, though, my birthday marked the beginning of the last month of it, and today we were going to celebrate.

They'd halfway set the kitchen table for breakfast already, and Ms. Mae was just about done fixing up the cake she'd baked especially for me, smoothing over the edges of icing with her fingertips, making sure it was just right.

"*Haaappy* birthday to you . . ." they started up singing together as soon as they saw my feet coming down the stairs. "Happy birthday to you . . . Happy birthday, dear Travis . . . Happy birthday to you."

Each candle, all twenty of them, she lit as I approached the cake with a big smile across my face, thinking hard on what it was I was going to wish for this year before I blew them out. And don't blow it, I thought, and of making it count, too, whatever it was going to be this time.

We sat down with the cake displayed on a stand, too early to think about eating any of it, not on an empty stomach before breakfast, so no need to cut into it. And that suited me just fine, leaving it there to look at a little while longer. It was perfect, too nice and too much work gone into it to just mess it up right away. Buttercream frosting, the color of the house, not with any coloring or from a can but as she'd mixed it with love herself, covered the cake like a cloth. She'd piped some out, too, more fancy around the base of the cake, and in a pattern alternating between yellow and blue and brown. Sprinkles didn't match but made it her own, with a blank space left on top for my name, written neatly in cursive, all for me.

"Thank you," I told her, in disbelief. "This is . . . so nice of you, really. I mean, you shouldn't've done all this."

"But I did," Ms. Mae answered me. "It's yer birthday. Course we was gonna make it special."

Mr. Joe gripped my shoulder with his wrinkled hand, gave me a newsprint-wrapped present, rigid and shaped like the harmonica he'd spit into on the front porch sometimes. So when I tore off the paper and saw it was a pocketknife, I must have looked surprised.

"From my pocket to yers, son," he said, half-smiling, unsure if it was the right thing to give me. "My name's there," he sighed, turning over the knife in my hand, running his finger over 'JT' engraved into what felt like maybe bone carved into a handle. "Oughta be fine, though. Least that way you ain't gonna forget who gave it to ya, when yer using it to cut stuff: twine it's good for, and even some small twigs out in the yard, and apples, too—I used to slice em real nice with that there. Or whatever yer wantin to do with it, if you're even wantin it."

"No, no, I love it, I do want it. But are you sure?" I asked, reading his initials, how the letters were not something he'd done himself on a whim but scrawled there by a professional. And it felt heavy in my hand, substantial, like it meant a lot to him.

"Course I am. Every man needs himself a knife like that one. And if you take good care of it, it'll last you as long as you live."

I gave him a firm handshake and a pat on his back. "I will. I'm gonna take real good care of it, Mr. Joe. Thank you for this, really. It's somethin special, ain't it? Wow." I carefully pulled out the blade, about as long as my finger, saw it scratched up in spots but not so much I couldn't see the light in the kitchen up above us shining down.

"And from me," Ms. Mae said, "next time we go to town together, I'm gettin you some new socks. You just pick out whatever pair of em you won't."

"Ah, that's so nice. But this cake you made, that's more than I'd of expected this morning, really."

"Well then, you got to see bigger, honey, cause the cake was gonna practically bake itself, even without you wonderin. So you think it up, bigger next time, hear me? And you never know, you might just surprise yourself."

"Maybe that's what he was wishin for, Mae, when he blew them candles out. Got every one of em too didn't he? Lord knows I wouldn't a been able to catch every one of mine."

"Maybe if you'd got only twenty of em like his, Joe."

"Em hm, yer right. Guess then that'd make me a young man again."

"I bet you'd like that, wouldn't ya?"

"Shoot naw," he told her, leaning forward. "No regrets, darlin. Notta one." And he pecked her on the lips.

Ms. Mae jumped, spooked by the front screened door slamming shut. "That the wind again? Or's it somebody real this time. Maybe a ghost I guess it could be, I oughta say—or maybe I ought not to. Way that's got me movin in my night gown," she said, scooting out from beside Mr. Joe, who stood back unfazed by the popping sound.

I poked my head out through the open kitchen and looked down the hallway. "Nope. Just the wind. Feels nice."

Being summer now, both the front and back doors were open to allow such a breeze to bluster clear through the house, causing curtains to twist and dust to collect in whirls around the corners of the front rooms, mail to fly off the entry table, and Ms. Mae's blood pressure to rise. The heat didn't help it, either. She'd kept her pills at arm's length since spring, not stepping far from a chair she could sit down in, up next to a table to set a glass of water and bear her arms onto.

"I just don't know how much more I got left in me, Joe," she grumbled. And they exchanged a troubled glance that had become all too common to see in their faces.

"Think ya might oughta sit this Sunday out, dear. Whataya think?"

"Maybe so. Maybe catchin my breath'll get me ready for next week. So much to get down anyway."

"What's next week?"

"We got the market comin up. You know that, Joe. Gotta get everything ready for it. Ain't even halfway done with all I gotta do."

"Let me handle some of it," I told her. "I've got two hands, and I know how to use em."

She giggled. "I know you do, honey. And I oughta use em more than I do, hadn't I? Well, suppose I should, but first, I'm gonna need somebody to help me get this pan of biscuits ready to go in the oven."

Mr. Joe rolled his eyes at her, at me. "Now, I was just fixin to ask you . . . Since when do we need all this food for breakfast, Mae. And for lunch, for dinner. War's over. You ain't feedin no army."

"I'm feedin us, though, ain't I? Besides, Joe, he's still growin."

He looked at me again, hoping I might back him up, but I wouldn't dare. I couldn't take this from her, the giving side I loved seeing for a change. As long as making food, more than plenty, was making her happy, who was I to tell her to stop doing it? I held my tongue and turned away. What I was going to do to help was hook the screened door shut, stop it from slamming.

Some Sundays I went to church with them, but mostly I felt too restless to sit and listen, through not just a sermon but uncomfortable stares I got from those who'd known the Tilletts better than I did. It seemed they'd taken me for some kind of bum and Mr. Joe and Ms.

Mae as fools for letting me board with them for little to nothing, or how I figured they probably put it, taking them for fools, too. Anyway, if they knew them so well, I wondered, then why'd none of them ever come out to the house for a visit? In all the time I'd been staying on this farm, not one person had stopped by, not even just to say hello to them.

I hooked the door tight and checked my handiwork on the screen wire, where there'd been big dents and crinkles, a rusted patch in two places, and a hole that let in mosquitoes and flies before I fixed it. Food left out on the kitchen table once attracted them, ten at the time it seemed, and the sugary lemonade on tap since May, which brought ants, too, but still. And just then, thinking about what was next, I saw a wasp outside looking to make a nest, or maybe it had already made one and was on its way back. There was more work where that came from. I knew my way around.

Turning back, each time I'd look down that long hall stretched straight through to the back of the big house, I felt lucky to be living here. Flowers colored in wavy smears out every window you walked past, and I'd come to know the names of all of them: asters everywhere, all different kinds; blazing star by the porch; mountain mint still in bloom, going in and out of the shade; coneflowers as tall as me, colored purple and red and yellow; milkweed, but mostly by the pond; and black-eyed Susans, a name that made me think of Mom.

The hall let out onto another porch, smaller than the front but big enough for a couple of wicker chairs and a matching table wedged between them. I'd catch myself deep in thought out there a lot, mostly on early mornings when I knew the hot sun couldn't find me yet. The view was as far and wide as a parking lot in Siler City, an open field of grass I'd cut every Saturday, up to the wood line that grew tall and endless, for miles and miles, how Mr. Joe had described it.

Ms. Mae was particular about the laundry so she did all of it, including mine. I, of course, put what little clothes I had away, and made my bed every morning, hearing her in the laundry room, which shared a wall with my bedroom, in there humming gospels and yelling out for Mr. Joe, only on occasion, to get in there and help her. And because her voice carried throughout the house, through walls, he always came, or I did.

I thought if I knew every square inch of this house I'd know more than the church folks did. After all, home is where the heart is, right? Getting to know them through getting to know the house maybe seemed like I was snooping. But the way I saw it, in doing so, I'd be able to know what needed my attention before they brought it to me.

In their bedroom, for instance, an old vanity table, an antique Ms. Mae was proud to label it, one of its legs had broken, had to be repaired, along with the bolt that somehow rusted to the screw and washer it was tightened with. I ended up fixing them all—plus an oil shine. "Restored it to its natural glory," she'd said, and "What else can you fix up for me?" I added extra padding to the stool she'd not sat on in years, and replaced the broken mirror that swiveled above it. With an odd job like that, I studied trinkets she'd set out, not just on her vanity table but all around the bedroom, things that told a story.

Needlepoints she'd done so long ago the colors had faded, of the same flowers planted out in the yard, hung crooked above sun-bleached greeting cards from friends, most signed and dated in the days after their daughter and Little Mae died. I held of her alternating wristwatch—the other around her wrist, waving in the air at church—made of gold-plated alloy metal, with a face the size of a nickel. My grandma never cared about telling time, and she never wore rusted hair clips crusted in rhinestone like Ms. Mae did either. In a basket she kept all of them, ones I'd not seen her wear once.

Their family history spanned from sepia tintypes mounted behind ovals in propped-up, gilded frames to blurred black-and-whites showing that even the camera couldn't capture with sharpness how happy they'd been trying to pose in front of it. It was the 40s and 50s then, next to a lone color print of a little girl on picture day. She was smiling with pigtails and looking away from the lens, probably to her mother, the Tilletts's daughter, the happiest and proudest mother there that day, how Mr. Joe would mention her smile to me again and again, almost like I didn't hear him the first time, or the second. On its frame she'd Scotch-taped a tiny pink flower, her pan-greased fingerprint still stuck to the backside of the tape. I wondered when she'd put it there, if it had been before or after the last supper she'd made for the girl, an occasion that meant so much more to them than any other. Knowing the set-up likely hadn't changed a bit, I could see them down there in the kitchen, Mr. Joe holding her hand while Ms. Mae ate her own cooking without saying a word after they found out about the accident, if she could even eat.

A little closet shut in just beside the vanity, where inside, along with mostly her dresses and skirts I'd never seen her wear, Mr. Joe's oversized suit jackets and matching ironed pants hung. He'd aged thin, making them ill-fitting now, although he continued wearing them to church, laid out for him on their bed by Ms. Mae, like every other decision he made, forgetful as he was of even something as simple as which shoe went with which. Which made me wonder about how Ms. Mae would make sure she said his name almost every time she spoke to him, Joe, and was she just saying it or was she telling it to him?

The room beside the one I was in, across the hall from Little Mae's, stayed empty even though it had been set up for somebody to sleep in the same as mine, to the point, without a lot of attention given to these four walls or any other kind of decoration left behind. There was one thing I noticed, however, while patching the plaster ceiling once, after a leak in the attic I'd fixed had done a bit of damage, something *had* been kept in there. Up and down the door jamb, seen only when the door was open, lines were drawn in pencil and pen, colored markers, even carved sometimes. Like a six-foot-eight-inch tall ruler, the wood charted the growth of what looked like several different people over many years, each one of them inching taller from the measurement taken the year before, until they just stopped. None of them had grown taller than I was, not in this house. The marks must have been put here on their birthdays, I figured, as time capsules kept on display instead of being buried with the rest, or eventually painted over after they'd gotten too old to keep doing it. Each year of someone's life was here, measured from the shortest to tallest—or was it the longest? Who were they? What happened to them?

At the end of the day, after eating one more slice of my birthday cake, I guess it was because I'd never had lines like those made of me on any door in any house I'd lived in, I stood there in that same spot as they had, with my back straight and head held high above the past, and left my mark. I couldn't know if it'd mean something one day, next year even, or whether it would be painted over in time. But at least for the time being I knew where I'd been, that this day meant something, and it was made special.

chapter 23

Mom said she'd been saving up some extra cash for a while, since before I'd turned fifteen. The next day I was turning sixteen so I knew exactly what she was saving for. Without even seeing the car, I hugged her, hard. From the front seat, what I imagined as a kind of chestnut-colored leather, I looked back at the road I was leaving behind in the rearview mirror and the smile this brought across my face, uncertain as I was that it even warranted a smile yet, let alone that the money would be spent on anything for me at all.

"Damn, you just can't be surprised, can ya?"

"So can I drive it? Where is it?"

"No, no, Trav. Gonna have to wait til it's yer birthday. And the car ain't even here, hon. But, yeah, I'm pickin it up after I get outta work tomorrow. *Then* you can drive it."

"Really! Yer really gettin me a car, Momma?"

"See, what'd I tell you? It whatn't like I hadn't been planning on it all along."

"Can I pick up Tommy in it? Take him for a ride?"

"I don't see why not? You drive as good as any man I know."

I hugged her again.

"Now, listen to me, don't get too excited, it's nothing fancy."

"Can it do all the things that other cars can?"

She laughed, coughed out her puff of cigarette smoke. "Yeah, Trav, course it can. It's got a gas pedal and a steering wheel . . . Decent enough engine under the hood. It's an old Cavalier. Those things run forever."

So then leather seats were off my list of expectations, I thought, though what was I thinking? I wasn't expecting a car at all, so what difference did the seats make?

"And, you know, there's a bit of rust here and there, round the back paneling, you'll see, some above the tires. Shouldn't be too much to fix that up, though. I figured you could put some of yer own money into it. Make it yours. Something yer proud of."

Alright, so then it's radio was probably busted, and some quarks with the way it handled the road, minor issues left unresolved, like maybe I should expect a back window that couldn't decide whether it wanted to stay up or down—same for the lock on the driver's side door, looking past the handle for it that didn't open or shut the way it was supposed to.

"What color is it?" I asked her, still excited.

"It's a kind of whiteish, maybe almost beigey-lookin color," she said, and her voice turned on me. "It's what I could afford, Trav."

"No, Momma, I'm so excited about it. Thank you! You really got me a car!"

She could see how happy I was and balanced her cigarette down into an ashtray, pulled us closer together by the same hand she'd been smoking with. And my head was pressed up next to her checkered shirt, so close to my face it was blurry when I looked at her. It smelled of Pall Malls and her favorite perfume, same as she'd worn since the day I was born.

"I'm so proud of you, you know that?" she said, the sound of her voice garbled.

"I know, Momma," I told her.

"Yer gonna be sixteen," she said, reaching for her drink on the table in front of us. "Sixteen years . . ." And she picked the cup up over me and took a swig of it, when I could smell it, and hear the melting ice shift at the bottom of the glass. A drop of condensation landed on the crown of my head. "That's a long time, ain't it?"

"Yep," I sighed.

"My baby boy, almost a grown man. Practically are already. And, listen, I know that I ain't been the best mother, and I ain't been much of a replacement for your daddy, neither, but I try. I won't you to know that. And to give you something to show you, how much I love you."

"You tell me enough."

"And I ain't never gonna stop. I mean it, too, Trav. Really, I do, but I don't show it. Things ain't perfect, I know—all of this. Don't always turn out how we hope it's gonna," she said, picking up her cigarette, waving her hand over the room. "We get by, though, don't we? It's not much. Though we are *not* poor. Never let anybody tell you otherwise. You and me, we got love. That's right. Money can't buy it. You love me, right? You do, doncha?"

I nodded my head, freed myself from her side, and smiled.

"Despite all of that, and this . . . Me, I'm still yer momma . . ." With a cigarette stuck to her lip, both her hands were gliding when she spoke to me, in her sweet spot, she called it, I could tell she was getting there. She'd talk this way whenever she was still warm and fuzzy, before it turned to fire. Before she'd just soon burn it all down to the ground.

"Yes, I know, Momma. I love you, too."

Even though I was well aware of this slow-burning sentiment of hers, how she must be feeling, the fact remained that she'd just downed her third drink I think it was—a stiff one at that. Next she'd get up from the table to pour herself another, followed by another, and her footing would change, her stance behind the counter when she made them, each time the same as the last, before it didn't matter how she was mixing and pouring her poison.

Just for the moment, in her hold, the feeling of her arm wrapped tightly around my side was enough for me. It was possibly her limit, too, one she'd not had for drinking but did for showing her affection. Even so, knowing she meant it in that moment, I was thinking about how tomorrow, in addition to the car, she would be gifting me with an opportunity to leave even sooner than I'd anticipated. Then, with the dirty-colored Cavalier, and what little money I had saved up to buy a car myself that I could put towards something I hadn't even thought to think about yet, I'd get the hell out of dodge. Maybe it wasn't going to be enough to get me far, but gas money alone could go a long way. Tiffany and I talked of putting whatever we'd each set aside together, to maybe move in with each other if we ever got the chance. Just a few months spent renting a place to live in and our whole outlook on life could've changed.

And the extra cash Mom said she'd been saving, I wondered about, how she'd spend more than what little she said she was making at her job and so it most likely wasn't coming from it. Had she actually stashed away some of the money from those checks Dad said he put in the mail and got so angry with her for spending on things she shouldn't have been? I doubted it. He was the last person she'd give credit for buying me the car. I already hated the thing, even without this further proof as to why I should have.

Mom and I sat at the table for a moment without saying any more about it. She finished smoking the last of her cigarette, running her other hand through my hair like it needed cutting, until it was a butt in the ashtray and time to get up and fix herself another drink. I watched her walk, and the walls to see if they were guiding her outstretched arm yet. If only she knew when to stop, I told myself, wishing I had the courage to tell her. An alcoholic, that's what she was, of course. She knew it long before I did, what word to call it, how it should be handled, and still, she'd kept me guessing all that time.

I looked away from the idea, the feeling that there was nothing she needed me for, not really, and tried smiling about the car I was getting, the thought that a future wasn't so far away all of a sudden. And

"*What?*"

"Yeah, she's at the damned hospital. Been there for I don't even know how long. Can you believe it? That was the sheriff. Probably drunk as a skunk, maybe worse, maybe doing something else besides just drinking, I dunno. I don't know how else she coulda done it. Now I guess I gotta figure out how to get over there . . ."

Right as I said that, the phone rang again and it was Tiffany. I told her what had happened.

"Trav—I'm so sorry. But listen, I'm gonna get Tracy to take me in her car with her over to yer house—she's gettin off in ten minutes—and then she'll take to you the hospital to see yer momma—all of us."

"Are you sure?"

"Yeah I'm sure. Just hold tight, alright?"

"Alright, then," I told her.

Pacing in and out of the kitchen after we hung up, I frantically searched for something else to think about. What, I didn't have a clue, anything I could think of to distract from the image of Mom in my head: drunk in the front seat of this car I'd never seen but saw differently now, wrecked rather than joyriding in on my birthday. I saw her trapped in what was left of it, mangled up, whiteish, beigey-colored metal, rusted and defective, her being freed from it by the jaws of life.

"What'd she do . . . What'd you do, Momma?" I said aloud, and I took hold of my chest, real dramatic, caught up in the moment.

"She made it out alright, thank God. Right, Trav?" Tommy said, sitting me down in the same spot I'd been sitting the night before, right beside her. "Just relax."

I nodded my head then shook it. "You don't get it, Tommy."

"It's gonna be alright. Probly waitin for you to come down there, and after makin sure she's good to go, bring her home. He would've told you so otherwise, on the phone, wouldn't he've? Tiffany's on her way, so let's chill out, alright, and see what's what when we get there."

And just that quick, she was outside, pulling up the driveway in Tracy's car. Usually cool under pressure, even Tracy looked stressed out. I thanked her for coming, for doing all this, going out of her way.

"No big deal," she said, blowing cigarette smoke. "I ain't busy."

Tiffany put her arms around my shoulders and made sure I knew everything was going to be okay. That based on what I'd told her, it already was. She didn't get it either. Whenever Mom messed up, consequences soon followed, not only for her but for the both of us.

When we got to the hospital and rushed inside, I immediately spotted the sheriff's uniform, heard his voice, same as the one speaking to me so matter-of-factly over the telephone. He elbowed the rib of the cop standing beside him sipping coffee from a styrofoam cup, both of them laughing about something. I'd expected he might have looked tired by now, like he'd had plans of his own tonight, but when I said hello, he looked wired, before composing himself to lead me and my high hopes to where my mom was. Along the way he began to fill me in on what exactly had happened, explaining how he'd had to handcuff her to the bed because of it and so not to be surprised when I saw them jangling from her wrist.

"She's fine," he told me, patting me on the back. "Was awake like I said, least when I called ya. They mighta given her somethin, though."

I thanked him when I caught sight of her, out cold and slouched in the bed, and he left me alone with her. I wasn't all by myself, though, seeing a man I didn't know with his weight leaned against the wall just outside the doorway she'd been taken through. Not quite out of earshot, I felt his eyes on me, nervous, unable to wake Mom up so I could speak to her more about what was really going on, despite already hearing the truth.

Maybe in his mid-forties, the man reeked of sweat and cigarettes, his greasy hair swept under a ball cap that had stained from all the times he'd worn it that way. The same went for his short-sleeved button down, blotched with sweat under each arm and yellowed around the collar.

"Hey, hey. Yer her boy, right? One she was gettin him to call?" he asked me, shifting his weight around and then walking into the room without asking. "Sorry bout what happened with yer momma."

"Okay. *Who* are you?"

"This here's the owner of the car, son," the sheriff said, stepping back in with a fresh cup of coffee for the man.

"Oh, alright, so, then . . ." I said, confused, dumbfounded by the whole situation.

Tiffany walked into the room with Tommy, who was acting like he'd known what was up, knowing less than I did, of course, but when the officer sat me down to listen to what I needed to hear, so did he. And Tiffany stayed, standing there behind me, unfolding her arms and wrapping them around my neck as the story continued.

Mom had actually driven away in this man's car without fully paying for it, so the sheriff had been told and so was telling me, along with the man, slurring with glassy eyes, interrupting the sheriff at every turn with more than enough detail, to prove he was telling the truth. Even his jeans were greasy, at both knees, and his filthy boots had likely been worn through every season of his whole life, left on this way without ever taking them off.

"What she did was she just took off in it," the man sighed.

"I know, I know," the sheriff said. "Now, hey, Lonny, won't you go on and have a smoke out front? How bout it? I'm gonna finish up in here with Travis. I took your statement so we're good to go, alright?"

I kept listening but looked over at Mom, her bruised hand—her smoking hand—cuffed to the railing of the bed just as the sheriff had described. She must've been a nightmare before she went to sleep, I thought. Her nose was swollen, broken probably, and half-hidden by white tape. Bruising spread over both sides of her cheeks. They'd stitched her up already in places that needed to be, and made her peaceful, had her on a drip of something, whatever was in the sacks of fluid strung up over her shoulder. Monitors blinked and beeped her vitals. Tubes strung in and out of her, one in her free wrist intersecting another plugged to her nostrils and laying over another disappearing underneath a blanket splayed over her body. She didn't look like my mom at all, but had become some kind of alien being, captured from the cratered dirt outside her fallen spaceship, now struggling to stay alive. ET is what she was, and I was like the kid who'd been looking after her in secret for so long. It had finally caught up with her, with both of us. And strangely, I felt her only from afar, like it might hurt me too if I were to touch her.

"Ah, man, she does look pretty beat up, don't she," Tommy said.

"You think?" Tiffany answered.

"She's very lucky," a nurse said to us, interrupting the sheriff. "Came in with a concussion. Due to the state she's in, we'd have had to hold her overnight anyway, honey. She was gonna return home til we found out about what had happened—I guess what Sheriff Johnson's made his mission to see to."

"Hey, I'm not the one who—"

The nurse glared at him, and he stopped talking. "I guess it's whatever terms the police department may or may not have is what's gonna send her back home," she continued.

"*Terms?* What do you mean?" I asked.

The nurse stepped aside, finished with what she'd been tampering with around Mom, and let the sheriff finish.

"Son, your mom has stolen a motor vehicle, driven it recklessly, under the influence. Crashed it."

"She stole a car?!" Tommy asked.

"Yes, she sure did," the sheriff told him.

The owner of the car kept himself in there with us, his stink, still smelling up the room, not leaving us alone. He was never going to go away, I thought, nor was a mess this big.

"I don't think she did, *steal* it," I said. "Now, can't she just pay the guy the rest of his money so we can move on," I asked the sheriff.

"Well, then . . . Hm . . . I dunno. We can't not do something bout her reckless driving, now, but I know yer momma, boy, and I don't see why it can't clear itself up like that—if the man she was gonna buy it from has some of the money and just not all of it."

And the man was tensing up again, ears burning, about to butt in.

"Lonny, you hear that?"

"What's that?" he said.

"How much did you say she was short?" I asked him.

"Bout two-hundred bucks, that's right. And listen, your momma's gonna be just fine, and that much'll settle things up right. Met me up at TJ's for a drink fore she took off. Was gonna give her the car for the cash and we got to drinkin some more, and as things go," he sighed, shrugging at the sheriff. "But yep, just up and snatches the keys right from me, like she won em in a game, makes a run for it. In bad shape cause of it. Maybe she didn't half know *what* she was doin. I shouldn't've made matters worse than they was. Whataya think, now, sheriff? The money's paid up, it ain't like no kind of grand theft auto or nothin."

The sheriff looked at me with his eyebrows raised, shrugged his shoulders.

"No, I get it, I do. I've got some I can pay you. So then you'll go away," I asked him, and the sheriff for confirmation, "and it won't be her stealing his car, if he gets his two-hundred bucks?"

"If I got somethin to say about it, sure," the man said. "Lynn's up at TJ's a lot. I seen her there. Yeah, we shoot the shit from time to time. That car, though, was like it was gonna be the gift of a lifetime to ya. Ah shoot, kid, I'm sorry."

"Where's the car now?"

"Oh, the car's totaled," the sheriff said. "Yessir."

"Two-hundred more than she gave you already—*for a totaled car?*"

"Yer momma and me was supposed to square up on the Cavalier. We had a deal. And I delivered on it, but—"

"Alright, alright," I told the man. And I was seeing what little money I'd put away in a tackle box that had belonged to my grand-dad. Before saving cash in it, the latch hadn't been opened since I was twelve, so I never thought there'd be any concern over its safekeeping.

I told the man I'd pay him his money, that I was good for it. So long as he let this whole thing slide, as a simple misunderstanding. He agreed, we shook hands, and then he finally left.

"I can't believe this," I said. "Well, actually, I can. Obviously something like this was gonna happen."

"You know it ain't your fault, right?" Tiffany said.

"I'm not so sure about that."

"Naw, it ain't, and neither is she. But it's all gonna work out, Trav. Happy Birthday," she mumbled.

"Wait, what time is it?" I asked her.

"Shit," she said, "it's almost 10:30! Daddy's gonna kill me."

I walked her outside where she found Tracy still sitting in her car.

I came back and sat down next to Tommy in the waiting room, where we spent the rest of the night talking about what had happened, how crazy it was, before he started dozing off, when I looked up at the clock on the wall and saw that it was now well after midnight, no longer my birthday.

chapter 24

A few months after Ms. Mae baked me a cake, she was out on the front porch swing, like any normal afternoon, when suddenly she died. If ever someone's heart stopped beating, simply gave up, I used to think it would happen with a great big fuss, a fight before it was all over with. The person would not go quiet or gently, but sound an alarm. Maybe one day—because I knew the day was coming—she was going to collapse with a pitcher in her hand, glass shattering all around, screaming out for help from a puddle of tea. That or she'd feel it in her chest, something odd, her pills out of reach or otherwise proving worthless in that moment, and then she'd cry out for Mr. Joe, tell him it was time.

She'd made us pimento cheese sandwiches, plated them up with some potato chips and pickles, and we ate outside on this unusually warm day. Mr. Joe and I'd gone back inside the house to look at something he'd wanted to show me, that I might be able to figure out how to fix. Time must've slipped right through the cracks, because we looked at each other, like we both knew something was off, missing, not just her voice but the sound of her footsteps throughout the house, shuffling and sliding, sometimes kicking their way around. No, the house was dead silent, but for the birds outside the front door wide open how we'd left it.

Out on the porch, the swing had long stopped swaying, and her eyes were closed, her neck bent just enough that her head was resting onto her shoulder. For someone who'd never seen a dead body before, I thought then, as morbid as it might've been, hers wasn't a bad one to start with, seeing as how she didn't look dead at all, but like she'd fallen asleep. The only way to tell at first was by the way her body wasn't slowly rising and falling, trembling when she breathed. She was so still, so peaceful, I thought it couldn't have happened any other way, not for someone as kind as this old woman.

I stood there, glued to the threshold, watching Mr. Joe lean and then cry over her body. He'd taught me everything that I needed to know about taking care of the farm, in order for my weekly routine to get started right away every Monday morning without assistance, after he showed me what not do before I ever did it, what to do right if I'd done it wrong. I looked back over the year I'd spent under his wing, back to that first week when he knew that I wasn't as experienced as I claimed to be, unable to even articulate how I got here, let alone where I'd come from. But my efforts had proved solid and reliable, so he'd told me, and he was easygoing enough that it seemed to come as natural to me as it did him. But his crying, this was the first I'd seen him do it, and I watched him like it was another lesson. He didn't know it, of course, but in his own grief and his restraint, he taught me how to handle it. Never to will the tears, when to hold them back, and when to let them come as they wanted to, until they were through.

By late that evening, his eyes puffed up and nearly shut, with no appetite to speak of, he was sitting down at the kitchen table and laying out her funeral, and what must've been future plans for his own. With him occupied, the old house at rest and making no sound, I crept through the pulled screened door to see if by some spooky or supernatural means Ms. Mae was still out there swaying in her porch swing. But no, not even the wind had moved it since they'd come and taken her away.

The leaves were changing, I noticed, the day of the funeral. I wore the cleanest pants I had and a button-down with paint speckle on one sleeve, the only one that I had. Mr. Joe lent me a blazer to cover it, to look at least halfway decent, he said. "Presentable enough!" I wasn't sure what the turnout would be like for the Tilletts, expecting church family and no other, none that I knew. Expect for maybe Ronnie, if he didn't have another passenger he was taking somewhere, more important than the one going to Heaven.

Mr. Joe and I ended up being the only real family in attendance, and although I wasn't, I sat up front right next to him like I was, in a row just for us. The funeral parlor could fit a lot more, so the other folks sitting around, if I tried to count on my fingers, would truly only amount to a handful: The parlor's owner, *his* son, a few women from the church who came despite the rain they complained about having to get out in; if the helpers who'd brought the casket inside and sat sipping free coffee in the back didn't count. So yeah, the turnout was sad, especially for such a happy woman. And maybe it *had* been the weather, I wondered, windshield wipers slapping there and back the way they did. It's a wonder we made it, with Mr. Joe's cough that'd persisted, and a chance of isolated thunderstorms. I imagined that even though it was her time, according to Mr. Joe and the church ladies, it wasn't really. Right on time was never not too soon. But she was with Jesus, and there was no questioning him. While she'd deserved better, to pass during a window of opportunity for more to show up, for the weather to get in line, on a day when formality could have extended into the service, in service to her and that of her maker, I imagined she was looking down and thankful it hadn't been a whole hoopla. No frills. Kept simple, humble even. Naked as she came, she'd say. She hated no one but strongly disliked any gossip. There would be none of that, not today. No mention of it again, I wouldn't think, not after they put her in the ground.

Mr. Joe and I stood shoulder to shoulder and thanked anyone who came for coming, invited them over for what was actually leftovers from the last dinner she'd made, along with the dishes the church ladies brought for he and I, opened up and served on the kitchen table. By then, however, the rain had gotten worse, clouds turned dark, day into night, so we shut the front door and locked it. Never did anybody knock on it, or ring the doorbell, which I'd just got to working again the week before she died.

When the clouds finally parted it was late and so it didn't matter. Mr. Joe scooched himself up to the edge of the front porch in his favorite rocking chair, same as I'd first met him. He was worn out, I could tell, and a bit out of sorts from the way I knew him now, with a rolled-up cigarette in between two shriveled fingers, nursing a glass of something that burned my nose when I picked it up off the porch floorboard and sniffed it. Never had I seen him smoke or drink, more disdain for it I'd heard from him.

"Hey, how bout it . . . Pull up a chair," he said to me, long-winded. "Go on and fix yerself one too, then. Stay a while. If ever there was a night for it."

I didn't want any but after slinging out the last bit of milk I had left I pored myself a glassful of whatever it was, to give him a partner in crime just this once. I coughed and couldn't hardly stop when I took a swig. "What is this?" I sputtered.

He chuckled. "Son, that there'll grow hair on yer chest. Also good for cleaning up just about anything under the sun."

It tasted exactly as he'd described it, like it wasn't meant to be tasted but used to strip furniture or set fire to something. Even so, it seemed to fit the mood he was in.

I slid a chair up beside his and sat down in it. "I'm so sorry bout Mae, I don't—"

"What's there to be sorry for, son? I swear, ain't nobody I've ever known said they're sorry more than you do . . . cept for maybe Brenda Lee, way back in the day, and I never knew her, course I didn't, but she sang a song about it, bein sorry, one I'm sure you ain't heard before. But thank you all the same. Really. And I'll tell ya something, too, maybe you are feelin sorry bout it, cause Mae, she whadn't just mine to lose but the both of ours," he said. "She was everybody's!"

"That's right," I told him.

Raising the spit-swallow of drink he had left, he said loudly, "Here's to her, to me, *and* to you. To any person still standing on this earth who knew Mae and now has to keep on going without her." And he clanked his cup with mine, emptied it.

"Yes," I said, still coming up for air, against the burning in the back of my throat like nothing I'd ever experienced.

"*Yessiree*," he smiled, the cracks of his lips wet and his chin shiny.

"How do you drink this stuff? *Whew!*" I huffed.

"It ain't for the faint-hearted fella, son, that's for sure. We've only got this smidgen left here anyway. I didn't even know we did, neither." He held up the jar, looking through the glass with his sideways stare. It glowed under the porch light above us. "Say, tell me somethin, what's really been keepin you here for as long as you have?"

"What do you mean?"

He smirked through the glass jar, settling it back down on the porch, his crossed expression I hoped wasn't an indicator for the words that would continue to flow out from him. "Son, you must want some kinda life other than this one, or mine I should say. I'm so old I hardly know, from then to now, the year I was born—I know it was after the first world war cause my momma use to tell me how she was out there in the fields pregnant with the rest of em, pickin up the slack for a whole nation, since everybody'd done gone off to fight the Germans. She whatn't a smoker, neither, but since my daddy'd been brought up doin it, gettin a little piece of land here and there, fore it got so big they was really gettin by, she and my aunt, even my little brother—not tall enough to reach the top step over yonder—he was out there with em, too."

"You mean, the tobacco?"

"Yep, been doin the job since I was big enough to walk—not as much then as I got to doin as I got older of course, which was a whole lot more than I do now, hadn't done in years, not since it pretty much dried up. I was in diapers . . . pickin worms. Got pictures round here somewhere. Only reason I remember. It was hard work but worth it when it was worth somethin. Round this time actually, the only break from being out there doin somethin. Even in November, it's about planning the next year. Old habits die hard, I guess."

"Wow, so what happened to it all?" I asked him.

He snapped his fingers. "Just like that, it seemed. Gone."

I gazed out into the night, beyond the front porch steps through the trees that still screened us from the road, the beginning or the end of the gravel driveway, whichever way you looked at it, grayed in a sliver of moonlight before it vanished into the thicket.

"But you like it, doncha? I can see in all the time since you been out here that you've sorta come into yer own. I could be making it up in my head, God knows, I just don't think you'd be here if you didn't wanna be. Mighty capable you are, son, really. Could be doin anything else. I gotta tell you that. Mae always tellin me, too, about how much of a pleasure it's been to have you here with us."

"Oh, well, yeah. I do, and thank you, sir, for sayin. I should be thanking you, for lettin me."

"It ain't like you been here for nothin, now, son. I've said it before and I'll keep on sayin it. Earning more than yer way is what. I'll say this, too, been less a tenant and more the son we didn't get to have—didn't get to see grow up, I guess is better said. You don't make it hard to wanna have you around. Used to be folks coming and going, though they hadn't for some time, but not you. It's a lot of land to look after, too. Some folks don't know what to do with it all, how to see to so many acres. And anybody comin for it."

I took a shallow sip of my drink and smiled, feeling good to hear him say that, and mean it, too. He wasn't just saying it because he was feeling what I was feeling, the numbing sensation come over my stomach, up to the tips of my fingers. Time was a funny thing out here on this farm, when four seasons meant so much more than they did elsewhere, and with someone who appreciated it as much as I did. It made me forgetful of why I'd come here, neglecting any plans for a future I might otherwise have had if I'd up and left empty-handed. This, here, could be my future, I thought.

"Tell me the truth, then," Mr. Joe said. "Had you never done nothin on a farm before? Really? Not a day in your darned life . . ."

"Well, no, I hadn't. I meant what I'd said. On the telephone."

"What was that, then? Remind me, now."

"That I was a quick learner."

He chuckled. "Sure are. More than that, though, you brought life to this place. It's funny, saying something like that with Big Mae dying, but it's true. You know somethin, I reckon she might notta lived to Easter Sunday if it whatn't for you showin up when ya did."

"And it seemed like she was getting better," I said, slumping in the chair, catching a blurry glimpse of him in the corner of my eye, wondering where he was going with it, if it was to bed soon or staying put, and for how much longer.

"So, then, tell me somethin else, why was it you come over here in the first place? I don't remember why it was you said you did."

"Well, honest, I came looking for something, was trying to find it. I don't think I really knew what, though. It hasn't been an easy road, I have to tell ya."

"Mm hm, I hear you, I mean . . . Well, now, what was it, then, what were you doin before?" He sat up straight in his chair and looked at me. "Here, you want me to go in and see if I can't find something for ya," he said, taking my empty glass.

"No, no. That's alright, really. I don't want anything else. I've seen what that stuff can do to a person."

"Oh, Lordy, and I've been shovin the bottle at ya like it whatn't nothin to it."

"That's alright."

"I couldn't a known, now could I? You ain't told me much about yer growing up. Yer parents? And I think you said you ain't got brothers, sisters . . ."

"That's right, I don't. And maybe I'm a bit of a loner or somethin. Somebody said something once about me being a highwayman, but back when I was a teenager, and—"

"Oh—I don't think they knew what they was talkin about when they said that. Maybe messin with ya's all."

"My momma's had issues all her life. Drinking too much, and I got into it with her quite a bit back home, mostly cause of it. I dunno, I guess we hope somebody we love'll see it for themselves, wanna make a change. Even more when we ask them to. If they don't then it hurts worse that way, maybe. Yeah, but my grandma, and my granddad, both of em died, I told ya, or maybe Ms. Mae it was."

"Ah, right, son. That's not what we want when we're young like you, is it? But you sure got a good head on your shoulders. Musta come from somebody. Most of em yer age round here are up to no good. Yep. And what about yer daddy?"

"Oh," I sighed. "He's out of the picture. Was hardly ever in it. Mostly me and my momma. Only made more of a mess to have to clean up."

"Well, then, it sure seems to've worked out alright. A brother of mine got caught up in all sorts of the bad stuff, Ronnie's daddy—you met Ronnie. Yeah. Drinking, too. I myself mighta once had a thirst for it but, well, not no more. Don't judge me for what I done tonight. What I say. Just like things left unsaid, so there are those we bury, hoping they won't get found. Not even by our own diggin hands sometimes."

I'd lit myself a cigarette as he was talking and just listened to the space between his words, and the quiet that fell over them afterward. It was a strange semblance to the hidden and unspoken, his way with words, how he must've had so many of his own, some he might just soon take with him to his grave.

"Could I have one of those?" he asked me.

"Sure," I said, lighting up the cigarette pressed into the wrinkled edges of his shriveled lips. "I won't tell nobody."

"I only stopped buyin em a decade ago," he said, smirking, slowly blowing smoke up into the dim light cast over our heads. "Now, then . . . carry on with your story," he told me slowly, leaning back in his chair. "I'm afraid if I sit here long enough, stewing, I'll start tellin you things I shouldn't be. What you might think less of me for."

"I doubt that," I told him, happy it was too dark to read the unclear expression on my face, thinking how right I was. "And well," I started up again, "that's pretty much it. But I left high school. Ended up in this rat's nest of an apartment with my girlfriend," I said to him, which was a lie but felt like the truth the way Tiffany and I had talked about doing it so much. "Her daddy wasn't as bad as mine, but only because she was a girl I think is why. We both worked at the same place for a while, before, well, I moved on somewhere else," I said, not saying Raleigh, not saying why, or how I left. "Those were some rough nights spent in that apartment—more like a room with a busted-up bathroom. It was the best we could do."

It was easier to talk about it than I imagined it would be, and so I told him more about what had happened with me and Mom, even some of things that had never happened before but had gone on in my head, because I'd never had someone to talk to about it, and about everything else, except all the things I couldn't tell him.

"I figure I learned young how to take care of myself, and so it made sense to go out on my own," I said, leaving it at that.

I looked over at him, after saying so much, and assumed he'd gotten tired of hearing me talk, or that he must have been so buzzed he could listen to anything and he was processing it. But the old man had drifted off with my rambling on about myself. It didn't seem it was interesting enough to keep him awake, not like him whenever telling his side of the story. And how long had he been, I wondered, long enough? He wasn't snoring, not yet. Was I talking to myself? Had I said too much, something I shouldn't have?

"*Mr. Joe,*" I whispered, waiting for him to return. His cigarette had put itself out without him taking another drag from it after that first time. His eyes, once I stood up and leaned closer to him to look, were shut and circled purple, still puffy. I gently removed the cigarette from between his slack fingers and tossed it into my empty glass. I wondered if I should wake him up or if he'd be okay out here alone on the porch, in this state, at his age. Of course not, I knew better, but he did look so peaceful, as peaceful as his wife had been. And he was breathing, I made sure, just sleeping like a baby.

The silence lasted for several more minutes. I allowed it, for me to finish my cigarette, wrap up my own thoughts about everything that had happened. I could only hear moths thumping up against the light bulb above me. And nowhere out there was another light on. Had there been, it'd shine like a beacon, I thought.

Down the porch steps I tiptoed in my shoes, careful not to disturb the old man. Soon I'd press on him and then take him by the arms, carry him back into the house. He'd tell me goodnight, maybe not remember much of the night come morning. But first I'd stand here, alone, breathe in the cool air and think of what it might be like to be him, to have made it to his age and propped up in a favorite chair on a porch that had long outlasted those who built it. I thought of generations come and gone from this land, the blood, sweat, and tears, the secrets, not only theirs and the ones that came before them, but his own he'd alluded to, altogether scattered across these parts and kept out of sight if not forgotten. And so where was I in all of it? Where was mine? I wondered. Was it far from here? Had it been so deeply embedded that I didn't need to find it, or was it that I didn't even know it had been here with me the whole time?

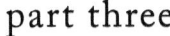

part three

chapter 25

Todd's green truck became Tommy's green truck. *Sellers Fix-its* was painted over in a color that didn't quite match, with a dull finish that made the blotchy squares stand out even more over each of the truck's shiny doors. Failed attempts at covering something up is what it looked like, and proof it had once belonged to someone else. He had no problems driving it, though, having just gotten his license and considered the old truck a gift that he'd have never been given otherwise, since his dad started driving a brand spanking new Ford F250 XLT 4x4.

With the truck came the idea to one day start his own business, something having to do with lawn care, when he'd hide the evidence again with: *Tommy's Tree & Garden*, maybe. But then all of that got put on hold, everything did, when in November, we were out riding on a Tuesday after school, sunny but too cold to have the windows rolled down. The A/C was shot to hell, though, so our breath kept fogging them up, that is until we picked up Tiffany and she cracked them just a hair, enough that the glass cleared but also to let in a whistle of freezing air. Wedged between us, she didn't have to feel it, happy and humming along to the perfectly-tuned radio that somehow got more stations than it used to. She'd had her last blowout with her daddy that summer and at eighteen was living with Tracy from work. I was now seventeen, still, and envious, of Tommy's truck, too. And it must have been this newfound confidence he had that got him to talking more about what we ought to do next.

"We're what, fifteen-twenty minutes outside of town?" Tommy asked. He squinted out through the windshield at the road, looking at the center line like it might be leading somewhere.

"Yep. Something like that," I replied, unsure if he was even trying to listen to me or couldn't over the radio Tiffany had turned way up.

"Okay, now, hear me out, alright: What if—even if it's just to do it, for real this time—we didn't go back. Not tonight, not ever. But just kept on drivin. I mean, I got almost a full tank," he said, lowering his eye to the gauge lit up. "What if, say we just kept on, all the way down 421?"

"A what if? That's what it is, Tommy. What it'll have to be, you know that. Let's don't and say we did," I said to him, eyeing the gauge myself. "And you ain't got but a half a tank. Don't lie."

Tiffany laughed. "Well I say why not—if I'm the one yer askin." She dialed the radio down like she heard in Tommy's voice something serious I hadn't. "Where's it gonna put us at anyway? Would it take us that far, I mean?"

"Yeah, course it would," I told her. "Even if we just went on for a while, that'd be all the way . . . down to the beach, I guess."

"Why don't we then?"

"Well, it don't make any sense, for starters," I said. "We'd just end up runnin outta gas."

"Well," Tommy said, looking to Tiffany between us to back him up on this, "then we'd just get some more. Fill it on up once we run out. Come on, why not? Give me a good reason why we shouldn't just take off. And why the hell should we ever go back."

"*What?* Come on, what are you saying?" I asked him. I knew what language he was speaking; it was something I'd have said not that long ago, I'd just kept my mouth shut for the time being, tried toughing it out until tomorrow. But, really, I'd not stopped wondering whether it was ever going to come. I'd have given anything to do just what he was wanting to do when I was him, when I'd just turned sixteen, if only . . . to leave, and like he said, never go back.

"I don't know, Trav," Tiffany said, squeezing my arm. "Maybe we don't think too much about it? Maybe we just see what happens? See where the road takes us?"

"Why would we do that when we already know where?"

"*Really?*" Tommy said. "Yer gonna act like you ain't never said nothing to me like this before? I swear, if you was the one drivin, you'd be all for it. It has to be your idea."

"No it don't. Don't be like that, Tommy."

"Why not just do it, then?" he said, thumping the steering wheel. "Finally. . ."

"You ain't gotta get all fired up about it. It's Tuesday. It's cold. The beach is gonna be—"

"Amazing. That's what. It's gonna be amazing," Tiffany said. "Come on . . ."

"It's also gonna be real dark by the time we get there."

"So we're goin then," Tommy said, smiling. "Sure sounds like it."

"Yer the one in the driver's seat. If you got the gas to burn."

I lit a cigarette and Tiffany looked at me, transferred the same widened eye she'd given him, excitement but also reserve, only a little hint of panic. Her lip stuck in her teeth with the thought of driving so far, on such a whim. And at the same time she was trying to break herself from laughing at how Tommy was painting a picture of us literally driving off into the sunset. I could hear those thoughts running through her head now, and I'm sure she could hear mine. Her nails were digging into my skin, clutching my arm, and pulling us closer. It could have very well been her plan to let his play out however it would, which most likely could amount to no more than a night out, a joyride, going along with it for the sake of Tommy and his feeling all grown up.

Even still, she got right down to it, asking: "So, alright, what then? We just drive? And what would we do once we got there? Where're we gonna stay?"

"Wherever. We do whatever we want. We'll find some place to stay. Even if we have to sleep in the back of the truck."

"I'm not gonna sleep in the back of this truck," she told him.

"Keep in mind we got jobs to get back to," I said.

"I know. I don't need to hear you reminding me about it again."

"Listen, I intend to go one day, you know that. Just not today. Not now." I huffed smoke and looked over at him, both of them. "But yeah, I guess let's see what kinda miles this thing's got left in it."

"Didn't even get to leave a note. But hell, writing's been on the wall, right? *I'm* not going back," Tommy hollered out, and then he smiled from ear to ear. The engine kicked up a notch underneath his stomped foot, his yelling along with the words singing on the radio after he turned it up even louder.

Tiffany grinned, picked my hand up between us and held it into hers, laced our fingers together and hit the seat with it like she was glad I'd given in. I turned and looked at Tommy, back at her, to let her know that I knew damned well he wasn't driving us to nowhere until the tank ran out, filling it up, then driving some more, until what, we reached the Atlantic? No, I shook my head with a smile, and kissed her quick before he could tell us to stop.

If there'd been any planning for it, and I wasn't so sure there had been, he'd probably imagined only the two of us driving away together one day, thick as thieves, blood brothers, starting over in someplace where we could've been anybody. Tiffany wasn't so much a wrench in it as she was the right tool to get me to follow through with it. Tommy wasn't the one making me believe in myself the way she was, having me trust in someone outside myself, so he ought to have been happy to have her along for the ride—because that's all this was, all it was supposed to have been.

With this decision made, the ease I'd felt at first, when we'd gotten into the truck late in the afternoon and had no destination in mind, seemed lost. The focus was instead on when it was going to stop, this silliness that turned to dread and now loomed with each mile that went by, every minute feeling longer than the last. I tried not to show it, though, resting my back into the seat, gripping Tiffany's hand more tightly, and I watched the highway pass alongside us like it was with fresh eyes. Although willingly this time, it still didn't feel like it, but once we kept going underneath that 87 overpass that took you south towards Fayetteville and then Lumberton, I *was* seeing it for the first time. Of course, that didn't make the highway look any different than the thirty-something miles of it we'd just ridden on, but being stuck behind a tractor trailer truck did put things into focus, allowing signs to be clearly read: 'Welcome to Harnett County.'

"Man, this dude is really slowing us down," Tommy sighed.

Every time he thought to pass the truck, as soon as the center line broke, either he couldn't because of somebody coming head-on in the opposite lane or he chickened out. I didn't egg him on, not for a second, afraid he might panic, steer us off the road or straight into the side of the truck, that or get us pulled over for speeding. It wasn't just the ticket I was thinking about but the 12-pack of Budweiser sitting cold on the floorboard between my feet. Tiffany had sweet-talked a twenty-something-year-old into getting it for her with what little cash we had on us at the first gas station Tommy saw after picking her up, forgoing more gas in the tank for beer to drink wherever it was the three of us were heading next. That seemed forever ago now, almost forgotten until we got here, the middle of nowhere.

"Hey, just—why don't you just turn off up there, on the left, and we can take it from there," I suggested, before he did something he shouldn't have, and to hold us back from getting too far away too fast.

Frustrated, he veered more than turned, didn't bother to use his blinker, and then slowed down some to stop the wheels from catching the curb. Tiffany reached out her arm and held on to the dash, looked at me like she wanted to laugh but didn't.

"Alright, we made it," I said to him. "Now where're you takin us?"

"Just keep ridin," Tiffany said. "I'm gonna have to pee soon. Maybe go up some, find us a dirt road we can go down."

"There ain't anybody out here lookin," he said to her.

"You don't *know that*," she talked back. "Just—there, go up that road, on the right."

He did what he was told, went right, then again, hung a left, and for what seemed like two or three more times, before the asphalt turned to gravel and then red dirt that was too hard to stir up. It wasn't dark yet but the horizon line ahead of us was changing colors, deep oranges and fading into a cloudless black and blue sky, with a half-moon rising through it.

"There. Right here's good," she finally said.

The road rattled under the tires and a clay ditch rolled out into a flat spot where grass wasn't growing, where a tree had been cut down, its wide stump left behind. I looked around and saw there were no signs posted anywhere telling us not to trespass, and an arch in the woods opened up, like it was inviting Tommy to park up beside it.

"Go in just a little more," she told him. "Right here, yeah."

I creaked open the door and stepped down from the truck and she scooched out after me. Tommy looked toward us, deflated, like he knew it wasn't going to amount to much, his grand scheming.

"Why you couldn't've done this before, at that gas station, I guess we'll never know . . ." he said.

"What's up, man? Chill out," I told him. "I gotta pee too, anyway."

He turned the engine off and got out. "Well then, why don't we all just have ourselves a pissing contest while we're at it."

"There you go," I said, patting him on the back. "That's the spirit."

Tiffany scurried ahead of us and into the woods a piece, squatted behind a tree. She was hardly visible through the overgrown under-brush, the stickers and crisscrossed tree limbs dead and lying around, pine straw pilled up as thick as fallen snow.

Here there weren't as many cars driving by—if any. None in fact,

I noticed, had passed since we parked and got out. Nor where there any other signs of life: houses, people, animals or otherwise, anything open for business or even out of business, there was none of it. Highway 421 wasn't even a thought, a reminder of it left to listen to if you tried to hear it, like the sound of a seashell, adrift from the ocean it washed away from.

"What're you so mad about?" I asked Tommy. "One minute you were fine—"

"No, I know, I guess I just—I dunno. Yer pretending like it's my fault, coming out here, like wanting to go somewhere else was so crazy, so stupid to even suggest—"

"No, I'm not, that's not what I said. No, I know it's not crazy. It's just, right now, this very minute, just took me by surprise is all."

"*You* were always the one who talked about leaving."

"Well, you know, things have changed."

"*What's* changed? Your momma hadn't? Least not cause she wanted, but she—"

"She ain't never gonna change, I get it, I get it, alright."

"No, it's not her, I know that, it's her," he said, and he pointed toward Tiffany. "She's made you think things was gonna change."

"Listen, I understand yer wantin to leave. I've said it before, I know. But yeah, okay, then, she's made things a lot better. None of it matters, though. You know we ain't drivin all the way to the damned beach, camping in the sand, under the stars, starting over . . . all that shit. Listen, we're just having fun. That's all this is, and you know it. So quit acting like it's anything more. Cause it ain't. Least act like yer havin fun. This was *your* idea, after all. Not mine."

"Seems like she don't see it that way," he said. "Maybe you oughta tell her that."

"*Where are we* . . ." she said, sighing, holding a colored rock in her hand, excitement on her face. "Can we stay a minute? I wanna pick up some more."

"Go for it. Why not?" I said.

Tommy flung his hand at my chest with a smug grin.

He and I walked after Tiffany, and I decided I wouldn't bring it up again, instead enjoy what last bit of light we had left, enough to see her dig through the dirt with her fingernails, turning over odd rocks in search of nothing and for no reason other than to kill time.

Tiffany slowed her pace and fell back into our silence.

"Why the long faces, boys?"

"No, it's nothing," I said.

"I was just tellin him how we shoulda done this a long time ago. Least attempted to do it. But I guess it took me gettin a license to drive fore we was makin the first move," he told her.

"That's right," I told her through my teeth. "Let's get on it with, then. Should we keep on going? Where're we goin? What's next?"

"—Hey, wait, look! Up there . . . Y'all see that?" she said.

A long, graveled drive took shape under a mat of weeds that had mostly covered it up, and the rough impression of it, gray rock and grit, went on up a hill and into a tunnel of gutted trees where it faded into dirt. It reemerged the further we walked, and there, finally, I could see, and I guess what it was she had spotted and brought us here to confirm, at its farthest reach: the roof of a big house, revealed in pieces, through shades of low sun beaming between skinny pines up ahead in the distance.

"Whoa," Tommy said, arching his neck, waving all around to try and see better. "Yeah, I see it! That's a house up in there, ain't it? Let's go check it out!"

"Wait! Hey—" I cried out to him, trying to holler. There was no way of knowing if we were alone, and if we weren't who we were about to be face to face with.

"Don't worry, ain't nobody out here," Tiffany said. "Look at it. You can tell. Least this means *he's* not going anywhere else," she said.

"You don't think so?"

"*Come on*, now, *seriously?*" she said, pointing ahead at Tommy, skipping like a kid through grass up to his shins, his knees in some patches. His breath was excited, in stacks, stuck there in the sun even when he'd run away from it, trying to catch it when he made it to the house.

The cold was biting at my ankles, my face and hands. Tiffany's teeth were chattering. I hugged her and we walked huddled together behind Tommy as he stood for a moment and studied the outside of what looked like a mansion grown up in the middle of the woods. It seemed impossible that such a place had ever been here, and how there'd been a way to get to it was a mystery, though we'd just solved it, if there'd even been anybody else trying to find it.

What may have once been a lawn was still here, mostly cleared, but had become overtaken by saplings and tall grass and what were now dead wildflowers in rumpled clumps. Brown everything, specked with black seed pods and yellowy shreds of wet fescue. The sun was setting behind the house and so the windows were near black, reflecting only the gloomy, trampled earth we stood surrounded by. There was an eerie feeling to it all, one that I felt in the pit of my stomach. I wanted to leave right then, seeing as how the house might well be haunted. The ghost looking out at us from behind any one of the dozen or more windows along the front of it wasn't happy about our being here.

"Where'd he go?" Tiffany said.

"Oh—Tommy?"

We unlocked arms and Tiffany called like his mom: "*Tommy?* . . ."

We walked around toward the side of the house, were a sunroom or porch or some kind of fancy place to be had caved in and looked dangerous to even attempt to enter into. "He's not in there," I said under my breath. Then I heard something inside the house and I stopped, frozen, afraid to budge. "*Tiff* . . ." I whispered. "*Wait.*"

I put my hand on my heart, breathed in slowly, still not moving a muscle, when Tiffany leaped through the grass, over a concrete slab of something broken, and took off around toward the front of the house.

The door jarred open with a loud choke. "Hey!" Tommy shouted from behind it, and he scraped over dirt and debris, stretched a leg out to walk over a gaping hole in the old wooden floors. "Forget the beach! Let's stay here!"

Tiffany carefully walked up the porch steps to meet him.

"Guys, come on, no. Don't go in there," I said.

"Too late," Tommy said.

The porch was deep and wide, spanning the width of the whole front of the house, a large part of its ceiling broken away, where maybe birds had taken cover, or any other animal that needed a place to stay. Droppings of some kind collected in every corner and sprayed brown and black above each of its windows. Panes were cracked in some but mostly intact. Nests stuck into nooks above every column that still held it up, between what was left of the railing that looked to be from another century, from old movies on TV about times like these.

I wasn't as nervous about going inside, possibly lured in by the grandness of it all, but looking up to see the ceiling above my head, right as I stepped through the door, sinking, black and crumbling, strips of wood poking out everywhere, I worried about venturing in too far. I did, anyway, seeing how most every ceiling in every room of the house was in this shape or worse but had remained there.

"This is crazy," I heard myself say, in awe of the stairwell, the half-fallen chandelier that must've greeted people with the same expression as mine, once upon a time, of course.

We went into a small living room with a fireplace, in between two other rooms along the left side of the house. It was filthy, trash piled everywhere, newspapers on the windows and writing scribbled up and down the plaster walls. Puffy chairs a kind of sea-foam green color sat side by side, with two couches covered up. A TV, older than any I'd ever seen, was out and still plugged in on top of a rolling table, where board games stacked in shelves underneath. Golden mustard yellow carpet, shaggy and caked with ceiling crumbs, spread wall to wall.

The kitchen was further in, toward the back, behind a bathroom with a toilet that was black inside, walls that once had been tiled but now were smashed and torn off, in piles like shattered glass on the plywood floor. Emptied canned goods filled the sink to its rim. Soggy boxes of food that'd dried stiff and stuck to each other were in the cupboards, where raccoons may have scavenged through. And mice most definitely still had a home here.

"Looks abandoned or somethin," Tommy said. "Super old, all this stuff. Like one day they decided to just up and leave it seems like. Ain't no way somebody's livin in here. Hadn't been for a long time."

Vines may have been the only thing keeping one half of the house standing. And as if to deliver us a message, a black bird cawed loudly, out of nowhere. I jumped back and Tiffany yelped, as it spread open and flew up through a break in the fallen down heap.

"Okay! That's enough," I said. "There's no lights or anything else we got on us to see with. It smells like shit. And there's definitely some kinda animal *or animals* livin underneath all this. Come on, it's starting to get dark out. You don't seriously think we're staying here?" I said, leading us toward an opening off the kitchen.

Tree limbs scratched against the house in a gust of wind, battling up against another porch, where rusty easy chairs turned upside down and a glass table was all there was left, along with half the floorboards. Dirt and rock was exposed, and tree roots grown too far. Tommy took a step and fell through, not so far he couldn't catch himself, pull up out of the opening, but enough to finally shake him.

"Yer right. Let's don't and say we did," he said, laughing.

"Thank God . . . I mean, like we were what, just gonna find us a bed to sleep in upstairs? Fat chance. Did you see how rotted the steps were?" Tiffany said, already out in the grass searching for something she could pick up and hold in her hand. Then she yelled out: "Look, over there, is that a barn?"

"You got enough keepsakes already, didn't ya? I don't know if I'd wanna bring anything back from this place."

Tommy laughed and walked off. "Might have cooties . . . Hey— where's the beer at? We didn't bring the beer with us, dammit."

"Where're you lookin?" I asked Tiffany. "I don't see it."

"There," she pointed, pulling me close, lining our sights.

"What're you lookin at?" Tommy asked. "I can't hardly see nothin back here."

"Oh, *that?*" I said, pointing. "That's way back there, Tiff. No, come on, now . . . We don't need to go all the way over there."

But she was already on the move, stepping over and under anything in her way, leading us to what was a small, squat looking barn, unlike every other, its roof high and pointed, its wooden boards a mishmash of lengths and widths and ways it had been put together. It was almost like whoever had built it was making it up as they went along. It seemed bigger the closer we got to it, its red color not as red as it possibly once was but more brown, darker in the twilight. It was even scarier than the house, and looked untouched by time.

"This is so cool," Tommy said, walking around all four sides.

"It's damned creepy is what it is," Tiffany said.

Turning back, I could just barely make out the house, and I tried making sense of where we'd just come from, if I could recognize where the road we parked on was. With so much overgrowth, the barn almost swallowed up by it, I couldn't see myself out of it, tangled up until I realized the only thing trampled on was our own footpath through the tall grass and boggy dirt. Everything else was undisturbed, totally forgotten about it seemed. Us too, I reckoned, if we didn't get the hell out of here.

"Hey . . . listen . . . The *beer's* in the truck, you said so yourself, and *we're* out here, *where* we shouldn't be . . . *when* we shouldn't be . . . It's only gonna get darker. Can we just go already? I almost can't even see my hand in front of my face. And it's gonna be a bitch gettin outta here, back to the truck. We should just go now, fore it gets worse."

"He's right. I'm sorry, Tommy," Tiffany told him.

"What about the beach? We ain't gotta stay here, I mean . . . But let's go somewhere else, do somethin, then. Come on, I get it."

"Alright, that's fine, but let's make it somewhere in the direction towards home. Can we? All this ain't goin nowhere any time soon.

Maybe we plan on comin back or goin someplace farther out even? When it ain't late. When we ain't got school in the mornin?"

"Since when do you give two shits about *school*? And if we plan on it we'll never do it, you know that."

Tiffany gave him a pat on the back, urging him to pick up his feet, and he did, mopey but willing and able enough to lead the way. I followed behind, as we slowly but surely came out of the brush and through the woods, onto a different dirt road that totally bypassed the broken-down house.

"Are we goin the right way?" I called up.

"Supposed to be," Tommy hollered back at me. "*Why*, you got a better idea?"

chapter 26

On a Sunday, Mr. Joe was stricken with a terrible pain in his chest that turned out not to be the heart attack he feared he'd been destined to die from. It was, however, a stroke, the doctor said, and this is what caused not only the tightness he described but the numbing sensation when he tried gripping his hand or moving his arm and leg. He'd also become confused, disoriented, and even more weak—not so much that he couldn't drive himself with no exception, hands shaking, all the way to the hospital that morning. "I'm fine," he tried telling me, slurring. "But still, somethin ain't right."

Ever since Ms. Mae died, I'd learned a revised set of tasks to prepare for a day like this, how to look after things alone, if only for an overnight, "Cause that's all this is," he'd said to me on the way there. "Lord help me." It was November again, and I'd not had a whole lot to do, except feeding the animals, a task that took three times as long as it had the year before. There were goats now, and twice as many chickens, eggs to sell on Saturdays, four different types of preserves, too. Canning came easy and then often. Not to mention all the crops I was in the middle of rotating.

It was then, not long after sunrise, when I was out sowing that he stumbled up to me, quiet and taking hold of his arm with one hand, mumbling and whispering that he'd like it if I could go with him. I didn't know where, not until he started to walk and I could see it for myself that he needed to go to the hospital.

"Once we get back, yer gonna be able to get some of this stuff taken care of?" he asked me on the way. "Even if I'm stuck upstairs in the bed for a few days, right? Least til I'm on my feet again."

"Em hm, yessir, that's right," I reassured him, knowing it was with or without his help that I was able to accomplish most things around the farm in need of getting done. He'd been so generous, and I'd returned the favor, so much so that it felt like we'd always been doing it this way, seeing us through to next year. Still, he was the farmer in my almanac and I'd never planned anything this far in advance on my own, what could very well come next, after him.

By midmorning, he was up but slumped sideways, still awake though, after a nurse brought him a plate of food he made sure not to complain to me about until she'd gone out from his room. "If we whatn't so far from the house, I'd get you to run down there and get me somethin to eat and bring it on back."

"I can," I told him. "You want me to make you some breakfast? I surely will, if that's what you won't me to do, Mr. Joe."

He paused for a second, looked past me like he'd forgotten what he'd asked me for, then he said, "Naw, this'll do alright for now. I'm gonna quit my belly-aching bout it. She was nice to bring it to me in the first place, after she done already did it once this mornin. Ain't gonna give it another thought." Sighing slowly, his arm hardly budging, he forked at the gray mush and scrambled eggs that looked chewed and spat out. "They're talkin like they're gonna have me home later, anyhow. Maybe tomorrow."

"Oh?"

"Yep. Sure did."

After sitting with him for another hour, I looked at his breakfast plate again and saw how it hadn't been touched. And by lunch, he wasn't hungry at all, requested only something cold and wet, for his cotton mouth, and whatever was enough to take something for his headache without making him feel queasy. I spoke with someone about this, about why he seemed to be getting worse after he'd just been getting better, and I was told it can happen this way, that he'd been experiencing some of these very same symptoms, not to the extent he was today, for some time. He had a history he'd not fully shared with me. The only thing I'd known about, his ever not taking care of himself in the past, was his smoking a pack a day, every day, from the time he was ten up until he was told he shouldn't. And maybe he'd drunk more than he should but he wasn't a drunk, he'd told me.

"The Lord Jesus Christ has me under his wing now," he whispered to me then, and again today, pale and stiff in his hospital bed.

Sometime in the late spring after Ms. Mae had died, I could've sworn that Mr. Joe had gone to join her. I found him sprawled out in the front porch swing on his back, all fours spread out over it, arms hung down, like maybe he'd gone out like a light right there the same way she did. It felt heavy, peering over him, thinking he was a goner. I could see his weathered, sunburned chest, bones across it, his shirt half open, and his heart beating. His flat stomach was filling with air slightly then shrinking back down into the ruffles of striped shirt, sweaty and not changed in days. You're still with me, ya old fart, I thought. I called on him, said his name several times, but he didn't respond. Even when I peeled his eyelids back, his cloudy, farsighted eyes looking straight at me, he didn't budge. Maybe the only thing strong enough to pull him up from it was more to drink. He was out of sync there for awhile, off his rocker. But in time he'd come back to himself, apologized for his behavior, that I had to see him that way. I told him not to apologize to me, that it was mild by comparison.

At around four o'clock, a lady was standing with me out in the hallway, telling me his condition had worsened, and good news wasn't looking like it was going to come. "I think you'd better get the family together." And she rubbed my arm. "It might be gettin time to, honey."

I didn't say he didn't have any family. I couldn't prove it, nor could I that he'd become like family to me, so maybe I was it. I didn't say anything. I drew a blank. In such a short span he'd gone from wide awake to half asleep to talking to barely able to speak. When she left me, I peeked into the room and saw him struggling to breathe, his chest rising up and down, rapid, panting like a stray dog.

The last time I'd seen someone in the hospital, even been in one, it was Mom, her handcuffed to a bed just like his. Tubes everywhere, too. And all around both of them these same lights were blinking, but so were his eyes; hers weren't. Not until early in the morning, before five a.m., did she finally open her eyes. She'd made it though, come out the other side in once piece. Nobody told me then how I needed to prepare myself for her death. Mom was as tough as the sheriff had said she was, only tougher. I feared Mr. Joe was giving up the fight, that or he'd lost it a long time ago and I was only now realizing I'd been watching him die from the sidelines since the day we met.

I came in and sat down in the chair beside his bed. "Talk to me about what we need to get done tomorrow." I wanted to coax him out of it, bring him back to life if I could.

His eyes winced and opened slowly, then he kept them open. "Welp, I guess since we done got it all graded—shoulda got done already if it ain't been—now we oughta get them hands tied up in there. Ones that ain't cut short. Huh? Get em ready to store up. Then I think we talk more about whether or not we're re-chinking this time around. Doncha think?"

"What, now?" I asked him, not understanding a word of it.

"Well rain's comin. Can't stop the weather, son."

"What're you talkin about, re-chinking? Tying hands?"

"After every last bit of its been done sold off, cleaned it out, that's when we start gettin it done. That's right," he mumbled.

He wasn't looking at me, or listening, and his arms were twitchy, his fingers gripping but not holding onto anything.

"Mr. Joe? *Mr. Joe?*"

"What? *What is it?*" he said, seeming to snap out of it.

"What're you talkin about?"

"Oh, I dunno . . . Woo boy, it's all mixing together in here," he said, using his right hand to point with a long finger at his head. "I'm layin here, maybe lost in it, tellin *you* what to do like yer listenin to me tell ya what to do. You ain't doin nothin with somethin that ain't there, now are you? Ain't nothin left to do is there?"

"What do you mean?" I asked, carefully placing a cup of water on the tray table wheeled up beside him.

"*Tobacco.* Season's bout down for, ain't it? If there was one left. I told you there ain't been for some time, though, so don't listen to me when I talk. I'm sorry."

"Oh. I guess. I don't know."

"I can smell it, son. When I close my eyes, it's curing. God awful heat. The hottest thing you ever felt in yer life. Summer's barren down on top of it." He stopped talking to cough and then stared out like he was really where he felt himself going to. And I let him stay there, picture a place that reminded him of somewhere other than this sterile hospital room. He liked to be in the dirt, always did, always will, he'd say. "Yep, that's right," he moaned, drifting off.

A nurse quickly popped her head in and looked sad to see me sitting there. I shrugged and half-smiled, a helpless look of saying I didn't know what to do without saying it.

"*Mr. Joe?*"

"Summer's when we lost our boy, ya know. Maybe it was in June, I wanna say. I reckon had you asked me not but five years ago I'd a told you what day, and the exact time he died, too. Yeah, this was a long, long time ago. You hear about them folks in church playin with snakes, getting themself bit, but a little boy, out with all of us, pretending like he was toppin and suckerin in the fields?" He chuckled, his eyes glassy saying this, and paused to catch his breath. "That's when I guess he—now I wanna say it snuck up on him, but knowing a snake, it was the other way around—come right up on one, a copper-head it musta been, done gone and went. Probly coolin in the shade is all, just right up next to the woods is where it was, where we found him. I think had we got to him quicker it woulda gone another way. This is 1954, you see. That's right, there we go. I know I still know somethin. Whatn't but eight years old. Be old enough to be yer daddy were it not for that day. It only takes one second, son. Can change yer whole life. It sure did . . . I did. Mae, too. Crushed her. I think her heart really got a crinkle in it then and it took all them years for it to catch up with her. The both of us I guess it did."

I wasn't going to say I was sorry, he wouldn't allow it. "Yer right. And I don't think there's nothing you could do about it, neither."

"Well, now, I thought I might could. And I did. I took out my pocketknife—that one I gave you—and I had dropped to my knees, down in the dirt beside him. Was gonna lance it, he was so swole up where it had bit him, and he couldn't talk no more, or maybe he could but was without words. He was seeing God. I think something happens to a person then, you know. Before it all goes away, this place, it's gonna slow down, nice and easy."

"Em, like when yer just fixin to fall asleep? And can feel yourself getting close, and if you allow it to, it happens."

"Yeah, cept you don't wake back up."

"Em hm, that's true." I looked at him, at the way his lips were quivering, crusty and cracked, the distant look in his eyes.

"You wanna know somethin, my own daddy," he mumbled, coughed, and I stood up with a napkin and wiped around his mouth, "so darned warn-out at the end of the day—every single day he was—he hardly ever said a word to me and my brother. The stubborn old man he became to us, somebody I barely knew when he died. He took just about every word of it with em to the grave, whatever it was that made him go quiet. I never heard the house so silent in my life, til the day my boy died out in that field. But he taught me everything I know, my daddy did. Not only out there in that dirt, but making the drink, too, the one you took a taste of. Devil's blood's what it is, son," he said, sighing. "Folks made a livin off it too, a whole trade before my time. It's no wonder this land's cursed. All sorts of bad is buried in it."

"My grandma told me our family had a curse."

"Imagine she whadn't lyin, neither. Old folks'll tell ya the truth, son. And I suppose every one of em's got something, just don't know what to call it. Ain't no different. It is what it is, regardless. You know what else, I see a lot of myself in you, I really do. Yer young enough that ya don't have to make the same mistakes I did. You got a lot left to go. I didn't have somebody like me tellin me nothin like this."

I smiled, patted his arm.

"It's the truth. I'm old." He giggled, then spit up into a napkin.

"So you think a curse can be broken, then?"

"Well, now, I suppose it can be. For it to be there in the first place it must've come into its own somehow, from somebody. Right?"

"Right."

"Yeah, and don't doubt what you know to be the truth. That's what folks are after more than anything, you hear me?"

I did but I didn't understand what he meant by it, that maybe he didn't and was just talking, to prove he still could, to both of us.

A different nurse leaned into the room and then walked in.

"You alright in here, Mr. Tillett? Comfortable enough for ya?"

"Hey, honey. Yeah, I'm alright. Got my son here with me now, so all's well—better at least."

"Oh, alright, now. Hi there."

I did the same thing I'd done for the last nurse, and I didn't deny what he'd said, sure I was that he'd pictured me that way to make himself at ease with the situation, or his mind had. In some strange sense, his forgetfulness and make-believe was maybe in preparation for what he said was his eternal ever after. And I wasn't going to meddle with *that*.

But when the nurse stepped out, he mumbled to me, "Now, I ain't tellin her that cause I'm layin here seein my dead boy sittin live and in the flesh next to me, now. Should something happen to me, I want you to know, even though we ain't really kin, yer my next of kin. Jargon is jargon, but really, you are. I done put it in writing, too."

"What? *Mr. Joe . . .*"

"Well what, then? Who else you see sittin in here with me? My brother sure ain't. And I figure my nephew ain't good for nothin, cept bringin you out to the house the way he did. I ain't gotta know somebody all my life to known em, son. I think you know what I'm talkin about. You were put there beside me for a reason. Yep, I'd say that about sums it up. The county's not gonna take hold of it, nope, that's for darned sure. Besides, there's more than a house— one some might see as a tear-down the way folks is doin em today. I told you bout how much land there is, and all there is to know about it, least most of it I did," he said, winking, trying to. "No, but really, as long as I got breath in my lungs, I'll say what's right and what's wrong. This is the right thing to do. I feel it in my bones, boy. You hear me?"

"I don't know what to say."

"You ain't gotta say nothin," he said. "Nod yer head so I know I made sense, what I was tryin to say."

I felt tears welling up. I shook my head and gripped his arm.

"Besides, I ain't dead yet. But when I do die, you need to know that you still got a room to stay in." He took the hand he'd been able to move and placed it on top of my arm.

"Telling you thanks don't mean the same thing as saying I'm grateful. I am, truly. And it's not me saying goodbye, neither."

"No, I know that. There's plenty of time for all that."

"Heavy stuff," I said, wiping the tears from my cheeks.

I pulled away from him and sat back down in the chair, watched him refocus his attention toward his breathing. The conversation seemed to have tired him out, grayed his skin some, and I remember wishing I'd been a doctor so I could do more for him. But what I'd done, continued to do, seemed enough. We quieted down and stayed silent, with just the TV up on the wall talking over us. I couldn't tell if the moment where he'd close his eyes and never wake up was starting to happen or not. Maybe I was beginning to get tired myself, of watching, waiting, wishing for him to suddenly stand, healed and ready to get back in the truck and go home. He'd believed it when he told me he would be by now, and so had I.

After a little while, I drifted from his room, out into the hallway, and through the waiting room, finally exiting the hospital for fresh air outside in the parking lot. Out of the way from everybody, I curled my back and lit a cigarette, and I saw how the sky was turning dark, every shade of blue. And it had gotten cold out, with my breath on top of smoke, night come down on me so quick it seemed. It was quiet, crickets, no real emergencies left to attend to for one of the nurses, smoking alone out there with me. Who knew this feeling more than she did? I wondered. I hung back my head, blew out slowly into the bitter air, and felt a shiver.

Though I'd only just seen them, as I stood there, I was remembering Mr. Joe's hands, strained and wrinkly but still precise, reaching and sifting through the dirt. Calloused since the day he began using them. Well-worn and giving. I saw them together in prayer, in times of rejoicing, and also in despair. Over his eyes or the back of his neck, and in his pockets whenever he was timid or skeptical. They spoke for him when he couldn't speak, and they touched others even if he couldn't feel it. I would forget what they looked like, what he looked like, I knew this much was true. One day I'd wake up without the thought to try to remember, not just Mr. Joe but this time in my life, these days I'd spent here, those that led me here, the grace that I'd been given, but I'd never forget how it felt. And for now, I thought, I'd remember it all, while I still could.

When I walked back into the hospital, I still believed he'd be there, in his room, awake in bed, ready to leave. But he wasn't, he'd gone home without me.

It was pretty much by the book after that, waiting patiently before then being told what next steps were going to be, who I should call, where I should go for this and that, like being read a to-do list out loud rather than any sympathies for what had just happened or salutations when it finally came time for me to leave. They were kind nonetheless, and maybe I was under the wrong impression of how it would be, in some kind of state, shock it was maybe, but I wasn't shocked. "People died," so I heard Mom telling me again whenever he first told me this was going to happen. And he'd prepared me for it, too. Still, I hadn't been for being handed over his "personal effects," neatly folded inside a large plastic bag: his shirt and blue jeans, the jacket that had hung up on the back of the door like he'd soon need it, even his tennis shoes, the socks he'd been wearing tucked into them. Seeing all of it, without him, I wanted to cry, but I couldn't. Tears were not coming.

I made it out to his truck, where he'd parked that morning, and I peeled open the bag I'd been given to reach inside for his keys. I couldn't recall ever driving the truck, oddly, having always gone somewhere with him, or with Ms. Mae, in her car, sometimes driving hers if ever I was going at it alone or when she couldn't drive herself and insisted on going with me. The ring of keys felt cold in my hand, was several rings, actually, in a wad of about a dozen or so different keys of all shapes and sizes. He drove a Chevy C20 long-box pickup the same color as the grass this time of year, just beginning to tan and almost turn metallic in the morning dew. It was six or eight of the keys he had on him that belonged to GMs, though, keys on one ring by themselves and much smaller than the ones on another ring with a bunch of other keys I assumed went to the house. He had a key for just about everything, and I knew from one Chevy to another that a different key was used for the doors and the ignition and the trunk, so I thought nothing more about it in that moment. Instead, I just opened the door to the truck he never bothered locking, set the bag of his things in the seat beside me, and tried each one of them until I got it to start. When the engine sounded I sat with my hands on the steering wheel, felt of how substantial it was, this, the loss, and too, what I'd gained from the old man.

The radio was barely turned up and I didn't mind the quiet. I needed it, really, in order that I might could hear my thoughts as they came rushing to my head. Just drive, I said to myself, and so I did, out from the parking lot, feeling the strangeness of driving the truck for the first time, fiddling with the lights before finally turning off onto Highway 421, back to where I'd come from.

Then, at the first red light I came to, I swear, if I didn't almost run it, get myself hit in the middle of the road. But I'd slammed on the brakes, and when I did, the bag of Mr. Joe's things slid over the wide seat, spilled out across it, one shoe clunked into the floorboard and the other hit the door. I cussed under my breath, adjusted the rearview mirror, my expression washed in red from the traffic light waving in the wind. I could've cried right then and there, I thought, seeing myself for the first time that day, perhaps longer, unrecognizable as I was in this driver's seat. And I'd been in this mystery I couldn't figure out, even for myself, like I'd lived as someone else in all that time on the Tillett farm, in Polk before that. Maybe I ought to stop trying, I wondered, just let it happen, let it come on me whichever way it wants. With that, my face warmed, my eyes burned, and I hit the gas and kept on going.

Through the windshield a half-moon was shining back in on me, only a little, but enough to guide me, when next I looked over at the scattering of his things, the shirt sleeves reaching down off the seat, a belt unfurled. Then I saw what must've been his billfold sitting there beside me, fat and separated from the creased back pocket of his blue jeans he'd always kept it in. I picked it up and held of it in my hand, how soft the leather was, how it probably had been with him for as long as the pocketknife he'd given me. And for some reason it felt familiar, holding another man's billfold. Something wasn't right, I thought.

At the next stop I inspected it as closely as I could in the dim cab, before halfway opening the door at the same time I was pulling off to park the truck. I got out quick and ran around so I could better see what I thought I'd seen, with Mr. Joe's billfold held up to the front headlight. And I realized that it *was* his. It was not Mr. Joe's. It had never belonged to him. I slumped down in the dirt, in a cold sweat, and rubbed my fingers over his initials branded into the dark brown leather: 'TLW'. Inside was a random business card from a body shop in Lumberton, along with bits of paper I'd last seen when leaving his apartment. Reading his handwriting now, it made me heave, and I dropped the billfold, threw up in front of the truck. His license was gone but would've only made it worse, more real, confirm it, though there was no denying it belonged to my dad: Turner Landry Wains.

Nothing else that I remembered remained, like that picture of us, the one he'd kept of me and Mom and him, taken when I was little. Had he thrown it away, or had Mr. Joe? And his keys, too, the ones to the Chevy, his apartment, I checked and there they were, hung on the key ring in the truck's ignition, all along. Seen but unseen.

chapter 27

Tommy's truck was exactly where we'd left it, of course, but we weren't altogether where we were when we left it there. He was still stuck in his head, and Tiffany was someplace else too, Alaska maybe. Lost myself, I was not only feeling put out by the whole thing between us, being sidetracked tonight in this land that time forgot, but also ending up back on this road I couldn't remember how we'd gotten to in the first place. Nightfall had turned everything upside down, and when we finally got into the truck, it seemed hours had passed, the whole day gone by, though it was maybe only seven, almost eight o'clock when we saw the Siler City city limit sign.

"Should we just call it a night, then?" Tiffany asked, and she patted the plastic-bagged 12-pack of beer on the floorboard. "These'll stay cold til next time."

"Yeah, alright," Tommy told her, defeated, tired, I could tell. All of us were.

"Can you just drop me off at Tracy's?"

"Yeah. Course," he said.

She and I didn't say a word after I opened the door and let her out. When we kissed goodbye it was as though we'd talk about it later.

I got back into the truck and told Tommy I was sorry. He said he was too and then turned the radio up. We didn't speak about it, instead listened to the last couple minutes of the song we'd started singing along to until he turned onto the end of our street.

"You wanna come in for a beer?" I asked him. "We can sneak some into my room."

"Oh—yeah, sure, that'd be cool."

But as we came up on my house, Tommy eased on the brakes, and I noticed there wasn't only the one car parked in the driveway. Then, with light from the picture window cast out over the other car, I saw it, sure as night, the Chevy.

"Ain't that yer momma's old car?"

"Yeah, looks like it."

"Then don't that mean—"

"Yep. Sure does. Wonder what he wants."

Tommy parked in his driveway and, without waiting to be sure of ourselves first, both of us got out of the truck. I did stand there for another second, though, staring at our house from across the street, seeing if I could make out anything that might be going on inside through the window. But the curtains were pulled shut, without a single shadow other than the back of the couch pushed up under it, with nobody sitting on it. And the sunrise-shaped window at the top of the front door was too high and cut away from any other clues of what was going on behind it.

"You still want me to go over there with ya, or just—"

"No, yeah. I do. Why the hell not? I ain't lettin my daddy stop us from doin what it was we was gonna do. Gonna show up like this—and what for? What does he expect I wonder. Nothing's what he's gettin from me."

"There you go," Tommy told me, reaching inside his truck for the beer. He took hold of the 12-pack and slid out several cans.

"But maybe we ought not bring any in with us. I mean—"

"Oh, yeah, yer right. Good idea."

I led the way and walked up the front step, was just about to open the door when I turned to Tommy and asked him if we should not go in. "You know, maybe we oughta go back over to your house. Or somewhere else even? I dunno."

"Come on, man. Don't worry about it," he told me. "Do like you said. Fuck him."

It had been a while since I'd last seen my dad, since he'd last seen me. A lot had changed. *I* had changed. Mom had tried to but had not, and I guessed I'd be hearing all about it. Even before the door opened I thought I would, at least a little bit of their bickering about something or other. But it was quiet. And when I reached to turn the door knob it was locked.

"*That's* weird," I told Tommy, and I knocked on the door several times, then banged on it.

"*Somebody's* home," Tommy said, looking back at the Chevy and leaning around me, spying like he might see something more than I could through the curtains.

"Well, duh," I said.

I kicked the bottom of the door with my foot a couple times.

Over my shoulder, Tommy jumped up and down, tried looking through the window. "Oh, they're comin. Yer momma, I guess it is."

The door cracked and stopped short of opening up all the way. "*Trav*," Mom said through it, speaking in a low gravelly voice and showing only half her face. Even just from the neck up was enough for me to see she'd been crying, that there was blood smeared and dried crusty under her nose, a busted lip maybe. She looked spent.

"Momma, *come on*. What're you doin? Open the door. What's goin on? Dad did that, didn't he? Momma, did he do that to you? I know he did, the—"

"*Shh*, keep yer voice down."

"What are you doing? . . . Let me in. Why're you actin like this?"

"Just—"

"Are you alright," Tommy asked her, stepping closer.

"Listen to me," she said, coughing, starting to cry, "y'all have to—"

Her hand lost its grip on the door and so I pushed in on it, careful not to hit her with the back of it, worried for her but also unsure about what he'd done to her and might do to me, to Tommy.

"What happened to you? What'd he do, Momma?" I asked her, coming into the house with Tommy. I didn't hear Dad or see him anywhere. "Is he gone? Did he leave? Why's the Chevy here?"

Mom turned in and locked the door shut behind her, pressed her back against it. "He's here, Trav." Her nose was more swollen than I thought, broken even, and her eye bruised, slick with blood above it, too, but not like it was from a gash or cut on her face but more she'd swiped or smudged it off onto it. And I could see spatter on her shirt, the knees of her faded blue jeans blotted red. Then I saw some on her hands, still shaking, scratched and cut up, with more than one broken fingernail. And on the door, a handprint, the lock. Blood was everywhere, the floor and walls leading up toward us in the entry, and back through to the house where she'd come from to let us in.

Tommy hadn't stopped to take in all of these details like I did, and so he found him first, when I heard him in the other room saying, "Oh, shit . . ."

"*What?*" I called out. "What is it?"

In the kitchen, Dad was laid out on the linoleum, his face covered in blood, so much I didn't know if it was him at first. I recognized his shirt, even torn and tattered, cut to pieces, with gashes made around the collar, into his neck it looked like, split open and with blood on the floor underneath where it must have gushed out.

"*Momma . . .*" I sighed, and I only asked her when, because it was clear what had happened, who had done it. And I just stood there stunned, staring at him, unable to look away from the bloody mess.

"I dunno. I guess, I guess it's been about an hour, since . . . I just—" She covered her mouth, wanted to scream, to cry out, but she couldn't. She just sat down in a chair and ran her hands up and down her arms.

"It's okay, *shhh*. It's alright," I said, kneeling down. I reached around her, squeezed tightly. She was flailing in my arms like she was still after him or he was after her, choking on her snot and tears. "Momma, calm down. Breathe, alright? Just try and relax." I thought if I reasoned with her some, waited for her to bring herself down, she might say why she did it. Even then, was there a reason to ask?

She did, or she tried, after she wiped her face off with her hands. "I couldn't stop doin it," she croaked out, wheezing, hysterical and bursting into tears again. "This'll be it for me, Trav. This is it."

"*Shhh*," I said. "Momma, calm down."

There were so many cuts she'd made, but the one she'd landed right to the chest, where blood had completely soaked into his shirt and bled down the side of it, if it wasn't his neck then that had to have been the one that ultimately did him in. And she must've turned the kitchen lights off afterward in a panic, because everything was sort of murky and dulled down, with only the lamp in the living room left on. That is if it wasn't me somehow making myself believe it wasn't a shock to see, unreal, not actually happening, given how surreal a scene it truly was. With so much blood around him, maybe tacky by now it wasn't at all shiny, not the way it had mirrored the sky coming in through the Sellers's front door. Or how I'd later see it pooled on the cement floor underneath those florescent bulbs in Polk, after fights and stabbings, illuminated when somebody had bled out.

"What happened, Ms. Lynn?" Tommy said, wide-eyed and arched over Dad's body, examining the knife on the floor beside it, before he was turning his gaze toward her and then me.

I shot him a look like it was stupid to ask. It was *the* question to ask, but for me, I knew the answer. It wasn't only that he was dead and Mom had done it, that she'd stabbed the man to death, but it was the last half of any of the arguments they'd ever had in the past, my whole life leading up to it, the one that had not yet happened but now finished them all. It was the fix. Problem solved. For as much as I'd wanted to believe he'd left us alone and would never return, that I was older now and so he couldn't get to me, to Mom, I knew this day would come. Only a matter of time. Not if but when. Honest, I'd seen it happen sooner, just like this, only the other way around. I was glad my dad was dead and my mom had survived, that both of us had.

Tommy shrugged. "*Sorry . . .*"

"Come here," she told him. "Get back. Don't get too close to it. You don't wanna get any of it on ya. You too Travis, don't go over there. I'm not lettin nobody do nothin to neither one a y'all, hear me? I did what I thought I had to do. Was defending myself."

I loosened my grip around her and stood up, peered into the kitchen. She stretched her arms toward me and tugged on me like I was going to go against her. "I won't, alright," I told her. "But yer gonna have to talk to me, Momma. This ain't good."

Although relieved to be alive, at the same time she was fearful for what was going to happen next. The sniffling stopped and she faced forward, straighted up, enough to start telling us what went on before Tommy and I got there. "You know, I didn't have a clue the bastard was drivin up. Just waltzes in here like he owns the place, as usual. Said he did. That it's his to take and he's gonna this time. He was gonna take this house, Trav, right out from under us. Well that sure got us goin. Set things spinnin. Right then and there. And I hadn't had a drop to drink. Not one damned drink, Trav. You hear me?" She lowered her head, put her face in both hands.

"I hear ya, Momma."

"No, but not him. No sirree," she said, raising her eyes and looking through us into the kitchen. "Here he comes, this son-of-a-bitch, hell on wheels, drunk as all get-out. On a mission, I swear, like I've never seen him before. I mean, I'm surprised you can't smell it in the blood."

I did, and I couldn't stop smelling it.

"Said he'd been up at TJ's, so yeah, of course you had been, I thought, and so here we go again. Musta just socked me square in the face for whatever it was I said to him. Boom!"—she slammed her fist into her palm—"I'm tellin you, I just couldn't. When I felt that, I could not do it. Not for one more second. I couldn't tell ya how I got to the kitchen, chasing me into it's what he did, after he done knocked me down and was pulling of my hair, like he was gonna start slamming me. I think he did, too, cause, I swear, I thought he was finally gonna kill me. Yep. That was it for me. I was lucky I'd been in here fixin dinner, cause I just, I dunno, I guess I just snapped, Trav. I got that knife right there off the counter and . . . well, that was the end of it. And he acted like he was gonna turn it on me, too, but I didn't let him. I just kept on. I couldn't stop myself til I knew he whatn't."

I looked over at Tommy to see how he was hearing all this, and he was taking it in, same as I was, with little effect, every word of it. If anything, a quiet strength was behind his glare, one that may have matched some sense of resolve I must've shown, had he looked. But his eyes stayed glued to Dad, scanning over every blow Mom had made, recreating in his mind her vague account of killing him.

"Every bit of what you see right there's cause of me, cause of what I done to him." She pointed to him, shrugged her shoulders. And she started to choke up, but then kept on talking. "I ain't sorry for it, neither. For what I did. Cause I didn't have no choice. It was me or him. I had to do it. But Trav—" and she began sobbing "—what I'm sorry for is what's gonna happen next. To me. To the both of us. I just know they're gonna take me from you, sweetie. Put me away somewhere. Maybe try and fry me for it. Ain't nobody gonna believe me. Just like that woman down in Florida's been on the news."

"Don't say that, Momma. That's not gonna happen."

"You don't know that, sweetie."

"No, it's definitely not," Tommy spoke up, "cause like you said, you was only defending yourself. It ain't just cause of you that he's layin there dead, but for what he did to you. So why—"

"Is that what it looks like, though?" Mom said, holding back tears. "I mean, he definitely slapped me around some, got me in the jaw, like I told ya. But—"

"Momma, yer nose is bleedin. This whadn't the first time. Dad did this to you, and so who's gonna question you bout that? It's the truth. I know what you mean, though, like you said, they *are* gonna question you. They're gonna question what you say to em. No matter what. But not if they don't? So long as there's no questions to ask, how can they?"

"Whataya mean? It's the police," Tommy said to me. "They're *gonna* have some questions. And a lot of em, too, that yer gonna need to answer to," he told her.

Mom looked at me. "Even more for them to have something to say about. Yep. That's right. They're gonna come up with a reason even if the one I give em is right—not the right one they want. That's what's gonna happen. I mean—"

"No, that's what I mean, ya hear me? That's *not* what's gonna happen," I said. "Not if they don't even know about it. It's been over an hour already and they're not here so they don't know nothin."

"Not yet they don't," Tommy said.

"Don't you think if somebody thought somethin was up, suspected anything at all, they'd've called the police by now?"

Mom stood up next to me. "What're you sayin, Trav?"

"I'm sayin they ain't gotta know, Momma. It ain't happened yet, right? Listen, nobody knows about this but you and me and Tommy. Maybe Dad was never here. And if somebody says he was, it's that he came and went. Gone before anybody even knew he was. Don't nobody care about that man."

Tommy thought about it. "I see what yer sayin, I just . . . I dunno."

"It ain't that difficult."

"It ain't that simple, neither," Mom said to me. "How am I gonna fix this? What would I even do with him? I mean—"

"You don't have to do anything. I will. I'll take care of it," I said, crossing my arms and trying to speak with some kind of authority, like it maybe had been something I'd planned before, though I hadn't. Anyway, I wasn't fooling anyone. This was not something I could have possibly planned on.

Tommy took a deep breath. "*How?*"

"Well, I mean—I dunno, I guess . . . Him, we gotta get rid him for starters. Somehow. Then—"

"*How* though?" Tommy asked. "And where, I mean, I don't even know *what* yer supposed to do . . ."

"Well, I guess you ain't gotta worry about, then, now do ya?"

"Whataya mean I ain't gotta worry about it? I'm right here. I'm not just gonna stand back and watch. Course I'm gonna help you, Trav."

"No yer not," Mom said, stepping between us. "And neither are you. Neither one a y'all's gonna do anything. Don't even so much as touch him. You hear me? This ain't like some movie on TV."

"Hey—wait, wait," Tommy said. "Yer gonna have to do something with that car, too. The Chevy. Aren't ya?"

"Oh, well yeah," I told him.

"Boys, boys, listen to me. I did this. I should . . . I don't know, it's on me. I fucked everything up. I did. Every bit of it's all my doin. And he's yer daddy, he—I took him from you, Trav. Bad as he was. Still, he's yer father. I'm so sorry." She was crying again. I could see how helpless she felt, unsure, confused and at the same time resolute about what had to be done about it.

"You know he whatn't a father to me, come on. If you just could clean up . . . How bout that?" I told her. "That's all you've gotta worry about. You took care of *him*, so, yeah, that's it. Not a single spot left behind. Every bit of it. Like it never happened."

She went numb and glared forward, with no more tears left to cry, out of steam. Tommy left us alone and went into the front room.

"All that blood, Momma, on you too, get it off of ya. Burn everything if you have to, I dunno, but don't let not one thing show that he was ever here, that this happened, alright? It's gonna be okay," I said to her. "Okay?"

I didn't know that to be true, how could I? Or what I was going to do. Panic set into my chest, swole up in my throat. I might soon throw up myself, I thought, if I didn't figure something out. This wasn't going to magically go away. Dad wasn't suddenly coming back to life, as another person, apologizing for what he'd done, to tell us he deserved this then walk away, out of our lives for good. For as sick as

I felt, I felt it my bones, what I had to do.

I went into the front room. "*What's up?*" I asked Tommy quietly. "You okay? I mean, I know that's a stupid question to ask but—"

"No, no, I'm alright. I'm not but I am, I dunno. It's crazy is what it is. Seeing all that. I guess I thought I'd feel some other kinda way about it, but I don't, honest. We just gotta figure out what to do about it. Yer momma's gonna fuck it up if we don't, you know that. We shouldn't even be talkin to her about whatever it is we do. You think?"

"Oh, I dunno about that, I—"

"She's not right, Trav. Look at her. She's out of it. What are we gonna do? Like you said, we gotta do somethin with him."

"And the Chevy," I whispered. "Well—"

"Trav," Mom called out. "I'ma stop all this and just call the police."

I walked toward her and hugged her. "No, don't. Don't you dare do that." I unhooked the phone from the wall in the kitchen. "Don't say anything to anybody. I'm not gonna either. I'm gonna fix this, and Tommy's gonna help me, like he said. And that's that. You hear me?"

She didn't say anything, until it clicked, and she said, "I think there's a tarp around here somewhere. In the crawlspace, maybe."

"Alright, then," I said, and I left her there alone in the kitchen, her opening and shutting cabinets, collecting rags and a towel, taking her shirt off, still with blood on her bra.

Tommy followed me outside, around to the side of the house. "What're we doin?" he asked.

"We're gonna wrap him up, and I'm gonna pull the Chevy round to the front—the other way, with the trunk up close—and we're, I guess just gonna put em in it. What else?"

"What about my truck?"

"We can't put him in the back of yer truck, Tommy. Out in the open like that."

"And where are you gonna take it?"

"I dunno, I was thinkin about where we just were, far from here, out there enough that nobody's gonna know about it. I mean, it's gotta be out in the boonies somewhere like that. We can't just bury him in the backyard."

"I know that, but—"

"No, no, that's it. It's perfect. There was nobody around. It was in the middle of nowhere. Up in the woods like that. Not the house but that barn we saw, that one covered up like it was, ain't nobody gonna know. We put him in there. *And* the car."

"Are you sure?"

"Yeah. You got any better ideas?"

He looked at me, with eyes I'd not seen before, amazed, I think, that I was coming up with it the way that I was, on the spot, with no fear. I was, however, scared, to death. If I showed it, though, the whole plan I was convincing myself to believe in, and for Tommy to play a part in, might fall apart.

"You can drive yer truck there?" I asked him. "You remember where it was, how to get there? And I can, I guess just follow behind you in the Chevy. Then, when it's over, we come back in yer truck."

Tommy took a deep breath. "Yeah. I can do that."

He and I moved quickly after that, unraveling a tarp we found covered in dirt and spiderwebs, over the clean part of carpet that met the linoleum in the kitchen. Mom insisted I put trash bags over both my arms and hands when I picked Dad's body up by his shoulders, Tommy his feet, and lugged him over onto the tarp. We tightened it around him as much as we could, careful not to get any blood on us before we struggled to carry the weight of him through the house and into the entry.

I'd already found the keys in Dad's front pocket and pulled the Chevy down the driveway, slowly, making sure no one was out when I wheeled it around and reversed it back up to the front step. It took me turning two different keys before the third one I tried opened up the trunk.

"Alright," I said to Tommy, sighing, and with one last look out through the half-open front door, I held of his head and neck under the tarp and led Tommy and the rest of him out and over into the trunk. "A little more," I whispered, wedging the sides of him into the space, trying to hold it together as I maneuvered him in.

"*There.* Is that it?" Tommy said under his breath.

"He's in there," I sighed, slowly lowering the trunk and locking it. "I'm gonna get into the car, then, wait for you to pull out. Alright?"

"And yer just gonna follow me, right?"

"Yep. That's the plan."

Mom knew what we were doing, but I didn't tell her where we were going. I went into my room and put on a ball cap, came into the kitchen before I left. "I love you, Momma," I told her. "Don't worry."

She raised up her head, down on all fours scrubbing, and wiped tears from her cheeks. I think she was still in shock, not only from what she'd done, but from what I was about to do. "Please be careful," she said to me, like I was only going out for the night, to maybe watch a movie, or for a burger and fries with Tommy. No longer were we those boys, though, maybe we'd never been.

Highway 421 along the way back to this place was a blur, and it wasn't until we passed under the 87 overpass Dad had taken us on back when he took me to Lumberton, which I'd seen again only an hour ago, that I started to look alive. I was a dead man driving a dead body, it felt like. If I got pulled over it was *all* over, I'd reminded myself, thinking how having beer was the least of our worries on the road that night. And Tommy, seeming to be lost ahead of me, kept making turns I couldn't remember, once we made it to Harnett County, confusing the turn-offs for roads to turn on to. I didn't know the difference myself, completely unsure of how we'd gotten ourselves here then and now. Eventually it got so bad, being so dark out that it was hard to even know if it was still his truck in front of me, before the brake lights lit up and I was stopping behind him.

"Do you know where we are?" he yelled out to me, stepping down from the truck and rushing at my window I rolled down.

"Tommy . . . What're you doin? Get back in. Just drive. I don't know. I can't see anything. These roads, they all look the same to me. You don't remember how you got us there?"

"No, I mean, I thought I would, but—"

"But what? Where are we?"

"Close, alright. I know that. We're close."

"Come on, don't do this to me, Tommy. You know what I've got in this car. Man, just get back in and let's drive some more, see if we can get somewhere."

"Alright, alright," he huffed, freaked out finally, after he'd already agreed to something he maybe shouldn't have, possibly second-guessing his decision. Maybe that was why he pulled way off the road not but a minute after we got back onto it, came running back to me again.

"Tommy! What's goin on?"

His eyes were red and his hands were shaking. "I can't do this."

"What do you mean you can't do this?"

"I'm sorry, I just—"

"Hey, hey, slow down. Listen, just listen to me. There's nobody here, if that's what yer worried about. Same as it was. Only it's even darker now."

"Yeah, exactly. I'm lost. I don't know where we're going. What the hell we're even doin out here. I just wanna go back."

"Here," I told him, and I reached over and unlocked the passenger side door. "Get in with me. We'll drive together—just up a piece. It don't matter. Alright. If we see it, we see it, but you remember, it's somewhere. Yeah?"

"Yeah," he said, "alright." He opened the door and got in. "Wait—" He hopped out, ran to his truck for the shovels he'd tossed into the back of it before we left, and then got back in the car.

We didn't drive for more than another minute or two, before I saw a muddy embankment with tire tracks or maybe it was a tractor or plow's, and the Chevy's headlights shot straight through the thick treeline, into an opening that reminded me of the one we'd come upon before. There wasn't a real path made to drive the car on but I did anyway, right into the woods. I worried we might get stuck, but it didn't matter, if that was the idea, to leave this thing wherever we could, so long as it wasn't out in the open. But then right up beside the worn-down grit a barn lit up, just like the one we'd seen.

"Is that it?" I said.

"I dunno. I think so. It's so dark. I mean—"

"Whatta we do now? Do we just—"

"I don't wanna do this anymore, Trav."

"Alright, then," I said, sighing, wishing it were different. And I got out of the car and took a look at the barn, the way it was half-fallen in, much like any on of them we'd seen, that I had seen since, clearly hadn't been gone into in God only knew how long. It was hard to even tell what it used to be, and there wasn't anything but more trees leading toward it, and darkness. There could have been more, but I didn't see anything else but the barn, a way out. "I say we just leave it here?"

"*Here? In there* you mean?" Tommy asked out the window rolled down. "Are you sure?"

"Well, yeah, I mean, looks like it's not gonna be for somebody to find. So long as we leave it like we found it."

"We could burn it down?" he said.

"*No* . . . That would only cause somebody to really come lookin for it, Tommy. Come on, let's hurry up."

He reached into the back seat where he'd slid the shovels, and when he brought them up, one hit the steering wheel, the horn, echoing out a loud but short honk through the woods.

"*Shit!*" I whispered, and I froze, listened out. I didn't hear anything but what little leaves remained on the trees, rustling in the wind. "I'm gonna get the car up close to that door. Can you try and get it open?"

He jammed a shovel into its side, worked it around some, tried easing the door until he forced his way in, almost breaking it off. I was done talking to him about it, though, and so with the car backed up I got out and opened the trunk. Little remained left in the barn, but stuff was strewn all over, old rusted metal, chains hanging down, wooden crates lining a wall. Still, in its center, there was room for us to start digging, where we might could narrowly fit the Chevy and shut the door.

"You think maybe this is a bad idea?" he said.

"Yer really gonna ask me that right now?"

"I'm sorry. Sorry . . . Least we outta flip the headlights off, huh?"

I slung the shovel down to the dirt and walked toward the car. Under my feet I heard the ground crunch, twigs snapping, and ahead of me I could hardly see anything outside the dim fan of yellow light the Chevy was throwing out. I flipped the headlights off and my eyes had to adjust. The moon gave something to see our way around in, hardly enough, but the trunk light was still on, keys in the lock. I looked down at the bundled tarp, at how Dad's hand had uncovered itself during the drive.

"I'm gonna go ahead and roll him out," I said to Tommy, but he wasn't paying me any mind, frustrated as I was, sick to my stomach.

When I moved him, the tarp came completely undone and the image of his body didn't look real. Already I had made myself see it differently, so that I could do this, handle it, bury it, like it wasn't somebody I knew. His hair was tangled and limp over his face, wet with blood, stuck in spots. When I reached for him I touched his hand, and a coldness transferred from it onto me, came over me, and went back to him, to being my dad: dead in the dirt. For as much as I'd wanted him gone from our lives, seeing him this way, it wasn't like a win but more a loss. I wasn't sad but I wasn't happy about it either.

Left inside the trunk was a red and black bag on its side, something like he used to get with his Marlboro Miles, heavy when I pulled and unzipped it. That's when cash tumbled out, bands of it, more than I'd ever laid eyes on.

"Whoa! What's all that for?" Tommy said, reaching from behind me. "This is a shit-ton of cash! What, he rob a bank or somethin?"

"Naw, he ain't robbed no bank," I told him, stuffing the money back inside and zipping the bag shut. "But it's another reason why he whatn't never heard from again. Right? . . ."

I had no time to wonder about the money, or to reflect more on all that had happened between Dad and I, because a light caught my eye, set off like a prism though the woods. Whoever it was seemed far from us but was coming closer, and fast, so much it felt like they were in there with us, right when I dropped the bag back down into the trunk. What sounded like heavy footsteps came up outside the barn, and then yelling: "What're ya doin?! Best not be stealin from me again!" A light shined into the cracks of the barn, then straight through the Chevy.

In a flash, I was ducking behind the car and hearing Tommy holler at me, "Run! Look, he's got a gun. Go, go, go!" Shots were ringing out. Tommy ran off quick, and then I went for it, too, circling around in the dark, making it out past the barn, running as far as I could get, so fast I didn't feel the switches of stickers grabbing at my arms and legs, or the low-hanging branch I hit my head on.

"That's right. Ya better get! Hear me?!" The man's voice trailed behind through the woods. "I done called the police once. They're on their way. Yer trespassin! Stay out here if ya wanna get yerself shot!"

My heart beat in my throat. I was shaking so bad from adrenaline I thought I might have a heart attack and die, but I kept on running, finally reaching a field. I hunched down and inched across it, afraid I might be seen. I could see another light on in the distance but I had no idea where I'd gone off to, where it could be coming from.

"*Tommy*," I called, trying to without calling attention.

A beam of light scanned over the blackness, grasses turned silver, the boggy mess of cold stink I was in up to my ankles glistening. And it was the silhouette of someone far away, standing there, making me feel trapped, unsure where to go from here. I wasn't so sure he could even see me, though. I could hardly see myself. I worried about what he'd seen in the barn. That he might tell someone about it. But what could I do now, other than keep on running. Once the light died down, I whispered, "*Tommy?*" And I listened for an answer, for any sound out there other than the night.

Rocks crunched behind me, like tires through it. And I could see high beams, breaking through the trees and dust kicking up ahead. I ran for it, didn't turn around to see if the man was after me or not, and when I shot out the other side it was right as Tommy's truck rode by. I yelled for him and the brake lights lit the tracks behind him red.

The passenger door swung open and I got in, slammed it shut as he floored it. "Ya just gonna leave me or somethin?" I said to him.

"I whatn't leavin you! I found my truck and was tryin to *find* you."

"Well then I'm glad I saw you. We gotta move. He was right there."

"No joke," he said, breathing heavy like he'd run a marathon, and he was cradling his arm up close to his chest.

"What is it? What happened?"

I flipped on the light over us and caught a quick look at him, bleeding, his shirt sleeve sopping already, before he flipped it off with his other hand. "Don't do *that!* Not til we're back on the road," he said. "But could ya get a good look at? I mean, I think maybe I hit somethin when I was runnin, or I dunno what. What's it look like?"

"Like you got shot in the arm is what it looks like."

"Oh, damn, no way."

"Bastard musta got you. Damn it," I yelled, slamming the dash with a fist. "We just took off. Left it all there. What're we gonna do?"

"Where's the bag? What about all the money? You didn't get it?"

"No I didn't get the bag of money. That ain't even the half of it, Tommy. What about the car? My daddy?"

"No, yer right, yer right. Shit . . ."

After some time spent trying to find our way, Tommy steered us back onto the highway, aimless but heading home, without any clear picture of what the future held for either one of us. And we sat silent, under the radio's broadcast of election night news. President Bush was conceding, saying over loud applause, "I just called Governor Clinton over in Little Rock and offered my congratulations. He *did* run a strong campaign. I wish him well in the White House."

chapter 28

I thought driving Mr. Joe's truck around a bit before going straight back to the house might clear my head, help me to situate myself some, at least so that I could rest easy tonight. But my mind raced. And I was replaying the night Tommy and I rode up and down these back roads in the dark. I'd seen them in the daytime and even still they either looked like no other road I'd ever been on before or just like every other. This time around, though, knowing what I knew now, that it was him who'd been out there in these woods, shouting at us with his flashlight and gun, I tried to see if there was something I'd missed, what I'd not paid attention to or even overlooked since my time spent on the Tillett farm seemed to have overshadowed even the blackest night of my life.

Then it got late, and I was exhausted, running over every second of what had happened again in my mind, not forgetting how I'd spent most of the day at the hospital, and so I took the truck on home. I'd not been here alone like this, never without one of them to greet me: Ms. Mae in her swing; Mr. Joe in his rocking chair. And the house was totally dark inside, leaving that morning without a light left on. With only a slice of moonlight to show me the way up the front porch steps, I practically crawled. I felt sick still, and I just wanted answers, which I'd never get, to questions I'd never asked.

I pulled back the screened door and the one it covered, walked into the house and flipped on the light in the entry. Then it was the TV in the next room, to give the house some sound, some life. It was almost ten on the clock in the kitchen and I figured *The X-Files* was still on, though nearly through. Mr. Joe had tuned into every episode up until now, and so I came back in and sat down on the couch, dialed over to it as he would've done already.

A sky at sunset, like the one I'd just seen, with clouds scattering in the far horizon, played on the screen. And Agent Mulder was talking, only his voice at first, over the scenery, more reading what sounded like poetry: "At times I almost dream . . . I too have spent a life the sages' way . . . and tread once more familiar paths."

Then he appeared, standing in a grassy field, a shirt and tie on, as always. Against the moody, changing sky behind him he looked somber, and in his hands he held two old photographs, portraits, like the ones upstairs on Ms. Mae's vanity table, maybe even earlier.

"Perchance I perished in an arrogant self-reliance an age ago. And in that act, a prayer for one more chance went up so earnest, so. Instinct with better light let in by death that life was blotted out not so completely . . . but scattered wrecks enough of it to remain dim memories, as now, when seems once more . . . the goal in sight again."

The screen faded to black, the credits came up, and I was stuck there, sitting with it, finally crying as *Star Trek* began afterward. I looked around the room I was in, out the windows that only reflected it back at me, the couch I was siting on, the pictures on the wall, colored the same as whatever flashed on the TV screen. Mr. Joe had left this to me, I thought, for a reason. He wouldn't have, would he, had he known all along? How could he have possibly?

I got up from the couch and walked back into the kitchen where I'd tossed the keys and my dad's billfold on the table. A chair was pulled back and so I sat with it, these things I had laid out in front of me. I would've remembered removing Dad's billfold from his pants, and I never saw Tommy do it. There was never anything said about it. And I knew I'd left his keys, the car, him. I studied each of the keys in my hand, swiveling away which of them I knew went to exactly what—his truck's, this house, the Chevy's—from those I'd never seen: two keys that looked smaller than all of them.

I went back outside and through the truck, Ms. Mae's old car, and started digging around the house for what he'd said were the plans he'd made, put in writing, and sure enough, right upstairs, in the drawer of Ms. Mae's vanity table there was a folded up set of papers he'd written as he'd described, locked in a box that, had I thought to look for there first, I'd have saved myself another couple hours of searching for the tobacco barn in the dark, out in the cold.

I took a flashlight from the kitchen drawer, the same one he'd used to search with, I figured, without a gun. According to an old land deed, also inside the box upstairs, its lines drawn lightly in pencil and hardly legible, there'd been outbuildings marked at some point on this property. It spanned a great distance, like I'd thought, and with so many places to look it had to be out there, somewhere. There'd been several barns, in fact, proof of a once booming business, across acres and acres of land he owned and gave away. Too, I remembered him telling me how at night, he'd sleep with one eye open, that I should always do the same. "Somebody's gonna try and take what ya got. Give em what's comin to em first, fore they do, though."

It must have been well after midnight whenever I first stepped off the back porch, that or a time warp I'd fallen into had made me forget for how long I'd been out here searching. It didn't seem as dark as it was when I began looking, nor was I tired from all the walking and feeling my way through it. The day I'd just had was behind me now, and I was bound and determined to find what these keys in my hand belonged to, telling myself how I wasn't going back until I did.

The woods seemed impassable at first, with sun giving the most attention to those fledgling spruce and juniper trees lining the edge of what had always stood as a wall I could not climb, nor dare show interest in crossing, not if I wasn't alone. Rarely I had been, but now, breaking through it, to where shade blocked out most of the daylight, I was making stride, my eyes seeing the night. However, these boots I had on weren't made for clopping through wet mud, and I kept getting myself stuck in patches of thriving thorns. An owl, hooting someplace far away, either up ahead or behind me I couldn't perceive, further put things into perspective. I was so small, treading with caution a much vaster, wilder land that I only had loose impressions of to guide me. And had they been drawn up before or after the old man's memory began to fade? I wondered.

There was a shed that had long since toppled over in pieces, another next to it that had nothing but old paint cans and motor oil jugs inside, a 10 gallon drum rusted shut. Random metal parts stuck out and caught my foot as I passed, and a crusty mop had me lean down and touch it just to make sure. And then shanties that still stood, their foundations crumbled, led the way toward barbed wire that stopped me from crossing over into the next property or leaving this one. A muddy embankment I tripped into and almost couldn't get out of stopped me in my tracks. Even with it seeming next to impossible to see which way I was going, I kept going, and eventually I saw something.

The tobacco barn, the color of the blood that had dried up inside, it was upright and covered in dirt, nearly hidden behind buckthorn, its roof rotted and kudzu growing into it. This was it, I'd found it, I thought. Years later, today, not for the first time but it felt like it was. And maybe because the sun was rising, or that my eyes had adjusted as much as my body had to the cold, I was seeing it stand out strangely, so clear, but also not how I had envisioned. Boards along the outside of it were crooked and crude, hammered in at different times, different shades of red, lengths that didn't matter, and nail-heads rusted all over like they'd cried. No windows to see into it but shaped for the kind of work I'd been told was done inside. Pines were growing closer to it than I remembered seeing them, almost blocking

the big door Tommy had jimmied open, which was now boarded shut
and padlocked. It had to be, I thought, this was the one.

I looked all around me, waited for a moment to pass before I
moved another muscle, feeling my insides shift, the dead silence of
the woods weighed heavy on me. I could see nothing but the night,
and the next day coming up like a ring of fire. Nothing obstructed the
vantage except for memory. You could feel it, the strong sense that
no one was watching you out here. No wonder we picked this place,
I thought, and at the same time it's a wonder we didn't get caught.

Not only had Mr. Joe never said a word to anyone—my being free
to stand there was proof he hadn't—it seemed like he had helped
us cover it up. The car wasn't here, of course it wasn't, nor were any
tracks still in the mud where I'd parked up close to the rickety door.
I tried one of the keys, and then another, to unlock whatever he'd
done with what we'd left behind. I pulled it, only getting a little give,
but once I got it, enough to see in, I shined my flashlight. Shadows
reached deep, extended up the insides of the walls of the barn, where
all those old chains and rusty tools still hung, grown ten times the size
they'd been before by the light. And the smell was nothing but dirt
and dust, not decay or death. Angling the flashlight downward, the
Chevy's front fender stopped the beam. There it was, almost exactly
how I'd left it, but not quite.

I folded myself to fit in through the opened door and then gave it a
good kick to get the rest of it out of the way. Just a hint more light let
into the barn, plenty to put any doubts I'd had to rest. And I hadn't
any, not anymore. This was it, one thousand percent. A layer of brown
grime had settled over the car. It had never been sparkly but it shined,
once upon a time. Its luster was lost, and so was the air in its tires.
After so many seasons of neglect, under rotting vines and water leak-
ing in, obviously not driven a mile since the day it was deserted here,
I was surprised I didn't find it worse off.

I took the wad of keys out of the padlock and unwound from it the
set I knew had belonged to the Chevy: its doors, ignition, the trunk. I

keyed open the trunk, not sure what I'd find inside, and there it was, not the bones of my dad but his bag of money. I unzipped it to check if the cash was still there and sure enough it was. I don't imagine a single dollar had ever been taken from it, if it had even been opened. I took the bag out and shut the trunk back down, locked it.

I thought of the key that went to the glove box but had gone missing a long time ago, when I was little. That's maybe why I opened the passenger side door first, where I always used to sit, to get in now and take everything in. It was more than I could've remembered, too much to reflect on, but I allowed the memories spent here to begin again, to take me back. I noticed my hands shaking as I fiddled with the glove box, and my eyes burning the longer I sat and looked around at all of it, being a kid again. I had to get out. Underneath it, I thought, must be where Dad's body was buried. Had the old man actually taken it that far, though, I wondered.

I dropped down to my knees, felt around through the dirt and flashed light over what I couldn't get to on my stomach. I searched across the surface of the barn floor, for any spot that looked dug into or covered back up, anything. But it was like it had never been touched.

I pulled myself out of it, from reaching even deeper for some clue as to what had happened after I left him in here. If there was something else I missed, could have done differently, had I not seen it? No, it was over now, I told myself, and I stopped looking back. I stopped smelling the blood, and exhaust fumes filling the tobacco barn that night, how cloudy, my judgment and my outlook on life, to just stay here for now, set free and able to start over again. Even as it was finally beginning to blue outside and I was dusting myself off, I couldn't sit still with my back up against the Chevy, feeling like I didn't deserve any of this. But really, who did?

chapter 29

Mom had given me a dollar to spend.

"*A dollar?*" I said to her, shrugging in my blue *Star Wars* T-shirt.

"That's plenty, Trav. Now go on, pick you out somethin."

She unleashed me then into the crowded Kmart and I began my hunt for the perfect item to buy with my one dollar bill. Before hesitating at how little I had to spend I'd made the decision to not begin my search for something that *I* wanted but instead end it with a present I found to give to her, to show how much I loved her, as much as a dollar could afford.

I wouldn't find it in the toy aisle, I wouldn't even walk down it. And housewares, being too much for something that wasn't worth half of what it cost, Mom'd said, and too practical anyway, there was no reason to look there. Tools, forget them, I wasn't getting something for my dad after all. So then I went to the place where all the pictures of women were smiling up on the walls, posed and pretty, looking down at me. They'd made up their faces, bright eyes and bronzed skin, frizzy waves of blond and brunette hair, some glittery and others with neon-colored clips to match their clothes like those hung up in the next department over. Strange, I thought, but they looked so happy plastered up there like that, wherever they really were, however it was in real life didn't matter. This is what it was all about, I remembered thinking, what she would want, and I figured this had to be the right place to look for what might have the same kind of effect on Mom.

"Hi there. You lost, hon? Or can I help find you somethin?"

"I got only one dollar I can spend, and I wanna buy my momma somethin with it," I said to the young woman. She looked close to her age and I knew she'd know something maybe I didn't.

The woman smiled at me and asked what she was like, my momma, that she wanted to determine for me the best option for her, something that fit within my price range. "I'm sure we can get her somethin."

In the car driving back home, Mom asked for me to show her what I'd bought. I pulled out of my pocket a tube of lipstick, which had actually cost less than a dollar—not including tax I don't think. The nice lady at the counter had given me the go ahead and sent me on my way with it.

"Wet 'n' Wild," Mom mumbled, reading the label, sort of funny at first, but then she seemed sad by it, spinning it between her fingers.

"*You don't like it*—I thought you'd like it? So did the lady. Sorry, Momma, I—"

"Oh, no. No, no, I do. I love it. I do. And it's a real pretty shade, itn't it? I just, I dunno, Trav," she was saying, and with tears coming to her bright white eyes, "I just wadn't thinkin you was gonna go in there and get *me* something, that's all, sweetie. Course you did."

I glanced away from her, then back at her, unsure but smiling.

She leaned her head out the window she'd keep down all summer, put the lipstick on right then and there. And her face lit up like those women in Kmart's did when she looked in over at me. "*How do I look?*"

I don't think she really liked the shade because I never saw her wear it again. She kissed me on the cheek and I left the neon-pink lips there for the rest of the weekend—into the next week I would've had she let me keep them with me a little longer—for as long as it lasted, which had actually been for a good while, until I forgot all about it.

This was nearly fifteen years ago, a lifetime in the way we lived, a whole nother person I could have been. But here I sit, in the Chevy, in the parking lot outside the diner where she and I arranged to meet at, halfway between the farm and the place I'll never stop calling home. And she told me on the phone how she'd decided to move out of that house of ours, out of Siler City, but that it wasn't going to be so far that she didn't still feel it. It would never leave her. But she'd get there, make it somehow, die trying.

She was here early, inside already, slouched in a booth. Maybe because I'm seeing her through the windshield, in profile, or maybe because she really has changed, that she's almost unrecognizable to me now. And not just since the last time I saw her but all these years later, from driving us around in this car, how I pictured her then and what she might be like today, the way I saw myself sitting here someday, as hard as it was to believe I ever would be, without her in the seat next to me.

I'd cleaned off the Chevy and fixed it up as best I could, with what little knowledge I have about old cars. I do know it's worth a lot, if not to someone buying it from her then to Mom. The tires are good for it, any dings and dents weren't tough to get out, and the cracked windshield had already been replaced a while ago. I maybe couldn't give it new seats, or lessen the mileage that had been put on it, but I did manage to get the glove box to work the way it should. A new lock and key, to match the old one. That's where I found the lipstick, stuck in there, and for no good reason, still brand new but melty like an old crayon in its tube. All that time I'd wondered whether it was wrong or right. Whether I'd been.

Sun shines brightly this morning, and it's clear skies, mostly birds, except all the cars and trucks whooshing along on the highway behind me. The rearview is a blur. And the radio's on but turned down low:

"'We're better than we were four years ago,' Clinton said in a final election-eve speech on Monday, making the promise, if given four more years, 'we'll be better off still.' And to a crowd gathered in New Mexico, one of six states visited in *his* final push for what has become an insurmountable climb to the White House, Dole said, 'I need your votes. There's still time.'"

I turn the engine off and take a deep breath before getting out of the car. She looks nervous inside, sitting still, not looking up, not once, to see me coming. But as I walk in, her face instantly melts, her eyes pink and watery behind glasses she's wearing.

"When'd you start wearin glasses?" I say loudly to her from the entrance, bracing myself, trying to hold back tears of my own before coming any closer.

"*Trav*, hush," she says under her breath, waving me over. Then she stands up and hugs me tight.

"Hey, Momma," I whisper in her ear, through her long wavy hair that smells just like her, how she always did.

"You musta didn't see me when I pulled up," I tell her, pointing out the wide glass window beside her booth at the Chevy.

"*What?* Travis, no . . . That's it, ain't it? What're you doin drivin that thang around for?"

I sit down in the booth opposite her paper placemat and cup of coffee. "Don't worry about it, Momma. It's all fine."

She sits and then stretches her arms across the table. I do the same, reaching my hands toward hers, so that our fingertips touch.

"I'm glad you called," she says. "Finally. I didn't know if you were ever gonna." She laughs and wrinkles curl around her nose and eyes. "I kept that bill paid up like it was my job."

"Yeah, I know. I'm sorry. Like I said, it's just been something I had to get through, this time, you know. But I'm here now."

"And it matters. It does," she says. "Besides, I knew it whadn't gonna last no way, whenever you and Tommy got back from wherever it was—well I guess it's where yer at now, right? Where you drove here from. Or are you even gonna tell me?"

"It really don't matter, Momma."

"I guess yer right. I believe you."

"I thought I could, but like you said . . . I dunno. I shoulda said something, I know I shoulda, but yeah."

"Still, last I saw you, you was in Polk. And I told you then, and I'm tellin you now, if you needed money—if you ever do—I'll help you out. Best I can, sweetie. I ain't got a lot but enough that you ain't never gotta steal from nobody. No matter how hard it gets. Don't ever do that. Hear me?"

"Yes, ma'am, I promise," I tell her. In the seat beside me I'd set the bag of money, more than I'd thought could possibly fit into it, than I knew how to spend, and so I knew I'd keep my promise. "You look good, Momma."

"Thank you. Yeah, I'm doin pretty good, I'd say. Considerin. Ain't had a drink. God as my witness. Hell if I ain't had a reason to, but I hadn't. More reasons not to, I'm told."

"Somebody say that to ya?"

"Yep. It helps to hear it," she says, sighing and sipping her coffee. "Yer skinny. You needa eat you somethin. Whataya wanna get? Pick somethin." She pulls up a menu at me. "Anything you want."

"I'm not all that hungry. And I don't know how long I can stay."

"Oh. Alright. Well what else, then? Fore I don't see you again for however long it's been. What about Tiffany? You didn't tell me what happened. You get a hold of her?"

"Yeah, I did."

"You tell her what I told ya to?"

"I did," I say, and I smile, which makes Mom smile. "And I'm supposed to be seein her. I think soon. I dunno, though. Depends, I guess. She wadn't happy but—"

"—Hey, is that Tommy?" she says, putting her hand on top of mine, looking out the window at his green truck pulling up right next to the Chevy.

I could barely make out his face from the scruff, through the glass. I'd hoped he might not be alone but he was. "Oh, yep. Looks like it."

"Well damn, I guess yer gonna wanna go on, then, aren't ya?"

I turn my hand over and show her the keys to the Chevy I'd been holding onto. "Take em," I tell her, leaving them there between us on the table.

She picks the keyring up into her hand, makes a fist around it and chuckles. "They feel the same."

"Do they?"

"Yep. Now you know I can't drive that thang. As much as I wanna."

"Who says? It's yer car. Always has been."

"Well I know that much, but—"

"No, I mean, the title says so. It's in the glove box. It's got yer name on it, Momma."

"Yer lyin."

"Naw I ain't, neither. Come on."

"*Right now?*"

"No. Tomorrow—next week. Course, come on."

"Oh, well—lemme get my pocketbook," she grumbles.

"I got it," I tell her. And then I take out from my jacket Dad's billfold with my initials on it, so she can see it for herself, leaving two dollars behind on the table.

Mom holds my arm coming out from the diner, as Tommy steps down beside his truck with a grin.

"Hey Tommy," I say to him.

"*Who're you?* Do I know you? My momma told me not to talk to strangers . . ." He laughs and then, as we come nearer, hits me in the chest with his arm before half-wrapping it around me. And he glances down at the bag I'm holding in my hand. "Damn, Trav."

Mom hugs him. "Hey Ms. Lynn. Look at you."

"And you," she says to him. "I ain't seen you since—well, now, not since you moved outta yer momma's. And now she done moved out, too, Pam, hadn't she? I told Travis I'm outta there, soon as I can."

"So, the Chevy, safe and sound," Tommy says.

"I guess so . . ." Mom says. "A Honda can't compete, can it?"

"Naw it sure can't," he tells her.

I walk around and open the door for her. She stands there a second, taking in its interior, the smell of it, before sitting down in the seat. Her hands smooth over the wheel, and she runs a fingertip across the dash, down the metal console. She has a smile on her face but it has nothing to do with the Chevy.

"Hop in!"

I hesitate but then do, clicking open the door—my door—and get in next to her. Tommy leans down and tilts his head to look into the backseat.

"Where're we goin?" she asks me, brushing away tears from her cheeks. And she takes one hand off the wheel, places it on the seat.

"We're there, Momma. We made it."

She starts to cry. I look out the window at Tommy turning away, getting into his truck.

"You go on, then, alright," she says to me. "And you call me."

"I will."

"I love you."

"I love you too, Momma," I tell her, reaching my arm around her.

I step out of the Chevy and walk around the truck, see Tommy wiping his hands over his face before I get in.

"You alright?" I ask him.

"Yeah, I'm fine," he says, choking on the words. "It's just . . . a lot, that's all."

I set the red and black bag on the seat between us. "And there's that."

"That there is," he says, smiling. He lifts it up by its strap with one hand. "Heavy, ain't it?"

"Yep. Sure is."

After a moment, he asks, "What's next?"

"Well, I guess I figured we'd pick up where we left off."

"Yeah?" he says, half-smiling. "And where's that?"

"The beach."

He laughs and then cranks up, reverses us out of the parking lot.

I see Mom stand up beside the Chevy. She's waving her hand, rubbing her eyes, and I wonder if she can even see me when I wave back, or when we're pulling out onto the highway and driving off. Still, she turns around and looks long, watches me, until I'm gone.

www.ingramcontent.com/pod-product-compliance
Lightning Source LLC
Chambersburg PA
CBHW050017120726
47903CB00006B/1808